THE SECOND WIFE

Rebecca Fleet

BLACK SWAN

TRANSWORLD PUBLISHERS
61–63 Uxbridge Road, London W5 5SA
www.penguin.co.uk

Transworld is part of the Penguin Random House group of companies
whose addresses can be found at global.penguinrandomhouse.com

First published in Great Britain in 2020 by Doubleday
an imprint of Transworld Publishers
Black Swan edition published 2020

A CIP catalogue record for this book
is available from the British Library.

ISBN
9781784163457

Typeset in 11/14pt Sabon by Jouve (UK), Milton Keynes.
Printed and bound in Great Britain by Clays Ltd, Elcograf S.p.A.

Penguin Random House is committed to a sustainable
future for our business, our readers and our planet. This book
is made from Forest Stewardship Council® certified paper.

MIX
Paper from
responsible sources
FSC® C018179

1 3 5 7 9 10 8 6 4 2

For Saskia

PART ONE

Alex

September 2017

It's past midnight and the lights along the pier are jumping points of static, reflected in silver glimmers on the sea. I'm walking fast, into the wind. Salt spray scatters across my mouth and filters between the buttons of my shirt. My shoes pound the promenade, the sound shuddering up into the silence. Out of season, at this time of night, the place is deserted.

An ache is spreading in my muscles and the beer I've drunk is making me unsteady, but I'm buzzing with satisfaction. A good night – the right mix of business and pleasure. Happy clients, down from London for the evening. And tonight it was easy: the barman seeing me straight away in the crowd, a table clearing as if by magic, the conversation quick-fire and slick because we were all on the same page. I can still feel it, that powerful sense of calm and fluidity – feel it shining around me as I walk like an aura, like star quality.

I turn the corner, away from the seafront and up the

hill that will lead me home. Natalie is probably asleep on the sofa by now, with the television still on. I'm thinking about dropping to my knees, pushing the hair away from her neck and watching her eyes half opening, her lips moving silently in the tail end of a dream. That slight pretence of resistance as she turns her head, in that way I still find maddeningly exciting.

The last song I heard at the bar is repeating in my head, a needle scratching in the groove. Shadows curl out from the side roads and on the horizon dark clouds are stirring, lurking strangers. I start to hum the song under my breath and walk briskly in time to the beat, pushing away a faint flicker of unease. Another five minutes and I'll be home.

Left, right, left again. I know this route by heart and I'm used to walking it blind: the streetlamps space out and fade away around this point, leaving me to travel the last few hundred metres in total darkness. But this time it's different.

A light is coming from somewhere, strangely tinged, drifting around the corners of the streets and casting everything into surreal semi-brightness. And the smell is different too – the salt sea air cancelled out and compressed into something earthier, sharper. It is not until I reach the top of the hill and see the hollow of the streets below that I realize what it is. Something is burning.

I stand there without moving, looking down. A blaze of red and gold, shockingly vivid, rising into black coils of smoke. Fire engines circling, stick figures of people gravitating towards the centre and gathering in groups, watching and waiting. And then I'm running as fast as I can.

The taste of smoke is in my mouth. My eyes are smarting with it, aching in the wind, and when I wipe my hand across my face ash scatters on my skin like soft black snow. It's so bright I can barely look. It's ripping up the walls, guttering the windows, taking it all. And they're inside. My child, my wife.

I'm running towards the gaping hole of the entrance, driven by instinct, but before I can reach it I feel a hand clutching at my arm. A voice is sobbing out my name, over and over again. It's Natalie – her black hair wild and dirty, mascara streaked across her cheeks. 'Alex,' she's crying. 'Alex, you're home.'

The house looms behind us, an angry, dangerous mass of light. She doesn't know what she's saying. Home is the last place we are.

I clutch her to me, feeling her body shaking with trauma, but the relief is only partial. I'm still searching, wildly scanning the faces in the crowd for Jade. 'Where is she?'

Natalie draws breath shakily. 'I don't know,' she whispers. 'I – I couldn't find her.'

For a moment it doesn't compute. I'm waiting for something more, something that will make sense of what she's saying. I look into her eyes and she looks back blankly. Tears are starting to trickle down her face.

'Couldn't find her?' I repeat stupidly.

'I looked everywhere,' she says, her voice trembling. 'Everywhere!'

I spin round and look again at the house – the flames luminous and cartoonish, rising up to the sky. And now it clicks. 'So she's still in there?' I shout. 'My daughter's been fucking left to burn?'

Natalie opens her mouth to reply but I don't want to hear it, and I back away from her reaching hands, shoving her violently to the side. I run up to the black hole where our front door used to be, but I know it's useless. Even from several feet away, the smoke chokes me and makes me splutter, bending over double, my eyes streaming and smarting. It's too late. Trying to go farther now is a suicide mission, nothing more. A shout is ripped from my throat – the sound ridiculous and impotent. Panic is flooding me like poison. This can't be it. There has to be some way I can get in there.

I strain my eyes to peer inside the house and this time I see the shadow of a man in what looks like a bulky uniform jacket and helmet, struggling against the flames. I catch my breath, staring at the indistinct shape. It feels like hours, but it's probably only a few seconds before I see that he's carrying something in his arms. I see the shape of a pale arm hanging down, the fall of fair hair. It's her. There's a crushing sensation in my chest, a physical pain I wouldn't have thought possible.

The man is emerging from the fire, his head ducked down, and he's holding my daughter – I see her face in profile as he stumbles out into the air, a vivid slash of red across her hairline. Her cheek is miraculously and perfectly clear, but her eyes are closed and her lips are white, and she isn't moving.

'Please stand back, sir.' I've lurched forward again,

6

fighting my way to her side, but the voice is authoritative and firm and it gives me pause. I swing round and see a paramedic in uniform, gesturing towards his colleagues, who are swarming around Jade at speed, blocking her from my view. 'Let them do their job.'

'She's my daughter.' I can barely get the words out. My eyes are sore and despite the strange heat of the air I'm shivering violently.

The man places a hand on my shoulder and grips it. 'They got her out,' he says.

I nod, looking into this stranger's eyes, feeling an odd moment of connection. Still gripping me, he steers me carefully around the group, then holds me back at arm's length as he bends in and speaks quietly to one of his colleagues. A moment later he beckons me forward. 'She's unconscious, but breathing,' he says.

His words give me a sick, dizzy swoop of relief. I have no idea if it's really warranted or not, and by the looks of it, nor does he. Good news, bad news. Neither of us knows the difference.

'What are they doing?' I manage to ask. A man is bent over Jade, performing what looks like a quick succession of compressions on her chest. Another is checking her pulse. I have no idea what these actions add up to. Whether they're futile, or whether they're going to save her life.

The paramedic squeezes my arm, a brief unspoken moment of solidarity. 'They'll do whatever they can. You can come with us in the ambulance to the hospital, along with your wife. She was in there for a while – they'll want to check her out too.'

7

I glance round and see Natalie being guided towards the ambulance, tears streaming down her face. Guilt and anger rush up through me, too tightly bound together to unravel. I nod, following the men as they lift Jade carefully on to a stretcher and carry her to the vehicle. I slide into the seat at the back, clasping my hands tightly together as I stare at her motionless face. I know I shouldn't touch her, but I've never wanted to hold her so badly in my life.

The ambulance lurches forward and all at once we're whizzing through the streets, faster than I'd expected. Here in the back it's hot and windowless, and I close my eyes, feeling a lurch of nausea. I can smell Natalie's perfume in the air, the cool, seductive scent she always wears. Something about it acts as a trigger, forcing my eyes open again. She's staring at me, mutely appealing for forgiveness. I can't quite give it yet, but I reach out my hand and touch the back of hers, briefly stroking the skin.

'What happened?' I ask quietly, but she just shakes her head and raises her hands in a strange, useless gesture, grasping at nothing as if she is looking for the answer in the air around us.

'What happened?' I say again, my tone rougher this time.

'I don't know,' she says at last. 'I don't know how it happened.'

The ambulance weaves on and above our heads the strip lights are flickering, brightness ebbing and flowing like the aftermath of a camera flash. Next to me, Natalie shifts in her seat, leans forward and clasps her hands together, blinking fast, whispering to herself. I look at her profile, her clenched jaw. This woman with the trembling hands and the tears drying in streaks . . . My wife, but not the mother of my child. Not the one who would have found her, no matter where she was.

The time in the waiting room passes at random speed. I find myself staring at the moon-faced clock on the wall and watching the second hand spooling round, each tick deliberate and fluid, stretched to ten times its length. At other times I look away for what feels like no more than an instant, and when I look back I find that half an hour has passed.

I keep seeing Jade, lying there in the Intensive Care Unit – doctors swarming around her, machines flashing and whirring. The image is clear and static, bright with pain. When I cannot turn it over in my head anymore, I tune out. I simply sit and stare at the things around me – the soft, green-covered chairs, the grimy cracks between the tiles, the people moving past outside.

After a while I go over to the vending machine, look at the bright rows of cans and bottles, and fumble in my pocket, digging out the change from my last round at the bar. I count out the money, feed the coins one by one into the slot and listen to them rattle, punch a number at random and watch the can fall. Its black and red design is ludicrously familiar, but I can't for the life of me remember what the drink is called until I raise it to my lips and taste it. It's a tiny thing, but it shakes me. In the space of an hour, everything has changed.

I've felt like this once before – in another hospital, with Heather when the cancer had ravaged her body, at the

9

end. The knowledge that this would happen, that it *was* happening, and that I had no power to stop it, was enough to floor me. I remember looking at Jade, only five years old, as she played on the edge of the hospital bed. Her bright blonde hair swishing neatly back and forth as she danced her toys jauntily along the sheet, and the uncertain little smile on her lips as she glanced at her mother, expecting her to react – and yet not quite surprised when she didn't. I've thought about it a lot in the intervening years, that moment when I saw innocence and knowledge fighting for place behind her eyes. And the sterile cool of the corridor afterwards where I held her, her body heaving with silent sobs because on some level she'd understood that this was the last goodbye. In that moment I'd vowed to protect her. For ever. And in the nine years since, I've done OK. Until now.

'Mr Carmichael?' A doctor is waiting in the doorway; a small Indian man with a neat grey beard, his eyes searching and kind. 'I'm Doctor Rai. Can I come in?'

'Yes. Yes, of course,' I say. The can is suddenly cold and heavy in my hand, and I set it down. I'm searching his face for clues, trying to find some meaning. 'Has something happened? How is she?'

The doctor motions for me to sit down, then sits beside me. 'I'm afraid I don't have much in the way of a concrete update for you yet,' he says, 'but I wanted to keep you informed. As you know, Jade is unconscious. She's in what I would define as a state of coma.'

'Coma?' I repeat sharply. It conjures up years of stasis, a slow vegetative decline. 'Why? What's caused it?'

'It's most likely that your daughter's current state is a

result of smoke inhalation,' the doctor says. His voice is peculiarly soothing, at odds with his words. 'We'll know more when we have her test results. We're carrying out a brain scan, and we've taken blood samples to check for a variety of things, but most pertinently carbon monoxide poisoning. In the case of fire-related injuries, this is always a risk, and one of the highest.'

'How big a risk are we talking?' I ask. I'm trying to keep my voice steady and authoritative, matching his own.

The doctor tips his head gently and a little diffidently to one side, as if to indicate that this risk is one that is difficult to calculate. 'Jade is stable,' he says, 'as far as she can be. In the worst-case scenario, there may be permanent brain damage. But we have no reason to believe yet that that is the case. It is equally probable that the coma is largely triggered by shock and could last only a matter of hours. There is a broad spectrum of possibilities at the moment, which I know doesn't help you. All I can do is assure you that we are doing all we can to keep her safe and to address the issues as they present themselves.'

I want to question him more, but I don't have the expertise to know what I need to ask. 'When can I see her again?' I ask at last.

He puts a hand on my arm. 'You have had a traumatic night, Mr Carmichael,' he says, 'and you'll be in the best position to support your family if you are able to get some rest. In any case, my colleagues will need to remain with Jade throughout the next few hours to perform additional tests and to monitor her condition.

I would recommend that you return here in the afternoon, during the official ICU visiting hours of two to four p.m. Of course, if there is any change before then, we will contact you right away.'

Slowly, I nod. The clock ticks. I realize that I'm blinking in time with it, my fingers twitching the rhythm into my palms. The synchronicity feels other-worldly, and for a moment I wonder if I am dreaming all of this. He's right that I need to rest, but I can't imagine ever sleeping again, and it strikes me that I have nowhere to go.

'There's someone here to see you before you leave,' the doctor says, as if he has read my mind. 'A representative from the local housing authority, who'll be able to shed some light on your position in the wake of tonight's events. I can point you in her direction, but I'm guessing you'll want to see your wife first.'

'Of course,' I say, perhaps too quickly.

The doctor nods. 'I believe she's stepped outside for some fresh air. My colleague has finished her examination, and she's satisfied that there's no significant damage.'

'I'll head out then,' I say, wheeling away from him to cover my confusion. The truth is, I realize as I walk down the buzzing strip-lit corridors and follow the signs for the nearest exit, that I'm not sure if I want to see Natalie or not. I want her to be OK, of course I do, but I can't get past the image I have of her in the middle of that furnace, knowing Jade was somewhere inside it getting closer to death by the second, and turning away. I don't think I could have done it. Logically, I realize I'm probably being unfair. I wasn't there, and I'll never know how

I would have acted. Maybe our most primal instinct is survival, not protection. But that particular truth isn't generally something you have to confront, and there's something ugly about it – an essential selfishness stripped bare.

As soon as that word comes into my head I feel bad. There's nothing selfish about what Natalie has done in the past couple of years, coming into a ready-made family of two, taking on a child rocked by trauma and bereavement. Jade hasn't always been easy to live with, particularly since the onslaught of puberty – and it's been made all the harder by not knowing how much of her defiance and sulkiness has been normal, and how much of it springs from something deeper, the absence of her mother making itself more keenly felt. Natalie has dealt with that and slotted into her life so neatly that the cracks can barely be seen. They are there, those cracks, beneath the surface. There are times when I've felt that I'm the only thing holding them together. But for the most part it works, and a lot of that is Natalie's doing.

I push open the heavy double doors and step out into the cool night air and it's just at that moment, when my feelings are softening, that I see her. She is standing at the far end of the car park, silhouetted leaning forward across the metal railings, looking out on to the road beyond. Smoke rises from the glowing end of the cigarette she holds, a tiny firefly shining against the dark night sky. I stare at the dot of brightness, and for an instant I see it again – the flames rising up, engulfing the walls of the house, the smoke pouring blackly through the empty windows, the enormity of it all.

When she hears my footsteps she turns, her face pale and haunted, staring across the distance between us. She stubs out the cigarette on the railing and tosses it to the ground, folds her arms uncertainly in front of her as she watches me approach. Her eyes are wide and glistening, waiting for a signal. And as I cross the last few feet the coldness that has collected around my heart melts away as if it was never there and I'm trembling with love for her and I realize I need her support and her comfort, now more than ever before.

She reads my face and throws her arms around me, hugging me tightly, and we stand like that for what seems like several minutes. The wind whips at her coat, sending it billowing out and enfolding us.

'I'm so sorry,' she whispers. 'I can't explain what it was like. The heat and the shock. I stayed in there as long as I could but I knew I had to get out or I was going to die. I knew it.'

I nod, my face pressed into the soft sweep of hair at her collar. I think of what I asked in the ambulance, the empty circling of her hands. 'I just don't understand how this happened,' I say. 'I'm not angry, but if you know, you have to tell me. If you have any idea . . . If you might have left a candle burning, or a cigarette. Anything. It happens all the time.' Dimly, I realize how ridiculous this sounds. Something like this happens once in a lifetime, or not at all.

Natalie shakes her head vehemently, drawing back. 'There was nothing,' she tells me. Her voice is low and hoarse with the effort of sincerity. 'It was just a normal evening,' she says after a while. 'I watched some television, read a book. I remember looking at the clock at about half eleven, and then I fell asleep on the sofa. I must have only been asleep for half an hour, maybe even less. I don't know what woke me. But I realized straight away. I could hardly open my eyes. I'm not sure why . . . The smoke, or the heat, or something else.' Still holding her, I feel a shudder pass abruptly and violently through the length of her body. 'It was just a normal evening,' she says again. 'If there was anything to tell, I would tell you. You know that, don't you?' She is still trembling slightly, biting convulsively at her lower lip, her eyes liquid and shining.

Slowly, I nod. I know she wouldn't lie to me. 'I shouldn't have gone out,' I say. The thought is a knife to the heart. 'If I had been at home, this would never have happened.' At midnight, I would probably have still been awake. I would have been there to see whatever had happened, to prevent it.

Natalie shrugs, not understanding. 'That's crazy,' she says softly.

The wind is picking up, sending drifts of dried-out autumn leaves scuttling across the car park from where they have collected along the tree-lined road beyond. I turn around and see the lights from the hospital windows, rows of bright squares shining out from the shadows. Glancing at my watch, I move away from her.

'We should go back,' I say. 'The doctor told me there's someone who needs to speak to us.' I am already walking back towards the flat grey building.

The woman from the housing authority is in her fifties and comfortably plump, with greying hair escaping from

15

an untidy bun and bitten fingernails. I try to keep my mind on the forms she is pushing in front of us, the relentless questions and explanations, but I haven't slept in twenty-four hours and the information is falling through me. I know I'll remember very little of this tomorrow.

'And just to confirm,' she is saying, 'it's been the three of you in the property? The two of you and your daughter?' Her eyes flick awkwardly from me to Natalie. We've only been married six months, and she hasn't yet changed her name. Even in this day and age, it seems that's enough to raise a question. It pisses me off that her conventional little assumption is correct.

'My daughter,' I say, 'yes.'

'Ah,' the woman says, nodding furiously, clearly relieved to have understood. 'And it's a joint mortgage? Fifty fifty?'

I launch into the details of the mortgage agreement, making an effort to be clear and concise despite my exhaustion. I know I'm on safe ground. Comprehensive house insurance was one of the first things we sorted out when we moved in together: battening down the hatches, protecting what we could. I even remember Natalie talking about what we were doing. *You can't prevent disaster,* she had said, *but you can make sure you're ready.* It has taken a while to prove her right, but here we are.

'I'm sure I can source the paperwork,' I finish. 'If it's been destroyed in the fire, then everything should be on record electronically. I'll put you in touch with the insurers.'

'Perfect,' the woman says, scribbling in her notebook, then glancing up again. 'But right now, the priority is to make sure you have somewhere to stay. Do you have any family or friends nearby who could accommodate you temporarily?'

I look blankly at her. My family, such as they are, are hundreds of miles away in the wilds of Northumbria, and it has been years since our contact has extended past a dutifully scrawled Christmas card. Natalie's are no better – her father long since dead, her mother estranged. The friends I have in this town live in cutely compact cottages, stuffed to the rafters with their possessions, or in chaotic flat-shares. 'No,' I say, a little curtly. It's not pleasant to realize that you have no plan B.

The woman just nods, as if this is expected. 'In the short term, it seems best that we place you in a local hotel or bed and breakfast facility,' she says. 'We have links with several. I've already made some initial calls, so I can give you some options and if you have a preference we can arrange a transfer right away. Of course, it won't be clear just yet how extensive the damage to your property is, and how long it will take to rebuild. It may be that we have to look for another option. But for now, does that sound good?'

'Yes, that makes sense.' I draw the papers she is pushing across the table towards me, run my eye quickly down the short list of local hotels and B&Bs. 'Do you mind where we stay?' I ask Natalie, but she shrugs and shakes her head. I try and visualize these places, but nothing comes to me. This town is full of tourist traps, and when you live here they're like white noise. I pick a name at random: the Sea Breeze hotel. The street name sounds familiar; I don't think it's far from the hospital, and I want to stay as close to Jade as possible. 'This one, if it's feasible,' I say to the woman.

She nods again, the soft flesh of her chin wobbling earnestly. 'That should be fine, Mr Carmichael,' she says. 'I'll call them again now to confirm, and then I'll book you a taxi. It's a nice hotel. Very homely.' As soon as she says it her lips press fractionally together; a tiny moment of self-chastisement, a mental reminder that our home cannot be so easily replaced.

'Don't worry,' I say.

Less than an hour later dawn is breaking and we are in the back of a cab, riding along the deserted coastal road. I close my eyes against the crisp September sunlight striking through the glass. Rows of houses whip past in pastel streaks of colour, blurring into one.

'Here you go,' the cabbie sings out, swinging the car towards the kerb. I raise my head and stare out at the hotel. I've definitely seen it before. I remember noticing the collection of little shells and sea-polished pebbles lined up unevenly along the windowsill. It looks OK. Homely, as the woman said. Under normal circumstances, I might have said something scathing about its old-fashioned facade, maybe walked on to somewhere slicker and smarter. But it doesn't seem to matter now.

Climbing out of the taxi, I follow Natalie to the door and wait. It is only a few seconds before it swings open and a man is standing there. Around forty, with sandy hair falling to his collar and several days of stubble

18

peppering his face, a sky-blue checked shirt and faded jeans.

'I've been expecting you both. Come in,' he is saying as he ushers us over the threshold. 'God, what an ordeal. I can't imagine what you're going through.'

Natalie murmurs something; without hearing, I nod. I don't have much time for platitudes, but all the same it is somehow comforting to know that what is happening to us is so easily categorized – a legitimate tragedy.

The man is leading us upstairs, pushing open a bedroom door and waving an arm vaguely in its direction. 'Lots free at the moment,' he says. 'End of season, you know. I thought this might do. Quiet, and you've got a good view of the sea if you want it. But let me know if anything isn't right. Anything you want, I'll try to get. Don't stand on ceremony.' He is seconds away, I think, from saying that we should make ourselves at home, and having to drag himself back from the social faux pas. I had never realized before how casual these mentions of home are, how much they pepper conversation.

I step into the room. Faded yellow-painted walls, scuffed cream carpet underfoot. A little lamp in the shape of a seashell and a vase of flowers beside it, blue petals scattered on the bedside table like confetti. The air in this room is light and empty. For an instant it makes me dizzy, a strange mixture of sickness and relief.

'I'll let you settle in,' the man says. 'If you need anything, just ring down.'

When he has gone I go into the bathroom and find

Natalie leaning out of the open window and smoking another cigarette, her hands shaking in the morning breeze. She half twists round, holding out her free hand to encourage me to join her, but I shake my head.

'I'm going to try and sleep for a short while,' I say, 'and then get back to the hospital.'

'Sure,' she says. 'I'm going to have a shower and then I'll do the same.' She stubs out the cigarette half smoked, brushes it aside. 'I don't want this.' She stands up and moves towards me, sliding in underneath my arm and pressing her face briefly to my shoulder; a wordless little moment of comfort that touches my heart.

While she showers I close the bedroom curtains, but the room is still light. Sitting down on the bed, I shrug my suit jacket off and turn out the pockets, laying them in neat little piles on the duvet. A wallet containing my credit cards and around seven pounds in change. My mobile. My pocket organizer and pencil, a packet of tissues, a small photo of Jade on the beach laughing and screwing her eyes up against the sun. A bunch of keys that I could throw into the sea now for all the good they are to me. For all I know, this is all I have left. My possessions, caught in the circle of my two hands. The thought is bleakly fascinating.

I pile the items back into the pockets and lie down, placing my hands behind my head and closing my eyes. Despite the nervous energy pulsing through me, I feel myself falling almost at once, sucked down into a black hole of exhaustion, and I don't try to stop it.

*

When I open my eyes again and reach for my phone I see that it is past midday. I have slept for almost six hours. There is no fog of doubt or uncertainty. I know exactly where I am, exactly what has happened. A shutter has been pushed up over my eyelids in an instant, moving me out of the dark and back into this frightening clarity.

'Shit,' I say aloud. I jab at the phone, dialling the number of the hospital. I've been left no messages, but that doesn't necessarily mean anything. Hospitals are chaotic places, the left hand often not knowing what the right hand is doing. As I listen to the phone ring I'm thinking of Jade, alone in that unfamiliar place, with God knows what happening while I'm not there. How could I have slept for so long?

Eventually I get through to a doctor in Intensive Care and without preamble he tells me that Jade is still unconscious and that there has been little discernible change, and that they will be happy to take me through the test results so far when I return at two. It's a relief, of sorts.

Visiting time isn't far away, but the couple of hours I need to fill stretch ahead, flat and directionless. Next to me, Natalie lies with her eyes closed, an arm extended above her head. The curve of her left breast is exposed, the skin pale and clear. I remember the pulse of desire I felt last night on my way home, that urgent need to get to her. An echo of it is still there – dampened down, a sick parody of itself. I think about pushing the thin fabric of her vest top away and losing myself in her for a few minutes. But I'm already lost and there doesn't seem much point.

I ease myself out of bed and push open the little bedroom window, leaning out and looking across the seafront. The water is almost still, rippled faintly by gusts of wind. Seagulls are swooping on the horizon, rising and dipping as if pulled on invisible strings. A couple of tourists wander along the promenade, arms desultorily swinging. The woman is wearing a strappy red dress that reminds me of one of Natalie's, and I wonder for a moment if I'll ever see her in it again. Something in me recoils from the idea of us wearing the clothes we might retrieve from the house. I can imagine the smell of smoke clinging to the fabric, and it doesn't feel like something that a quick wash would solve.

I pull my shoes and jacket back on. Silently, I move away from Natalie and slip out of the room, filled with a new sense of purpose. I can go to the shops and buy some clothes for my family, enough to see us through for a short while until we know where we are. It seems like a pitifully small act, but God knows there isn't much I can do for Jade or Natalie right now, and at least it's something.

I head inland up the Western Road towards the shopping centre, realizing that it's the first time I've been there in well over a year. Natalie usually handles this kind of thing, and I soon remember why. It's easy enough to pick out some basic things for myself – a few shirts, a pack of boxers, a couple of jumpers and pairs of trousers, a warmer jacket – but when it comes to my wife and daughter I find myself standing aimlessly in front of rails and rails of clothes, staring at them like a fool with absolutely no idea what I should be buying.

Colours and patterns and fabrics and styles are all mixed up like a jumble sale and I can't see the logic.

I try and think about Jade, about what she wears when she isn't at school. A little flashback: walking with her in town one day and her head turning to look at a girl's flowing skirt, a covetous gleam in her eyes as she squeezed my arm. The skirt was bright blue, I think, and dotted with small sequins. *Hey, Dad, that's nice, isn't it? You could get me one like that for my birthday. Or, you know, whenever.* I remember us laughing, me exclaiming at the brazenness of the request. But that's not the sort of thing you wear for an average day around the house, or that you'd take to a hospital. The longer I stand there, tinny music screeching from the speakers and the harsh lights flickering above my head, the more I start to panic. What kind of father am I, that I can't even fucking remember what my daughter likes to wear?

'Can I help you at all?' a sales assistant pipes up. She doesn't look much older than Jade herself, and for a moment I experience a sharp, irrational pang of jealousy that she's here, bright-eyed and bouncy in her uniform, and my Jade is lying unconscious halfway across town.

I dampen it down, forcing a smile. 'I'm just looking for some basic stuff for my daughter,' I say. 'She's fourteen, about a size ten I think. I'm at a bit of a loss.'

The sales girl takes pity on me and before I know it I'm being whisked around the store, having various items showcased, and her confidence rubs off on me. I leave with a couple of bulging bags – mostly jeans and long-sleeved tops, with a few things for Natalie thrown in. I'm on safer ground with her, feel pretty sure about what she will like. I can't help buzzing with pride as I glance down at the bags, walking swiftly back down towards the beach. I suppose the bar for achievement is set pretty damn low right now.

I've still got an hour to kill and I decide to wander along the beach before going back to the hotel, breathe in the fresh air. There is little or no sand on this part of the coast and the soles of my shoes slip unsteadily between the stones, making my progress slow.

I pass the small beachside stall that seems to stay open all year round. The owner, an elderly grey-haired man with a paunch and a red striped apron, stares out towards the sea with glazed eyes, shut off. I glance at the billowing bags of pink candyfloss, suspended from the roof of the stall and swaying in the breeze, and wonder if I should buy some. I'm light-headed, and I know I should try and keep my strength up, but food feels strangely irrelevant. The man eyes me warily, cocking his head to one side, but I shake my own and wheel away, walking towards the sea. I wander along the beachfront, looking out on to the churning water. My mind is blank and for a few moments I just stand still, the wind blowing into my face and the waves rising and falling in relentless rhythm.

A sly tremor of instinct passes over me, raising the hairs on my neck. It's that strange, primal feeling when you know that someone's eyes are on you, and when I turn round I'm unsurprised to see that I'm not alone. A man is standing motionless at the far end of the beach, the direction from which I have come. Sun streams across him, casting him into silhouette. I can't see his face, but something in the set of his shoulders and the angle of his body tells me he's watching me.

I stare back, half raising my hand; whether in query or warning I'm not sure. He pauses, and then turns and walks slowly and deliberately away down the pier. He doesn't look back. I walk up the beach on the diagonal, reaching the road by the traffic lights. But by the time I'm there, he's long gone.

As I head back to the hotel I tell myself that it's no surprise if I'm paranoid. This is an abnormal situation, and it's natural for my responses to be heightened. As if to make my point, when my phone starts to ring and vibrate, I almost jump out of my skin.

I answer it quickly. 'Hello?'

'Mr Carmichael? This is Doctor Rai.'

'Yes?' I glance at my watch, but it's still only twenty past one. I spoke to the hospital less than an hour and a half ago. 'Has something happened?'

'Jade has regained consciousness,' the doctor says, and with the words I let out a breath that I hadn't even realized I was holding. 'She is still very weak, of course, and we have numerous tests still to do. We'll need to monitor her here for a few days at least. But it is very positive that she has come round relatively quickly.'

'That's great news,' I say, barely able to register the negatives in what he has said. It's only now, when I know it isn't going to happen, that I realize that part of me thought she might never open her eyes again. 'I'll be in straight away,' I add, hearing my voice crack, but for once I'm not ashamed. If there was ever a time for emotion, it's now.

I race down the main street in search of a taxi, and it's only when I've flagged one down and have climbed into the back that I remember Natalie. I send her a quick text to tell her the good news and ask her to meet me at the hospital, and in seconds she's sent one back, saying she'll be right behind me. I look at the kisses and exclamation marks with which she's peppered the message, and I feel the last of the poison around my heart starting to drain away. She may not be her mother, but she loves Jade. We'll get through this together, all of us.

I repeat this to myself as the cab carries me along, and by the time it reaches the hospital I've almost succeeded in pushing down the niggling little thought that has sprung up time and time again since the fire: the awareness that when it came to the crunch and I was faced with my wife in front of the burning building, we didn't pull together. I blamed her, told her she'd acted wrongly. My first instinct wasn't solidarity, but division.

Jade is lying on her back with her face turned towards the doorway, and when she sees me coming towards her smiling, her face flickers weakly in response. With deliberate slowness she blinks, then extends a bandaged hand across the white sheet.

'Hi Dad,' she says.

'Darling,' I say as I sit beside her, stroke my fingertips gently across her arm. 'Thank God you've woken up. I'm so happy to see you.' Words don't scratch the surface in this situation, I realize. I can feel all this emotion

26

rising up, choking my throat, stinging my eyes, and I know that if I let it out it would overwhelm her, frighten her even, so I swallow it back down and just smile again, as reassuringly as I can. 'How are you feeling?' I ask. I think of the brief conversation I've just had with Doctor Rai; the names and results of tests that I find almost impossible to keep in my head. The picture he painted was inconclusive; at best, vaguely reassuring. I realize, with a jolt of shamefaced awareness, that I want my daughter to look me in the eye and tell me she's going to be OK.

She moves her head from side to side, thinking about it. 'I'm not sure.'

I swallow down my disappointment. 'I brought you some clothes.' I open the bag that I brought back from the shops, fan a few items out on the bed to showcase them, a conjurer parading his wares. 'Of course, I can't guarantee that they're the height of fashion. You probably won't want to be . . .' I cut myself off. *Seen dead in them*. There's something about the casual turn of phrase that still feels like tempting fate.

She doesn't seem to notice my slip, or to pick up on my jocular tone. 'Thanks.'

Her voice is faint, and there's a distance in it; I realize that she's not quite with it, not quite present in this room. I'm conscious of having to be gentle with her and take things slowly, but maybe she doesn't want small talk, and it feels disingenuous to ignore the elephant in the room. 'Do you – do you remember what happened?' I ask tentatively.

Jade nods immediately. 'The fire.' She glances away

27

for a moment, staring at the shaft of sunlight breaking through the curtain. Tiny motes of dust are spiralling and sparkling in the air. 'I was frightened,' she says. 'I didn't know what to do. It was so hot in there.'

'I know, sweetheart,' I murmur, feeling its uselessness. 'Natalie said she looked for you, and that she couldn't find you. Where were you?'

'I was hiding,' she says, so quietly that I have to lean forward to hear her. 'I was in my bedroom. In the wardrobe.'

Frowning, I look into her face, the seriousness behind her dark blue eyes. It is as if she is waiting for me to understand the gaps between her words. 'Because of the fire?' I say at last. 'You were hiding because you were frightened of what was happening?'

Minutely, she shakes her head. 'Because of the man,' she whispers.

'The fireman?' I ask. Even as I speak I know that isn't right. The firemen came later, after Natalie would have started searching, and in any case it makes no sense to hide from someone who is trying to save you.

Jade shakes her head again, and for an instant impatience crosses her face. 'No,' she says, and closes her eyes. I watch her – knowing she is exhausted, not wanting to push her, but with some instinct telling me that I should ask again. Before I can speak she opens her eyes again, looks straight into mine. 'The man in the house,' she says clearly.

'Who?' My voice sounds harsh and abrasive. I clasp my hands together, trying to calm myself. 'Who do you mean?'

28

She stirs restlessly on the pillows, half lifting her shoulders in a shrug.

I force myself to speak calmly. 'You're telling me that there was a man in the house last night?'

Jade brings her wrist to her forehead and rubs it slowly across, wincing as she does so. 'I don't know,' she whispers. I can see the shadows underneath her eyes staining red, as they always do when she is about to cry.

'I'm sorry,' I say quickly, 'I don't want to upset you. It's just that this could be important.' Until now I've mentally filed the fire as a freak accident, perhaps a moment of tragic carelessness, or even some bizarre electrical fault. The possibility of an intruder hadn't even crossed my mind. 'If there's something that could help us understand how this happened,' I try again, 'then—'

'Found you!' Natalie's voice cuts through the room and she rushes in, swooping down on Jade to embrace her gingerly. She's holding a large bouquet of cheerful multicoloured flowers that she sets down on the bedside table. 'I'll get you some water to put them in,' she says. She's trying to sound upbeat, but I can tell that she's nervous. I mentally curse myself for the way I acted last night. It's been hard enough for Natalie, navigating Jade's hormonal ups and downs over the past couple of years and trying to remain calm and loving in the face of her teenage defiance, without my putting it into her head that now she's let her down in the worst possible way.

I glance at Jade anxiously, but she's smiling, seemingly happy to see Natalie. 'Hey,' she says. 'Thanks. I never get flowers.' She keeps looking at the spray of colour,

I notice, seeming totally charmed by the novelty, and I feel a little unexpected stab of jealousy that I wasn't the one who thought of bringing them.

'Nor me,' says Natalie, shooting me a mischievous glance before rolling her eyes at Jade. It's a game they play sometimes, this ganging up on me; in the early days it was an easy way for the two of them to forge an alliance, and sometimes it seems that these bonds need to keep on being strengthened and reaffirmed. But today I'm not really in the mood to play along. I can't stop thinking about what Jade has said to me, and it strikes me that Natalie needs to hear this too.

'There's something you should know,' I say. 'Just before you arrived, Jade was telling me that she thinks she saw a man in the house last night.' I look at my daughter, hoping she'll cut in and explain further, but she just bites her lip worriedly, staring at me, expecting me to solve this mystery.

'A man?' Natalie repeats. 'I don't understand. What man?'

I glance at Jade again, but she remains silent. 'She isn't sure,' I say, 'but obviously it's something we should talk to someone about.'

'Who?' Natalie asks blankly.

'Well, the police,' I say. 'If someone broke into the house, then they should know about it. It seems too big a coincidence for this to happen on the night our house caught fire. It's possible that whoever this man was . . .' I trail off, conscious of Jade, and not wanting to upset her further, but surely this can't be anything she hasn't thought of already. 'He might have done it deliberately,' I finish quietly, angling myself towards my wife.

She doesn't reply at first; her eyes flick from side to side, as if she's considering what I've said, and then she gives a tiny, imperceptible shrug. 'It's not possible.'

'What do you mean?' I ask.

She clears her throat and speaks again, louder and more decisively this time. 'It's not possible that there was anyone in the house. I would have seen them, heard them. I dozed off on the sofa, yes, but I'm a light sleeper, you know that. There's no way I would have slept through somebody breaking in, especially when I was sitting there in the room right next to the front door.' She stops, looks away. I have the sense that a thought has struck her, but whatever it is she doesn't seem inclined to share it. She just looks back at me, raises her eyebrows a little and shrugs again. I've seen it before in her, this kind of silent, defiant certainty. It's hard to push back against, and often I don't care enough about what we're discussing to try. But this isn't some idle debate about party politics or an after-dinner chat about an interesting moral dilemma. It's quite literally a matter of life and death.

'So how would you explain what Jade saw?' I ask, as calmly as I can. I shoot my daughter a little apologetic glance. Under normal circumstances we wouldn't be having this kind of conversation in front of her, but this is far from normal, and she's already too deeply involved to be cut out.

Natalie breathes in sharply through her nose, folds her arms in front of her chest defensively. 'It's hardly any wonder, is it,' she says, 'if she's confused?'

'I don't think that's entirely fair,' I reply tightly, straining to keep my voice under control. 'There's a world of difference between being physically and mentally exhausted, and hallucinating something that never happened. I don't think we can just dismiss—'

'Please.' Jade interrupts me, her voice suddenly weak and sounding very young. 'I don't want to talk about it anymore. Just forget it, OK? Forget I said anything.'

Her face is white and drawn, and I'm reminded that she's been through a horrific ordeal. The last thing she needs is to listen to us arguing. She needs stability right now; a loving family. And by the sounds of it, she's told me all she can for the moment.

'All right,' I say with an effort. 'We'll leave it for now. What do you want to talk about?'

For the next twenty minutes we chat about safe topics – which of Jade's classmates she wants to come and visit her, who might go through to the finals of her favourite reality show – until it becomes clear that she's getting tired and the doctor is lingering at the door, subtly sending a message that it's time for us to leave. I bend over the bed and hug her goodbye, breathing in the scent of her hair; hospital shampoo, a sharp peppermint tang. For some reason the unfamiliarity of it brings a lump to my throat and I have to fight to make my voice cheerful when I tell her that we'll be back to visit her very soon.

Outside in the corridor I take Natalie by the arm and draw her aside against the wall. 'What was all that about?' I ask quietly.

To her credit, she doesn't try and pretend that she

doesn't know what I'm talking about. 'I'm sorry, Alex, but I'm not going to go along with something that I don't think happened.'

I take in the unblinking levelness of her gaze, the slight lift of her chin. 'I'm not saying you should, but I don't appreciate you intimating that my daughter is lying.'

She flinches a little, her face clouding with hurt, and already I'm regretting that 'my', but it's too late to take it back now.

'I never said that,' she says carefully.

'Well, one of you is,' I fire back.

Natalie gives a short bark of laughter and shakes her head. 'Really?' she says. 'It isn't possible that we're both telling the truth? That she *thinks* she saw a man in the house, and that I *don't think* there was anyone there?'

I'm silent for a moment, confounded, because when she puts it like that of course it's obvious – she's right. This doesn't have to be black and white, and yet that's where my instincts naturally went: slotting my wife and my daughter into opposing positions, pitted directly against one another, with myself as arbiter and judge.

'I'm sorry ...' I say slowly, sorting through my thoughts.

It's her cue to take the moral high ground and accept the apology, but to my surprise she doesn't. Instead she steps back, wraps her arms around her body and scowls, her eyes blazing. 'This is you all over, isn't it, Alex?' she hisses. 'You don't look for the most likely explanation, you look for the one that's going to cause the most hurt. It's not my fault you're so fucking suspicious—'

'Hold on a minute,' I interrupt, struggling to catch up. This kind of aggression isn't like Natalie, and it throws me off base, but even more disturbing is the sub-text behind what she's saying. *Suspicious*, I think. The truth is that I hadn't gone so far as to *suspect* anything, not yet, but now that the word is in my head the inference is clear. If Jade is right in what she's saying, then an intruder isn't the only explanation. It's also possible that if a man was in the house, he was there because my wife invited him. And I can't help wondering why it is that she's got to this theory so much faster than I have, as if it was there in her head all along.

Natalie

September 2017

GETTING ANGRY IS AN effort. I've barely slept in twenty-four hours and there's an ache running down the length of my spine, and my mind feels fuzzily light, as if I could spiral out of it at any time. It would be easier to fold. I could tell him that I'm sorry and that I understand why he might not be thinking straight right now – even that I can understand why he might be suspicious, though I've given him no reason to be. But instead the blood rushes to my head and all those words spill out of my mouth.

And actually, it helps. Everything that has happened in the past few hours jostles inside me and fuses into this one simple point of anger. It's the oldest story in the book. Never mind the fire, the trauma that his wife and daughter have gone through – when it comes down to it, what's *really* eating away at him right now is the thought that I might be fucking someone else. It's so stupid that it almost makes me want to laugh.

'Hold on a minute,' he says, but then he just stands there, his mouth hanging slightly open, giving me this hurt puppy look that I've seen a few times before and which usually disarms me. Not this time. He looks ridiculous. And that only serves to ratchet the anger up a few notches, because I don't want to think of him this way. This is Alex, my husband, the one I idolize, that I've always put first. The one I'd do anything for. But right now he just looks like a man, and a pretty ineffectual one at that.

'Yes?' I prompt, knowing that there's an edge of sarcasm in my voice and not bothering to soften it.

He takes a step towards me, then back again, as if pulled by invisible strings. His hands rise helplessly for a moment. 'I don't know what to say.'

I look at him again, more carefully this time. He looks exhausted – deepening shadows beneath eyes red with crying, his skin almost grey under the harsh neon strip lighting. His shoulders are hunched, making him seem smaller than his six feet. I try and remind myself that he's gone through an ordeal, too. But at the same time the images are flickering in the back of my head of where *I've* been: the flames rising up, bright and savage, the unbearable heat and the smoke rushing down into my lungs, making it hard to even draw breath. There was a moment there when I didn't think I was going to get out. When everything went soft and dream-like and I could see my feet moving but they didn't seem to be going far or fast enough, and I thought, *I'm going to die.* And when you've gone through that, doesn't that earn you a bit of slack? A bit

36

of understanding? A tiny bit more than 'I don't know what to say'?

There's a breeze coming from somewhere, cutting through the thin layers of my clothes and finding its way to my skin. I wrap my arms around myself, squeezing tight. 'Well,' I say, 'I'll just leave you to it for a bit while you try and figure something out.' Before he can answer – not that it looks like he's miraculously found the right words in the last few seconds – I turn on my heel and march down the corridor. I think I might hear him asking me to wait, but I'm not sure enough to turn around, and as I push through the entrance doors and find myself back in the outside world with the autumn sun bright and cold on my face, I realize he isn't going to follow.

Automatically, I hail a taxi and ask the driver to take me back to the hotel. It'll cost me my last five-pound note. I realize I need to call the bank, ask them to send me a new card. The thought is exhausting and I lean my head back against the seat, closing my eyes as the taxi carries me along. There's something in the way it slips and turns along the coastal road that gives me a weird pang of déjà vu. Whatever it is, I can't catch on to it. A beat, and it's gone.

Once I'm in the hotel room I climb on to the bed and switch the television on, but I know instantly it's hopeless. The picture is distant and static and it's like I'm looking at a different world. I can't think of anything except what's happened. The gap between how things should have been, and how they actually turned out. I should have been awake when Alex came back, the lights dimmed attractively low, a drink waiting for him on the table. I should have been there to welcome him in and chat about his night, make small talk about his clients for a few minutes before I slipped out of my clothes to reveal the new black silk underwear I bought a few days ago. I'd stood in the shop, sliding on the bra and feeling it smooth and tight against my skin, imagining his reaction. My hands on myself, stroking the fabric, thinking about the look he'd give me before he reached forward to touch it for himself. I don't even know where that underwear is now. They changed me out of my smoke-drenched clothes last night, put me in some standard issue hospital gown that felt scratchy and stiff, and then gave me a basic zip-up top and jogging bottoms this morning that are about as far away from sexy as you can get.

Well, things don't always work out the way they should. You never know what life is going to throw at you, and I should know that by now. All the same, I allow a few hot tears to escape. I hardly ever cry these days. You reach a point where it feels a bit irrelevant – doesn't bring much release. But it's something to do. Jade pops into my head, and that makes the tears come quicker. I should have known he would blame me. I can see why he would think that I should have tried harder to get her out, but he wasn't there. I wonder what he would have done. Would he have sacrificed himself for her? Would he have stayed in there, searching and searching, until it killed him? He thinks he would have, I can tell that. But he'll never know.

I think about sending him a message – something

along the lines of how I love Jade too and I'm glad it looks like she's going to be OK – but I can't quite bring myself to do it. Maybe I'll wait a while. I'm still hoping that he'll make the first move when he realizes how stupid he's been; not over Jade, but over these sudden suspicions that I've been sneaking some man into our home to shag while he's out. I try and summon up some of the anger that came to me in the hospital, but I can't. Now it just feels sad. I'd never cheat on Alex. On anyone. He should have known that, from the very first time we met.

I close my eyes, and I'm back there. Waiting at the bar in a crowd of people, trying to decide what I wanted to drink. The sudden awareness of a body close by that felt different from the rest; the minutest brush of a coat sleeve against mine, but something that electrified, set my senses on red alert. It sounds overblown and dramatic, but even then I knew that whoever this was next to me, it was someone I wanted to know. I looked up. Saw him there, tall and broad, staring at me, his lips curving into a smile and his eyes sparkling. 'Buy you a drink?'

I nodded. It was instant and powerful, this leap of interest. But a few seconds later I saw the wedding ring. *No fucking way*, I thought. So I made my face cold and angled my body away from him. 'I'm not interested in married men.'

For a moment his eyes clouded with confusion, and then he glanced down at his hand. He folded his fingers into a fist, the pale gold band standing out stark against his skin. 'No, no, you don't understand,' he said, the words falling over themselves in his hurry to make himself understood. 'I'm not married. That is, I am, I was, but I'm a widower. My wife died years ago.'

I paused, and I could feel it trembling on the tip of my tongue, words I knew were inappropriate, but something told me he wouldn't mind. 'Well,' I said at last. 'That's good.' And then we were laughing together in quiet complicity; both of us knowing it was crass and disrespectful, half appalled, but secretly glad that we were on the same page.

An hour later I was in his bedroom, kneeling on the white cotton sheets, the windows wide open and the scented air rushing in from the sea. When he took his shirt off there was a light film of sweat on his skin, smelling salty and sweet. He pinched my nipples in his fingers, so hard that it made them red, and I pinned him down to the bed, my long hair falling over his chest, and made him look at me as I pushed myself down on to him, gasping with the relief. There was a warm breeze rolling softly over my skin, and I moaned, feeling his hands stroking and teasing, relaxing into a rhythm that built and built until he was holding me urgently, bringing me down to meet him. And with a shock I found myself wanting to please him, startling myself with the force of this discovery. He wasn't afraid to look me in the eye and face what was happening. And afterwards as I lit a cigarette he lay back against the pillows, still watching me, and lifting a hand to brush the hair from my face. It was dark outside, there was a small lamp shining in the corner of the room, and his face was half shadowed.

I took the hand and pulled it forward in front of us,

running my finger over the ring. 'Can I ask – why do you leave it on?'

He hesitated for an instant, and then reached across wordlessly with his other hand, a swift movement, pulling the ring up and away, off his finger and folded into his palm. He placed it on the bedside table. Not a careless act, not dismissive. But decisive, all the same.

Then he kissed me again and I felt his arms slide underneath me, arching my back up against him. I couldn't help thinking, in the back of my mind, that it was all a bit slick. A bit well practised, maybe. It flicked through my head, the thought of him doing this at other times with other women – the ring sliding on and off like a magic trick. Now you see it, now you don't. But I wound myself around him, clinging on tight. If he didn't mean it now, he would soon.

I wait in the hotel room for what feels like hours, but when I glance at the clock I realize it's only been about forty-five minutes. I scramble off the bed and go over to the window, pushing it open and craning my neck down to watch the street below. In a minute, I tell myself, I'll see Alex walking up the road, his hands stuffed in his pockets, a determined roll to his stride. Coming to find me. The picture is so clear in my head that the street's continued emptiness is a shock. Well, not emptiness. There are people scurrying past, cars winding their way down the road, but none of them are him and they might as well be cardboard cut-outs.

I'm not used to Alex disappearing on me – usually when we argue he's the first one to reach out. He isn't

41

someone who needs a lot of personal space. I was surprised, right from the start, how easily he let me in, and how quickly we became close. My cynicism on that first night hadn't been justified, and to my surprise I'd found that I was the one pushing back. I wanted him, but I didn't trust closeness, had seen how it could fall apart and blow people to pieces. I had my walls up. But once I saw that he wasn't going to run, I let them all down. I gave myself up to it, more than I'd ever thought I could.

I lean forward on the window ledge, resting my chin on my folded arms and feeling the wind blow coolly across my face. I'm remembering how it was, the morning after we first slept together. I was showering in his bathroom, luxuriating in flashbacks from the night before, when I noticed a bottle of pink raspberry-scented shower gel balanced on the edge of the bath. I was surprised by how quickly my stomach dropped – how much I realized he could hurt me, even then. I carried the bottle into the living room, still naked and dripping from the shower, and held it up quizzically.

'You don't strike me as the pink shower gel type,' I said, making my voice casual. I wasn't going to scream and weep, not after one night, no matter how I really felt.

He looked instantly guilty, and I braced myself. 'I knew I should have told you earlier.'

I laughed, though it was an effort. 'Easy come, easy go. She's still on the scene then?'

'Still on the scene . . .?' he repeated, looking a little mystified, and then it clicked. A strange look flashed across his face: half relief, half offence. 'No,' he said. 'The shower gel belongs to my daughter, Jade. She had a sleepover with her friend last night, but she lives here with me. She's twelve. My late wife was her mother.' He paused as if he was waiting for a reaction, but I didn't give him one; I was scrambling to readjust, and I wasn't sure how I felt. 'Like I say, I should have told you earlier,' he said. 'Of course, I understand if you don't want to take things any further. All the same, it would be a shame.' A beat of silence. I was conscious of how close we were standing, the air warm and soft on my naked skin, my eyes on his own intent gaze. He shrugged. 'I thought there might be something worth pursuing.'

It was the confidence with which he said it that got me. He did a good job of pretending that he could take it or leave it, but his eyes said otherwise, and when I pushed him back on to the sofa and climbed on top of him in answer, soaking his shirt with the water from the shower, so did his body.

I didn't meet Jade for three months, and by then I felt secure, so safe in the knowledge that Alex was crazy about me that nothing could faze me much. When it happened, it was low-key; an after-school kitchen dinner, Jade balanced awkwardly on a stool and knocking her legs together as she prattled about her day. A small girl with her fair hair tied up in plaits and a habit of blinking fast when she was nervous. On the whole she seemed younger than I'd expected, but once or twice I caught her watching me when she thought I wasn't looking, her eyes narrowed thoughtfully in surprisingly adult evaluation. I couldn't tell what she was thinking.

'Your dad talks about you a lot,' I said at one point, when Alex had left the room. 'He's always saying how proud he is of you.' He hadn't said that, in fact, not explicitly, but it was obvious he was. I'd been doing some watching of my own that evening, and I'd seen the way he looked at her, hanging off her every word. For some reason, I hadn't expected him to be like that.

Jade smiled, looking down at her feet, but said nothing. I thought at first that she was embarrassed, but it also struck me that maybe there was just very little for her to say in response. I'd stated a fact, like the sky being blue.

We made conversation for a while longer, until her bedtime, and when she rose to go upstairs she came forwards and shook my hand, formally, as if we'd just concluded a business meeting. 'Thank you for coming,' she said.

'Thank you for having me.' Impulsively, I let go of her hand and went for a hug instead. I pressed the narrow bones of her shoulder blades against my palms, smelled the sweet, fragrant smell of shampoo in her hair. I wasn't sure what I was supposed to be feeling. Part of me had wanted to fall in love with her at first sight. She was Alex's daughter, and if she mattered to him then she mattered to me. But there wasn't really anything there inside me to catch on to, not yet. I told myself not to be disappointed. Expecting maternal instinct for a twelve-year-old I'd never met before was a stretch. She was fine, quite sweet in fact. And those little flashes of evaluation ... They were no surprise. She'd be wondering who I really was, this cuckoo in the nest who'd arrived from nowhere. Wanting to protect your territory was something I could understand.

When she had disappeared up the stairs I turned to Alex with my eyebrows raised. 'Well?'

'Good,' he said. 'Very good.' He was brimming with suppressed excitement and I saw that to him this meeting had been invested with even more than I had realized. I looked into his eyes and I had the sense of something let out of a trap. Green light, permission to take off. He pulled me against him and kissed me without another word, and later he ripped my clothes off and fucked me on the sofa, his hand over my mouth to keep me quiet while she slept upstairs. I could see the possibilities shining in his eyes, the knowledge that now this could really go somewhere. In that moment I knew that no matter how awkward it might be navigating my way into this pseudo-mother role, it didn't matter. I could do anything, as long as it got me this.

Afterwards we lay together quietly for a while, his hand stroking rhythmically up and down my side, the movement and its repetition soothing me and sending me close to sleep. When he spoke it was a surprise. 'Tell me about you,' he said. 'I mean, before I met you.'

It was the first time he'd ever asked anything like that. He was a man focused on the here and now, who didn't see the point in mulling over what was gone – it was one of the things that had drawn me to him. All the same, I understood the question. Now that he was sure this wasn't just a fling, he wanted to dig deeper, make sure he understood who he was sharing his life with. It was a bit pop psychology textbook, but it made sense.

I shifted up on my elbow, rolling over so that I could look him in the face. 'I'm not sure where to start.'

He shrugged, brushing my hair away from my face. 'It doesn't really matter. I don't know anything much about your childhood. Where you grew up, your family. What happened to you as a teenager, when you moved here and why. Everything that got you here.'

I laughed. 'Everything?'

He half smiled, acknowledging the impossibility. 'Yeah, if that's all right. Seriously, though, I want to know.'

I took a moment to think, arranging things in my head. And then I told him everything I could think of. The lonely childhood in a remote country village, unalleviated by the presence of siblings; the evenings spent watching my parents entertain their friends over dinner while the conversation flew over my head. The aimless summers that I filled with television, drawing and complex imaginary games. The gradual unfurling of purpose and passion as I worked harder at studying and discovered a love for design. The teenage nights spent drinking with friends in meadows under the stars, the move to London in my early twenties, the years of flat-sharing with fellow design students, the job hunts and the break-ups and the bumps in the road that led to the bar job I was doing at present, just filling in time, waiting for something better. It wasn't a particularly remarkable narrative, but Alex's attention didn't waver. He listened quietly, occasionally interjecting to ask a question, and when I eventually stopped talking the sky had darkened outside the lounge windows and I could see our reflections in the lamp-lit glass. He took me in his arms again and rested his chin on my head. I could hear his heartbeat, steady and even against my cheek. He didn't have to say it. I knew that he felt closer to me, not just physically; we were finally moving into a new phase where lust wasn't the only thing binding us together, where he felt he really knew me.

Later, when he was asleep, I lay there and wondered if anything I had told him was actually true. I concluded that it wasn't. I probably hadn't needed to go quite so far. I could have left some grains of reality nestling in there, amongst the lies, but somehow it had felt easier to go the whole hog. And yes, I felt guilty. I didn't want him under false pretences. But sometimes it's a question of need. I loved him, but I didn't trust him yet, and I wasn't sure if I ever would.

Alex

September 2017

I'LL JUST LEAVE YOU *to it for a bit while you try and fig-ure something out.* Those last words Natalie fired at me before she left the hospital rattle around in my brain for a while. There's an uncharacteristic sarcasm to them, a brittleness I've rarely glimpsed in her. I've always believed that when people act like this – defensive, flipping the situation round on you – it's generally because they have something to hide. Try as I might, I can't get the images that are flooding my head out again. My wife sidling to our back door, her finger to her lips as she lets in a stranger; his hands rough and urgent on her body. And I can't help thinking of something else she said before she left. *You don't look for the most likely explanation, you look for the one that's going to cause the most hurt.* But what happens when those two things are one and the same?

I remind myself that Natalie has never given me any reason to doubt her. Up until this moment, there's

48

nothing I can pinpoint that even hints at her having wanted to look elsewhere, and the strength of my instinct about this makes no real sense. Of course, I can't help thinking, it's probably true what they say: guilty people are often the most suspicious. It's an uncomfortable thought, and I shake it off. What's past is past.

In any case, I know I won't be able to rest until I've satisfied myself that she has nothing to hide. The only way to do that which I can think of right now is to go back to the house, look through her things, whatever might be left of them, and see if there's anything to fuel my suspicions. It's not a pleasant thought, but it beats sitting around in the hospital unable to see my daughter for hours while the doctors perform tests, or heading back to the hotel for another barbed conversation with my wife. I shrug on my coat and make for the exit.

Twenty minutes later I'm at the top of the hill and staring down at our street, searching for the house. I can see the flickers of red and white tape blowing in the breeze, and the dark jagged outline that already looks oddly familiar, overwriting the memory of what used to be there. Slowly, I walk down towards it. As I get closer I see that there are two men there, dressed in boiler-suit uniforms and patrolling the building; one is holding a hammer and chisel, bent over a jutting expanse of wall. A vague stirring of memory; something the woman from the housing association said last night. They'll be carrying out a structural assessment of damage, trying to determine if the foundations are sound, deciding whether to rebuild or rip up.

'I'm Alex Carmichael,' I say as I near the men, and the elder of them turns round instantly, obviously recognizing the name. 'This is my house. You're doing the assessment?'

The man nods, wiping a dust-blackened hand on his overalls before extending it for me to shake. 'We're just finishing up. Got some tests to do back at the lab, but we've done quite a bit on-site. The deterioration isn't too bad,' he says. 'The majority of it's cosmetic. Could have been a lot worse.'

'That sounds positive,' I say automatically. And yes, I can see that it could have been worse, on almost every level. But right now, standing in front of what looks like wreckage, it's hard to feel grateful.

I glance up at the house, and when I look closer I can see the staircase through the burned-out windows, stained and charred but still apparently solid. 'Is it possible to go in?' I ask. 'I was hoping to take a look round. See if there's anything I can salvage, to take away with me for now.' It's true enough, but it's not the whole truth. The reality is that I'm looking for more than keepsakes. I've never been through Natalie's things – have never had any reason to – but I can't shake the feeling that if she's hiding anything, then now might be the time to find it.

The man half shrugs. 'Not for me to say. It's at your own risk, like.' I can tell he's going through the motions. I nod briskly and turn away, my hand going automatically to my pocket for the front-door keys before I realize that I don't need them anymore.

I step into the hallway, and the smell of smoke is still

50

there, collecting instantly in my throat and making it hard to breathe. Out of the corner of my eye I see the kitchen – a nightmarish collection of blackened rubble and stripped wallpaper, with bizarre patches of random clarity: the silver utensils pot on the worktop with a green spatula poking out the top, seemingly untouched. I remind myself of what the man said – and yes, I can see that a lot of this is cosmetic damage. But still, I can hardly connect it to the room where we all used to collect at the end of the day and chat: Jade on the kitchen stool swinging her legs, recounting the latest exploits of her hapless friend Susie and making us laugh; Natalie stirring a pot at the cooker with her hair tied up at the nape of her neck, the steam rising up and flushing her cheeks pink. I remember just a few days ago, when Jade had left the room to call a friend, stealing up behind my wife and putting my lips to the place where her hair met her skin, sliding my hands easily around her waist, feeling that spark of desire as she pushed back against me. It's like another country, viewed on a TV screen from far, far away.

I move on, reaching the staircase and making my ascent. It's our bedroom that I really want to look around, but as I step on to the landing my eye is caught by Jade's room first. The carpet is stained and there's a jagged hole burned into the far wall, but as I scan the room I note with relief that a lot can be saved. The little collection of swimming trophies she keeps on the windowsill is almost clean, and so are the bundles of jewellery and make-up on her dressing table. Gingerly, I ease open a drawer and find a sheaf of papers, and the sight of them pristine and untouched is enough to bring sense-less tears to my eyes. I'll come back here tomorrow with a couple of cases, I decide, collect together more of her possessions and take them to the hospital.

Swinging round again, I notice her mobile, poking out from beneath her pillow – I have no idea if it will be work-ing, but I slip it into my pocket anyway along with the charger that is plugged in at the wall. After a moment's hesitation, I also take Sidney, the soft toy rabbit that Heather bought for her when she was only a few months old, and which still nestles at the end of her bed, covered with a fine layer of dust but still salvageable.

Carrying Jade's things, I turn and go to my own bed-room, and I wince. It looks more brutal in here – the wallpaper ripped away in streaks, the floorboards charred and jagged, every surface stained with soot that feels smooth and oily against my skin when I touch it. I almost walk straight out again, but my eye is caught by the wardrobe – the door swinging open, and a collection of Natalie's scarves and bags bundled at the back, look-ing at first sight to be undamaged.

I hesitate, and then I pick my way towards it, walk-ing softly and slowly as if the room is a coiled snake that could unfurl and strike. Crouching down, I pull some of the handbags from the wardrobe, then retreat to the landing, emptying them into my lap as I sit down on the floor. I sift through the contents: a couple of compact mirrors, an almost used-up lipstick, a spiral-bound notebook full of shopping lists and half-written reminders, a load of train tickets and supermarket receipts. And then I find something else.

The photo is faded, a thick white line across the centre as if it's been folded hard in two, then smoothed out. It looks to have been taken inside some kind of bar or nightclub: slick metallic surfaces, spotlights picking out the rows of glinting bottles. I don't recognize the place, and I don't recognize the exotic-looking man lounging on the stool with his elbows resting idly on the bar. He's young – in his late twenties, perhaps. His arms are bare and muscular, the skin taut and olive-coloured. He's sitting next to a woman, and for one stupid moment I'm not sure whether or not this woman is my wife. She looks similar, at a glance, although younger. But when I look more closely I see that she's someone I don't know. The curve of her mouth, the colour of her eyes, the height of her cheekbones – they're all slightly different. She's looking straight at the camera but her expression is flat, as if she doesn't want the photo taken.

I look back at the man beside her. By contrast, he's barely looking at the camera, but there's a kind of contemptuous curve to his mouth, a sly knowledge in his slanting, challenging gaze, that shows he's aware he's being watched, and that he expects it. The muscles of his arms are tautly defined. I can imagine those arms lifting weights in the gym; can imagine them swinging a punch that finds its mark. I can imagine them pinning down my wife. Even in print, there's an indefinable energy that radiates off him. I don't know who this man is, but I don't trust him. And I don't want his picture in my wife's handbag.

I fold the photo back along the crease and press it

down hard, then shove it into the pocket of my coat. My heart is beating fast and unevenly, and I realize that the palms of my hands are wet. Of course, this proves nothing. It's just a photo of a man and a woman, probably from years ago. And yet it's unnerving, this glimpse into something of which I knew nothing. I go back into the bedroom. This time I excavate further, pushing the tangle of bags and scarves in the wardrobe aside and reaching a small pile of folders. Most of them are labelled: Finances, Household, Birthday Cards.

I flick through them briefly but their contents are just as mundane as the labels suggest. All except for one, and even that is nothing exceptional at first sight. Just a few old documents: a certificate from a music exam, a couple of schoolbooks, a torn-out article from a newspaper. The only unusual thing is that they relate to someone I don't know. The name that pops out at me from all the papers is Rachel Castelle. Rachel Castelle has passed her Grade 4 piano with merit. Rachel Castelle has been feted in the paper for winning a local tennis tournament. Rachel Castelle has meticulously cut and stuck and annotated and put together a school project about Tudor history. There's no reason for me to be worried by these things – they certainly aren't the sordid evidence of infidelity that I feared I might find – but somehow they add to the strangeness. A childhood friend, perhaps, or a relative. Perhaps even someone who's died.

The thought makes me replace the papers, feeling a little ashamed. Taking the photograph is one thing, but it feels wrong to be rifling through Natalie's things like this – and besides, I don't think there are any more answers to be gained here, not yet.

Slowly, I pick my way back downstairs and go out on to the street, blinking in the sudden harsh daylight. As I shield my eyes against it, I notice that the workmen have been joined by a lean man in his thirties with a shaved head and wearing police uniform, who eyes me a little suspiciously as I emerge.

I stride up to him and offer him my hand. 'Alex Carmichael,' I say. 'This is my house.'

'Oh, right.' The policeman shakes my hand and mutters a few perfunctory words of condolence. 'I was going to contact you in any case, now that the initial investigation into the damage is concluded. You've probably seen already that the house seems to be salvageable. If you want to rebuild and renovate then it should be doable. Are you sorted with insurance?'

I nod, mentally adding the need to contact the insurance company to my list. But we entered into a watertight plan when we bought the place, and it's the least of my worries. 'That's all fine.'

He nods. 'The other major point of the investigation is locating the cause of the fire, of course,' he continues. 'We've discounted all the usual suspects – dodgy wiring and electrics, that kind of thing. But we've turned up something else which is more unusual.'

'And what's that?' I ask abruptly.

His narrow eyes flicker in my direction. 'The burn pattern isn't typical.'

I must look blank, because he turns and gestures up at the house, his hand tracing an invisible line down its

55

centre. 'Normally, you'd see what looks like a V shape. It basically indicates the fire spreading out from a central point, almost like an arrow pointing to the source. As you can see, there's nothing like that here.' I follow his gaze and see that it's true; the external walls are darkly pockmarked with burns, like paint splashed randomly on to a canvas. I stare at them as if I'm trying to make sense of an optical illusion, expecting to see some order rising from the chaos.

'The reason for that is clear when you look a bit deeper,' the policeman says. 'What we've established is that this fire had multiple points of origin. It wasn't caused by a freak localized explosion or anything of that sort.'

Multiple points of origin. I turn the phrase over in my head. 'And that indicates what exactly?' I ask, though I'm pretty sure I know.

'It's usually a good indicator that we're dealing with a case of arson. Not a certainty. Not at this stage. But enough to kick-start a deeper investigation. It's best for you to be aware.'

'Right,' I say again. 'But you're not suggesting – I mean, obviously you're not suggesting that we set fire to our own home, are you.' I deliberately don't make it sound like a question.

The policeman twists his mouth briefly in a smile, straightening up and moving a little away from me, signalling his detachment. 'You'd be surprised what some people do,' he says. 'Mostly to cash in on the insurance, you know. Get a nice new revamp on their property.' His tone is casual, but there's an inference I don't like.

I smile back tightly. 'That is surprising, yes.'

'Well,' he says as he begins to stroll up towards the workmen, 'we'll be in touch.'

My head is whirling as I walk back up the hill, trying to take in the implications of what he's said. If someone did set fire to the house deliberately, then surely it's a sign that the man Jade saw *was* an intruder, and that he's the one responsible. When I think of my family under threat in this way, my suspicions of Natalie seem reprehensible, and irrelevant. But then I think of the man in the photograph, my sense that there are things about my wife of which I know nothing – and I'm unsure again, my thoughts spinning off wildly, taking me down paths I don't want to follow.

When I get back to the hotel dusk is falling and our room is empty. I go over to the minibar and take out a miniature of gin and a bottle of tonic, pour myself a glass and swig it down in three gulps. For a few seconds there's a buzz, but it soon fizzes into nothing. I could drink my way through the entire minibar and it wouldn't solve this. I need to find Natalie and talk to her.

I already know where she'll be; when we've argued in the past, she's always told me afterwards that she went down to the seafront to be alone with her thoughts. There's something calming for her in facing the water and forgetting that anyone else exists. I walk fast down the esplanade. The sun is sinking on the horizon, a blaze of virulent pink and gold splashed against the darkening sky, and I can barely make out the coastline beyond the rocky beach. I strike out across it all the same and make for the water's edge, sea-slicked pebbles crunching against my boots, my breath blowing out ahead of me in fine clouds.

It's only a few minutes before I see her, sitting huddled on the rocks with her knees drawn up. Her dark hair is blowing behind her and as I get closer I can see her profile as she looks out to sea. She looks shut off, absorbed in her thoughts.

'Natalie,' I say, but she's already turning her head and I know she's seen me. More than that, she's expecting me.

Natalie

I SEE HIM FROM a way off, but I pretend I haven't. It's ridiculous, because I've been waiting for him for hours, but all of a sudden I feel like I need more time. I've been so lost in thoughts of the past that returning to the present, with all its sudden complications, is a wrench.

'Hi,' he says quietly, perching awkwardly on the outcrop of rock. He reaches out his hand to where mine is resting, but in the same moment I've brought my own hand up to push my hair away from my face, and he's left grasping at nothing. It's just a silly little hiccup of misalignment but his expression flickers with hurt and he curls his fingers swiftly back into his palm.

'Look,' he says after a moment. 'I'm not stupid, Natalie. I know how traumatic the fire must have been, but it seems like there's something else going on here. And I have to say, when I think about it, it isn't even just since the fire. You haven't seemed yourself for . . . for a while now.'

His gaze is serious and intense; he's not playing around. And for an instant it's as if I've spiralled out of my own body and am coolly looking down at myself, my own voice clear and present in my head: *This guy loves you, but he doesn't know who the hell you are. He doesn't know you at all.* And yet he's not stupid. He senses something.

I must take longer than I think to formulate an answer, because Alex shrugs impatiently, and then, as if he's made a snap decision, he rummages in his coat pocket and pulls something out. 'I found this in the house earlier.'

I peer forward in the semi-dark and when I see what it is my heart stops. It's strange, because of course I've looked at this photo hundreds of times. I probably only looked at it last week. But this time I wasn't expecting it, and it's bizarrely and painfully out of context – here on the rocks in the cold with my husband, whose hand is trembling ever so slightly as he holds it out to me.

'Are you having an affair with him?' he asks bluntly. His tone is a challenge but the look in his eyes tells a different story. He's terrified I'm going to say yes.

Something washes through me: a kind of darkly amused horror. He doesn't know just how improbable – impossible – this would be. I can't help giving a brief, humourless snort of laughter. 'God, no.'

'Then why do you have this picture?' he asks. 'And who's the woman? You've never mentioned either of these people to me, have you?'

Slowly, I shake my head. 'No, I haven't.' My mind is whirring and I realize I've thought about this moment several times, or variations of it, and yet I have absolutely no idea what I'm going to say. When you've kept so many secrets from someone for so long, it changes the shape of your life. I can't imagine how it might shift again if I let them out, and I'm not sure – not at all sure – if I want to, or if I even can.

'And that's not all,' Alex says. He doesn't sound angry, exactly. More frightened, behind that prickly, defensive edge. 'I found some other stuff. A load of papers about someone called Rachel. You've never mentioned her to me either. It feels like there's all this . . .' He raises his hands helplessly into the air, encircling us for a moment. 'All this *stuff* coming out of the woodwork, and I don't know what any of it means, or even if it means anything at all, I don't . . .'

He carries on talking but I'm not truly listening. My mind has snagged on the sound of the name in his mouth. *Rachel*. I never thought anyone would look me in the eye and say that name ever again. It's shocking. Exciting, almost. I can't just pretend this isn't happening, or try and fob him off. And all of a sudden my head clears and I know what I have to do.

'I'm going to tell you something,' I say abruptly. 'Something that I didn't intend to tell you now, or at all.'

Alex is motionless and watchful. 'What? Whatever it is, Natalie, you *can* tell me. It won't change how I feel about you. I love you – I know you.' Our faces are close together and his lips are inches away from mine, his breath sweet and cool on my face.

'You don't know me as well as you think you do,' I say at last.

61

He waits a little, then frowns. 'What do you mean?' he says slowly.

I draw in a breath and the night air rushes into my lungs. My head spins lightly. Am I really going to do this? 'When I was younger,' I say, 'I was someone else.'

'Well,' he says automatically, configuring this into something he can understand, 'we all change. We all do things that—'

'No,' I say. 'I don't just mean that I behaved differently, or that I did things I wouldn't do now. I mean I was someone else entirely. I had a different life, a different name. All the things I've told you about my past, my childhood – they weren't real.'

I've been speaking with clinical precision, because it seems the easiest way to get through this. The only way. But now I cut myself off and I'm staring at him, waiting for his reaction.

He frowns again, looking puzzled and lost. I can tell he hasn't fully taken it in.

'Those papers you found,' I say. 'They're mine. I mean, they're me. About me. Rachel . . .' I shake my head, aware I'm not really making sense. 'She's me,' I say. 'I'm her.'

He stares at me. 'Rachel?' he repeats. Softly, as if he's trying it out for size and finding it somehow lacking. 'But . . . I don't understand. Why?'

'I want to explain this to you,' I say, 'but I need more time. Like I said, I didn't think I'd ever be doing this. It feels so strange.'

'Join the club.' It's a weak attempt at flippancy; he forces a smile, clearly lost at sea. 'Look, you're landing a lot on me here. This is . . . You're scaring me. Did you – did something bad happen?' He grimaces, as if he's just heard how childish the words sound.

I half nod. But no, I'm not ready to go all the way, not yet. 'Yes. Something to do with my sister. Sadie.' I glance down at the photograph, which he still holds in his outstretched hands. The painted-on smile, the slanted eyes, the cheekbones that are angled and defined, the same as my own. He follows my gaze, and I know he gets it.

'I didn't even know you had a sister,' he says flatly.

'I don't,' I reply, and the conviction that I'm speaking the truth floods through me viciously. 'Not really. Not anymore.'

PART TWO

Rachel

IT'S ALMOST ELEVEN AT night and she's alone in the flat. At times like this, when she's tidied up and dimmed the lights and is wandering slowly back and forth through the rooms, she likes to shift into make-believe. Part of this fantasy is that the flat is actually hers. She's somehow come into enough money to buy it, in this exclusive part of London, just overlooking Covent Garden market. Everything she sees and touches belongs to her, and no one can take it away. In reality the flat belongs to Martine, a friend from uni who promptly went off travelling after they graduated, her father's seemingly limitless wallet acting as the wind beneath her wings. But Rachel knows she's been lucky to be chosen as the friend who gets to look after the flat and pay a nominal rent, and in truth this isn't the most important part of the fantasy. The real key to it – the thing that keeps her coming back to this compulsive little ritual – is the idea that she lives here alone.

Now, as ever, it's an illusion that is difficult to sustain, because everywhere she looks the evidence to the contrary hits her. The black smudge on the wall behind the cooker where Sadie once threw a charcoal-stained frying pan in a drunken temper. The ground-in marks left by cigarette butts that pepper the floor of her bedroom, like ink shaken from a pen. The deeply grooved scratches along the beautiful parquet floorboards in the lounge, which Rachel doesn't even know the origin of. They weren't there, and then they were. She's aware that she should be doing more about all of this. Trying at least to do some damage limitation, scrub and shampoo and paint until things look a little better. But she's paralysed – unable to stop picturing Martine's look of horror when she finally returns to her nest, unable to imagine this not happening, or do anything to stop it.

She completes her slow circle of the flat and glances at the clock again. Five past eleven. She has no idea when Sadie might be back, or even where she is. She's probably at a club, mingling mindlessly with people whose names and faces she barely knows, treating them like her best and oldest friends. Rachel thinks, briefly, about the well-trodden paths that Sadie might go down tonight: causing drug-fuelled trouble out on the streets in the early hours, or ending up at some weirdo's flat and crisis-calling her to come and get her out, or having a run-in with the police. She even thinks about some of the darker possibilities, ones that haven't yet happened: Sadie lying broken and crumpled in the corner of a back alley, raped or mugged or left for dead. And then she lets the idea that her sister might never come home alight and settle, just for an instant, and she feels the familiar, sickening pull between devastation and relief.

It's not possible that she really remembers much about when Sadie was a toddler, as she herself is only a couple of years older, but nonetheless there's a whole host of pictures there, real or imagined, locked away in her head. She remembers, or has been told often enough that it's become synonymous with memory, her sister following her around everywhere she went. Even dutifully waiting outside the bathroom door while she went to the toilet – a dumb and faithful Labrador awaiting notice and praise.

When they were young Sadie was called her shadow. It was a nickname that stuck for a while, and then gradually people stopped using it. Not just, she thinks in retrospect, because her sister stopped following her around, but also because it started feeling more and more inappropriate as Sadie grew and blossomed and brightened. It soon became blindingly obvious that she was no one's shadow. In fact, she had a tendency to cast everything else into negative, without even meaning to. Rachel has a vivid memory – and this one is definitely real, has been revisited time and time again like a nervous tic despite its embarrassing lack of relevance to adult life – of climbing the small wooden steps of the school assembly hall that led to the stage. She's on her way to collect a trophy at prize day, possibly for swimming or art. And there in the front row is Sadie, beaming and clapping her hands furiously until her palms are red and sore, radiating triumph and praise. And the eyes of the teachers and the parents are gradually drawn to her, fond with approval and indulgence, so that by the time Rachel actually collects the trophy no one really seems to be looking at her at all. It's not Sadie's fault. Not exactly. But this is the way it is.

As a child, she is conscious of a growing resentment, even if she can't give it a name. A tightness in her chest when her sister leaps into view, a kind of hot itchiness spreading inside her when she watches her holding court. She knows that she, Rachel, is superior in many ways. She's cleverer, more talented, more practical. She can't quite put her finger on why this neatly assembled little tower of qualities doesn't seem to count for much in the face of whatever her sister has – and again, she can't give it a name. They even look quite similar, similar enough to be acknowledged as siblings at a glance. Sometimes she studies her own oval face in the mirror, half consciously comparing it to her sister's slightly more heart-shaped one. The colour of their eyes, the mouldings of their bones. Similar, but not the same.

When she thinks about the single incident when this resentment coalesced into something tangible, it has the quality of a dream. A stifling summer morning, the dawn just breaking through sun-drenched curtains, the air hot and thick. She stretches her limbs in bed, feeling the stickiness of the sheets against her skin. Quietly, she slips out of bed. The feel of the carpet warm and soft under her feet, making it easy to move without noise. She and Sadie share a room, in those days. Her sister is sleeping, one arm flung carelessly above her head, her breathing deep and regular, her eyelids moving minutely with dreams. She sits and watches her for a while. Cross-legged on the carpet, her eyes narrowed in the glare of the sun. Her sister's hair spills like a fountain across the pillow. Shades of pale brown, gold and something close to red, interwoven into a complex pattern.

When the thought strikes her, it feels calm and mellow. Nothing sinister. She moves on her hands and knees towards the box of arts and crafts supplies, rooting through until she finds the scissors. And then she crouches by the side of Sadie's bed and lifts a strand of hair gently, held between her fingers, and snips. It falls to the ground silently, a whisper of colour. No skies fall, no thunderclaps crash. So she reaches out again and takes another strand, a little thicker this time, and cuts again. And soon there becomes something gently compulsive in this easy rhythm, and the gradually growing pile of softness by her feet, scattering like thread. She is surprised by how deeply her sister sleeps. It feels as if they might stay here for ever, lost in this little ritual. So much so that when Sadie stirs and opens her eyes, it takes a moment for her to catch up with reality.

She glances down at the scissors in her hand, looks at the fallen hair on the carpet. There is more of it than she thought, and when she looks back at her sister she realizes with a sense of impending doom that she has made a mess of this. The hair sticks out jagged and uneven, cut in some places almost to the scalp. She opens her mouth to give some kind of explanation, even though she has no idea what that might be, but by this time Sadie is screaming, her eyes round and accusing and terrified, and she can already hear the thump of their mother's footsteps along the corridor, the bedroom door yawning open and the drawn-in breath before the storm erupts.

After this storm has passed, the incident is covered over – quickly, shamefully. Rachel is excused on account of her youth, although the truth is that at six years old she's just treading the boundary of accountability and in her heart she knows that she meant to do what she did, even if in the moment it didn't feel strictly wrong. Sadie has a professional haircut, a gamine crop that actually makes her look even more striking than she did before. Their parents, with their usual ineffectual misjudgement, eventually turn it into a funny story. Occasionally, Rachel is referred to as 'the hairdresser in training'; an indulgent, slightly patronizing dismissal of whatever driving force might have led their daughter to mutilate her sister's appearance while she slept. It's an infrequent but unsettling reminder of something she barely glimpses out of the corner of her eye; the knowledge that no matter what she does, it will have little effect on Sadie's hard, glancing power. Their roles are set, and she can do nothing about it.

Despite these uncomfortable undercurrents, they're close as children. Exploring in the woods near their home, digging holes in the mud and filling them with water, making sculptures out of bits of wood and leaves. Drawing pictures of each other, elaborately signed and dated. Holding midnight feasts in their shared bedroom, giggling over the stash of crisps and biscuits they've patiently built up over months of covert swiping from the store cupboard. But these things can only take them so far, and by the time they are in their teens this closeness has begun to feel precarious and difficult to sustain, a needle jolting on a record.

Sadie at thirteen looks years older – her body already taking on tightly provocative curves, her face carefully made-up to suggest wanton sophistication. She starts bringing home boyfriends, randomly selected strangers who share little except a certain rough diamond quality and an apparent devotion to her. She makes friends with the kinds of girls who Rachel dreads passing in corridors. The sort who whisper and roll their eyes and smoke cigarettes at the back of the school playing fields. She realizes, with a kind of dawning dread, that her sister is one of them – more than that, she's the queen. Rachel herself is no laughable swot. She's clever but she's pretty too; she should be able to hold her head up high and walk without embarrassment. She shouldn't have to train her gaze straight ahead and ignore the piercing glares of her sister and her friends as they stand lolling against the school lockers with their skirts hitched up, a ridiculous mean-girls parody. And it's true that they don't really come near her, those girls, but there's a sense of sharks circling, ready to swoop if they sense blood.

At home Sadie increasingly acts as if she owns the place; crossing the room to turn off the television with a snap, frequently announcing that she's so fucking bored here she could die, stinking the place out with cheap hairspray and perfume. Their parents steal looks over the dinner table at their changeling daughter with the rainbow-streaked hair and the long, glittering nails, and bewilderment is written all over their faces. They have no idea how she got here. Even less how to bring her back into the fold. It is Rachel's role to act as the intermediary, interpreting her sister's moods and mumbles and haughty stares and translating them into something their parents can understand. It's a tiring role, and for the most part a thankless one.

And yet there are moments, even in those days . . . The odd precious time when the distance between them unaccountably drops away and they're conspirators again. She remembers a movie afternoon, soon after Christmas when the weather is too cold and wet for Sadie to want to venture out. They huddle under blankets together and light the fire and watch films that they're ten years too old for, and there's a kind of fuzzy nostalgia binding them together and briefly lighting a spark of intimacy. One evening, they go to a concert together to watch one of the few bands they agree on, and they dance wildly in the crush of people, laughing breathlessly with the effort.

And then of course there are the times when Sadie's mask slips and she shows a kind of helpless vulnerability that Rachel can't help but respond to, no matter how calculated she fears it might be. The – vanishingly rare – occasions when a boyfriend dumps her, rather than the other way around, and Rachel is called into her room to witness her face wet with tears, her eyes sending a mute appeal. She grows used to the painful tug of emotions that wrestles inside her at these times; the desire to push her sister away and snap that it serves her right to be the one who is hurt for a change, combined with the need to cuddle and comfort and take this hurt away. Somehow it always seems to be the gentler impulse that wins, even though she knows that this closeness won't last. Her sister might not love her, or even like her very much, but she needs her. Of that she's sure.

When she's away at university, those three years unencumbered by anything but her own purpose and her own desires, she starts to think that things may change. The uncomfortable tightness of the threads between herself and Sadie seems to loosen. She no longer feels the same sense of duty or responsibility, and she's free to be herself. She has boyfriends, makes new friends, goes to parties. And when she sees her sister, less often now, they do seem to get on better. So when, after she's graduated and Martine has temporarily gifted her the Covent Garden flat, Sadie asks casually if she can stay for a short while, it feels easy to be gracious. Churlish to be otherwise.

It takes her longer than it should to realize that Sadie's assurance that she'll be out within a fortnight, three weeks at the most, is completely empty. Her nineteen-year-old sister has nowhere to go; no job to speak of, no money, and she's spiralling further and further off the rails. Their parents are hundreds of miles away, and in any case are as distant emotionally as they are physically. It dawns on her gradually that she is now Sadie's sole carer. The person in charge of her and her well-being, in charge of keeping her in line. And she's totally unequipped for the task.

Rachel settles down in the armchair by the window, looking once more at the clock and seeing that it is almost midnight. She's been lost in her thoughts for a long while. She stares out at the street, and at the shadowy outline of her own reflection in the mirrored glass. She's thinking about what happened last night. She was alone in the flat again, and driven by something she can't now define – perhaps a mix of boredom, defiance and curiosity – she had gone to Sadie's wardrobe and started rifling through her clothes. She had pulled out a tight red dress, the sort of thing she would never dare to pick up in a shop, and before she knew it she was sliding out of her own clothes and pulling it over her head, feeling the fabric stretch and cling to her body. She looked in the mirror, and the woman she saw looking back wasn't quite her, and not quite Sadie either, but some bizarre mixture of the two. She was attractive. Sexy, even. She examined herself more carefully, feeling the rush of power and confidence settle over her like mist, and she thought, *So this is what it feels like to be her.*

She clears her throat and shifts uncomfortably in the chair, glossing over in her mind what had followed. The sudden movement behind her, the sharp, piercing realization that she was no longer alone. *What the* fuck *are you doing, Rachel?* A strange look on her sister's face, as if she were trying to decide whether to swing in the direction of horror or amusement, before she dissolved into drunken laughter. Tossing herself down on the bed, her arms stretched behind her head. *Just put it back when you've finished.* And Rachel already scrambling out of the dress, her cheeks hot, not caring if her sister saw her naked, because even that was preferable to this.

She gets up and crosses the room swiftly, turning the lamp off with a snap. She's going to bed.

Sadie

1999

IT'S FRIDAY NIGHT OR Saturday morning, some indistinguishable time between the two. Sadie took the wrong night bus and she's walked in the dark for what feels like hours in her four-inch heels, her tight silver skirt and a heavy black jacket that she thinks may belong to a man she was dancing with and which smells of cigarettes and sweat. It's taken so long to get home that she's wishing she hadn't bothered and that she'd crashed at the man's place, although he would have wanted sex and she isn't in the mood. It's never easy to tell what effect the random cocktail of booze and drugs she downs on these nights out will have on her; sometimes she's horny and insatiable, wanting to fuck anyone who comes within a hair's breadth of her, and other times the whole business seems sordid and pointless and her body feels like an old coat that's been left out in the rain for too long.

She staggers the final few yards towards the tall

building where the flat is, stares up at the first floor. It's only when she sees the unfriendly dark square of window that she realizes she's forgotten her keys again. She pulls her mobile from her bag but it's dead.

'Rachel,' she croons, softly at first, then louder. 'Rachel!' She picks up a handful of gravel from the little artificial flower bed that sits at the base of one of the elegant lime trees flanking the road, and throws it in the direction of the window, but her aim is indiscriminate and she's shocked and amused by the way in which it scatters. 'Rachel!' she yells again. Her voice sounds surprisingly loud, shattering the silence of the street. She sees a couple of lights switch on in neighbouring buildings, a couple of shadows angrily flickering behind curtains; a window banging shut with a muffled curse. But she's got what she wanted – the front door of the building is swinging open and Rachel is standing there in her pyjamas, rubbing her eyes and gesturing her over the threshold.

'Shhhh,' she hisses, pulling Sadie by the arm and closing the front door behind them. 'Get upstairs. For Christ's sake, do you know what time it is?'

Time to get that stick out of your arse, Sadie thinks, but instead she makes some vague noise of apology and stumbles up the stairs in the dark, falling through the door and heading straight for her bedroom. She sinks down on the bed, fumbling with the straps of her shoes. Something isn't right; they snarl up in her fingers like barbed wire, resisting detangling. In the end she gives up and simply throws the jacket off her shoulders and lies down, rolling on to her side and seeing that Rachel is still watching her, standing in the doorway with her arms folded.

'This has got to stop,' Rachel says. 'If you must go out, can't you at least remember your keys? Or stay somewhere else?'

Sadie tries to think of an intelligent response but instead she starts giggling. It's something about the 'if you must go out' – as if going out is the sort of thing that you'd only do if you had a gun held to your head and you couldn't see any way out of it. 'It's the weekend,' she finally manages to say. 'This is what people do, Rach. You should try it some time.'

'Thanks, but I'm all right,' Rachel snaps, and with that she's gone, flouncing back to her own bedroom and shutting the door with a bang.

'Night night,' Sadie calls in a saccharine falsetto, wanting to have the last word even if it doesn't mean much. For an instant, the idea flits through her head that she is hungry. She wanders back into the open-plan living room cum kitchen, boils the kettle and chucks a handful of pasta into a pan, then some tomato sauce she finds in the cupboard into another. But somewhere along the line she must fall asleep, because some time later she wakes to the smell of burning and sees that the pans have boiled dry and that there are oxblood-red splatters all across the hob, dark and volcanic. She stumbles across and switches it off, then wanders back into the bedroom and throws herself down on the bed.

She catches sight of herself in the long low mirror on the dressing table, and stops. She has always liked looking in mirrors. It's not that she's vain. She takes no pleasure in what stares back at her: the heart-shaped face with its pouty, slightly asymmetric mouth, the blue-green eyes fringed by long, curled lashes, the cheekbones that give the kind of startling definition that means it's almost impossible to take a bad photo of her. Seeing herself is an anchor, that's all. Ever since she was very young she's been prone to a feeling of weightlessness that can attack without warning – a sudden spiralling away from the world, leaving her momentarily unsure of who or where she is. Looking in the mirror brings her back down. Here she is. Her face is grimly familiar. Nothing has changed.

But for once the sight of herself doesn't soothe her. Instead she takes in the rumpled clothes, the long expanse of thigh where her skirt has rucked up, the long, caramel-coloured hair damp with sweat and the fine spattering of rain that she's walked through – and she has the strangest feeling that none of it belongs to her at all. She's a heartbeat away from toppling down into that dark sense of dread, the one that sometimes waits for her around the corner and sinks its teeth in when she least expects it. Rolling over on to her stomach, she presses her face down hard into the pillow and starts counting to a hundred, but before she even reaches fifty she can feel herself losing her grip and the world switches off again.

When she next peels her eyes open, sunlight is streaming through the window. She's still fully clothed, one shoe hanging half off. There's a sour taste in her mouth like bitter apples. She can smell bacon cooking and hear the sizzle as it turns in the pan. She drags herself off the bed and combs her fingers through the tangled mass of her hair, shaking it out behind her. Sidling to the door, she peers through the crack. The hob that looked like the scene of a murder a few hours ago is bright and sparkling, and beneath the cooking smells she can just pick up the sharp citrus scent of cleaning spray. Rachel is standing there, her hair in a tight high ponytail, dressed in what looks like some kind of Lycra jumpsuit.

'Any left over?' Sadie asks cheerily. She finds that it's best to skate over incidents like last night. Part of her hopes that perhaps they seem as hazy and unreal to her sister as they do to her.

'If you want.' Rachel doesn't turn around and it's hard to gauge the frost level in her tone. 'Thanks for clearing up,' she says. 'Again.' This time the frost is unmistakeable.

'Sorry,' Sadie says, because it's very easy to say, even if she's no longer sure of its value.

Now Rachel turns around, wiping her hands at her sides and taking Sadie in with a quick flick of her eyes, head to toe. 'You know, Sadie, I'm less than three years older than you.' She pauses, as if she's waiting for her sister to pick up on some unspoken meaning, but Sadie's mind is blank and it hurts to try and think, so she just nods, and after a while Rachel exhales and turns back to the bacon, easing it out from the pan and slapping it between the slices of buttered bread.

'After this,' she says, 'we should go out and do something.'

'You and me?' Sadie queries. She and Rachel spend a

lot of time in each other's company, what with living in the same house, but they rarely socialize. A quick flash of memory: hours spent wandering around the shops in their early teens, trying on unsuitable and increasingly off-the-wall clothing until they were doubled up in hysterics in the changing rooms, laughing so hard at the sight of each other that they could barely breathe. She's no longer sure who these people were.

'Yes,' Rachel confirms. 'You and me. Going out somewhere, like sisters do. I've got nothing much on today, and I assume you haven't either. So let's do something.'

'Okaaaay.' Sadie advances cautiously, taking the sandwich Rachel offers her, trying to divine if this is somehow a trap. 'Camden?' she suggests, because she knows that her sister doesn't like the place; the aggressive individuality of it, the rough diamond feel of the streets.

There's a fractional pause, but then Rachel nods. 'If you like.'

'All right.' Backtracking now would seem weak, though she doesn't want to go out at all. Her head feels as if it's being splintered by a thousand subtle knives and she can feel the arches of her feet aching in protest at the long rambling walk last night. Even the autumn sun at the window is too bright and vivid. She eats the sandwich in silence, feeling the bacon crunch and stick against her teeth. When she swallows her throat is raw.

'Come on then,' Rachel says briskly. 'Go and have a shower, and let's get changed and go. Twenty minutes.'

'Yessir,' Sadie mumbles, but the sarcasm is lost on Rachel, who has already turned tail and hotfooted it into

82

the bedroom. She's regretting having fallen in with this plan, and as she drags herself through to the shower and stands underneath the fall of warm water, tipping her head back to wash the grime from her hair, she's already looking forward to going back to bed.

Four hours later she's dead on her feet, trailing round the streets of Camden with Rachel at her side, the whole world suffused in a haze of exhaustion that makes it seem as if she's walking through a computer simulation, liquid and insubstantial. They have visited some shops, reconfirming their wildly different tastes. They have exchanged soundbites about their equally wildly different lives. Rachel has even tried to suggest a visit back to Durham to see their hermetic parents, who have barely left their house in years, which Sadie has treated with the deadpan scorn it deserves. It has all been painful, so much so that she has coerced Rachel into visiting a pub and downed three large glasses of wine in the space of an hour while Rachel watchfully sipped a single gin and tonic. She had hoped the alcohol would take the edge off but it's only sharpened her sense of fruitlessness.

'Sadie,' Rachel cuts into her thoughts as they walk. 'I know things are difficult. I'd be finding it tough in your position – with no real job, no sense of routine. But you've got to start sorting yourself out. You can't stay in the flat for ever. I'm already scared about what Martine's going to say when she gets back.'

Sadie nods vaguely. She's well aware that she and her sister have different views on acceptable standards of living. It's odd how something can matter so much to one person and so little to another.

'To be honest,' Rachel continues, 'I'm not sure how much longer I can keep this up. I'm tired of it. I barely sleep. You come in at all hours and don't care how much noise you make. You shout at me and try and pick fights. I've had the police round about five times already complaining about your music, or the run-ins you've had with people. I'm always having to make excuses for you. The neighbours all hate us. I don't . . . I don't want to live this way anymore.'

It's a well-worn speech. Her sister speaks simply, with sadness. Sadie shoots a look at her, and she notices that she looks exhausted, with faint violet stains beneath her eyes and pale skin. For the first time she grasps the edge of something – the sense of what it must be like to worry about someone in the way Rachel does. The helplessness, the impotence. She doesn't like it, this thing she's brushing up against.

'You're right,' she says eventually. 'I know, I need to change some stuff.' She doesn't really have any idea what she can change or how.

'Yes, you do,' Rachel says, 'and it needs to be now. It's scaring me, the way you've been acting lately. It's like you've got no off switch. I do care about you, but it isn't easy, trying to deal with you when you don't seem to—'

Sadie never hears the end of that sentence, because all at once they have rounded the corner of the street and he's there, coming out of the tall black building with the painted letters, kicking the door shut behind him. A stranger in studded leather jacket and black jeans, maybe thirty years old, very tall and olive-skinned, his black hair shaved at the sides and swept into a stiff peak. He's walking towards them, faster and faster, and in seconds he's close enough for her to see the flat gleam of his eyes, dark grey like gunmetal; the contemptuous curve of his lips that softens, as he reaches her, into what seems like invitation. And all of a sudden the world has blazed into colour and all her nerves are on edge, leaping into action with the kind of eagerness she wouldn't have thought her body capable of just seconds before.

He thrusts a flyer into her hand, and she takes it. *Kaspar's*: the letters dark red and vital against the black background, the downward stroke of the K cutting down like the slash of a knife. She looks up at the black building behind them, and sees that stroke mirrored there, in crimson paint against the wall.

'My club,' he says. His voice is accented, harsh and exotic. 'You should come along some time. Yes?' His eyes sweep over her, unchanging, for an instant. Mutely, she nods. He is so close that she can smell his aftershave, the spicy cinnamon scent of it crawling over her like smoke.

'See you there,' he says, and then he's gone, abruptly pushing past down the street. The speed of it has jolted her so much that she has to blink hard, willing the world around her to settle back into its familiar lines. Her head spins. She is more drunk than she thought she was.

Next to her she can feel Rachel's eyes on her, sharply assessing and probing. 'Something wrong?' she asks.

'No. No.' The words don't come out easily; she can barely wrap her tongue around them.

Rachel glances at the club. 'I wouldn't bother,' she says. There is a brief, tense silence as they continue down the street. 'And as for him,' she says, in a tone that Sadie knows is meant to be final and cutting, demonstrating absolute contempt, 'he looks like seriously bad news.'

'All right,' she snaps. 'I don't care. He's nothing to me.' She sets her teeth and clenches her hands into fists in her pockets. She has slept with on average two men a week since she was fourteen years old. They cycle through her life with bland predictability, one much like the next. It has been a long, long time since she has felt this sick, instinctive pull, these tremors of lust racing through her body like speed. It has come to her now with such force that she feels knocked out. *Be careful*, she thinks. She already knows that she won't be.

Late that same night she's back in Camden, inching slowly forwards in the queue for the club. She slips past the bouncer and inside the heavy black doors, wriggling out of her jacket and flashing the flyer with its promise of free entry at the bored-looking girl behind the desk.

The girl examines it briefly, then glances up at her. 'Did you get this from Kas?' she asks.

Sadie hesitates, but she remembers the name of the club and quickly puts two and two together. 'Yeah,' she says confidently, and as she speaks she notices a letter lying at the edge of the desk next to the girl, the name on it printed in block capitals: **KASPAR KASHANI**. She commits it to memory, and there's something bizarrely exciting about this new knowledge, as if already she's one step closer to him.

'Through you go then,' the girl says, dipping her head, losing interest, and Sadie nods and moves on into the club.

Under the hot red spotlights, her white lace dress glows ultraviolet and bright, dramatically picking out the lines of her silhouette. She sees herself in the mirrors as she worms her way through the crowd, and her heart is hammering, sending her giddy with the thrill of the lights, the music, the scent of sweat and marijuana. The bassline throbs through her, making her instinctively sway her hips, feeling men's hands brush against them as she passes. She rolls a little white pill in her fingers, and pops it into her mouth. Her lips are sticky with thick red lipstick. When she licks them, the sweet chemical taste lingers on her tongue.

She has spied him already, up by the DJ box, and she keeps her eyes on him. Laser beams pass across his face, casting it in neon light. Seeing him again, she is struck by the iconic familiarity of that face, reminded of posters and photographs – Elvis, she thinks, only darker, with Persian skin and eyes. He is staring out across the crowd, unsmiling. As she draws closer, her eyes trace the muscular curves of his body, pressed tight against a white T-shirt. She is there, right in front of him, not speaking, keeping a few feet's distance.

She dances, feeling herself carried along by the heady rhythm of the music, her eyes half closed. She feels his stare alight on her, the spark of recognition, and it sends a shiver down the back of her neck. Sweat trickles down her back. She's breathing hard and fast, still moving to the beat. When she dares look over, he is still looking her way, unblinking, his strange, hooded eyes inscrutably brittle and cold, and for a moment she feels afraid.

He speaks to her, raising his voice above the music. 'What's your name?'

'Sadie,' she says, and she has to come closer to make him hear her. 'Sadie,' she says again. She can feel the heat coming off him, prickling around him like a force field. She knows how this goes. How it has always gone. He'll take her hand and draw her towards him, pull her into a kiss. They'll go back to some dark back-room and do whatever they want, and then he'll be out of her system and she'll move on.

As he studies her she feels herself trembling, half holding her breath. And then he nods and turns away, swinging back to give her one last cool, appraising look before disappearing into the crowd.

The morning after that first night she wakes up and her thoughts are instantly full of him: the scent of him inches away from her, that last long look. *Kaspar Kashani* . . . The five smoothly flowing syllables of his name drip into her mind in a relentless repeated rhythm. She hears them in his low, roughly accented voice, as if whispered into her ear. The thought of him obsesses her, grips hard and won't let her go. She sees it again and again in her mind's eye, that moment when he turned around and walked away from her. The unexpectedness of it, the way it immediately sharpened her desire into need. This has never happened before.

She wants to talk to someone, and Rachel is the only one there, so she gets up early and joins her for breakfast, ignoring her look of surprise.

'Morning,' Rachel says cautiously as she pours her cereal. She's already dressed, in the leggings and crop top she wears for her morning runs, her hair tied up in a neat ponytail. 'Didn't think I'd see you before I left. What did you get up to last night?'

'Oh,' Sadie says, and she hesitates for an instant, teetering on the edge of the precipice before she falls and hears herself say in a casual voice that belies her eagerness, 'I just went to see Kas.' It's the first time she's spoken his name aloud and the shape of it is new and luxurious in her mouth, sending a brief ricochet of erotic possibility through her body.

'Who?' Rachel asks blankly.

'You know,' Sadie says. 'The guy yesterday, from the club.'

Rachel sets down her spoon with a clink, her eyes wide. 'No,' she says. 'You didn't.'

'Didn't what?' Sadie asks airily. She knows she's making this sound like more than it is, and even that is exciting, the sense that her sister believes that something could happen between herself and him. Still, she shrugs and shakes her head, relenting. 'Nothing like that,' she says. 'The club is pretty cool, though. You should come down with me some time soon, check it out.'

'Right,' Rachel says doubtfully, raising an eyebrow as she returns to her cornflakes.

'No, really.' As the suggestion takes root Sadie realizes

she means it. She can't go back there time and time again on her own; it would look desperate, pathetic. And she doesn't trust any of the women she hangs around with enough to call them real friends, the type who wouldn't try and hit on Kas themselves or show her up by recounting some embarrassing anecdote that makes her look bad – and there are plenty of those to choose from. Rachel may be straight, but she's her sister. She knows she wouldn't want to hurt her.

She feels a sudden rush of affection, even love, and even though she knows it's at least partly chemical – the drugs from last night still buzzing round her system – it's enough to spur her on. 'You used to go out sometimes,' she continues persuasively. 'Until you got this job. We don't have to go during the week . . . just weekends. It could be something we do together.'

Rachel frowns, and Sadie knows she's weighing up that 'it', wondering whether spending nights in a crowded club while her sister pops pills and cosies up to men is what sisterly togetherness is all about. But eventually she nods. 'OK, I'll come with you next weekend. But I'm only coming because I'm worried about you. I meant what I said yesterday. You need to change the way you're behaving. In the meantime, if I can't stop you then at least I can be there.'

'Great!' Sadie says brightly, before she stops and realizes that what Rachel has said actually isn't that great; it's depressing and defeatist and sucking the fun out of everything. At least she's going to come, though, and don't actions speak louder than words? So she gives her sister a dazzling smile and reaches for the cereal, remembering that she hasn't eaten in almost twenty-four hours and that that must be why her hands are shaking and her heart feels like it's on fast forward.

And so they go to the club the next Saturday night, and it's obvious from the instant Rachel steps through the door that she hates it, but she stays nonetheless. They dance for a while, and Sadie drinks less and takes fewer drugs than usual. She pretends it's because she wants to show Rachel that she can be responsible, but in reality she wants to keep her wits about her, look out for Kas so that she can be seen behaving in the right way. And up to a point, it seems to work. It only takes half an hour for him to notice her, and when he does he moves swiftly towards her, buying them drinks and asking if they live nearby. Rachel is monosyllabic, her expression shuttered and suspicious, and before long Kas is ignoring her almost completely.

'Your second time here. There is something about this place you like?' he asks Sadie. His tone is oblique, lazily charming. His eyes flicker up and down her body, never quite settling.

'Yes,' she says. If only he would look at her properly, then she could show him exactly what that something is – give him the brazen, unblinking stare that has worked on so many others. But he doesn't, and there's something unmistakeably deliberate about the way he's holding her at arm's length. She knows this game, has played it, but never from this side of the fence.

He smiles, reaching out an olive-skinned hand and slowly pushing his fingers into her hair. She stands rigid, trying to slow her breathing. His fingers re-emerge with something between them; a bright twisted stream of ribbon. 'Yours?'

She laughs, trying to be casual, though she can still feel the touch of his skin against hers, as if it has branded her. 'No, I don't think so.'

He crumples it into a little ball between his finger-tips, then puts it in his pocket, and for a moment he does look at her. She feels the full focus of his attention on her, intense and overwhelming. 'I hope to see you again,' he says.

'Maybe,' she fires back. 'If you're lucky.'

For a moment he looks a little incredulous, regarding her steadily. She hears the echo of her flippant words hanging between them, and it comes with the queasy, dawning realization that none of her usual patter will work on this man. She has always been the one in control, without even trying; it has always been so easy. She cannot even imagine what it would be like to be with someone like Kas. Someone who will not jump when she clicks her fingers, panting after her like an eager dog on heat. She thinks about those hands that were close to her just moments ago, thinks about them slipping underneath her clothes and claiming her body, and desire floods through her again, making her feel almost sick.

'Well,' he says. 'Until next time.' And he gives her a brief glittering smile and nods at Rachel politely before he walks away.

As soon as he is gone Rachel tugs on her arm, putting her mouth close to her ear. 'What a creep. Come on, Sadie. You can't possibly think anything else.'

'You don't know him,' Sadie says, dismissively.

'No,' Rachel acknowledges, 'and nor do you.'

And in this, Sadie thinks, she isn't wrong. And so she watches him, carefully, throughout the rest of the night, trying to glean what she can. He moves across the dance floor, behind the bar, out to the reception, never staying anywhere for long. He talks to various men, one-on-one, short intent conversations that look professional. There is something distinctly deferential in the way the other men behave around him. Their stances, the angle of their heads, the movement of their hands. She sees it, and she understands that he is the boss. Not only of the club, but of the people in it.

At almost two a.m., when the crowd is thinning out and the music is winding down, she sees his attention caught by something behind the bar. One of the barmen is swigging cheekily from a bottle, laughing with a couple of the punters. It looks harmless, a brief jokey interlude before he turns back to his work, but she can see at once that Kas is not happy. He strides over to the man, puts a hand on his shoulder and leans in. The two of them stay there for almost a minute, a little frozen tableau, and she's suddenly aware of how tall Kas is, six foot four or maybe more, and how his presence dominates. She cannot hear the words that he speaks into the barman's ear, but whatever they are, they are enough to make him blanch and pull back, nodding urgently. She sees that he is trying to mumble something in return, but Kas cuts him off instantly, his hand reaching out again and this time gripping harder. The man's face twists in pain, and he nods again, his eyes downcast, until Kas breaks away and walks back across the dance floor, not looking back.

Sadie watches him go. She has stopped dancing and she's aware of a thin film of sweat all over her body, but her skin feels clammy and cold. It is important, she supposes, when you are in charge of people, that you are able to keep them in line. She thinks back to her old school, where some of the best teachers were those who had the respect and admiration of the pupils, but who were also strict enough to command a little fear. If you have this power, you use it. That's natural.

Rachel

1999

SHE DOESN'T ALWAYS GO into the club. Most of the time, in fact, she just drives to Camden late at night and waits in the car park opposite until Sadie emerges. She sits there watching the minutes tick by, trying to warm her hands against the ineffectual fan heater, waiting. At first she used to switch on the little light above the driver's seat, spurred by a childish fear of the dark, but one night it occurred to her how it would look from the outside; a beacon advertising her presence to whatever ruthless stranger might chance to walk past. Since the thought entered her head she hasn't been able to get it out, and so now she just sits in the dark.

Sometimes the thought of this silent vigil is too much to contemplate, and instead she joins Sadie inside. She can never decide if this is better or worse. At least in there she can watch her sister, keep an eye on whatever is going on. But she doesn't like to be in the same room as Kaspar. There's something about him that she instinctively mistrusted from the start, but over time this instinct has hardened into knowledge. It's not that he's ever done anything untoward as such, not that she's seen. It's subtler than that, more ingrained; she's simply frightened by the person that he is. She finds it impossible to understand why Sadie is unable to see what she sees, but she's given up trying to make her. Instead she makes it her business to watch him.

Slowly, she grows to understand that he is at the centre of a network that does not advertise itself. Like a set of concentric circles, some are allowed into his inner force field, and others are kept at the fringes. There are many men who drop in and out of the club from week to week, seemingly at random, but the strange thing is, she soon becomes adept at knowing which ones are part of Kas's circle. There is something indefinable that groups them, something she cannot isolate despite many attempts.

At the heart of the circle is a man called Dominic Westwood. He is short and stocky, with white-blond cropped hair, hard, glassy eyes and curiously pliable-looking features, as if he has been fashioned out of Play-Doh. It takes three visits for Rachel to notice him, but once she does, it seems he's there all the time – observing from a distance, exchanging looks with Kas across the club. She starts to notice them talking in corners. She is unsure of the nature of the bond between them, but she quickly realizes that it is well established. In much the same way, it seems that Dominic has noticed her, recognized her link to Sadie, whose growing closeness to Kas he has clearly acknowledged. When the two of them fall together into one of their cryptic conversations or intense exchanges of glances by the bar, Dominic often seeks Rachel out, despite her efforts to put him off. They are thrown together by default. He has never indicated any sexual interest in her, and it's for this reason only that she talks to him at all. At least if he is there, he keeps the others at bay; men who circle silently and speculatively, waiting for their chance.

'How did you and Kas meet?' she asks Dominic one night, some six weeks in, as they sit together by the bar.

Dominic shrugs and his eyes slant away, in some brief private moment of remembrance. 'He's always been around,' he says, 'but I only got to know him a couple of years ago.'

This answer tells her nothing. Rachel pushes the heat of her hair back from her face, feeling her forehead damp with sweat. 'You started working here with him?' she asks. As she speaks, she realizes that she is not entirely sure, after all, whether or not Dominic works at the club. He is always there, and sometimes behind the bar, but there is a layer of distance; he observes, rather than participates. It does not surprise her when he shakes his head.

'He did me a favour,' he says. 'Helped me out of some trouble. After that, well.' He shrugs again, and downs his drink. Rachel wants to probe further, but she has detected something new in his voice – a chilly note of self-protection that warns her off. She repeats his words to herself. She is reminded of a fairy story: the princess who, once saved from peril by the handsome stranger, was magically bound to him for ever.

The comparison feels faintly ridiculous, and without thinking, she smiles.

Dominic gives her a swift, sly look. 'And of course, I've known Melanie for a while,' he says.

Rachel frowns slightly, trying to place the name. All Kas's associates are men, as far as she is aware. 'Right . . .' she says, in a tone that she hopes conveys understanding.

'Yeah,' says Dominic, nodding. 'His wife.' The keenness of his eyes tells her that he wants to see her reaction.

She keeps her face straight, though inside her stomach is churning. She's almost certain that Sadie has no idea that Kas is married. They rarely discuss him – they're both too aware of their fundamental differences of opinion – but it would take a blind woman not to see that her sister is obsessed with him, and to a degree Rachel has never really seen in her before. 'I didn't know he had a wife,' she settles for, her tone off-hand.

'She's in tonight,' Dominic says casually. 'First time in a while. Look.' He jerks his head in the direction of the DJ box. 'Over there. Red dress.'

Rachel looks, and sees a tall woman, five foot ten at least, with olive skin, wavy dark hair, an angular face and a rake-slim figure that speaks of self-possession and denial. She's leaning back against the box, her arms folded, looking dispassionately out across the club. For a second her gaze snags on Rachel's, and she gives her a quick hard stare of dismissal.

'Why are you telling me this?' she asks.

Dominic smirks as he motions towards the barman

for another drink. 'Just making conversation, babe.' He manages to make the endearment sound like an insult. 'You want another?' He nods at her near-empty glass.

Rachel shakes her head. 'I'm not staying.' She slips off her stool, scanning the crowd for Sadie. She soon spots her, dancing aimlessly in the centre of the crowd, her expression flat and glazed. She doesn't look as if she's enjoying herself. She only comes here, Rachel thinks, for him.

She pushes through the dancers to reach her sister's side, touching her on the shoulder. 'Sadie,' she says, putting her mouth close to her ear. 'Can I have a word?'

Sadie looks vaguely put out, but shrugs and nods, allowing herself to be led to the side of the dance floor. Now that they're away from the spotlights, Rachel can see that her make-up is running; sparkled shadows of dust collecting beneath her eyes, a smudge of red lipstick spilling on to the skin beneath her mouth. She looks damaged, and inexplicably beautiful. 'What is it?' she asks.

'Dominic just told me something,' Rachel says. There doesn't feel like a good way to say this, so she just spits it out. 'Did you know that Kas is married?'

Sadie's face twitches, as if she's been slapped. 'No. What do you mean? He isn't.'

'That's not what Dominic said.' For a moment Rachel thinks about pointing out the woman in the red dress, but thinks better of it. 'Anyway, I just thought you ought to know. I know there's nothing going on between you two, but . . .' She trails off, unsure of how to continue. She senses that for Sadie, confronting the fact

99

that she isn't having an affair with a married man might be even more humiliating than having an affair with one that she believed to be single.

She expects Sadie to snap something back; conversation with her is usually quick-fire, shoot first and think later. But she stays silent – a slight frown furrowing her brows, her eyes distant and lost – and then abruptly turns and marches back across the dance floor. Rachel can see she's heading for the reception area, where Kas is likely to be. She stands indecisively for a moment, then swiftly follows her sister. The reception is round a sharp corner, and she lingers diagonally across from it, shaded by the dim corridor lighting. She can see Kas, leaning back against the wall and rifling through a stack of papers, so absorbed that even when Sadie moves next to him he doesn't look up.

'Kas,' Sadie says.

He whips round. 'What?' The word is barked and unfriendly, like an accusation. A split-second later, his expression relaxes. 'I am sorry, Sadie,' he murmurs. 'I thought you were somebody else.'

Sadie looks uncertain for an instant, then seems to collect herself. 'I just came to let you know I won't be coming in again.' Rachel can hear the slight crack in her voice that would be imperceptible to anyone else; the only sign that this is difficult for her to say.

Kas raises his eyebrows, but says nothing. It's impossible to tell from his face whether he cares about what she is saying or not.

'You never said you were married,' Sadie states baldly, but as soon as it's out she seems to lose confidence in her stance. She wraps her arms around herself, reaches one hand up to tug unconsciously at her hair. 'It's none of my business,' she continues more quietly, 'but . . .'

Kas comes closer to her, sliding a hand beneath her chin and lifting her face a little to his. He studies her intently, like a scientist with a strange and rare specimen. 'I thought you knew how things were,' he says softly, so that Rachel has to strain to hear him. 'Life is not always simple, Sadie. You know this.'

Sadie is staring up into his eyes, clearly completely taken in. 'I just . . .' Rachel hears her say, and then her lips move again with words that she can't quite catch. Kas nods, and for a moment their faces are so close that Rachel thinks they are going to kiss. A light shudder runs down her back. She's spying on them, doesn't want to see this, but she can't move.

But in the end Kas just smiles, and straightens up slightly, smoothing Sadie's hair back behind her ears, and then resting one hand each side of her head, keeping her in place.

'For now I can only say this,' he says. 'That if you were to stop coming here I would be sorry. And that your feelings are not only your own.'

Whatever the hell that means, Rachel thinks, but Sadie seems satisfied with it, dropping her gaze to the floor and nodding, a smile playing around her lips. Incredibly, it's as if she has got exactly what she wants from this exchange. She isn't disillusioned or angry; the news that Kas has a wife has been taken in, evaluated and dismissed all in the space of five minutes. And the way she's reacting isn't like her at all. She's never seen her sister look so – she gropes for the word – submissive. There's no fight or resistance in her body; she's pliable, apparently quite happy to have this man's hands on her and to believe every word that comes out of his mouth.

It's only now, watching this, that Rachel realizes she's wasting her time. There is no point in trying to control her sister. She'll do what she wants, with whom she wants, no matter what Rachel says or thinks or does. There's a sense of things shifting inside her – a weight lifting, but an emptiness too.

Quietly, she slips along the corridor by the wall and hurries towards the exit, though she knows they are too absorbed in each other to notice her. She grabs her coat from the cloakroom and walks back to the car in the light rain, her head bowed. She'll sit there until Sadie reappears, and then she'll take her home, but she won't be coming back to the club. Her sister is on her own.

Sadie

1999

IN THE HEAT AND dark of the corridor, their faces almost touching, she understands him perfectly. He's saying that their feelings are the same. That he wants her as much as she wants him, even if it can't happen. *For now.*

Mutely, she nods, and she's seized by the fervent desire to get away from him, because she doesn't want to shatter the unspoken perfection of this moment. She senses that it won't get any better than this, and so she pulls away and walks slowly back towards the dance floor, her limbs aching, a sweet dizziness spreading across her temples and sending the room reeling.

She's in the thick of the crowd again, her body moving to the music, the sweat trickling down her face, when she sees Dominic across the room. He's not alone. He's listening to a woman beside him, a woman with long, wavy hair falling down the length of her bare back who's leaning in towards him. She watches, never taking her eyes away from them until she sees the other woman turn from Dominic and stalk away towards the basement stairs.

Sadie picks her way over to Dominic, reaching his side and raising her voice above the thumping music. 'Is that her, then?' she asks airily. She can be this way with Dominic – flippant, challenging. She knows very well that telling Rachel was his way of telling her, indirectly, just to test her reaction.

Dominic smirks. 'She was asking about you, funnily enough,' he says. 'How I know you, how old you are . . .' He pauses. 'If you have a boyfriend.'

Sadie mirrors Dominic's detached expression, setting her jaw in a hard, uncompromising line, but her stomach is churning with excitement. This means something. For Kas's wife to have noticed her, to have bothered to try and find out more, she must on some level see her as a threat. 'What did you say?' she asks.

'Not a lot. I've not got a clue about your – love life.' The last words are ironically laced, framed by invisible quotation marks. 'How would I know if you have a boyfriend or not?'

'I don't.' As she speaks, Sadie realizes that she hasn't slept with anyone for almost two months now – the longest she's ever gone without it since that first awkward night in the upstairs room of a local pub five years ago, when she was only fourteen. She's had the opportunity, of course, could turn around right now if she wanted and catch the eye of some lingering Lothario who'd be only too happy to step in and end the dry spell. It comes to her that she doesn't want any of them, doesn't want anyone except Kas. The knowledge steals her breath. This is different from anything she's felt before. It's all-consuming, terrifying. She barely knows this man, but she wants him so much that it feels as if her insides have been brutally scooped out, leaving her hollow with need. Tears are suddenly in her eyes, and she glances away.

When she looks back, Dominic is still watching her, his lips faintly curled in a smile. 'You like Kas, don't you?' he says eventually.

The phrasing strikes her as strangely coy. She shrugs and nods, meeting his gaze.

'Can he trust you?' Dominic says then, and there is a new sharpness in his voice. All at once it is as if Kas is there, glinting behind Dominic's flat, dead eyes. She feels that she is being auditioned for a part she knows nothing about. The air is loaded with something she does not understand; some thickly cloying sense of compulsion and duty, of contracts and promises.

She turns the question over in her head. There is something second hand about it, as if Kas's needs and wants somehow render Dominic's own irrelevant. He is staring at her, unblinking, his pale hands held lightly around his glass. She does not know what warrant she is signing by agreeing, but she finds herself nodding and saying yes. *Yes, of course, he can trust me*. And once it's out, there is no taking it back.

Later, she looks back and sees that after those few words with Dominic at the bar, it all progresses with frightening speed and efficiency. At first it's inconsequential – the occasional request that she keep an eye on the cloak-room, or take a few orders at the bar, and she's flattered that they're comfortable enough with her to ask. It's only a couple of weeks later that Dominic beckons her into a corner of the club and passes her a small packet, tightly wrapped in silver foil. He names the sum he's after, directs her towards a man across the dance floor and thanks her casually when she trots back, cash in hand. Over the next few visits, she is passed several more of these parcels. She knows she's acting as a go-between, a handy buffer to render the transaction harder to trace, but it doesn't much bother her. She's bought drugs herself many times, although she's never sold them, and she can't see that much difference between the two sides of the coin.

December 12th. She's walking to the club through lit-up streets, Christmas lights twinkling and flashing across the night skyline, sparkling like cool blue jewels in the branches of trees. Anticipation runs through her like fever. There is ice on the ground, and the pointed heels of her shoes slip and skid on the treacherous pavements. She is wearing a tight black satin dress that pushes her breasts up like offerings, and she feels the frozen air lashing her bare skin, but inside she is burning. As she picks her way through the shining streets, she reaches into her bag and takes another pill. These days it seems as though they barely dent her consciousness, but the habit persists.

She walks up to the front of the queue and nods at the bouncer. She doesn't have to speak; they all know her by now, have been briefed that she is to be let in whenever she wants. She slips past the rope and smiles, seeing the jealousy in the eyes of the other girls in the queue; skimpily dressed, badly made-up, chewing gum or picking cheap nail varnish off their fingernails. She knows Kas would never look twice at any of them. Going to the cloakroom window, she slips her jacket off her shoulders. The air in this anteroom is cold and sterile. She glances at her watch. It is just past ten, the time when the punters start pouring in and the room heats up. Anticipation rushes through her and she throws open the heavy black door, the music surging up and enveloping her as she moves forwards, lights flashing and swooping above her head.

He's there, of course, and she sees him straight away. She has grown used to picking him out in a crowd; it's as if he has his own personal spotlight, constantly trained on him wherever he goes. He's leaning against the bar, his head tipped slightly back. Even at this distance she can sense a certain tension in the way he holds himself, as if he is preparing himself to fight. As she comes closer she thinks she sees some warning in his eyes, behind the unnaturally reflective gleam that comes off them. He barely seems to see her at first, and for a brief moment her mouth fills with nervous saliva, tasting bitter and sharp. She swallows and steps closer. She doesn't often approach him uninvited, but tonight she's feeling reckless.

'Sadie,' he says, smiling, his perfect, pointed teeth flashing at her for an instant. His full attention is on her, flooding her with warmth. 'I hoped I would see you tonight.'

'Did you?' she says, tossing her head. She knows her voice is level, even if she can feel her heart bumping against her ribs. While she is near him she feels herself become someone else, someone almost unrecognizable. She believes he likes this hardness in her – the sense that, like a glittering diamond, her beauty is the type that if used right could cut through whatever it touches. He admires a strong woman, she thinks, and so that is what she is when she is here. That is what she can be.

'Yes.' He reaches out and pulls a bar stool close to him, motioning her to sit next to him. Sadie smiles and sits, and in the same moment she sees Dominic, standing on the other side of the bar, swigging from a silver flask. She nods a greeting at him, but for once he does not respond. His gaze is intently on Kas and his closeness to her. For some reason, his lack of acknowledgement makes her shiver, as if someone has walked over her grave.

She drags her eyes back to Kas. He is leaning inwards, his breath strangely cool against her ear. 'You could help me out with something a little different tonight,' he is saying, 'if you wanted. Do you want to help me?'

Uncertainly, she nods. Kas has never asked her for anything directly before, and something in the question feels odd and unbalanced; she cannot think what she could possibly have that could be of use to him. He is very close now, and with an electric shock she feels one of his hands sliding lightly around her waist and the other coming up to cup her chin, twisting her face towards his. She can smell the sharp cinnamon scent she has come to associate with him, the merest echo of which can make her stop dead in the street, her whole body flooding with longing.

'I can trust you, Sadie,' he says. There is no hint of a question in his voice. He speaks with such assurance that she instantly thinks of Dominic and his strange, querying tone that night at the bar. She has the eerie sense that her words have been dutifully fed back, her name ticked off a list. She wants to reply, but her mouth is dry. The tips of his fingers are still resting underneath her chin, his thumb pressed hard against the line of her jaw.

He is silent a few moments before he speaks again, his voice quiet and low, so that she has to strain to hear him. 'There is a man coming here tonight,' he says. 'He is not here yet, but he should arrive in about thirty minutes. His name is George Hart. You don't know him. He doesn't know you. Look.' Swiftly, he pulls a photograph from his pocket. A man of around forty, white and thickset, sandy hair cropped around his temples. The photo has been taken from some distance, across a car park. A prickle of instinctive knowledge tells her that the man was not aware of it being taken.

'You see him?' Kas says. 'You could pick him out?'

She stares at the man's stocky frame, the good-natured set of his face. He is frozen in the act of unpacking a supermarket trolley into the back of a car. 'Yes,' she says.

'Good,' Kas says. 'George and I have been working together. He is a good man, but we have some business to discuss. He has agreed to meet me here in the club tonight, but I need to talk to him in private, alone. You understand?' He is talking smoothly and confidently, barely pausing for her response. 'I need you to approach him, and bring him to the basement stock room – you know it. Then he and I can talk in peace. Do you understand?' he says again, and this time it is very definitely a question.

Sadie runs his words back in her head. Her mind feels fuzzy and amorphous, as if made out of cotton wool. 'You can't ask him yourself?' she says. 'Why me?'

Kas shrugs, not taking his eyes from her face. 'It is better that it does not come from me,' he says. 'For reasons I do not understand, people are wary of being alone with me.' He shrugs elegantly and smiles, but the words send a chill down her spine. 'And as for why I am asking you . . . Well, surely that is obvious.' Now his gaze dips, deliberately sweeps her from top to toe, and despite the panic that is starting to throb inside her, she feels a sharp pang of desire. 'You can get him there,' he says, the conviction in his voice like a caress. 'I know you can.'

Sadie glances across the bar again. Dominic is still watching them. She looks back to Kas. 'This business . . .' she says, licking her lips. 'Is it – is it . . .' She realizes that she does not know exactly what she wants to ask.

'There is nothing for you to worry about,' Kas says soothingly. 'We will talk, that is all, and then he will go. And after that . . .' He lets his words trail off, smiling. She can feel heat radiating off him; she breathes in the scent of him and it makes her head reel. For a brief moment, she shuts her eyes. In the temporary darkness it feels as if he is enclosing her, his presence everywhere at once. She is not stupid, and she knows that she is about to mix herself up in something she does not fully understand, but fiercer than her fear is the need to please him, to do what he wants. It sounds so simple, and it is within her power to do it.

'OK,' she says, hearing the word fall into the tiny space between them, and he smiles again, drawing back. She sees his muscles visibly loosening, releasing tension.

'Thank you,' he says. 'Watch out for him, and bring him down in half an hour or so. I will be waiting.' He stands up, and, turning, as if struck by impulse, he takes her hand and brings it to his lips. The touch only lasts a second, but as she watches him move away she feels it still burning on her skin.

She recognizes the man at once. He looks out of place in this setting, dressed in an open-neck blue shirt and a pair of workman's jeans. Scanning the crowd, every now and then he takes a gulp of beer from his pint glass. Under the strobe lights, his hair is strawberry blond, and she can see a spread of freckles across his cheeks. He's doing his best to look confident, but she can see a hint of wariness in the way he looks around, his eyes darting back and forth. As she slips closer to him, she sees him briefly suck in his lower lip and tug on it, blinking, before he takes another swift sip.

She is right next to him now, and she sees him notice her automatically, in the way that men usually do. 'Been stood up?' she calls above the music. George Hart is not a tall man, but she tips her head back and looks up at him.

111

He swings round and stares at her. She can see that although his mind is elsewhere, he is flattered. 'Not sure yet,' he says briefly.

'Well,' she says, slipping on to the stool next to him, 'I'll keep you company while you wait.'

He frowns, looking her over dubiously. He is double her age; an open, likeable face, but nothing extraordinary. She holds her nerve. In her experience, most men are surprisingly easy to convince that they are stunningly attractive to women. It seems George Hart is no exception. She sees his face relax, and immediately she offers to buy him a drink. He asks for a whisky and Coke this time, and as he knocks it back, his tongue loosens. He drops Kas's name – 'the boss man', he calls him, vaguely waving his arm to encapsulate the club, and asks her if she knows him.

She shakes her head, but she cannot resist probing a little further. 'Are you friends?' she asks.

George Hart shrugs nonchalantly. She sees a flicker of pride in his eyes. 'You could say that,' he says. 'Known him for a while. He asks me down here sometimes, like tonight – free entry, you know? Seeing as he knows me. Been doing a bit of work for him, actually. Buying and selling? But as it goes,' he continues, 'I've decided to knock it on the head.' He leans in, gazing at her with drunken sincerity. 'Got a baby now, haven't I, and it's time to move on. Wash my hands of it.'

Uncertainly, she nods. 'Does he know?' she asks.

For a moment George's face looks haggard, doused in apprehension, and then his expression straightens. He waves a dismissive hand. 'Nah,' he says, 'but he'll be OK.'

'Right,' she says automatically. Before she can stop herself, the thought flashes into her mind. *He does know*, she thinks. *And that's what he wants to talk to you about.* For an instant, the words tremble on her lips. She looks at him. He reminds her of a kindly neighbour or a seldom-seen uncle; the kind of person she would normally treat with polite detachment and little more. A baby, she thinks. He has a baby. And even though she knows that this means nothing, really, that there must have been a dozen fathers or more who have slavered over her and been inside her, it somehow throws her off-track. She does not want to touch him, and she does not want any part of this. Something is telling her to walk away.

She almost does it. And then she thinks of Kas down in the basement, waiting for her. She thinks of what he will say if she goes back on her word, and the look of disappointment that he will give her before he turns away from her, for the last time.

George is starting to fidget and cast his eyes around the club again, watching out for Kas. She forces herself to speak. 'Look,' she says, 'I don't think he's around. In any case, if he is, you can catch up later. How about we go somewhere more private?'

Here it is. She reaches out her hand and places it at the top of his thigh. The material feels scratchy and slightly damp, the muscle beneath tensing under her touch. She glances up at him, her eyebrows raised invitingly; she feels her lips peel apart in suggestion. The moment is white-hot and electrically charged. She has forgotten, in this instant, who this man is; there is only the familiar rhythm of seduction, the cut and thrust of approach and response. George Hart hesitates for a moment, taking one final look around the club, and then he puts his hand on top of hers. The gesture is almost romantic, she thinks, considering the multitude of other places he could have put it. She wraps her fingers around his and pulls him from his seat.

'Come on,' she says, 'I know a place.' She guides him through the swaying crowd, her eyes fixed on the small red spotlight that signals the steps to the basement. She has never been down there before, but she has seen Kas emerging, always locking the door behind him. She knows that this time it will not be locked. Curling her fingers more tightly into the man's palm, she glances back at him. He looks confused and eager, almost grateful, and for an instant she is pulled up short. She is not sure, not sure at all of what she is doing. But now they are at the steps, and she is pushing the door open and slipping quietly in, unobserved in the dark corner, and pulling him after her. Together, they descend the staircase, and she sees another door to her right, left ajar so that dim light spills out across the floor from the room beyond.

'Here,' she says. George's hands are around her waist now, drawing her against him, as she backs against the door and pushes it open. He has lost his earlier finesse, his touch rough and almost aggressive. She leads him into the room, a small, stone-walled storage cavern, almost bare but for a pile of boxes stacked at one end, a corner table and a lamp. In an instant, as the door slams behind them, she sees Kas, standing silently in the corner, leaning back against the wall. Even though she has been expecting it, the sight of him makes her body jolt in shock. She gasps, and George immediately lets go of her. He swings round, and she sees him visibly stiffen and go still. He does not speak.

Sadie looks at Kas, but his gaze is fixed on George. In another moment, she feels hands on her shoulders, guiding her away. Twisting around, she sees that it is Dominic. He is pushing her back towards the door, and at first, her mind groping for comprehension, she does not resist. In the half-light of the basement, time seems to slow and stop; everything around her is motionless, and she hears the faint, muffled thud of music above, seeping through the ceiling. Her head swims. And then she is suddenly terrified. The fear makes her struggle, kicking out against Dominic, and she hears her own breathing coming hard and fast. Even as she resists she knows that there is no point. He is stronger than her, much stronger, and she is not sure enough of what she is fighting against.

After that everything happens very fast. She is pushed outside the door, and Dominic comes with her, closing it tightly behind them. He holds her only by the wrist now, but his fingers clutch around the bone like iron. He tells her to be quiet, and somewhere in the back of her head she thinks that this is strange, because she has not spoken a word. Her legs are shaking, threatening to collapse below her. They stand there together outside the door for two minutes, maybe three. Dominic's eyes never leave the dark summit of the staircase. She feels a powerful impulse to run, and the need is so strong that she shifts an inch or two towards the stairs. *Let me go*, she whispers, so quietly that she cannot be sure that Dominic has heard. He makes no reply, but his grip on her tightens. She looks at him, and sees his face calm and set, his glassy eyes fixed somewhere above her head, as if she is not trembling beside him, as if she is not there at all.

A knock comes from the other side of the door. With silent efficiency, Dominic swings round and pushes it open. Kas is there, his face oddly alert and searching. He says something that she does not catch. And then they are all inside the little room again, and for just a fraction of a second before the two men move forwards to block her view, she sees it: the shape of a body underneath a rough sheet of sacking, perfectly still. For a few hectic seconds, the pieces do not fit together. Her eyes flick around the room, searching for George, back and forth, each image like the snap of a camera inside her head. There is no one moment when she understands, only a deepening fear and shock that numbs her from head to toe.

She is shuddering; she doesn't realize how much until Kas puts his hand on her arm. 'Go back upstairs,' he says. 'Stay by the door for a few minutes, and then go home.' The words are innocent enough, but every one of them pierces her like a knife. She feels Kas's fingers under her chin, tipping up her face to meet his. 'You did well, Sadie,' he says. 'You will keep this to yourself.'

She thinks that there is just the faintest quaver of a question in the last word, a tiny rise in his inflection that seems to demand an answer, but she cannot make herself nod.

'You must understand, Sadie,' Kas says. He is very close to her now, his hands sliding down to grip her

116

shoulders, and he speaks intently, his voice low and steady. 'This is all a question of loyalty. Some people are disloyal. Those people are not worth caring about. They may be useful to make an example of, but that is all.' For a fraction of a second, his eyes roll over the sheet of sacking, before his gaze snaps back to her. 'And others . . .' he says. This time he looks deliberately towards Dominic, standing rigid at the doorway, his face expressionless. 'Others are loyal. Which are you, Sadie?'

Her head is reeling now. Everything in the room is turning fuzzy and bright, colours blurring in front of her eyes. A light film of sweat is collecting on her face. 'I'm with you,' she whispers, the words dragged out from somewhere because she knows they are the right ones, because despite everything she cannot help but mean them. And after a brief pause, a look of searching satisfaction, he nods.

She has to get out. Slowly, she backs away, and her fingers fumble for the door handle. As she does so, she thinks she hears Dominic speak to Kas, a low worried mumble. *Are you sure she* . . . She hears Kas's confident reply. And then her hand finally clasps around the door handle, and she propels herself out and away from the room, her legs carrying her up the staircase on autopilot in the dark. She pushes against the heavy black door, and it eases open, and she's back in the heat and noise of the club with hundreds of people swarming around her, dancing and drunk and shouting. She stands there frozen, counting seconds in her head. When she has reached four hundred she moves away.

As she pushes through the crowd, she feels the electric warmth of strangers against her skin and realizes that she is cold. Her eyes are stinging with tears, but they never quite fall.

Suddenly she's out on the street alone. She begins to walk, slowly at first, then faster, feeling the frozen air sobering her. For a moment, she wonders if she has hallucinated it all. But with every step she takes she can visualize the scene more clearly, like an amnesiac starting to make sense of what she has seen, and she knows that it is real. She feels a sick surge of exhilaration that she does not understand. She begins to run, and as she does so, the brightly strung rows of blue and silver lights along the streets seem to shimmer and shake above her head, as if brimming over with ominous secret meaning.

The week that follows feels double the normal length. She watches television, gets half-heartedly drunk, cancels plans with friends that she can no longer remember why she is still in touch with at all. Early every morning she wakes up with the same nagging sense of unease, like the aftermath of an instantly forgotten dream.

At first, when she replays those minutes in the basement in her head, they are clouded by shock. She can't quite comprehend what has happened, but she knows it should horrify her. And yet as the days go on, the shock slowly begins to recede, an ebbing tide sliding inexorably away from her. She begins to realize that nothing has changed. George Hart was a stranger to her. His existence on the planet had no impact on her. She has been close to death, been party to it even, and the world is still turning and her own life goes on. It hardens something in her, a tight little kernel of cynical knowledge which she'll never be able to pull out.

Late every night Kas texts her the same three words. *Speak to me.* She has learned that it doesn't matter what she replies. He never sends a second text. It seems that he simply wants to know that she is there. All the same, she replies to every one, and every night he stalks through her dreams.

On the fourth day, Rachel comes to her and sits down on the bed, dressed smartly in her work clothes but with darkish rings staining the skin beneath her eyes, and begins to talk about an opportunity that has opened up at her company. Just an internship, with minimal pay, but it could lead somewhere. She thinks Sadie should come in and meet her manager. She thinks it could be good for her. She gives her to understand, without quite spelling it out, that she has pulled some strings to arrange this meeting. And Sadie can't think of a good enough reason to say no.

And so it is that on the sixth day she's sitting in a glass and marble reception, listening to the sound of high heels clicking and echoing across the floor, watching the workers buzz back and forth talking to one another in a language that might as well be foreign. She is dressed uncomfortably in one of Rachel's suits; they're the same size on paper, but the curves of her breasts and hips make a provocative hourglass of the clothes that hang fashionably off Rachel's slim frame. Her hair is pulled tightly back from her temples, making her head ache.

Rachel is hovering next to her, glancing at her

anxiously every so often. 'Here he comes,' she hisses, gesturing towards a plump middle-aged man in clothes designed for someone fifteen years younger who is lumbering in their direction. 'Good luck, hope it goes well.' One final glance, and then she's hurrying off. Sadie sees in that glance – its mixture of fury and pleading – that her sister knows damn well that she's going to fuck this up. She thinks about walking away, but the man is already extending a hand and clasping her own in it, making his introductions and leading her away to a small windowless meeting room that takes her back to the basement she was standing in last Saturday night. She sees herself walking down those narrow steps with their glowing red spotlight, feels the cold stone wall of the cavern against her back.

'Maybe you could start by telling me something about yourself, and why you'd like to work at Kempton Price,' the man is saying, but Sadie barely hears him. She's thinking of Kas, leaning silently back against the wall, his eyes on George Hart and filled with that cool, strong sense of purpose; the tense muscles of his arms swelling beneath his white T-shirt.

The man is waiting, pressing the tips of his fat fingers together expectantly. 'Do you have any experience in this kind of company?' he tries when nothing comes. Behind his black-rimmed glasses, his eyes flick over her; the swift reflexive action that she's used to, although at least he has the decency to blush when he sees her noticing it. The apples of his cheeks briefly stain dark pink, as if he's been slapped.

Sadie clears her throat, groping for the answers that

Rachel has coached her in. 'Nope,' she says simply at last. 'I work in a bar, which I'm guessing is pretty different to this place.'

The man blinks, clearly wrong-footed. 'Well, it is . . . pretty different, yes.' He hesitates, frowning as if he's trying to work out what on earth it is he's looking at, and how she can possibly be related to the smiling, dutiful girl who does his accounts with such acumen and precision. 'Do you—'

'I mean, I suppose there's *some* overlap,' Sadie interrupts, and all at once she's starting to enjoy herself, relishing the chance to step outside of her head for a few brief moments. 'At the bar my job is basically to take people's money, which is kind of like what you do, right? And I have to be nice to a load of wankers – I'm sure you know what that's like. And of course everyone's pissed all the time, which I've heard isn't so unusual in your line of work either. So all in all—'

The man gets to his feet, gathering his papers together with a snap. 'Don't call us, we'll call you,' he says ironically, and Sadie sees with a flash of clarity that he's probably not so bad – that he's got a decent sense of humour and he's probably a good boss and maybe she'd be lucky to work here after all – but the possibility has already slipped through her fingers with those few badly chosen words and now it'll never come back.

'Wait,' she begins, but he's already ambling out of the room, raising a hand in a farewell salute, dismissing her from his life.

She follows and walks slowly back through the reception, glancing at the clock as she does so. She's been in the interview room for precisely a minute and a half. A record, even for her. As she crosses the gleaming marble floor, she sees Rachel, hovering behind one of the glass doors at the far end of the corridor, peering anxiously and uncomprehendingly through. She halts for an instant, spreads out her hands, palms up: *hey, I did my best.* But already Rachel is pushing open the door and marching towards her, arms folded, her lips compressed into a tight angry line.

'What the hell's going on?' she snaps. 'You were in there about five seconds. What happened?'

Sadie shrugs. 'Guess it wasn't the right fit.' She knows that her tone is too offhand; she should be sounding more regretful, conscious of the missed opportunity, but it's too late now and so she shifts her demeanour in the opposite direction, the slight tilt of her chin spelling out boredom and defiance.

Rachel stands looking at her silently for a moment, a frown splitting her forehead, as if she's trying to make sense of what she's being told. 'Nothing ever is,' she says at last. 'I don't know what you want.'

'I don't fucking know either,' Sadie bites back in response. Her voice is louder now and she sees Rachel glance around furtively, not wanting this to turn into a scene. She thinks about upping the ante, giving her sister what she so clearly expects and screaming in her face, but she doesn't have the energy. 'But it's not this,' she contents herself with. 'I'm not like you, Rachel.'

Rachel regards her again, a long evaluative sweep from head to toe. 'No,' she says flatly. 'You can say that again.'

The air between them hangs taut for a moment. At any time, Sadie thinks, one of them might say something unforgivable, something from which they'll never come back. She doesn't think it's going to be her, not this time. She can't quite muster the will to feel anything much. The disappointment in her sister's eyes is numbing her, just another layer of chilly insulation around her heart. She shrugs again and turns around, walking away.

As she walks down the street away from the office, the regret she felt in the interview room is already dissolving. She knows she couldn't have done it. Couldn't have got up to be at her desk by nine each morning and sat there for eight hours with her fingers flying efficiently over the keyboard, making chirpy, incisive comments in team meetings, even though she's bright enough. It doesn't matter. She's not even twenty and already she's rotten inside. Whatever it is that makes people human has been scooped out of her. When she glances down at her pale hands she's struck by the tremulous fragility of her skin, the improbability of this smooth, beautiful casing housing all this darkness.

Something inside her lurches. She's close to the edge, and she snatches gratefully at her phone when it buzzes, her breath catching in her throat when she sees Kas's name on the screen. It's much earlier than he normally texts her, and as she opens the message she registers that it's different, and that it's all beginning again. *Tomorrow night at the club*, he has written. *Be there. Delete this.*

When she looks back on that Saturday night, her memory is strange and cinematic, presenting only the edited highlights. Dressing in her bedroom at home, pulling on a short red dress and clasping a diamante choker around her neck. It is six days before Christmas, and the radio is piping out carols in the background, sweet choirboy voices raised in harmony.

The next thing she remembers, she is standing at the bar in the club, and Kas is there, pulling a photograph out of his pocket. *Felix Santos*, he says, and shows her a picture of a short dark man with black hair oiled to his scalp, laughing and pointing at a television screen, footballers frozen in action, across a crowded pub. *Got it?* She tells him yes. She feels no sense of surprise; she has known from the moment she received his message that this is how things will go. Then the slow patrol around the club, the seeking out of the man in the photograph with the dark, shining eyes. There is nothing in her head when she sees him, nothing but automatic recognition and the message it sends to her legs to move towards him.

It is even easier than the last time. In minutes she is leading him across the dance floor, down the dark staircase to the tiny basement room. This time the man does not freeze when he sees Kas. He swears loudly, and flies for the door, but Dominic is there. It is two against one, and the man is drunk and clumsy. There is no time for her to leave the room. She does not watch, but she hears the sickening crunch of bone and the last gasp of breath leaving body. She is staring at the back wall, watching the shadows slide along the stone.

They leave her there in the room and tell her to wait, taking the bundle of sacking with them. It is only Kas who returns. He reaches her in two long strides, peers into her face and asks her if she is all right. She looks into his eyes, and doesn't know what to reply. For the first time, she acknowledges that she is afraid of him. The realization tugs at her painfully, as if her own flesh and blood has revealed itself to be evil. And yet there is something else there still, impossible to beat down or strip away, the heady swim of lust that clouds her mind whenever he is there.

She closes her eyes.

'Hey,' he says. 'Hey,' placing his fingers at their corners and opening them. 'Sadie.' She looks back at him. 'Thank you,' he says, his voice low and caressing. His eyes have the flat, cool gleam of metal. She can see nothing behind them, not even her own reflection.

He pushes his body against hers suddenly, standing over her where she sits on the little wooden table against the wall. The shock of it makes her gasp. This is what she's dreamed of, wanted so fiercely for what feels like years, and even though it's all mixed up with the ugliness of what has just happened here – in this very room – it's euphoric, shocking her with its intensity, and it blows everything else out of her head like a hurricane.

His mouth comes down to hers, and she feels it move against her skin, his tongue flicking sensuously across her lower lip. He kisses her harder, slipping his hands around her waist and holding her against him. The sudden need floods through her, drenching her. She can taste his skin, the mix of salt and sweet, and when he slides his hand up beneath her dress she cries out as if he has slapped her. She hears him unzip the fly of his trousers, and wraps her legs tight around his waist, urging

125

him inside her. His teeth are grazing the skin of her collarbone, his hands encircling her thighs, and pulling her towards him. There is nothing in her mind now, nothing but the urgency of wanting him there and then, with no room for thought or delay. He stares at her as he enters her, and the power of his gaze, the liquid darkness of his eyes, forces a moan helplessly from her throat. Slowly at first, then faster, he begins to move his hips, his arms stock still and holding her there on the table. It is hard and brutal, setting all her senses on fire. *Come for me*, he hisses, and she does, and it's the best it's ever been.

But then it's over. And in no more than a second she feels everything drain away and she's back there in the room, her body numb and sore and with nothing to block out the reality of what she has done.

'Wait ten minutes before you leave,' he says, breaking away from her, doing up his trousers. She watches his strong hands wrench the belt into place. He throws her a brief glance before he leaves. It is not the sort of look you would give a lover; it is cold, searching, and it issues a warning.

She sits there in the empty room, feeling the cool air trickle over her bare shoulders and thighs. Ten minutes is not long, but it is long enough for her to realize something that should have occurred to her weeks before. It comes to her that Kas's interest in her is not, as she has always thought, because of her strength, her independence or her defiance. It is because of her weakness. He has recognized something in her that few people have ever seen: a malleability, a desire to please which will overstep normal boundaries. A willingness to do anything. She sees this with clarity now, but it is too late.

His text message wakes her the next day: *Best if you stay away for a while, baby. I'll be in touch X*. Over the next three weeks she looks at it again and again, wrenching drops of new meaning from it. He isn't simply telling her to stay away; he's protecting her, shielding her from something, and he's promising that he'll be back, that whatever it is between them isn't finished. She is his baby.

In those weeks she reworks those few minutes in the basement repeatedly, and just as with the text message, she soon finds herself viewing them differently. Perhaps the look he gave her when he left hadn't been cold after all, but simply intense – caught up in the passion they had just experienced. That at least isn't something she has to warp or refigure. She remembers every detail: the seamless fit of his body to hers, the speed and the violence of it, the pure perfect chemistry that has always eluded her before. It must mean something. It has to. She knows that Kas has made some bad choices, but it's part of the life he has grown up in; something that he has to do to stay on top and which he could leave behind, which he *will* leave behind, once they are together properly. Her thoughts skate around the truth, and when the images of those two men – George Hart, Felix Santos – slip into her mind she blocks them straight out.

Murderer. Sometimes she finds the word there in her head, clear and present. But she just lets it linger there for a moment, and the sound and the shape of it is so

127

unfamiliar that she can't connect it with reality and it fades away again. Surely that isn't who he is.

She goes through those three weeks on autopilot, barely speaking to anyone. After the disastrous interview at the office, Rachel snapped out a few crisp words about humiliation and washing her hands of the situation, and she's avoided her ever since. Their paths rarely cross, and when they do, Rachel behaves as if she's alone in the room, her jaw set in a hard, defiant line. When Sadie lets herself think about it, it hurts. So she doesn't, and it just becomes another thing to block out, another part of the churning white noise that fizzes constantly around her like static. There doesn't seem to be an end in sight, and so she tells herself that she had better get used to it – that this strange, sleepwalking stasis is how it's going to be for her from now on.

It's the twelfth of January before something happens to jolt her out of it. She's walking the streets around Covent Garden in the late afternoon as dusk begins to fall, staring at the market stalls, when she sees a little ornamental desk calendar propped up on one of them. It's the kind where you move little painted numbered blocks around to form the correct date, and as she looks at the curved figures of the twelve, something clicks. Her period is as regular as clockwork, and she was due on the sixth. She can't remember the last time she was late. And yet here she is, almost a week on, and her body is resolutely unprepared, with none of the usual twinges of oncoming cramp or the slight oiliness of her skin.

She stands quite still for a few moments, and then she turns and runs, back up towards the station and down a side street where she knows there is a chemist. She makes straight for the family planning section and snatches up the nearest test, then pays for it, fumbling with her wallet and snapping at the saleslady who is so slow with finding a bag that in the end she just grabs the test and rushes out of the store again. She makes a run for the pub across the street, elbows her way past the little clutches of people gathered outside. Swerving past the bar, she finds the toilet and locks herself in the cubicle, panting and catching her breath. Her bladder is full to bursting and she lets the stream flow, her fingers shaking as she holds the test in place and then stares at it, counting the seconds in her head. She has heard that most people like to hide it until the three minutes are up, to prepare for a moment of sudden revelation. But she isn't like most people and she doesn't take her eyes off the stick, and so she sees every millimetre of the change, the slowly shifting coloured molecules that start off grey and slowly coalesce into a pale pink line, faint but unmistakeable.

She holds it tightly in her hands, trying to breathe deeply. She's on the pill, of course, but she knows it's not foolproof. And yet this has never happened to her before. It's no coincidence that it has happened now, with him. It's meant to be. Her eyes fill up with tears as she tucks the stick carefully into her handbag and picks up her mobile. She's never contacted him unprompted before, but this is different. *Kas, I need to talk to you*, she types. *Can we meet as soon as possible? S xx*.

It's less than a minute before the phone buzzes in response. *I can be at Camden market in an hour. This is important, yes? You wouldn't ask otherwise.*

Something about the message unsettles her a little – there's a hint of a threat, an intimation that whatever this is had better be worth his time. All the same, she's thrilled at the prospect of seeing him so soon. She quickly redoes her make-up in the cloakroom mirror, painting her lips with strawberry gloss and drawing her eyeliner thickly. Her eyes are sparkling, and as she turns and pushes her way back through the pub and out on to the street she's aware that she's never looked so good – that people are turning their heads as she walks by and craning their necks to watch her, and a laugh bubbles in her throat because she's finally feeling happy.

The Tube takes a long time, wheezing its way between stops and frequently sitting for minutes at a time. At first she doesn't mind, but the longer she sits there, surrounded by irritable commuters sighing and fidgeting, the more the edge starts to wear off her elation. A sliver of doubt worms its way in, sharp and cool as a knife. Kas isn't a single man, after all. His situation is complex; it won't be easy to resolve. She tries to push the doubt away, to imagine them together this time next year ... Imagine him cradling their baby, a baby with dark olive skin like his and the same gleaming, liquid eyes. But it's hard to put him into this picture. For an instant, she's uncomfortably reminded of the fear that shot through her when he came back into the basement, the few seconds before he kissed her. Is this man cut out to be a father? Does she really want this, after all?

It's these questions that are still hammering in her head as she steps off the Tube and takes the lift up to the platform, and that she still can't find the answers to as she weaves her way through the streets towards the lock. She stops by the edge of the market, leaning back against the side of a juice stall, breathing in the sharp scent of freshly squeezed orange mixed with the faint sweetness of marijuana on the air. Something is closing over her, darkening her vision, and in that moment she has almost decided that this is a mistake. But as she pushes herself slowly away from the wall, preparing to leave just so that she can have a little more time to think this over, she sees him.

He's leaning against the opposite wall, scanning the far side of the street, the smoke from his cigarette curling elegantly up through the air. A dark jacket is slung around his shoulders over a tight black T-shirt and jeans that would look ordinary on anyone else. In the few seconds before he turns his head and sees her, Sadie gazes at him: the aristocratic slash of his cheekbones, the sensuous curve of his lip. Her stomach clenches and she can feel her heart thudding against her ribs, and by the time he notices her she's already hurrying towards him. As soon as she nears him she can smell his aftershave, cutting through the heavily scented air with its familiar note of cinnamon.

'Sadie,' he says, tossing the cigarette to the ground and grinding it out. He reaches out and touches the side of her face, a lazily charming movement. The cold of his fingers makes her shudder. 'I had meant to contact you before this. You know, it was only for your sake that I asked you to stay away. You realize this? In these matters, it is best to take precautions.'

She nods mutely, and for a moment she has to fight an

inappropriate urge to laugh. It's the unknowing irony in what he's said – the reminder of the one precaution he failed to take. She bites her lip, sucking in hard, and she sees his eyes flick coolly down to follow the movement before returning to hers. Desire rushes up through her body, and she takes a long breath. Kas is smiling faintly, his head tipped slightly to one side.

'So,' he says, seemingly more at ease now that he can see that she isn't angry or distressed, 'why are we here? I don't flatter myself that you only wanted to see me.'

'No,' she says, although he must know she'd walk over broken glass to get to him if there was no other way. 'I – I have something to tell you.' She hesitates a moment, feeling the space between them electrically charged with expectation. 'I'm pregnant,' she says at last. On the way here she's rehearsed several ways into this, but now they all seem redundant. 'It's your baby. There's been no one else for ages now.'

He is absolutely silent for more than ten seconds, and in this space she realizes just how long time can stretch. It feels like an eternity. His expression is entirely unread-able, his eyes narrowed thoughtfully and studying her, evaluating what she has just said.

'Well,' he says eventually. 'Life is full of surprises.' His tone is blandly neutral; he could be commenting on a news story of passing interest. When she doesn't reply, he smiles again, a little tightly. 'It is natural, I suppose, that you wanted to inform me,' he says, and she is briefly struck by the stilted elegance of the way he speaks, the only sign that English is not his first language. 'But I am not sure what you want from me.'

She swallows, tasting something bitter at the back of her throat. 'I thought that you would want to know,' she says. 'I thought . . .' She realizes that there is no point being coy. If she wants this, she is going to have to ask for it. 'I want to be with you,' she says, loudly and clearly. 'I want us to be together, to have this baby and be a family.'

Kas raises his eyebrows and smiles again, a glittering, incredulous smile that fades as quickly as it has appeared when he sees that her own expression has not changed. He brings the tips of his fingers to his mouth, rubbing lightly across the skin. 'Sadie,' he says quietly, so low that she has to lean in to hear him. 'You know that cannot happen. I am married.' For the first time, she is aware of the dull gold ring on his fourth finger; a plain, wide band that looks a little loose, as if it would be easy to slip off and toss away into the gutter.

'I know,' she says, forcing herself to remain calm. She takes a moment, looks beyond him at the brightly coloured clothes hanging from the roof of the market stall, swaying faintly in the breeze. 'But you and I, we have something, don't we? There's something between us that . . .' She trails off. She has never felt so young and so vulnerable. She has no idea how to express what is swirling inside her, the conviction that she needs him to feel as much as she does herself.

His face softens now, and he reaches out for her, pulling her against him, putting his mouth close to her ear. 'Something, of course,' he murmurs, and she feels him hardening against her thigh, his fingers gripping her waist. 'But one does not throw away a marriage for this kind of something, Sadie. You must understand that. I have my life. I have my duty.' He seems pleased with this word, listening to its echo, giving a brief nod to himself. 'I am sorry,' he says, releasing her, 'but you must see that this is impossible.' His voice is lightly regretful now, and he moves away, taking the warmth and the heat of his body with him, stepping back from her.

'But, Kas,' she says, hearing the crack in her voice and knowing that she is about to cry. 'I don't know what to do. I'm only nineteen, for fuck's sake. I'm not ready for a baby! I can't do this without you . . .'

He shakes his head, and he's backing off fast now, raising his hands palms outwards in an expression of defeat. 'If only things were different,' he says smoothly, 'but they are not, Sadie, and the best I can advise you is that you deal with the situation in the sensible way and put all of this behind you. Think it over, and let me know when it is done.' And with that parting shot he turns on his heel and walks confidently away, moving the crowds apart with the force of his stride. She sees the heads turn – the sparks of interest and apprehension that flare up around him – and she sees how he ignores them all, locked off inside his own force field, uncompromising, untouchable.

Rachel

12 January 2000

SHE'S DEVELOPED A KIND of instinct for when Sadie is in trouble – a prickly, uncomfortable sense that makes it impossible for her to sit still and which scratches at her whatever she's doing. Today it's more insistent than usual. She doesn't know where her sister is; she thinks she mumbled something about going to the shops round the Covent Garden market, but that was hours ago now and she still isn't back. In itself this isn't unusual. She's used to Sadie changing her plans on a whim and not bothering to inform anyone, but there's something about the way she's been recently – detached to the point of remoteness, but at the same time less defiant, more pliant than normal – which sets Rachel on edge. She doesn't know what to do about it, and ever since the disastrous interview she set up for Sadie at the office, which has resulted in more than one awkward conversation with her boss, she's felt less and less inclined to do anything at all.

She makes herself some dinner, watches a cookery show on TV. It's half past ten and she thinks about going to bed, but something tells her not to get undressed just yet. She finds herself glancing at her phone repeatedly, almost daring it to buzz, and when it does and she sees Sadie's name flash up on the screen she feels nothing but a kind of internal hardening, a knowledge that this is going to be a bad one.

The message is barely coherent. *Its all fucked what the hell am I going to do. Im in the three crowns where are you??* The name is vaguely familiar; Rachel has a shaky image of a black frontage, diamond-patterned windows. She's sure she's seen it before, on the way to the club with Sadie, and when she looks it up her suspicions are confirmed; it's a pub in Camden, not far from Kaspar's.

She looks out of the window. It's drizzling, slapping softly against the glass, and the tree branches that crisscross the streetlamps move sluggishly back and forth in the wind. She remembers being outside earlier, the startling cold of the air cutting through her clothes. There is almost nothing she would rather do less than go out again now, take the Tube across London and pull her drunken sister from a pub. Instead, she could have a bath, luxuriating in the heat and warmth, and then go to bed with a book and drift off into sleep, ready for work in the morning. She's still thinking about this possibility as she pulls on her boots and searches for a scarf. Why can't she do it? Sadie is nineteen, not quite an adult perhaps in the way that most people are, but not a child. If Rachel wasn't there, she would have to manage. These thoughts circle around her head, increasing in indignation with every rotation, but she still can't translate them into action. The old brute force of responsibility is propelling her, driving her out of the flat and down the freezing streets towards the station.

The journey isn't a long one but there are delays on the Tube and by the time she gets to Camden it's well past eleven. She has visions of Sadie cast out on the street, lying in a gutter. But when she gets to the pub it's clear that this isn't the sort of place that abides too much by last orders. It's a total dive, full of bruised-looking men who are barely even talking to their companions, just downing their drinks in vicious silence. She pushes her way past them, spotting her sister as soon as she turns the corner. She's sitting on her own at the back of the bar, dressed in a tight scarlet T-shirt with matching lipstick, mascara smudging the corners of her eyes. Rachel sees a young man hanging around, running an appraising eye over Sadie, but her sister looks up lazily and stares at him with such contempt that he hastily backs off, his expression wary, sliding off her like wheels off black ice.

Rachel wraps her arms around herself and steps forward. 'Not a good night, then?'

Sadie looks up with a start, her eyes dazed and unfriendly. 'What are you doing here?'

'You told me to come.' It isn't true, actually, Rachel realizes, but it might as well be. 'So here I am.'

A beat of silence, as Sadie takes this in, and then, inexplicably, she's laughing uncontrollably, almost bent double over the table, her eyes streaming. Her breath is coming in gulps, and as Rachel watches her she's no longer sure if this is laughter at all, or something closer to grief.

She sits down and reaches out across the table, pulling her sister's hands into hers. They hardly ever touch, and the contact feels strange, skin burning on skin. 'Tell me what's happened,' she says quietly, 'and don't even think about lying to me.'

Sadie looks surprised, almost offended. 'I wouldn't,' she says, and silently Rachel acknowledges that this is fair enough, because to the best of her knowledge lying isn't something her sister does a lot of, except perhaps by omission. She's never been concerned with covering up her behaviour.

'Go on then,' Rachel prompts. She can see that this isn't just a drunken panic. There's something specific, stirring between them, waiting to erupt.

Sadie draws in a long, slow breath and shrugs. 'I'm pregnant,' she says, 'and he doesn't want anything to do with it.'

At the same time as she registers the shock and dismay, Rachel is also conscious of a creeping little thought that it is a wonder this hasn't happened before. Because of course this is what happens to girls like Sadie, girls who don't give a shit about anything and who put their animal instincts above anything else. But it hasn't happened, not until now. And actually, her sister isn't stupid. She's cynical about men, wary of being trapped. So even as she draws in breath and asks, 'Who?' she already has a nasty feeling that she knows. There's only one person who Sadie would have dropped her guard like this for.

138

'Not Kas,' she says flatly in the wake of her sister's silence, and Sadie winces and looks down, acknowledging it.

'Don't be angry,' she mumbles.

'It's not you I'm angry with,' Rachel says automatically, finding that it's true. Right now, looking at Sadie's tear-stained face and the lost, glazed look in her eyes, she can't feel anything but pity. An image of Kas swims into her head; the hard, muscular bulk of him, the way that everything about him seems designed to intimidate. She can't imagine wanting this man anywhere near her.

'I don't want you to be angry with him either!' Sadie fires back. 'You don't understand. He can't do anything about it, his hands are tied. He's married to that bitch Melanie and he can't leave her, because he isn't like that. He doesn't just – shirk his responsibilities!' It's like she's reading from a script.

Rachel is silent for a moment, dropping her head into her hands and massaging her temples, gently pushing her fingers into her skin. 'Sadie, listen to yourself,' she says eventually. 'What you're saying is ridiculous. You're talking like this is a man with incredibly strong morals, but that clearly isn't the case. If it was, you wouldn't be in this position, would you, because—'

'You don't understand,' Sadie says again, her voice rising. She stands up, reaching a hand out to steady herself against the table. 'It's not him. It's her. I'm going to find her right now, I'm going to tell her everything.'

Rachel jumps up. 'Don't be insane,' she says. 'Why would you do that? He isn't going to thank you for it, you know. It's not going to change anything.'

'Yes it will,' Sadie argues. 'It will, because then I'm taking it out of his hands, aren't I? He can't do it himself, but I can do it for him. I know where he lives. I'm going to his house right now, I'm going to find her.' Abruptly she pushes the table away from her and strides through the bar.

There's a split-second when Rachel thinks that she might let her go. A weariness comes over her, settles like cloud. These mercurial spikes of anger that Sadie has are powerful, and she knows her well enough to realize that if she's fuelled by this energy then there's absolutely nothing that can be done to talk her out of it. But then she thinks about the reality of this situation. Her sister is stumbling out drunk, looking for a fight with a woman she knows nothing about, a woman who's married to a potentially dangerous man. There isn't a choice here. Just like she's always done, she's going to try her best to minimize the damage.

'Fucking hell,' she hisses under her breath, and she makes her heavy limbs move and hurry after Sadie, out of the bar.

Her sister has moved fast, and Rachel can see her swerving down a side street a hundred yards or so ahead, walking surprisingly steadily and with intense purpose. She makes herself walk faster to catch her up, reaching out a hand to grab her arm. 'Please, Sadie, stop,' she pants. 'This is such a bad idea. She won't even be there anyway, she'll be with him at the club, won't she?'

Sadie stops for an instant; a spasm of doubt crosses her face. But then she shakes her head firmly, pressing on. 'She won't,' she says confidently. 'She hardly ever goes.'

'Please,' Rachel says again, wrenching at Sadie's arm so that she has to turn towards her. To her own surprise, she finds that there are tears in her eyes, and she has to fight past a lump in her throat. 'Just come home, come home with me. You can put this behind you, Sadie. We can talk properly tomorrow, work out what's best to do about the baby. This doesn't have to be the end of the world. It could be a turning point! At last! You can move on, honestly.'

Sadie pauses. She's looking at Rachel thoughtfully, as if she's genuinely considering what she's saying; these words sinking in slowly and absorbing themselves through her brain. Rachel stares back at her, willing her to agree. Perhaps, she thinks, Sadie just needs one more push, something to get her over the line. 'Just leave Melanie alone,' she says calmly. 'She knows nothing about any of this. It isn't her fault.' And even as that last sentence leaves her lips she realizes it was the wrong thing to say, and that if she had just kept quiet, everything might have been different.

Sadie

12 January 2000

SHE STORMS ON THROUGH the streets, covering ground fast. She knows where she's going. Kas lives on Fraser Street – she's seen the address on letters at the club and she's walked around the nearby area many times, wondering if she might catch him there. It's not far now. She isn't so drunk as to be incapable. In fact, she's just drunk enough to be able to channel all this fury and conviction without inhibition, to get the job done.

It's true what she told Rachel, she thinks; Melanie won't be at the club. She doesn't want to support Kas. Not the kind of wife he needs. It wasn't Melanie he turned to when he needed help, was it? It wasn't her whom he trusted with the stuff that really mattered. She wishes she could tell Rachel this, but it's a can of worms she can't open. She just lets it add fuel to her own fire, strengthening her conviction. Of course Rachel doesn't understand. She doesn't have the full picture, and you can't make a judgement based on fragments.

As she marches on she thinks it all over again, playing her favourite game of reshuffling and reshaping, sliding the pieces into place. The way Kas touched her this afternoon when he first said hello, the way he pulled her against him and spoke into her ear, his lips hot against her skin. He still wants her. And the word he used when he talked about Melanie. *I have my duty.* Not love, she thinks, not love, duty. A duty is barely a choice. It's a responsibility. A burden. It's this definition she likes the best, the one that feels like it's starting to drain the poison away from her heart. He has this *burden*, and it isn't his fault.

She rounds the next corner and she sees the little plaque looming at the side of the road: Fraser Street. This is the place. She peers down the darkened alley at the houses cluttered together like dominos. There's something about the lines of dark gaping windows with their ragged curtains, the jagged piles of bricks unevenly skirting the entrances, that worries her. It isn't the glamorous penthouse she imagined. Now that she's here, it's harder to imagine walking up to one of these unfriendly doors and knocking on it to be let in. But then she hears the footsteps, clicking lightly up the other side of the street, sees the shadow of a figure, dark and indistinct at first, then revealed in a sudden brief burst of light beneath a streetlamp; long legs in sheer tights, black high-heeled boots beneath a shiny raspberry-coloured mac.

She finds herself shrinking back instinctively, out of the light, pulling Rachel with her. 'That's her,' she whispers. 'Look. She's going out somewhere.'

'Leave it,' Rachel whispers back, but there's a hope-less lack of conviction in her tone.

Sadie shakes her head silently, and then she turns and moves quietly, following Melanie back through the darkened streets. And Rachel is trapped too in this silence now, not wanting to attract attention to their presence, and with no choice but to follow after her.

She's going to the Overground station. Sadie realizes it as soon as she takes a turn off from the high street and strikes out up the Camden Road, although she can't imagine where Melanie would be travelling to at this time, almost midnight, and on her own. Perhaps she's going to meet another man. Sadie likes this idea – likes the thought of Kas's wife being an unfaithful bitch, no matter how unlikely it seems that she'd need to look else-where. It's a good ten minutes' walk to the station, but it seems that it's done in seconds, with nothing existing except this moment, the thrill of the chase and the sat-isfaction of being unseen. A couple of times Melanie hesitates, half turns her head, then walks on, drawing the cheap-looking mackintosh closely around her, her long dark hair cascading down her back in a tangled fountain. She quickens her steps a little as she reaches the entrance to the station, slipping over the threshold as if she's crossed a finish line.

Sadie reaches the entrance seconds later, and as she peers through the gateway she sees that the ticket hall is deserted and dark, the expanse of platform ahead com-pletely empty but for Melanie's tall thin shape patrolling back and forth uneasily. She's checking her phone, then tucking it back into her pocket, and Sadie knows that in a few seconds she'll raise her head and look in her direction. She can feel Rachel's hand on her arm, silently tugging her back, but she shakes it off and steps forward on to the platform, the wind whipping down the long tunnel and chilling her right through – and as she does so she realizes that she hasn't planned this at all and that she has no idea what to say.

Melanie must sense her presence now, because she looks around sharply, and there's a split-second where she struggles to place the woman she sees in front of her, then a dawning realization that hardens her expression. 'What the fuck are you doing here?' she snaps, and strides towards Sadie.

She doesn't answer for a few seconds, struggling to process what is happening. She has expected Melanie to be caught off guard, not to react so instantly and with such aggressive interrogation. And her voice is different to how she imagined, with none of Kas's subtle exoticism; a voice straight out of the East End, all hard edges and swallowed consonants. Sadie gathers herself, taking a moment to breathe in, feeling the cold air rush up through her lungs. 'I've come to tell you something about your husband,' she says.

Melanie tosses her hair back over her shoulders, folding her arms in front of her. She's half smiling, a lazily amused smirk that makes Sadie want to hit her. 'There's nothing you can tell me that I don't already know.' The words are edged with steel, even if her expression is light.

Sadie looks at her steadily, and she sees that this woman is older than she thought. There are tiny wrinkles

145

at the corners of her eyes and across her forehead, a faint roadmap that will only strengthen with time. 'I don't think you know this,' she says. For some reason, now that the time is here, the words won't come. Or rather there are too many of them, all jostling for prominence, forming a cauldron of cacophony inside her head. *He's cheating on you. I've slept with him. I'm carrying his child and he's staying with you out of duty, nothing else.* She doesn't know where the right place to start is, where will hurt the most – and she realizes, too, that there is no reason why Melanie should believe her.

The older woman is looking straight back, cat's eyes slanted, her expression bored. 'I don't play guessing games with little girls,' she says. 'Especially ones like you. You think you're special, but you're not. You're nothing to him. You can't think you're the first slag he's had some fun with?'

She is very close now, and Sadie can smell her breath, sweet like peppermint, as she speaks her words slowly and clearly. 'He used you,' she says, 'like so many others, and now he's thrown you away.'

Later, when she looks back, Sadie will find it impossible to unpick exactly what goes through her head when she hears those words, or why they hit their target so keenly. All that remains in her memory is the fury, the strength of it and the brute instinct it unleashes. Her hands rising up, her fingers curled like claws as she lunges at the woman's face. The savage gladness she takes in the way Melanie's heels twist on the platform, her thin legs crumpling like paper. And then in the next split-second she finds that she's defending as well as

146

attacking, raising her arm against a returning blow, pushing back against the force that is coming at her. The gathering sound in her ears of wheels rushing against tracks, the blaze of headlights igniting from nowhere out of the dark. An instant of panic that she sees reflected in the face of the woman just inches away from her own, because suddenly she realizes that they're close to the edge, very close. So close that anything could happen.

PART THREE

Alex

September 2017

WE SIT IN SILENCE for a while, my wife and I, side by side on the rocks. She's very close to me, but she's never seemed so far away. I find myself staring at her profile, picked out in silhouette against the darkening sky, and it feels as if I'm looking at a stranger. She's thinking about the sister in the photograph, I think. Sadie. There's all this knowledge, all this history, packed away inside her head, and I know nothing about it. Nothing at all.

'You and your sister weren't close, then?' I ask. I deliberately keep my tone casual. I have the feeling that at any moment she might snap this conversation shut.

She breathes in and out slowly, her gaze straying upwards as if she's remembering. 'We used to be,' she says. 'When we were young. We spent all our time playing together. Once we even wrote our initials in blood on a tree trunk because we'd read somewhere that if you did that then nothing would ever break you apart. We pricked our fingers with a needle to do it and I cried, but

151

not because it hurt me. Because I saw it hurt her.' She gives a little grimace, at once sad and dismissive. 'I grew out of that, though. If I'd cried my eyes out every time she did something to hurt herself I'd have never stopped, by the end.'

'So what changed?' I ask.

She shoots me a quick glance, her dark eyes meeting mine for an instant before she looks back out at the rolling expanse of the sea ahead of us. 'I suppose you could say we grew apart,' she says. 'We liked different things.' Her tone is dryly understated, as if she's making an in-joke, forgetting that I can't understand. 'We lived together, when she was nineteen and I was twenty-two. It wasn't what I would have chosen, but, well . . . It was complicated. I thought it would be OK. But it wasn't. I can't even tell you, Alex,' she continues, turning to me again, fixing the force of her gaze on me so that I feel almost suffocated by this intensity. 'It got to the point where I would lie in bed and I could hardly breathe, literally could hardly breathe, because I knew that she was in the next room and I couldn't bear it anymore, the way she poisoned everything.' She stops and takes a breath, looks down. Picking up a small polished rock from the scattered pile beneath us, she takes aim and throws it fast and precisely into the sea. It skims over the surface for an instant, sending salt spray up into the air, before sinking and vanishing.

'And the man in the photo?' I prompt, because I can see now that all this is connected, even if I don't yet understand how.

Her expression shifts with something that could be

displeasure or fear. 'He ran a nightclub. He was – involved with my sister. I'm not even sure how deeply. Not very, I suspect, from his perspective. But she was besotted with him, obsessed with him. She was very young, and he was so . . .' She hesitates.

'Good looking,' I say, glancing down at the sloping, aristocratic angles of the man's face. 'Don't worry, I won't cut your head off for noticing.'

'I wasn't going to say that,' Natalie says, a little sharply. 'But there was something – compelling about him, I suppose. Not in a good way.' For a moment she half smiles, but it drops from her face instantly. 'She would have done anything at all to be with him, I think. It didn't matter what he was like or how he treated her or anyone else – whatever Kas did, it was all right with Sadie. But he was married, of course, and he used that as an excuse, when in reality he probably never would have committed to her in any case.'

She has been speaking with passion, her face hotly lit by these memories, and I'm sitting as still as I can, not wanting to jolt her out of it, especially when she mentions the man's name. I don't think she has realized that she let it slip.

'And it ended badly?' I prompt.

She dips her head, a quick instinctive moment. 'Sometimes it's hard to tell, isn't it,' she says, 'where the line is between intention and action. Whether things happen because you want them to, or whether they just happen, and whatever you want is incidental.'

I try to wring out some meaning from this, but I'm

not sure what she's driving at. It's so unlike the woman I know to talk in this convoluted, sideways manner.

I fall back on a simpler question. 'Why did you change your name?'

She shrugs. 'I needed a fresh start. Sometimes it's the best way to move on.' Her expression is guarded, evasive. She brings her hand up to her mouth, pressing briefly against her lips as if she wants to keep anything else she might say inside.

She's not telling me the truth, I think, or at any rate not all of it. I don't think I've ever looked at my wife before and known that she's lying to me. It gives me a nauseous sense of disconnection. Like I'm losing my moorings on our life together.

'I suppose so,' I say carefully, conscious that it's all I'm going to get for now. She's told me almost nothing, but I can sense that, for her, even letting these bread-crumbs of information slip is more than she thought she would ever do.

She stands up abruptly, brushing her skirt down from the sandy rocks and reaching for me. 'Let's go back.'

I've been awake for most of the night, lying in the hotel room and listening to the faint splash of the sea beyond the window, crashing softly against the rocks. Several times I've tried to switch off, but I can't get beyond the strangeness of watching my wife sleep. She lies with her arms stretched above her head, completely still except for the minute movements of her eyes behind closed lids, flickering back and forth in dreams. I've always liked the hint of mystery she carries about her – it was one of the things that first drew me to her, this sense that there was more going on inside her head than she would tell me. In the light of what she's revealed now, it doesn't feel so seductive. Watching those tiny traces of movement, I find myself wanting to shake her awake and make her tell me what is going through her head, before any sense of self-protection kicks in. *Whatever you were thinking of, tell me, tell me right now.*

At around three a.m. she stirs, turns her head towards me and opens her eyes. There is none of the slight disorientation she often shows when she wakes; she's instantly watchful, expectant.

'How much of this is real?' I ask, without preamble.

She blinks slowly, reaching out a hand and running it lightly across my shoulder. 'All of it.' Her eyes flicker a little, as if she's trying to calculate something immeasurable. 'It's the past which isn't real,' she says, 'not this.'

I hear those words again and again, in the dead time after she falls back to sleep. Does it really matter what she did – who she was, even – before she met me, so long as it doesn't undermine what we've built together? But as the hours roll on and the faint purplish light of dawn starts to seep through the thin curtains, the less consoling those words feel. I don't like the idea that I've fallen in love with someone without really knowing them. People don't come to us as blank slates for us to project our love on to – they're complex, packed full of experience and emotion. It's their past that makes them who they are.

I think of everything she's told me about her life.

I hate the fact that I can no longer tell how much of it was true. And that I lapped it up readily, and that I've felt secretly smug ever since at having so easily got under her skin and figured her out.

I must have fallen asleep in the end, however briefly, because my alarm wakes me and I roll over to see that Natalie is gone. Her jacket is missing from the back of the chair. I heave myself out of bed, and as I do so I see the note, which she has left neatly folded on the dressing table. It's written in the distinctive violet coloured ball-point pen she uses – a colour that even now sets off a little Pavlovian reaction in me that dates back to the first days of our relationship, when she used to write me notes that she left around 'just because', veering from dirty to romantic depending on her mood. But this note is neither of those things. *I've gone out for a walk – I need to be alone for a bit and I didn't want to wake you. I'll be back later today so don't worry. I'm sorry about every-thing. Natalie.*

I read it a couple of times before scrunching it up and shoving it angrily into my coat pocket. There's something disingenuous in 'I didn't want to wake you' – as if I'd rather wake alone to find my wife has effectively thrown a grenade into our lives and then left without clearing up the wreckage. My daughter is still in hospital. Natalie landing this on me now is almost more than I can cope with, at a time when my defences are so low and I need to focus on Jade.

I have enough self-awareness to realize that this anger is partly a throwback, bred of guilt. I love Jade more than anyone, but I haven't always put her first. After Heather died, grief made me selfish, all the more so because this sadness was complex – a cocktail of regret, desolation and a small poisonous seam of relief. We had been headed for divorce, long before the cancer, although I suppose I'll never know how much the strain of her illness stood in the way of our fixing things. At any rate, there was a secret part of me that couldn't help but feel a burden lifted at the knowledge that I would never have to share my daughter. I've never really thought before about the fact that since Natalie has come along, Jade is the one who has had to share. Now of all times she deserves to take centre stage.

I shower and dress quickly, then call a taxi to the hospital. By the time I get there the morning visiting hour will have almost started. There's more traffic than usual on the roads and progress is slow. I find myself staring vacantly out of the window, watching the slow cycle of movement, the passers-by trudging along the seafront, shoulders braced against the wind, and the cars crawling past them.

When the squat, grey building looms into view I pay the taxi driver hastily and duck inside, hurrying along the gleaming white corridors towards the ward. Jade is half sitting, propped up in bed and staring at the small TV screen next to her, and I'm surprised by how much more alive it makes her look. I step forward, pulling her mobile from my pocket and brandishing Sidney, the soft toy rabbit – one in each hand, like a conjurer presenting his spoils. 'Morning, darling,' I say. 'I got you these last night, from the house.'

Jade's eyes light up and she instantly snatches the

mobile from my hand, bending her head over the screen as she taps in the pin code and waits for a tense second before she smiles in triumph. 'It's still working,' she says. 'Thanks, Dad.'

'That's all right. Thought you'd want it.' I'm still holding the rabbit. She doesn't seem to have noticed it, and her gaze doesn't stray from her screen as I place it down on the bed beside her. Its fur is bluey-grey and worn in places, the cotton eyes frayed. I remember the way she used to clutch it to her chest, unable to sleep without it pressed against her, and my heart clenches with what feels like something close to grief.

'Sorry,' Jade says, not looking at me. 'I'm just . . .' She trails off, her thumb skimming back and forth across the screen in the swift messaging motion I still haven't totally mastered. 'Sorry,' she says again, and places the phone down beside her on the pillow.

'Don't worry,' I say, 'I'm just glad you're feeling better.' But it feels like an effort, sorrow still weighing on my chest as I watch my daughter, so close to the child she was and yet so far away.

Jade clasps her hands in front of her. 'I am, a bit,' she says, 'but my head aches all the time. The doctor said it happens sometimes, when you've breathed in a lot of chemicals like I probably did. And I'm worried about the burns. I don't want scars. Do you think I'll have them?'

'I'm not sure.' I know from my conversations with Doctor Rai that it's unlikely these scars will ever heal completely. I've already been thinking about the livid red line across her temple, thinking about how she might

158

grow her hair in a fringe to conceal it if she wanted. But of course she'll still know it's there.

I try and think of something else to say, but I soon see that she's mentally moved on. She's staring at me with what looks like expectation, and with a flash of intuition I divine that she's thinking about our last conversation, and that maybe she wants it to continue.

'What you told me yesterday, about the man in the house . . .' I begin tentatively, and am rewarded by her lack of surprise. 'Can you tell me any more about what happened?'

She presses her lips together briefly, remembering. 'I was up late because I realized I'd forgotten to do my homework, so I was up doing it in my room and I saw a shadow moving outside the door – you know, when you can just tell there's someone there? The door was a little bit open and I bent back to look through . . . I thought it was Natalie, come to check up on me or something. But it wasn't. I only saw him for a second, because he moved straight past, but it was a man.'

The words have poured out of her fast and softly, and she breaks off to draw in a breath. 'I got up and went over to my wardrobe and opened it and I got inside and shut the door,' she says. 'Maybe it was a stupid idea but I didn't know what else to do. I thought I should hide. I don't know how long I stayed there, it seemed like ages. And then I realized there was something else wrong – the noise, like something crackling, and I could smell the smoke, and then I was even less sure what I should do, I didn't know if I ought to try and get out or stay where I was and I didn't know where

159

the man was and . . .' She stops again, pressing her finger-tips swiftly to her eyes.

'It's OK,' I say quickly. 'It's over.' I reach out and squeeze her knee gently.

'But that's not all, Dad,' she says, her voice muffled. 'The man – it's not the first time I've seen him.'

'What?' I say sharply. 'What do you mean?'

'I've seen him several times,' she whispers. 'On the street. Outside school. Never for long.'

'You're sure it's the same man?' I ask. I can hear the desperation in my own voice, the need for her to be wrong.

Jade nods slowly. 'I wasn't at first,' she says. 'When I saw him in the house, it was the first time I'd ever really seen him up close. But the more I think about it, the surer I am. I can't explain exactly how I know. I just . . .' She blinks, screwing up her eyes with the effort of finding the right words. 'I just feel it,' she says at last, the words barely audible. It's the kind of pronouncement that from most people I'd find laughable. I want facts, evidence. But even so, there's a cold, subtle chill of unease, working its way beneath my collar and bristling the hairs on the back of my neck.

My hand goes reflexively to my pocket. I don't have time to consider what I'm doing – I just pull out the photograph I've been keeping there, unfold it and show it to Jade, gesturing towards the man. 'Is this him?'

She only has to look at it for the briefest of seconds before she shakes her head. 'No.'

'You're sure?'

Jade nods vehemently. 'Yes. This man looks nothing

like that. He's got blond hair, almost white, like maybe he dyes it or something. He's . . . big. Not fat, you know, but just . . .' She gestures vaguely in the air around her shoulders, sketching out muscle. 'Big. He's not that tall. Not short, but not as tall as you. And he's – I don't know, he's got a funny sort of face. It's hard to describe.' She hesitates. 'A bit like it's made out of clay or something like that.'

'OK . . .' I say, trying to commit all these details to memory. I'm searching my mind for anyone I know who might match this description, but nothing comes. In any case, the essential facts are the same. If there was a man in our house on the night of the fire, then we need to track him down. 'You know,' I say to Jade, 'you will have to tell the police about this.'

She looks shocked at that, leaning her head back against the pillows, and I can see that our conversation has tired her. 'I hadn't thought about that.' Her eyes are uncertain, a little unfocused. 'Do I have to do it now?'

'No,' I say quickly. 'But maybe in a day or two, when you're feeling stronger.' Logically, my head is telling me that it would be best to report this as soon as possible, particularly in light of the barbed conversation I had with the policeman at the house yesterday, but I don't want to push my daughter too hard too fast. In any case, the police will take her more seriously when she's stronger. I know that short-term memory loss and confusion is a common side effect of the kind of trauma Jade has been through, and even though I don't doubt her, I can't help feeling that they might.

'Dad,' she says. She's lain down again, rolling on to

her side, and her left arm is reaching out, her fingers grazing the edge of the blue rabbit, moving back and forth against the worn cotton in what could be unconscious comfort. Her voice is half muffled by the pillow, her head averted from me as if she's embarrassed to say what's on her mind. 'Am I safe now?'

I'm still thinking about that question as I walk back towards the hotel. When your child asks you that, there's only one answer you want to give, and I gave it instantly, with the conviction I knew she needed. Turning it over in my head, I think it was true. Right now, in the hospital, protected and guarded by doctors and nurses day and night, I believe she's safe. But after that? When she's back at home – wherever that will be – going to school, tracing her own path through the world, and it becomes impossible for me to shadow her every minute of every day? I'm not so sure.

Dimly I register that my phone is ringing, and I dig it out and answer it without first glancing at the screen. 'Hello?'

'Alex?' It's James, my fellow manager at the office. It's a shock to hear his voice, clipped and professional, coming from another world. A surreal realization dawns: it's Monday morning. Work has barely entered my head since the night of the fire. 'Where are you, man? I thought you were in all day?' He barely pauses for a second before pressing on. 'Look, we've got a bit of a situation with the Cooler Cola campaign. The client's come back wanting to change the ads at the eleventh hour and they're looking to have a call to talk it through at one fifteen. I don't really want Gav and Carly to handle it on their own. I could sit in but you're a lot closer to the project than I am. So are you coming in?'

I should just tell him, of course. James lives and breathes our work but if I told him that my house has burned down and my daughter is in hospital, he'd be left with no choice but to tell me to stick on my Out Of Office and take all the time I need. And yet there's something about the way he's talking to me . . . There's no awkward sympathy, no embarrassed attempt to offer solutions, and I'm surprised at how much I need this right now. 'Yeah,' I say before I have a chance to consider further. 'I'll be in in twenty.'

Fifteen minutes later I'm at the office, tapping my key-card at the entry button and climbing the two flights of stairs. It's an automatic ritual, but today its familiarity feels poignant, as if I've just returned from years away – a traveller uncovering long-forgotten, dust-laden possessions, and finding some unexpected stab of emotion in what he might have once thought mundane.

'All right, Alex,' James mutters as I come into the office and make for my desk. 'Late one last night then, was it?' He barely lifts his eyes from his screen.

'You could say that, yes.' I sit down at my desk and then freeze, realizing I don't have my laptop. It must be in the house still, though I have no idea what state it's in. I can't understand how I didn't think to check, but the past few days have thrown everything up in the air, and some of the things that have slipped through my fingers

163

have been the ones I wouldn't expect. I stare at the desk in front of me, wondering what to do.

'Oi oi,' Gavin shouts jovially across the office, 'not with it this morning, Alex? Do some fucking work!' This kind of banter is two a penny in most ad agencies – we take a stupid sort of pride in smashing down the hierarchy barriers, and the fact that Gav is probably on thirty grand less than I am is no reason in our world for him to treat me like his boss – but right now it feels totally alien. I make myself smile, raising my hands in surrender.

'Come in without my laptop,' I say, 'what a prick.'

'Sure you haven't left it out on the piss again?' Gavin fires back. I lost my last office laptop a year ago, and have never heard the end of it. It had been half-inched from a coffee shop in broad daylight, actually, not abandoned on a piss-up, but I can't be bothered to argue the toss.

'It's all right, Alex,' Carly says, trotting up to my desk, brandishing the spare computer. 'You can use this one.' She smiles brightly, tossing her high blonde ponytail. She's had her roots dyed over the weekend, a strange light pink colour. She lingers by my desk briefly, clearly expecting a comment, but I just thank her and take the computer, forcing another smile, and she spins on her high heels and prances away again, her hips moving briskly in her tight tan leather skirt.

I fire up the laptop and connect to the server, downloading a few of the files from the cola campaign. A soft drink brand looking for a bold new TV and print run, something that will divert from their crazily high sugar content and reel in the young, trendy consumers they're after. It's the kind of project I normally love. I read over the latest version of the ads, look at some of the artwork. I can barely remember anything. My mind feels soft and woolly, my thoughts dripping slowly like treacle. There are too many other paths to wander down: the state of our home, Natalie and everything she's told me, the photograph still burning a hole in my coat pocket, my daughter in her hospital bed asking me if she's safe.

Take a breather, I think, when it's clear that I'm not taking the files in in the way that I should. I bring up the browser and log into my email. I run my eye down the list, taking in the familiar generic messages from sites I'm subscribed to, and then I see something that pulls me up short. An email from SRUK. *You have a new message.*

My first instinct is to delete it without looking. It belongs to a part of my life that's over. But there's something in the very strangeness of it – my account has been inactive for so long that I can't imagine who would be messaging me – that reels me in. Slowly, I move the cursor to the message and open it, then click the link. I haven't been on for over six months, but my fingers move swiftly in the shape of my password, as if it's been less than a day. There's a short, tight pause before the site loads, and as I wait I can't help but remember the feelings the sight of this black anonymous screen with its thin red lettering in the centre – SECRETROOM – used to stir in me. The impatient hunger, the addictive pull of its cheap thrill. The letters emerge, a dark curtain unfurling to reveal them one by one; their edges fuzzily scarlet, fizzing with mystery. The inbox at the top of the screen is showing five new messages. Even if it hadn't been so long, it would be surprising – on this site, there was never a lot of unsolicited contact from women. There was a kind of unspoken rule that the men were the predators here; it was up to us to make the first move.

I've never cheated on Natalie, not physically. I apply my own standards to myself, and I've always thought I'd find it harder to forgive a drunken one-off kiss at a party than several months of loaded conversations. For me, the physical is where it becomes real. And yet part of me knows I was always bullshitting myself about secretroom. It wasn't right. Why else would I have given it up before we got married? I wanted to mean my vows, and that meant turning out the dark pockets of my life and throwing out the trash.

The main reason I had done it in the first place was that keeping this small covert piece of myself hidden was a way of keeping real intimacy at bay. I'd been through the mill once before, with Heather. I was afraid to let anyone get close, and in some small stupid way these little forays of flirtation reassured me that I wasn't completely obsessed with Natalie and that, albeit in the most meaningless way, I might still be keeping my options open. But in the end I got tired of being afraid, and that's when I cut the chains.

I click on the inbox, knowing I shouldn't. Instantly I see that all five of the messages are from the same person: Cali. Of all the women I used to talk to on secretroom, she's the one with whom it lasted longest, and the last one I was in contact with, before I logged off for what I thought was the last time. I don't know why the connection stuck. With most of the women on this site, it was a one-off thing; a half-hour or so of dirty talk that served a primal purpose and burned out almost as soon as it had begun. With her there was something that had kept me coming back. Nothing emotional, nothing that deep. But something. A chemistry.

The messages are all brief and intense.

I'm waiting for you.

Can't get you off my mind . . . You want me to beg?

Tried a lot of others but there's no one like you. No one who gets me like you do. Come on . . .

Still waiting.

And the last message, sent yesterday morning, months after we'd last been in contact. *Are you OK?*

I stare at that last one, thrown off base. There's something different in its tone. Maybe it's just because I'm *not* OK right now that it feels so loaded. But this woman never really cared how I was, surely; we didn't even know each other. I saw into the darkest corners of her desires, but I never saw her face. She was barely real. She could have been a computer, churning out automated obscenities.

I flick back through the message history, my eyes furtively scanning the lines of text. I'd forgotten how much we'd said, how fast any inhibitions had fallen away. I'd talked to this stranger in a way that I'd never talked to anyone, including my wife. It's over, but it happened, and turning your back on something isn't the same as

167

erasing it. I'll never be able to do that. I'm thinking of this, feeling sick with guilt and trying to make it into something more palatable, when I see that the little box at the bottom left-hand corner of the screen is flashing with a message. *Cali is online.*

I move the cursor swiftly to close the window down, exiting the site instantly. My heart is thumping again, this time with panic, and I can't help thinking about the message that will have been flashing on Cali's screen at that exact same moment, telling her that I was back. That for those few brief seconds we were there in the same virtual space, the invisible connectors between us bristling with electricity.

Natalie

September 2017

I SPEND THE MORNING battling the panicky sense that everything is spiralling out of control, telling myself that this is all OK, everything can get back on track. But there's too much evidence to the contrary. The fire, Jade's hospitalization, and now this seismic shift between me and Alex; the split-second decision I've made to tear a hole in the fabric of the past and let it begin to spill through. In the cold light of day, I'm not sure I've done the right thing. I could have styled out the photograph, explained away the documents somehow. I can think on my feet. Maybe I shouldn't have given in to that impulse, powerful and seductive though it was, to let him in just a little bit more. It's too late now, though, and I need to figure out where to go from here.

There's only so much I can occupy myself with – my new card hasn't arrived from the bank yet and I only have small change on me, and it isn't the sort of day to sit outside and soak up the atmosphere. The sky is bright but it's the kind of brightness that almost hurts, light stabbing coldly down through the autumnal air. By lunchtime I'm bored and restless, and missing Alex. Leaning back against the iron railings flanking the road, I give him a call. He answers almost at once, his tone guarded and low, as if he's trying not to be heard.

'Where are you?' I ask without preamble. 'I'm sorry about this morning. I just needed a bit of space.' It's a cliché and it isn't even true. I thought I needed space, but all it's done is unsettle me.

A brief pause. 'I'm at the office. I came in to help the guys out with something.'

I almost laugh; it's typical of Alex to get on with the job, even when his life is falling apart around him. 'Can you take a lunch break? I'm not far from you, I could be there in ten minutes.'

He exhales before saying OK. I can tell he's still aggrieved at my disappearance, and the knowledge makes me walk faster, head down, anxiety thudding through my body with every step I take. The last thing I want is for him to be angry with me. I'd never show it, but so much of what I do and say is geared around him – trying to make him happy, trying to make his life perfect – that when things go off track it scares me.

When I reach the office I pull out my phone to call him again, but then I see he's already at the top of the stairs, jogging down towards me. As he opens the door, a middle-aged woman is approaching, ducking into the building, and when she sees us she does a double take.

'Alex,' she says, 'are you OK? I heard about what happened. I didn't think you'd be in so soon.'

'That's all right,' Alex says briskly. 'Thanks. I'll be in and out for a few days.'

The woman waits with eyebrows raised, her face awash with concern; clearly she's expecting or hoping for more, but Alex just nods tightly and moves on past, placing his hand on my back to guide me with him along the street. 'Great,' he says under his breath as we go. 'Now it'll be all over the office. That's my afternoon's work screwed. I might as well not go back.'

'It doesn't really matter though right now, does it?' I say, struggling to keep up. 'About work.'

He slows his steps for a moment, glances at me and sighs. 'I suppose not.' We walk in silence for a little longer, lost in our own thoughts. 'I probably wouldn't have gone back anyway,' he says eventually. 'I'll need to go back to the hospital. I was just enjoying it for a bit. You know, being normal.'

I nod, understanding. 'I get it, though it did surprise me. You didn't tell me you were thinking of going to the office.'

'Well, I didn't get much chance, did I?' he points out. 'You'd upped and left.'

'At least I left a note.' This is starting to sound like the beginning of an argument, and I quickly link my fingers through his. He squeezes them a little, letting me know that he too doesn't want to go down that road. It's a complex game we play, I think, this kind of cut and thrust; the balance of words and actions, everything open to interpretation and nothing entirely

171

unambiguous. It's a disturbing enough thought to keep me quiet on the way down to the seafront, and Alex seems content to walk in silence.

It's only when we've settled ourselves on one of the wrought-iron benches that flank the pier, looking out to sea, that I turn to face him, placing my hands lightly on to his knees. 'I am sorry. I know this is a terrible time for me to have added to your stress, and I know you must feel like I've lied to you.'

'That's because you have,' he says. His voice is mild, but there's a confrontational bluntness to the words.

'I know,' I say slowly. 'All I can say is that it does feel like another life. Genuinely. Part of the reason I never told you before was that it just didn't feel relevant. It has nothing to do with who I am now. It's dead and gone.' I've never really set it out like this before, even to myself, but what I'm saying is true. When I try and put myself back there, in those days, the memories have the quality of dreams.

'But is that really true?' Alex asks. 'Look, I went to see Jade early this morning. She told me some more about the man she saw in the house, and I believe it happened. And from what she says to me, it isn't the first time he's been hanging around.'

'What?' I'm jolted. 'She's seen him before?'

'That's right. Several times, apparently.'

I take a breath, taking this in. It's a shock, but almost immediately it starts to feel inevitable. Of course, she's seen this man before. It was naive of me to think otherwise.

'We need to take what Jade is saying seriously,' Alex

172

says. 'I know this is frightening, but you need to accept that there probably was someone in the house that night. You didn't lock the back door, did you?'

Mutely, I shake my head. The reality is that I rarely lock the back door when Alex is out; he's been known to forget his key on nights out and our street is quiet. 'Don't be angry.'

'I'm not. But we need to think about what this means.'

For a moment I glimpse something in the corner of my mind's eye; the idea of a man's silhouette, moving fast and quietly along the back wall, coming inside while I'm sleeping, intent on setting the house ablaze. I can see why the thought is terrifying, and why it might have drained the colours from my husband's cheeks, but I can't make it feel real.

Alex is watching me closely. 'Natalie, I don't think I have any enemies. I've been racking my brains for anyone who might have a grudge against me, and there's nothing, nothing that could be anywhere near big enough to justify this. But from what you told me last night, I get the sense that a lot has gone on in your past that I don't know about. I have to ask, is there anyone who might resent you?'

I allow a little bark of laughter to escape, short and bitter. 'Plenty. They were good at holding a grudge, my sister's friends.'

'Well, you need to be aware of this, then,' Alex says. 'Jade said this man was fairly short, cropped white-blond hair, broad shouldered. And that he had a kind of malleable face – that isn't the word she used, I can't remember exactly what she said, but that's what I got from it. Does that sound like anyone you know?'

I'm not sure what I should reply, but I find that speaking is difficult in any case. It's the precision of the picture he's painted, I think, that has knocked the breath from my body. From that description, anyone who knew Dominic Westwood would recognize him. I can see his face in front of me as clear as day.

'Maybe,' I manage. 'There was a guy . . . it sounds like him. He cared about loyalty, more than most of the others, I think. And he was probably infatuated with Sadie, too, which wouldn't help.'

'Really?' Alex says. He looks surprised, as if readjusting a mental picture.

'Most people were,' I say, and then I can't resist adding, 'you probably would have been, too.'

Alex laughs. 'Don't be ridiculous.' He frowns in amusement, but I keep staring at him steadily, and he seems to realize that I want him to take this seriously. 'Look, Natalie,' he says. 'I love you. Nothing that's happened here has changed that. I'm not interested in anyone else, and I wouldn't be even if she was the most beautiful woman on earth. Although, of course, that's you.' It's a cheesy line, designed to make me smile along with him, and I do, but then his expression straightens again. 'Look, you know we're going to have to talk to the police about this. If you think you know who this guy is, we need to inform them.'

Even the thought of involving the police brings a sour, nauseous taste to my mouth, but I know I'll never be able to make him understand. To Alex, the police are reliable and kindly, the obvious source of support in times of trouble, people who will help you and always do the right thing. I've learned the hard way that this isn't always true.

'I know,' I say, 'but I'd rather wait a bit longer at least, see if their investigation turns anything up. We don't actually have any proof he's involved. And it would be so much better if they found something beyond our say-so that actually tied back to him which they could use as evidence, something concrete and unarguable.'

'What difference would that make?' Alex asks, clearly exasperated. 'I mean, obviously it would be easier to convict him then, but why does that mean we shouldn't say anything now?'

'Because if they find him and speak to him on the back of no hard evidence, then he'll know that I've tipped them off.' I'm aware my voice sounds harsh and unfriendly, and I make an effort to soften it. 'Look, the bottom line is that we're safe for now. We're in the hotel, and Jade is in the hospital. Nothing's going to happen while we're all being looked after. Just give me a couple of days, please, just to get my head round this, because if we do go to the police, I'm going to have to talk about a lot of stuff that I've spent the past God knows how many years not talking about. It isn't easy for me, Alex.' Something inside me twists. I wish I could cry, but my eyes are achingly dry.

Alex must sense my distress, because he puts an arm round me and pulls me in towards him, letting me press my face against his chest. I feel his breath rise and fall in a heavy sigh, as if he's trying to weigh up what I've said, but before he has a chance to speak the shrill melody of his ring-tone leaps into life. He moves away from me, looking at the screen, and I see that it's the hospital.

'Yes?' he says sharply. 'Is everything all right with Jade?' There's a pause, and I try to read his face, which isn't crumpling in despair, but nor is it lifting with relief. 'Well, of course,' he says after a short while. 'I'll come down straight away. Yes. Thank you.'

'Has something happened?' I ask as soon as he's hung up.

He half nods. 'Physically, she's OK. But the doctor tells me that emotionally she seems troubled. She won't tell them what's wrong. It could just be delayed shock, of course. In any case, I'll need to get down there.'

'Do you want me to come with you?' I ask, then wish I hadn't.

He looks at me a little awkwardly, his eyes meeting mine for a beat before he glances away. 'You could, of course, but maybe it'd be best if I go alone for now. I'll call you, let you know what's happened.' He gives me a quick kiss on the forehead, clearly already preoccupied elsewhere. It's as if the conversation we've just had hasn't happened; it's been superseded, blown out of the water.

I watch him go, and I try not to let it sting. It makes sense that he'd want to see her alone first. He's her father, after all. I think of all the times I've seen them together; the silent bond of intimacy that flows between them like a river, the automatic understanding of each other. From what I can tell, they don't talk much about their feelings, but they're synchronized somehow. They seem to know what the other needs at any given time, a knowledge faster than thought or reason. Little things. A cup of tea, a carefully chosen DVD. A spontaneous walk on the beach, a quiet night in. I've tried to second-guess these little rituals, but there's no pattern to them.

My eyes are still on his departing back, but he's walking fast, reducing himself to a pinprick so I'm no longer sure if I'm still watching him at all. This just confirms what I already thought. He doesn't trust me to do or say the right thing, not like he would have trusted her mother. The thought sends a wave of sadness sweeping over me. The past few days are digging everything up, uncovering the bones of our family and throwing them into stark relief, and more than ever before it feels as if everything we've built together is more tenuous than I'd thought, and dangerously at risk of collapsing.

Alex

September 2017

THE BLUE CURTAINS ARE pulled round the little cubicle where Jade's bed stands, and as I approach I can hear the sound of muffled sobbing, an unsteady, relentless sound. Jade is lying awkwardly on her side, her face turned and pressed into the pillow. Her shoulders are shaking with the effort of repressing her misery, and I'm briefly pulled back to that time nine years ago – the five-year-old sobbing for her mother. I don't remember having seen her quite like this since those days.

Sitting down beside the bed, I reach across and gently place the flat of my hand on the back of her neck, stroking it. There's no jolt of surprise. She knows I'm there, but it takes at least another minute for her to lift her face from the pillow and glance in my direction, her eyes red and sore from crying. I can tell from her expression that she can't quite make up her mind whether she wants to pull me close or push me away. It's a conflict I've seen played out in her so many times this past year or so, since the explosion of hormones that has hit her. I move my hand down to her shoulder and squeeze it lightly, trying to transmit a signal. 'Sweetheart,' I say, 'what's wrong?'

She is silent, frowning ferociously, trying not to start crying again. 'Is it the fire?' I try. 'Or something to do with what we were talking about last time? About the man?' I'm guiltily aware of having done exactly what I didn't want to do – of having pushed her too fast, tried to get her to relive things that she isn't yet ready for.

Jade shakes her head, her breath expelling in a long tremulous sigh. 'You wouldn't get it,' she says eventually. 'You'd say I'm being stupid, so there's no point.'

'I wouldn't.' I'm trying to remember if I've ever dismissed her feelings like this, or if this is just casual teenage assumption. I don't think I've ever called her stupid. 'Whatever it is, it's obviously important to you. And that makes it important to me.'

Jade rolls her eyes faintly, but I can tell she's thawing. 'You say that,' she says, 'but ...' All of a sudden she breaks off, her eyes darting to where her mobile is briskly vibrating on her bedside table. She makes a lunge for it, but she's forgotten her injuries, and she stops herself with a wince of pain. By the time she's collected herself and reached across more cautiously, I've had time to look at the lit-up screen and see the start of the message that is revealed. The name at the top is 'Jaxon', and the message beneath is in almost indecipherable text speak: *Alrite babe im sorry I no u wuldnt lie 2 me I just scared ur goin* ... I can't read the rest of the message, but it's enough.

'Jade,' I say steadily, 'who on earth is this messaging you?'

She moves restlessly and frowns again, and for a moment I think she's going to swing towards defiance, but in the end she just droops her head down to her chest and rubs her eyes. She doesn't have the stomach for a fight.

'Just this boy,' she says, trying to sound offhand and failing miserably. 'We've been chatting for a few weeks online and, well, you know. We were going to meet up. But when I told him about the fire and that I was in hospital he didn't believe me – he thought I was lying because I didn't want to meet him after all.'

I wait, wondering if there's going to be an explosive twist in the tale, but it seems she's finished. I can barely credit a few unkind words from a boy she barely knows with the power to trigger the outburst I've just witnessed, but I force myself to remember how it is for her, at her age – how these early infatuations can swell and suffocate everything else out. But I'd thought we had another couple of years, at least. 'Jade,' I say again, struggling to keep my voice level. 'You're fourteen. *Fourteen*. I know that's not a baby, but it's also far too young to be talking to strangers on social media and agreeing to meet up with them. I mean – you don't even know anything about this boy. Only what he's told you. You don't even know what he looks like. I know you think you do,' I continue, raising my voice as she opens her mouth to contradict me, 'but in reality, you have no idea. Anyone can take a photo of a good-looking teenage boy off the Internet. He could be . . .'

I stop, unsure of how much I want to say. I've always found it difficult, trying to tread this line between instilling confidence and paranoia. I don't want my daughter to be a shrinking violet, jumping at her own shadow, and there's some sentimental part of me that still hates the idea of sullying her innocent acceptance of the world as a warm and cosy place, though some might say that that ship sailed a while ago. But safety trumps sentiment. The thought of some sixty-year-old pervert squinting lasciviously at a screen and messaging my daughter is enough to make up my mind. 'He could be anyone,' I say decisively.

'You don't understand,' she says. Her lips part as if she might say more, but in the end she just shoots me a sideways glance that looks thoughtful, a little calculating even.

'I think I do,' I say, 'and I don't like it. I don't know anything about this boy. Maybe, if he wanted to meet me . . .'

'You?' she asks, her eyes round and aghast. 'That's – that's not – I can't invite a boy to meet my *dad* for our first date.'

'Well, in that case, you should probably stop messaging him entirely.' I glance at the phone again, now in her hand, but she's angled the screen protectively away from me. 'I mean, for God's sake. Jaxon? It's the sort of name a middle-aged man would choose because he thought it sounded cool. I'm pretty sure it's fake.'

'Dad,' Jade mutters under her breath, shaking her head. I can't tell if I've rattled her or not. 'No one does that.'

'Unfortunately, that's not true.' For an instant, I'm tempted to say what I'm really thinking. Natalie, sitting huddled opposite me on the rocks, her lips moving into the shape of that new and unfamiliar name. *Rachel*. It hits as if for the first time, sending a tremor of unreality sifting down my spine. How different is this, really? How much difference does it make that I'm married to this woman, sharing my life with her, if the bedrock deception is the same?

But of course it's all a question of motive. 'I mean it,' I say firmly. 'It just isn't safe, particularly in light of what you told me this morning.' I pause, thinking about the unpleasant resonance in what I've just said. My daughter has told me that there's a strange man hanging around, someone she's seen several times. And now there's this 'boy', worming his way into her messages, trying to get close. Is this just the way things are now – potential danger curling out like smoke from every corner? Or is this more than coincidence?

Jade raises her eyes to mine, and I can see that she's got there at the same time as I have. 'Dad, you're wrong about this, I promise,' she says. 'And besides, that wouldn't make any sense! That man's never really come anywhere near me, not until the other night. If he wanted to talk to me then he could just do it. Why would he waste his time trying to meet up with me when he already knows who I am and where I live?'

'I don't know,' I say slowly. 'I suppose, if he wanted to catch you off guard . . .' I stop myself. Speculating about potential gruesome scenarios is only going to frighten her. 'You need to be sensible about this, Jade,' I say.

'I *am* sensible,' she says, a little grumpily.

'So take it slowly. Stop messaging this boy for a bit, and give what I've said some thought. OK? Will you?' I take a breath, aware I'm pressing the button on the teenage urge to kick back and defy. But she's sucking on her lower lip, her eyes flicking back and forth as she thinks, and after a few seconds she shrugs and nods.

''K,' she says. As monosyllables go, it's about as comforting as I'm going to get right now. She frowns, and for a moment I think she's going to say something else, but in the end she just reaches her arms out silently, dropping her gaze from mine as if she's almost ashamed to be asking for this comfort. I put my own arms around her and hug her to me tightly, hoping that applying this pressure will somehow transmit this complex cocktail of emotions: love, protectiveness, warning, chastisement, and all the rest.

Natalie and I have dinner downstairs at the hotel restaurant and drink a couple of bottles of wine between us in the bar afterwards, faster than we usually do. In another situation, I would look at my wife in the flattering candlelight across the table, the shadows playing over the inscrutable angles of her face, and be thinking about nothing but what I saw. I might even slip my hand on to her knee and let it ride up under the silk fabric of her skirt, suggest we go back to the room for an early night. As it is, she's the one who suggests it, and I can see from the sudden droop of her eyelids that it's only sleep she's considering.

I follow her silently back up the stairs and lie down on the bed, watching her strip off her clothes in front of the half-open window with the lights from the pier shining dimly through the glass and illuminating her outline. I can smell the perfume she often wears, the one that always makes me think of cut grass and rain. If I closed my eyes and she came at me in the dark, I'd know her by that scent. Not just by the pure smell of it – I've come across it in shops before and it's never been the same – but by the way it reacts on her skin. It's this kind of thing that tricks you and makes you think you know someone, I think suddenly. It's easy to confuse familiarity with knowledge.

When she's drifted into sleep beside me, I try to do the same, but I can't relax. It strikes me that what I need is to be alone. It's not that I don't want to be close to her, exactly. More that I want to feel like I have a choice.

It's for this reason, perhaps, that I start thinking about going to the house. It's not a pleasant place to spend time right now, but nonetheless there's a kind of homing instinct, boomeranging me back. And I'm also thinking of my laptop. I'll need it to keep an eye on things at work from afar, but it could be useful for more than that. My conversations with Natalie have been frustrating in the extreme. She's told me almost nothing about what happened in her past, but I have a nasty feeling that it was something big. If she won't tell me anything more for now, then I can at least try and use the very little I've got to find out more online. It's more than simple curiosity – it concerns me too, and Jade. It's not right of Natalie to keep me at arm's length, no matter how difficult it is for her.

I know from experience that I could spend hours lying here, fighting this disconnect between the exhausted heaviness of my limbs and the swift weightless whirring of my thoughts. It's a hiding to nothing. I could walk to the house in thirty minutes, and be back here in less than a couple of hours. Once I've made up my mind I climb out of bed and dress quietly in the dark. Slipping one of the room keys into my pocket, I go softly to the door and ease it open, a shaft of light from the hallway filtering through. Natalie stirs, her lips moving lazily in an inaudible whisper, but then she settles back against the pillow and is still again, and I slip out of the room and close the door silently behind me. I hurry down the corridor and take the lift to the ground floor, then step out on to the street. I feel a fleeting stab of guilt as I consider the possibility of Natalie waking up while I'm gone, but I remember the screwed-up note she left me yesterday; she didn't seem to care too much if I worried about her absence.

Half an hour later I'm descending the hill and the house comes into view. I'm struck again by the starkness of its blackened walls, a Hallowe'en nightmare against the orange gleam of the streetlights. I slip under the red and white tape, and I register how cool and empty the air inside is, now that it's abandoned. I flick the hallway switch on instinct, feeling stupid an instant later.

Instead, I pull my mobile from my pocket and activate the flashlight, moving forwards into the lounge. The tiny beam of light bounces dimly off the walls, throwing the room's cracks and crevices temporarily into relief. It reminds me of something, and it takes me a few moments to realize that it's straight out of a TV drama: the police entering a crime scene, scanning and excavating, uncovering some hideously mutilated corpse.

'Get a grip, you prat,' I say out loud. Now that I am here, the homing instinct that seemed so strong when I was lying in the room at the hotel seems misplaced. This isn't home anymore – it's a grotesque parody, incapable of offering the kind of comfort I need.

I go to our bedroom, in search of my laptop, and sure enough I find it tucked under the foot of the bed. Sitting cross-legged, I hold my breath as I press the power button, and exhale in relief when it sparks to life. I click on the browser icon at the base of the screen. The Wi-Fi here doesn't work any longer, but when I open the available connections I see the log-on for the pub down the road, for which I'm still in range, so I click connect and open up the search engine. I start off vaguely, hopelessly. I enter the names Rachel and Sadie, along with the word 'sisters', which yields nothing but a few amateur porn sites. I add the name of the man in the photograph that Natalie let slip, trying a few different spellings: Cas, Kaz, Kas. Still there's nothing. I scroll through pages of search results, my eyes starting to glaze over, the words fuzzing on the screen.

And then I remember another detail. A nightclub, Natalie had said. She had told me that the man in the photograph ran a local club – although I realize that I have no idea where 'local' might be, and it's partly this which is making this task so difficult. Something is nagging at the back of my mind, and I pull out the photograph from my pocket, angling it up to the light of the screen. There's a mirror running along the length of the wall behind the bar where Kas and Sadie are sitting, and reflected in it I can see a logo, painted across the opposite wall. The letters are blurred and in mirror image, but I can just about make them out: KASPAR'S.

Galvanized, I search again. At first it seems there's nothing new, but as I'm scanning another interminable page of results, I see a YouTube link. The name of the video is 'Promo – Blackout Club (ex Kaspar's)'.

I click on the link and play the video. It's a pretty standard club promotion piece: shots of a darkly spotlit dance floor against a thumping beat, gyrating scantily clad punters, rows of gleaming bottles behind the bar and overblown slogans flashing in luminous letters. YOUR NEXT BIG NIGHT OUT. CAMDEN'S NUMBER ONE DESTINATION. The description beneath the video reads, '7 days a week – R&B, house, underground trance nights – on the site of infamous 90's club Kaspar's'. I read it a couple of times, trying to wrench some significance from it, but although I feel I'm getting closer to something, it doesn't actually take me much further forward.

Scrolling down, I see that there are ninety-eight comments beneath the video. Most of them are inane, half-baked verdicts on the club: 'bangin', 'had sick night there friday', 'fuckin shite dont bother'. But towards the bottom there's a comment written about eighteen months ago from a user called LeonR: *anyone know what happened to KK??*

A little message below tells me that there are five replies. Quickly, I click to display them.

> **Jaz:** *still banged up mate*
> **LeonR:** *where he at?*
> **Jaz:** *belmarsh i think*
> **DJW:** *he aint getting out anytime soon mate lol.*
>   *Those were the days tho the club was quality*
>   *back then*
> **LeonR:** *thx*

Once again, it doesn't prove anything. Natalie didn't tell me Kas's surname, but there's a sudden tightness in my throat, a slipperiness of my palms, that tells me I'm on the right track. Returning to the search engine, I type in 'Kaspar's Camden'. There's surprisingly little – a defunct website that now simply states the domain name is up for sale, a couple of old and inconsequential forum comments – but I find a short, cryptic article announcing the club's closure in the year 2000 on behalf of the club's owner, Kaspar Kashani.

KK. There's no photograph, but it all fits. If what I've seen on the YouTube link is right, then Kas is in prison, and it sounds as if he's been there for a long time. I have no idea if Natalie knows this, or if it's linked in any way to her own past. I could ask, but something tells me that she might shut up like a clam, and I'm not sure I want to risk pushing her too fast.

Something brings me out of my reverie then, snaps my attention away from the lit-up screen to the darkness of the room around me. I'm on red alert. Listening.

There are always noises in an old house: pipes whistling, floorboards expanding and contracting. The house talking to itself, we used to call it. But crouching here in the dark with the wreckage of a half-destroyed home around me, the cutesy turn of phrase doesn't feel so appropriate anymore.

I listen harder, straining my ears. There's a creaking, yes, but it doesn't sound like the familiar, internal readjustments of the foundations. It's slower, more deliberate. Like footsteps across the floor below, not seeking to advertise themselves, but not tiptoeing either. An unhurried patrol, back and forth and back again.

As silently as I can, I close the laptop, tuck it under my arm and stand up. I creep towards the bedroom doorway, still trying to determine exactly what it is I'm hearing. There's a buzzing in my ears, the start-up of panic, and it makes it even harder to be sure. For a full ten seconds it seems there's nothing. I start to relax, already chastising myself, and then it comes again: another beat of pressure, like a tap or a knock against floorboards, and then a slow scrape which could be the sound of something being dragged across a table or shelf. A few seconds later, a muffled clatter, as if some light object might have fallen to the floor.

Drawing in breath painfully, I'm acutely aware of just how stupid I've been – coming to an unsecured house after dark, a place that I already know has been under threat. It comes to me that if I died here tonight, my last coherent thought would be that I was a fucking fool. Peering down into the chasm of the hallway below, I try to think. If I stay here, then whoever is downstairs is likely to come up eventually, and then I'll be trapped without an escape route. And the best-case scenario – the most likely one – is that this is some common or garden burglar, or even a squatter, looking for a sheltered place to spend the night. If that's the case, then they'll be easily scared off, and I have the advantage of surprise.

Without giving myself time to waver, I stride towards the staircase, no longer bothering to try and stay quiet. 'Get the fuck out of my house,' I say loudly, with as much aggression as I can muster.

The house is quiet. No response. The echo of my voice lingers, and I feel immediately ridiculous. I've seen countless reconstructions of unprovoked attacks and break-ins on TV, and I've often wondered why the victims so rarely scream. Surely if you're in danger, you react – make everyone in shouting distance know that you need help. But now I get it. We're conditioned to downplay. Even now, I'm not quite convinced that this is any kind of emergency, and the instant those words leave my lips I'm embarrassed.

I walk fast down the stairs, my footsteps clattering on each step, and turn the corner towards the kitchen, thinking too late of the torchlight on my phone. Without the streetlight shining through the window, the blackness is even denser than it was upstairs, and my eyes need a few seconds to readjust, before the outlines of the room form themselves into a more familiar shape. In those few seconds, I can't be completely sure of what I see – of whether the sense of something moving swiftly and fluidly through the dark like an escaping shadow is real, or just my nerves playing tricks. By the time I can see more clearly, it's gone. The burned-out back door yawns open, the yard behind empty. I step outside, feeling the coolness of the night sharp against my skin. There's no one around. But something feels different. A kind of tension, as if the air is holding its breath.

Back at the hotel I manage a few fractured hours of sleep, simply by virtue of forcing myself to empty my mind. Whenever I wake I turn my head to look at Natalie, but she's always motionless, her eyes closed, her eyelids unmoving and serene. I find myself reaching out in a childish impulse to hold her, circling my arm lightly around her waist and feeling the even rhythm of her breathing.

It's almost eight a.m. when I reach across the bedside table and check my mobile. It's been on silent and there's a missed call and a new voicemail from work. It's James. *Heard the news. It's no problem if you need a few days to handle things after the fire, Alex. Just let us know.* I hesitate, then type him a quick email saying that I appreciate it and that I'll be back in soon.

As soon as I know the pressure is off, my thoughts return to what I found out last night. Once again, I consider asking Natalie about Kas and his imprisonment, but I'm still unsure, and the unpleasant realization dawns that it's largely because I don't trust her to tell the truth. Until a few days ago I wouldn't have thought her capable of any major deception, but things are different now. There's a small, hard nub of conviction inside me that tells me that if I want to find out more about Kas and his

191

link to my wife, I'm going to have to do it alone, difficult though that may be. But as I think about it, I realize that maybe it's not so difficult after all. If what I read on the YouTube video is correct, then I know exactly where this man is – he's a sitting duck. I've never visited anyone in prison before, but there must be a procedure.

'Alex?' Natalie's voice, very close. I start, twisting my head back over my shoulder and seeing that she's lying propped up on her elbow, suddenly wide awake.

'Morning,' I say. 'What's up?'

She shrugs and rolls on to her back, passing her hands through her long dark hair. 'I don't know. I was dreaming, I think. I thought you were saying something to me.'

I watch her fingers moving through her hair, combing it gently from root to tip. 'Do you dye it?' I ask.

She stops mid-movement, a faint smile playing on her lips. 'Yes. But so do a lot of women.'

'I know,' I say, but all the same I'm stupidly affronted. I've always loved Natalie's hair, the way it shifts from dark brown to almost black, the perfect ripples of graded colour. Too perfect, I realize now.

'Does that bother you?' she asks. The bedsheet slips from her shoulder, falling down to expose the curves of her bare breasts, the hardened points of her nipples.

'No . . .' I say.

'Everything else is real,' she says softly, 'in case you're wondering.'

In another second she's in my arms, pressing herself up against me, her legs parting to wrap themselves around my waist. Her mouth is hot on my neck, the

scrape of her teeth teasing my skin. 'I know everything feels wrong right now,' she says, 'but I really
want this. Do you?'

I make some noise of affirmation, but even as I'm
kissing her, running my hands over the smooth length
of her back and feeling the softness of her skin against
mine, I know something isn't right. Maybe it's the guilt
of the thoughts I've just been having, the idea of making plans without her knowledge. I'm turned on, but
the message isn't getting through to my body. It's an
odd sensation – all the elements present and correct,
the same beautiful body in my arms that has roused me
countless times, and yet nothing's happening. Her
hand slips between my legs, and for a moment I think
about falling back on some reliable kick-starting fantasy, but on some obscure level it doesn't seem fair. To
her, or to me.

Her hand lingers on me for a few more moments,
gentle, exploratory; then she sighs and rolls away again.
'Not in the mood, then.' Her tone is light, but she turns
her face away and I see her shoulders tense, then hear a
shaky intake of breath.

'God, don't cry.' I lean across to touch her. This isn't
like Natalie – she's always been practical about sex,
finding the humour in it if things go awry, defusing any
awkward complications. She sees it for what it is and she
likes it; it's something I've always been drawn to. 'It
doesn't mean anything,' I try. 'I'm just stressed, you
know? There's a lot going on.'

She sniffs, wiping a hand across her face. 'I know
that. But all the same, it feels . . . significant. Like you

don't want me anymore because of what I've told you. Because of who I was.'

'I don't . . .' I begin, then stop. *I don't know who you were.* She's told me so little.

My silence seems to distress her even more; she's pressing her fists into her eyeballs, sobbing unevenly now. 'She's doing it again,' I make out. 'She's ruining it without even being here.'

'Who?' I ask, confused.

She shakes her head violently, as if she's driving unpleasant thoughts away. 'Sadie, of course. Fucking up my life once clearly isn't enough.'

Wrong-footed, I stroke her shoulder, trying to decide how to reply. 'I don't understand,' I start eventually. 'What makes you think this?'

Natalie takes her fists away and wipes her eyes, then looks me full in the face, her eyes red and sore. 'Because her own life's been a disaster. She'll want to ruin things for me. Whatever she's doing, however she's living, I can guarantee she'll have made a total mess of it. She doesn't know how to do anything else, and she'll want to drag me down with her. This all has something to do with her. I know it.'

'I see,' I say slowly, although I don't really, not at all. I'd assumed that in Natalie's eyes, any threat to us might be from Kas, or at least his associates. But it doesn't sound that way, not from what she's saying. 'But – why?'

For an instant I think I see something flicker in Natalie's eyes, but then it's gone. 'Because she's jealous,' she says simply. She sits up in bed, hugging her knees to

194

her chest. 'Look, I don't expect you to understand. And it's possible I'm wrong.' It's a meaningless little platitude, this last one, but her tone clearly signals a close to the conversation. 'I'm going to have a shower,' she says. 'And then I might go to the bank, see if I can chase up my card and get some cash out. Do you need me to get anything while I'm out?'

'I'm OK, thanks.' I watch her get ready. I'm uncomfortably aware that I want her to leave. I want to be alone, to follow up on my idea about calling the prison.

As soon as she goes, I get up and search for the visitors' number of Belmarsh Prison. Repetitive hold music crackles in my ear until a bored-sounding woman answers, who simply asks me for the prisoner's name who I wish to visit.

'Kaspar Kashani,' I say.

'Prisoner number?'

I hesitate. 'I don't know.'

'Have you got a VO?' the woman asks. When I don't reply, she sighs and clarifies. 'A visiting order.'

'No,' I say. I can sense she's on the point of cutting off the call. 'Look, I know this might be unusual, but is there any way that you or someone else can let him know that I want to see him?'

I can almost hear her shrug down the phone. 'We can pass on a message, yeah. But it's up to him. If he wants to send you a VO, then we can be in touch and you can set something up. Give me your details.'

I give her my name, number and email address. 'Can you please also tell him that he used to know my wife, and that I want to talk to him about her?' I say quickly.

'My wife's name is – well, he knew her as Rachel Castelle.'

'All right.' There is a scuffling sound which I hope indicates that the woman is writing this down. 'Got it. Don't hold your breath though, will you? I'm guessing that if he wanted to see you, he would have sorted it by now.'

'No, he couldn't really have done that,' I attempt to explain, 'because he doesn't have my details and . . .' I realize I'm talking to no one; the woman has hung up.

I breathe out deeply, trying to collect my thoughts, and then I notice the new email icon winking on my phone. With a shock I see that there is a new email from SRUK. I always appreciated that little touch of discretion they employed at secretroom, but now it's an embarrassment – a reminder that this kind of discretion is one I can do without.

Cali has sent you a new message, it reads. *To read it, click on the link below.* She's seen that I was online yesterday, just as I thought.

I open up the message. *So. You're back?*

That's all it says. Just a monosyllabic little communication from a woman I spent a few months exploring my fantasies with a while ago, idly looking to start things up again. I don't even know why I bothered to open it. I'm on the point of closing down the window when the little green icon flashes at the base of the screen.

Cali is online. There's something about the speed of it that makes it feel too coincidental. I'm not sure if there's a way to set up an alert on the site to let you know if another member is active, but that's twice this has happened now, and actually, this was always how it was. Whenever I wanted her, she was there. At the time, I'm ashamed to realize, that felt completely normal.

The chat box pops up, her words brief and inviting. *Come to play?*

I hesitate, then type a reply. **No. *Just checking back in.***

Checking on me?

Maybe . . . I type. I'm stalling, unsure of what I'm doing.

You were gone for a long time. A pause, neither of us typing. Then a single question mark: *?*

Thinking fast, I type: **I'm married. Did you know that?**

The little dots at the bottom of the screen roll for a long time, as if she's typing a lengthier message, then freeze for a second, and in the end all that pops up is *No.*

I love my wife, I reply. **I decided I didn't want to do this to her anymore.**

In the pause that follows, I try and project myself into her place, think about what a reasonable response might be if she had said something similar to me. I might simply log off – decide that this wasn't worth the hassle, that there were clearly some emotional complications at work that didn't warrant further trouble in a situation that was, after all, just about sex. Or at a push, if I was feeling horny and didn't much care what she felt about it, I might ignore what she'd said completely.

197

Write something dirty, something to entice her back in. Both scenarios sound plausible.

But Cali doesn't do either of these. After a few moments, another line flashes up. *Tell me about her.*

I stare at the message, its directness and simplicity. Her motive doesn't feel sexual. She hasn't said, *tell me about what you do to her, tell me about what you do in bed*. Something about it feels off.

She's waiting for me to reply, and when I don't, she doesn't lose interest and drop it. Instead I see the little row of dots moving again, seeming slower this time, more deliberate, before another message appears on the screen.

I want to know everything.

My fingers move by instinct and I close the window, logging off. I don't know why, but there's something about those five words that unsettles me.

I throw my phone aside on to the bed and go to the window, needing some air. The sea breeze blows into my face as I wrench it open and breathe in deeply, and I can taste the faint tang of salt on my lips. Leaning my elbows on the window ledge, I look out to the shut-down pier and count the black iron railings that flank it, my eyes leaping from one to the next. It's an old trick, a way of calming myself and focusing on something bland and simple. But this time it doesn't quite do the job.

It feels like only minutes that I stand there, but when the phone starts ringing I notice it's been close to an hour that I've been uselessly staring into space. I feel a quick flare of impatience with myself; giving myself the luxury of this kind of inactivity isn't going to solve anything. 'Hello?'

'Alex Carmichael?' a woman's voice asks. 'I'm calling from Belmarsh Prison. We spoke earlier? So, it's your lucky day.' Her tone is flatly edged with sarcasm. 'We passed your message to Mr Kashani and he's keen to have you visit. And he doesn't have a lot of visitors, as it goes, so he hasn't used up any of his slots this month. Do you want to set up a time?'

'God. Right.' With difficulty I try and focus. I'm vaguely conscious of a sickening, swooping sensation, not dissimilar to the point on a rollercoaster when you near the top and know that the downward plunge is not far away. 'Yes. Yes, that would be good. The sooner the better, I suppose.'

'You could do this afternoon,' she says. 'At five.'

Despite what I've just said, I feel a pathetic desire to turn away from the situation. But this isn't the time for childish histrionics. 'That works for me,' I say firmly.

'You can look up the guidelines on our website, if you want,' the woman says. 'Enjoy.'

I hang up, and lie down on the bed, rubbing my hands across my face. It's faster than I had expected, but the timing works; I could go to the hospital and spend the visiting hour with Jade, then travel straight up to London. I can feel a headache starting, aching in the depths of my temples. I have the sense that I'm straying too far into something I don't understand, but the old adage flashes into my mind: keep your friends close, and your enemies closer. That's what I'm doing here – getting closer, trying to put myself in the way of anyone who might want to destroy what I've got left. I tell myself this, and try and ignore another peculiarly

199

apt little phrase; that if you're playing with fire, you run the risk of getting burned.

That afternoon I take the train to Woolwich, then hail a taxi to Belmarsh. The prison stretches wide, a vast dark monolith. I glance up at the row of small windows running across the lower walls, but the glass is dark and blank, offering no clue as to what is inside. I linger for a few moments by the entrance, wishing I still smoked and had a reason to delay. As I do so, a thought strikes me and I take out my wallet, fishing out the small photograph of Natalie that I keep there. She's looking straight down the lens and laughing, standing by the sea in her bikini with the sunlight sparkling on her face. Having scanned the visiting guidelines online, I know I won't be allowed to take anything in with me, but I want to show Kaspar this. The sight of her is bound to provoke some kind of reaction, and it'll be more instinctive, more real than words. It'll help me to understand what his feelings towards her are. And maybe there's another reason too; maybe I want to get a sense, if I can, of how much she's changed.

I oscillate between possibilities for a moment, then decide to slip the photograph inside the waistband of my trousers, where it lies flat. I check my phone and see that it's almost five o'clock. Shoving the wallet back into my coat, I turn and make for the entrance.

As soon as I push my way through the heavy doors, an impassive official asks to see my ID, takes my photograph and scans the prints of my index fingers into the system. 'First time?' he says. 'You leave your personal possessions in a locker. You take in your VO and some money for refreshments if you want, that's all.'

I nod, beginning to turn out my pockets. The wallet stuffed with credit cards, a little pile of business cards, a pair of gold cufflinks. I find myself lingering over these items, wanting for some craven middle-class reason to show the official that I am a professional, but he completely ignores me and I feel like an idiot. 'Pound for the locker,' he mutters when I have finished, and I exchange my possessions for a smooth silver key that I drop into my top pocket.

'Thanks,' I say. The roof of my mouth is sticky and dry.

'No problem.' The official scratches the skin above his eyebrow, his fingers moving dully back and forth. He looks very young, no more than twenty-two. For an instant I wonder if he's an inmate brought out on remand, or performing some kind of rehabilitation duty. As if he has read my mind, he looks up sharply and shuffles up straight. 'Go to the main gate and show your VO,' he says. 'They'll scan you again and then show you to the waiting area.' He looks down, dismissing me.

I walk away from the visitors' centre towards the tall wooden gate farther along the front wall, where I show the documentation and consent to the scan. There's something relentless about the rhythms and rituals of this place that I can feel working on me. The door swings shut behind me, and I'm inside. It's strangely silent and deserted, and my footsteps echo on concrete as I walk to the waiting hall. Two uniformed officials are standing at the entrance, staring straight ahead as I approach.

'We need to search you, sir,' one says as soon as I am close enough to hear. 'Please stand straight and put your arms out to the sides.'

I stand still and try to detach myself from their hands patting up and down my body, insistent and hard. I try not to think about the photograph tucked into my waistband, but they don't seem interested in searching that thoroughly, just covering the basics. Beyond where we are standing I can see a handful of visitors, waiting in the corridor on red plastic chairs. One is a woman with a young toddler, who squirms and wriggles restlessly as he plays with a toy truck, running it up and down his mother's arm. Her arms are clasped around him, fencing him in, but she's looking only at the far door, her eyes fixed on it, waiting. A couple of chairs along, a man in his twenties sits hunched forward with his hands clasped, tapping his feet on the floor.

'Straight ahead,' one of the officials says, gesturing at the corridor. 'Just sit down and wait until you're called.'

Slowly, I do as I'm told. The toddler squeals and points at me, eyes wide and dark in his face, but none of the others turn to look.

I sit motionless, regulating my breathing. Now that I'm here, adrenaline is starting to thump through my veins. The place smells sharp, like spearmint disinfectant. Nausea throbs faintly in my head. I notice a vending machine and go across to it, fumbling in my pocket for the two pounds I kept. I feed the money into the machine and down a can of Coke, but it fights queasily for place in my stomach. I can't seem to settle down. My heartbeat shifts into time with the quick repeated tapping of the young man's feet on the floor, each tap thudding through me. I clench my fists, try to relax. There is a round plastic clock on the far wall, its face entirely bare and smooth but for two black hands bisecting the surface. On a little table in the corner, magazines and colouring books with crayons are stacked up in piles. A tall green plant in the corner winds its way towards the ceiling. I look at these objects one by one, grounding myself.

'Alex Carmichael?' When the call finally comes, it jolts me and I get quickly to my feet. A tall, stocky man in uniform is waiting for me, smiling tightly. 'I'm going to take you to a private room,' he says. 'I'll be waiting at the door, to keep an eye on things.' His face is neutral; it's impossible to tell if the statement is intended to warn or reassure.

We walk along a corridor painted in lurid peppermint green, hallucinogenic in its brightness. When we come to the door, it is polished metal, brushed like aluminium, a small grille set into it. The official stops, throws me a look. 'He's inside. You have an hour max,' he says. I think I catch pity and confusion in his glance, as if he's wondering how on earth I have got myself here and what business I could possibly have with the man on the other side of the door. Then it slides open and I'm looking in at the low metal table standing alone in the emptiness, with the chairs on either side, and Kaspar sitting there waiting.

He glances up when I come in, his expression expectant and watchful. Automatically, I register his looks: the refined mouldings of his face, the smooth olive skin pulled tight over his bones, the strange, dark, silver-tinged eyes glittering across at me. He's wearing a sleeveless white vest top, the muscles of his arms bulging, shining under the lights like iron. It's impossible not to notice his peculiar magnetism – it raises my hackles, and yet I can't help but acknowledge it.

I sit down opposite him. 'Thank you for seeing me,' I say.

Kaspar shrugs lazily. When he speaks, his voice is husky and accented. 'Let us say that I was curious,' he says. There's a second-language quality to his English, giving his speech a stilted yet oddly elegant air.

'I'll get straight to it,' I say. I refuse to let myself be intimidated by this man, although it would be surprisingly easy. 'I think the officials here told you that I'm married to someone you used to know.'

Kaspar inclines his head very slightly. 'Rachel.' His tone is contemplative and soft, giving nothing away.

'That's right,' I say. 'I don't know how well you knew her, or how much you had to do with one another.' I'm careful not to make it sound too much like a question; I don't want to give the impression that I'm interrogating him, but in my experience people don't like to let a silence stretch, so I simply wait, hoping that he'll elaborate.

The silence doesn't seem to bother Kaspar; he stares at me through unblinking, slightly narrowed eyes, one corner of his mouth turned upwards in a faint smirk. On the table, his hands rest coolly in loose fists. It's as if he's letting me know how easy it would be for him to knock me out if he chose, but that he's deciding to let me speak.

'You're probably wondering why I'm here,' I say at

last. Kaspar doesn't deny it, but nor does he show any sign of confirming it; he just continues to regard me levelly. 'Look,' I say, 'the truth is that I don't know everything about my wife's past. But I get the impression that relations between you were strained.' It's something of a leap in the dark, but from the way Natalie spoke about this man, I can't imagine anything else.

Kaspar tips his head back a little and contemplates me some more, as if turning these words over in his head. 'It is unlikely that they would have been otherwise,' he comments, 'given the circumstances. But all her actions were what I would have expected from a woman like her.'

'Meaning?' I ask, a little sharply.

He moves his mouth in a small gesture of contempt. 'She was not someone who understood the true nature of things. She had little imagination. She was very different to her sister.'

'Sadie,' I say, just to show that I do have some knowledge. I'm tempted to argue, push back against the slights to my wife, but I tell myself to hold off.

Kaspar nods. 'For all her faults,' he says, pausing briefly, giving the impression that he is running through their litany in his head, 'she is loyal.'

I register the present tense, wonder if it is significant. He certainly speaks as if they are still in contact, still part of one another's lives. But on the other hand, in a place like this time effectively stops. I can imagine that the past few years might have felt like a drawn breath, little more than a necessary bridge between the past and the future. 'My wife is loyal,' I say tightly. 'To those that she feels have earned it.'

Kaspar straightens up in his chair, looks a little incredulous. For the first time, I see him studying me with some genuine interest. 'Forgive me,' he says, 'but I am not sure you have, in fact, explained why you are here.' His tone is still light, but there's a kind of veiled menace to it that makes my blood rise.

'I'm here because I want to understand what happened back then,' I say. I keep my voice as low and controlled as his, conscious of the official behind the door.

Kaspar frowns, tipping his head to one side and rubbing a finger across the smooth slash of his jawline. 'Surely this does not matter now,' he comments.

'That's what I'm trying to find out.' I'm aware of an increasing sense of frustration, knowing this conversation isn't being played out on an equal level. Without knowing for sure if he has any involvement, I don't want to mention the fire, or the man in our house; it feels better to play dumb, assume that he has nothing against me. 'Look, you and I don't know each other. We have no animosity.' I pause briefly, giving him the chance to contradict me, but he remains silent. 'All I'm asking is for some information about the past that can cost you nothing to give. Anything you can tell me will help.'

Kaspar nods slowly, his eyes on mine. When he speaks his voice is calm, almost soothing. 'My friend,' he says, with a little tremor of irony, 'I will tell you only that I am serving two life sentences for murder. I will be in

206

here until the day I die. Not everyone is in a position such as mine, but everyone must serve their sentence. Even your wife.'

My heart is thumping, and I can feel the collar of my shirt damp against my neck. It's something about the casual way in which he says it – the throwaway acknowledgement of what he's capable of. 'What does my wife have to do with this?' I manage.

He shrugs faintly. 'Nothing. Everything. She is not exempt from consequence.'

I realize with increasing despair that he's playing with me. 'She has a new life now,' I say, trying to drag us back on to concrete ground. 'She only wants to live her life with me and my daughter – our daughter – in peace.'

Another long pause, before he speaks again. 'I cannot imagine,' he says thoughtfully, 'why you would think I would wish otherwise.' He leans forward, those odd grey-silver eyes boring into mine. Now that he is so close, I can smell the heat that rises off his skin, a faint note of cinnamon and spice. 'These things are *so insignificant to me now*,' he says quietly. 'What is done is done. Your wife is nothing to me anymore. My life is this.' He gestures around at the four walls of the small room encircling us. 'You would be surprised at how quickly everything else is extinguished.'

Despite the mildness of his expression, there's an indefinable malice about the way he speaks, and about the closeness that he maintains between us. I force myself to stay motionless, not wanting to be the one to move back. It's impossible to say if he is telling the truth. There is a frightening composure to this man that I sense I won't crack. I had imagined a thug, coarsely direct and indiscreetly verbose, not this regal-looking foreigner who makes it so clear that each word he gives me is a gift that he could easily withdraw if he wanted to.

'Then I'm sorry to have taken up your time,' I say. It's meant to sound ironic, but the words come out simple and unvarnished.

Kaspar regards me thoughtfully. 'Time is something I have plenty of,' he says at last.

I make as if to stand up, but as I do so I'm conscious of the photograph digging into my stomach. I want him to see it. There's the slightest chance that the sight of my wife's face might unlock something in him, maybe betray some emotion that he has held back up to this point. I reach down and pull it out, holding it between my fingertips. 'I have a picture of her,' I say. 'Rachel.' The name feels unfamiliar on my lips. 'This is how she is now.'

There's the faintest spark of interest in Kaspar's eyes – nothing much, just a brief instant of connection as he reaches one hand forward to take the photograph that I'm holding out to him. He looks at it intently for what must be ten seconds; a long time, in this room and its silence. I'm watching him, trying to read his expression, but it's frustratingly blank.

He tosses the photograph back at me across the table. 'It only remains,' he says, 'for me to say good luck to you, my friend.'

I snatch up the photo. It's clear that the conversation is over. He's leaning back in his chair, the vest riding up over the tight muscles of his stomach, signalling to the official through the small glass window. I think I can see a faint smile playing at the corners of his mouth now, but when he glances back at me as I stand up it's gone.

'Goodbye,' I say, and then I'm walking away, listening to my own footsteps echoing across the smooth polished floor, and forcing myself not to look back.

Natalie

September 2017

I'M SITTING ACROSS FROM Jade, trying to block out everything I hate about being in this place: the antiseptic smell, the harsh fizz of the lighting, the general air of lethargy and decay. We're watching the little TV above her bed, steadily eating the grapes I brought with me. We haven't spoken in about ten minutes. I had thought that Alex would meet me here, but I was held up on the bus and by the time I arrived, he'd texted me saying he had had to leave. Work again, I'm guessing. So it's just me and her.

While she's absorbed in the television I take the chance to study her. She's looking better, I think. The colour is bleeding slowly back into her cheeks, and everything about her – even the way she blinks – just seems a little less languid and perfunctory. In fact, if we were sitting somewhere other than a hospital bed, then the only clue I'd have that there was anything wrong with her would be the livid red scar running along her hairline and creeping down the side of her face. It astounds me, the speed with which she's bouncing back. The indestructability of youth.

Tentatively, I clear my throat, but she doesn't look over, her eyes trained on the screen. I have no idea if her concentration is put on, or whether this silence is an uncomfortable one for her. I know it's uncomfortable for me. Say something, I instruct myself. Doesn't matter how banal. Anything to break the deadlock.

'I've seen this before,' I say at last, gesturing at the film. 'She dies at the end.'

Jade shoots me a quick look, half amused, half outraged. 'Seriously?'

'No.' I smile, pleased to have caught her attention. 'Just joking. I've never seen it.'

Jade sighs, then reaches out for the remote control beside her and zaps the television into blackness. 'I have.' She rolls on to her side, pushing herself up on her elbow and propping her head on her hand. 'And she does, actually.'

'Seriously?' I echo her, thinking she's making a joke in turn, but she just nods, straight-faced. 'Oh. Well . . .' I try and think of something else to say. Making conversation with Jade is unpredictable; sometimes easy and unthinking, sometimes like pushing water uphill. I've always been conscious of this, but here more than ever. There's nothing to distract. The spotlight is on us, shining at full force. 'Your friends have been in?' I ask, gesturing at the little clutch of new get-well cards lined up by the bed.

Jade nods again. 'Yeah. Last night. They all had a nightmare with the history test yesterday. At least I didn't have to take that.'

'That's something,' I agree. Is she being ironic, or just stating a fact? I can't tell; don't seem to have that natural instinct for teenage mannerisms and moods. I can't remember much about how I thought and felt at that age. It's another life.

'Have you been back to the house?' she asks. There's no obvious change of tempo, but her eyes seem a little brighter and keener.

'I haven't, no,' I say slowly. 'Your dad has, but I don't . . . I'm not sure I see the point. Not until we find out how much can realistically be rebuilt, or how long it's going to take. Without knowing that, it's just staring at wreckage.' I take a breath, half expecting her to chip in or at least make some noise of agreement, but she's silent, and so I keep talking. 'And I suppose quite apart from that, I just don't want to. I remember reading an article a little while ago about a woman who goes back every weekend to the place where she saw both her parents shot, to place flowers or whatever, or just to, you know, relive it. I thought at the time, why would you want to do that . . .? And now I think it even more. No one in their right mind wants to relive trauma really, do they? I mean, I know it's not the same, what's happened here. But . . .' I finally wind myself up, realizing that Jade is staring at me looking lost, presumably wondering what the hell I'm on. 'All the same,' I say.

'I think you're right,' Jade says. 'I don't want to go back, either. I don't even want to live there anymore, even if they do rebuild it. It's all . . .' She moves her head restlessly on the pillow. 'I dunno. I can't think of the word.'

Tainted, I think, but I don't say it.

She's looking at me head on now, unfalteringly. 'Did Dad tell you?' she asks. 'About me having seen that man before, the one who was in the house before the fire.'

'Yes, he did.' I realize as soon as I've spoken that she's chosen a clever way of putting it. By framing a question, she's slipped the fact of the man being there under the radar, so that any answer I gave would be a tacit acknowledgement of it. I don't know if this is calculated, or if she's just got a natural knack for it, but either way I respect it. And of course she's right. Whatever I might have thought when she first talked about this, the truth is that I know she wasn't mistaken. In fact, I know more than she does – I know exactly the kind of man we're dealing with. The kind of man who's capable, not of anything, but of most things. And they're the most dangerous kind, in a way; they have something to prove, always feeling they have to make up for their little pockets of softness and shortcoming. Yes, Dominic Westwood could set a fire. He could light a match and walk away, as long as he didn't have to see the outcome of what he'd done.

My mouth is dry and I know that Jade is waiting for me to say something more, but it's an effort to get the words out. 'You think he's been following you.'

'I don't *think* it.' Jade's voice is briefly scornful, but there's a crack in it that tells me she's desperate to be taken seriously. 'It's not the sort of thing you imagine, is it. Maybe once or twice you might see someone around and think they were following you, but it was actually just a coincidence. But not this much. I've seen him, like, nine or ten times.'

'That much?' I say, my mind whirling. 'When? Doing what?'

Jade scratches the side of her face, glancing down. At first I think she's being bashful for some reason, but then I see with a light shock that there are tears brimming in her eyes. 'Not much,' she says, clearly fighting to keep her voice casual. 'Sometimes he's just hanging around the school gates, on his phone or whatever. Once or twice he's been on the bus with me. A couple of times round the shops when I've been hanging out with Katie or Sophie. He's never spoken to me. He just . . . stares at me. Not like a perv, you know. Just looking. That's all it is. It sounds stupid now I say it.'

'It's not stupid,' I say automatically. Internally, I can feel fury welling up, and I obviously don't do as good a job of hiding it as I think, because Jade looks startled, her fingers plucking at the bedsheets uncertainly. 'Sorry,' I say with an effort. 'It's just, well, it's not fair, is it? It's not right.'

'Not fair?' Jade echoes.

'Not right,' I repeat. I realize that I'm not sure how much Alex has told her, if anything. For all I know, she may have no idea that the man she's talking about has any connection to my own past. In fact, the more I think about it the more I'm convinced he hasn't said anything. If he had, then she too would be thinking this wasn't fair. She'd be asking herself the same question that I'm sure must be going through Alex's head: why her? If this man has some kind of grudge against me, why is it Jade he's targeting? I have an answer, of course. Because she's an easy target. A naive young girl who could be a convenient weapon of choice, given the right circumstances. I could

214

say this to Alex, maybe, but not to her. I don't want her wandering around in a permanent state of fear, on red alert.

'Anyway,' Jade says, her voice distant now. I can tell she's regretting this sudden show of vulnerability – it doesn't fit with our relationship. We get on, but she keeps me at arm's length. 'It'll get sorted now, won't it. If there's some weirdo been hanging round trying to torch my house and kill me, the police will be on to it now.' She speaks with what might be false bravado, but I suspect that there's a core of belief in her own words. Now that the drama of the past few days has passed, she can't conceive of a world in which justice might not be done, and in which the police wouldn't be there waiting in the wings like avenging angels if danger ever came her way again. She has no idea.

Impulsively, I lean across the bed and take her hand in mine. I feel her muscles stiffen for an instant, but she doesn't pull it away.

'I understand how you're feeling,' I say. 'I was luckier than you, but I was there too, at the fire. We've been through it together, and we're the only two people who know what it was like. It was horrible, but in a way it brings us closer, doesn't it? It's . . . bonding. Something like that. Don't you think?' I squeeze her hand, maybe a little too hard. And I find that I am holding my breath, really wanting her to say yes.

'Uh huh,' she says, but her eyes are blank.

That evening Alex and I order room service at the hotel. The trays arrive topped by silver domed servers, flanked by ostentatiously folded napkins, though the food underneath is likely to be pretty basic. The porter places our trays ceremoniously on the little table and retreats gravely without a word. I pull a chair up and sit down, smiling tentatively at Alex as I whip the servers off with a flourish.

'And tonight,' I say in a bad French accent, 'we have fillet of plaice with pommes frites. You are in for a treat, monsieur . . .'

Alex laughs, but there's no real warmth to it. He sits down opposite me and starts eating; fast, rhythmically, pushing forkful after forkful into his mouth in a way that suggests he's barely tasting it. After a couple of minutes he catches me watching him and shrugs. 'Sorry. Just hungry. I didn't get much lunch.'

I make a vague noise of acquiescence but anxiety is building within me. This wasn't how I had envisaged this evening. I'd hoped that we might be able to shake off everything that's been oppressing us, just for an hour or two, and that I could remind him what it was really like between us. The odds are against me, though, in this setting. I glance round at the sterile white walls, the bought-in furnishings. Staying in hotels is all right, when you've got a home to go back to.

'So you went to the office this afternoon?' I ask after a while, when Alex has demolished his fish and chips and is staring at the plate with a look of prickly dissatisfaction. 'How was everything?'

Slowly, he nods. 'All fine,' he says. 'Gav had a proposal he needed to get out the door and . . .' He trails off. Silence settles between us and he takes an audible breath, pushing a hand back through his hair and rubbing the back of his neck. 'No,' he says eventually. 'I didn't go to the office.'

I taste something sour at the back of my throat. 'You didn't? Where did you go, then?' Normally I'd make an effort to keep these words light and non-threatening, but right now I can't think about niceties. For a stupid moment, I think he's going to tell me he's been with another woman. But this is Alex. He'd never do that. So why lie?

He's looking me full in the face now, with something like remorse in his expression, and yet when he speaks again his tone is defiant. 'You didn't want to talk to me,' he says. 'You land all this on me, this stuff about you having changed your name and started a new life, about you having a sister I didn't even know about, and you talk around the houses about something bad that's happened in the past, but you didn't really want to tell me anything. How do you think that makes me feel, when my daughter's in hospital and my house has been all but burned to the ground and it sounds like it might be because of *you*?'

I gasp, feeling winded. There's a vicious emphasis on that 'you', and I've never heard him speak like this before. 'I'm sorry,' I begin. 'I would have talked to you – I will talk to you. It's just not easy, after all this time . . .'

'I know,' he interrupts, and his voice is softer now, the anger gone from his eyes as fast as it came. 'Look, I'm trying to explain why I did what I did today. I felt I needed to take things into my own hands. I did some research on the Internet, and I found out about the man you told me about – Kaspar. I found out where he was, and I went to visit him.'

He says it so quietly, with such unvarnished simplicity, that at first it doesn't compute. My body gets there faster than my mind does; my heartbeat quickening, my fingers curling into fists. 'You went to visit him?' I repeat. And saying it out loud brings it home. I look at Alex – my husband – and it's as if that other face is imprinted on his, just for an instant. My husband has been in the same room as Kas, today. Nausea swells inside me. 'What the hell were you thinking?' I ask. If I'd been asked beforehand how I'd feel if this happened, I wouldn't have been able to imagine it, but now that it has, it seems my overriding feeling is that it's my turn to be angry. I don't even know exactly why, can't stop to unpick it – there's only this white-hot sense of incredulity and rage, rising inside me. 'How could you do something like that?' I spit. 'How could you be so stupid?'

Alex pushes back his chair and glares at me. 'I'm trying to protect my family, Natalie. You and Jade. How can I do that if I don't have a bloody clue what's going on? I needed answers that you weren't giving me.'

'And did you get them?' I fire back. 'What did he say to you?' Trying to imagine this conversation is making my brain feel like it's about to explode. I don't want to know what they talked about. I don't want my husband anywhere near Kas, and yet another part of me is desperate to hear every detail. 'Did you get your answers?' I push him again.

He looks diffident for a moment, drops his gaze. 'Not entirely,' he admits.

'Well, there's a fucking surprise.' Abruptly, I stand up and go over to the window. This room feels hot and airless. I push the window open, savagely drawing in breath in the hope that the sea breeze will clear my head. 'Kas isn't the sort of man you just – just drop in on,' I say. 'If anything, you've probably put us in more danger. He's a maniac – he's a murderer.'

'I know that now,' Alex says. 'But I wouldn't have done, would I, if I'd hung around doing nothing?'

I'm silent, thinking, looking out across the rolling darkness of the sea. I can see Alex's reflection behind me, the shadowy outline of his body standing just behind me, so close that I can smell the aftershave he wears. 'I know what you're saying, but I still don't think you did the right thing.' My throat feels choked up and I realize I might be close to tears.

'You knew he was in prison, didn't you?' he asks.

I think about denying it, then shrug. It doesn't matter now. 'Of course I did.' I turn round to face him, leaning my head back against the wall. Memories are dragging me back. The polished, gleaming wood of the courtroom, with its strange orange-tinted light. The faces of the jury, neutral and expressionless, bored almost. And the sight of Kas in the witness box, the contained fury that shone out of him; the overt restraint with which he spat out every word.

'I helped to put him there.'

PART FOUR

Rachel

January 2000

SHE'S ONLY A FEW metres away, standing under the station's archway at the entrance to the platform, but it feels as if she's watching from behind reinforced glass, or through some remote TV link-up – as if this scene has nothing to do with her beyond the fact that it happens to be in her line of vision. She sees Sadie striding up to the woman in the shiny plastic red coat, sees the defiant tilt of her head as she begins to speak. She can even hear the words, or most of them. She listens and she watches, witnesses the brittle interchange of tensions, and still she is strangely detached. If she's conscious of feeling anything, it's the discomfort of the night air, the thinness of her tights an ineffectual barrier against the cold. She wishes she wasn't standing here.

And then everything changes.

Rachel sees her sister lunge forwards, her fingernails clawing indiscriminately at the other woman's face. The savage instinct with which the woman fights back

223

despite the precarious high heels she's wearing, her hands tearing at Sadie's hair. She sees that the woman is veering close to the edge of the platform, her feet slipping. It's the speed of it all which paralyses her, at first; the way in which the situation has abruptly kicked up a gear. And then she is momentarily distracted – seeing a gleam of light in the distance down the track, her eyes flicking to pinpoint its source. The train is coming.

This is the moment. This is the time at which she could – at which she should – step forward and issue a warning. She knows in that instant that if she were to do so, it would be enough. Enough to make both women turn, to catch them off guard; enough to break their scuffle and draw them away from the platform's edge. The course of action is obvious. Imperative.

But along with this realization comes another. In these few split-seconds, she realizes that what could happen here has the power to change everything. And isn't that what she's been waiting for, hoping for? For something to stop her sister in her tracks and reach the end of the collision course she's been hurtling on for years, no matter how violent a landing it might be? She finds herself flashing back over the past few years – the sickening lurching up and down of the rollercoaster that Sadie lives on and which she's dragged Rachel unwillingly on to as well. And the desire for something to make this stop is so powerful that it takes her over entirely.

And so she does nothing. Nothing at all. She continues to watch.

When she looks back, she will start to piece together

exactly what it is that she sees. Whether her sister's arm is raising itself in defence or attack, whether the way in which it swings sharply to the left across the other woman's body is calculated or involuntary. But right now, there is no judgement. She simply sees that movement, and its impact; sees the woman stumble and fall to her knees, skidding forwards, and then the slow-motion, vertiginous moment in which she tumbles on to the track. The perfect coalescence of this moment with the headlights' approach, impossibly fast, a blare of violent light and speed. And then the brutal, ugly jolt that the train gives, the slamming on of brakes that comes too late, and the screaming. She isn't sure who the noise is coming from; will never be sure. But it's shrill and loud and almost animal, and it drags her hard into reality – as if she's being pulled by her hair from her bed, from the deepest sleep she's ever had.

It's almost midnight but the train is half full and the passengers are gathering at the doors, their faces etched with shock and concern, stabbing at the door release buttons without success, mouthing at each other, trying to determine what has happened. The driver is running down the platform towards them. He is several coaches away, and Rachel realizes that he must have driven straight over the woman as he braked, that a single human body is nowhere near enough to stop a train in its tracks. It probably only takes ten seconds for him to reach them, but it feels like a lifetime, and in those seconds she looks at her sister for the first time. Sadie's face is white, unearthly. Her eyes are wide, blinking in staccato rhythm. Shock has made her expression unreadable.

But she's looking straight at Rachel, her focus unbroken, as if she's waiting for something.

Before she can think what this might be, the driver is there, his feet pounding to where they are standing. He's grey-haired, in his fifties, a small man with a paunch, dressed in a navy blue uniform. Despite the cold, he's sweating. She can see it rolling down his forehead, soaking the collar of his shirt.

'Oh my God,' he says hoarsely. 'What the fuck happened?'

Sadie wheels round and stares at him, and now she's crying, gasping for breath. 'It was an accident,' she shouts. 'It was an accident.' Her thin arms are wrapped around herself, as if she's trying to hold her body together. She moves towards Rachel and leans in, and Rachel finds that she is putting her arms around her, holding her in what must look like comfort – what is comfort, maybe. Even from the inside, it's hard to tell.

'I'm calling the police,' the driver says. His hands are shaking. He pulls a phone from his pocket and jabs at it, veering away up the platform, his voice hushed and broken as he begins to speak.

Sadie pulls back, her fingers plucking insistently at Rachel's arm. 'We should go,' she whispers jerkily. 'We need to go.'

Jolted, Rachel almost laughs. 'We can't do that,' she says. 'We have to stay here. We'll need to talk to the police, give them a statement. You can't just run off.'

'But it was an accident!' Sadie interrupts plaintively. 'I didn't mean – I don't . . .' Suddenly she slumps, looking around her vaguely. 'I need to sit down.'

At least this is better than running, Rachel thinks, and she sits down beside her sister on the platform and puts an arm tentatively around her shoulders. The concrete is smooth and cold, faintly sheered with ice. As she sits, she sees the blood. Spattering up the side of the track, pooling on to the platform less than a metre away. She isn't sure if Sadie has seen it, and she angles her body to block it from view. She's surprised by how cool her head is, how well she can deal with this.

Her sister is muttering something, her head dipped to her knees, her shoulders shaking. Rachel makes some small noise of interrogation, and Sadie raises her head and speaks more clearly. 'He'll kill me,' she says clearly.

There is a small, strange moment of silence. Rachel turns the words over in her head. They should sound melodramatic, but somehow they don't. 'What do you mean?' she says.

'Kas,' Sadie says. 'You don't understand. You don't know him. He'll kill me.' Her tears have dried up and her tone is soaked through with dread – fatalistic, certain.

'But it was an accident,' Rachel says. 'You just said.'

'That doesn't matter,' Sadie shoots back. 'You don't know him,' she says again. 'You don't know what he's done.' The words are pouring out of her now, as if a dam has been released. 'He's killed two people before – just the ones I know of – two men, George and Felix, people who used to work with him or for him, I don't know, and I don't even know why he did it, I think it was just to make an example out of them, to show people that they couldn't fuck with him and he wasn't afraid of anyone. I saw it, I saw it with my own eyes!'

227

'You saw it,' Rachel repeats. It's difficult to take in, this onslaught of information, and she feels briefly dizzy. She has always known that there was more going on in her sister's life than she was aware of, but she hadn't gone this far in her imaginings. Even now, she can't visualize what Sadie is telling her. The images that come to her are slapstick, almost comedic: Kas brandishing a gun with the sneer of a movie villain, her sister lurking in the background wringing her hands – or perhaps looking on, coolly and approvingly. It makes no sense.

Sadie is wiping her tears uselessly from her face, her fingertips streaking her cheeks with mascara. 'I love him, I really do,' she says, 'but he's a . . .' She pauses, as if she's testing the word inside her head. 'He's a murderer.'

She is quiet then, her breath coming more slowly, and Rachel finds herself matching the rhythm of that breathing, wondering what she can say. But then she glimpses a movement out of the corner of her eye and when she turns around she sees the policemen – two of them, in uniform, striding towards the train driver who is now sitting hunched by the edge of the platform with his head between his knees. She thinks he might have been sick. One of the policemen crouches down beside him, speaks to him as he puts a hand on his shoulder. And the other is walking in their direction; a tall man who looks barely older than they are, with strawberry blond hair and pale, barely-there eyebrows. His expression hovers uncomfortably somewhere between suspicion and sympathy.

'Good evening, ladies,' he says. 'I need to talk to you about what's happened here.'

Sadie shoots him a glance, terrified, antagonistic.

Peering up through the tangled strands of her hair, she looks like a wild animal. But Rachel nods and gets to her feet, letting her arm slip away from her sister's shoulder.

The room is small and cuboid; walls washed with watery khaki-coloured paint, a tiny window set into the door. There is a smell in the air that she can't quite place; some kind of disinfectant or bleach perhaps. Outside, she can hear footsteps and the occasional rise and swell of voices, echoing emptily along the corridor. The policewoman who curtly introduced herself as Karen pulls the little curtain across the window in the door and switches on a lamp in the corner of the room.

'If you're ready, Miss Castelle, we'll start now,' she says, coming back to sit on the other side of the desk. She is middle-aged. Greying hair curling neatly around a plump face. Small black-rimmed glasses. Her stare is neutral, impassive. Next to her is the young man with the strawberry blond hair. He's even younger than she thought, little more than a teenager; she can see the scars of acne on his left cheek. He looks across at her as he switches on the tape recorder. She sees the little red light winking and stares at it a second too long, so that when she looks away it's still there in her vision, a tiny, bright red pinprick suspended in the air.

The woman reels off a practised spiel that Rachel has heard on television, and which instantly slips from her mind. 'So,' she continues, 'perhaps you can tell us, in your own words, what happened at Camden Road Station tonight?'

In the minutes that they left her here alone, Rachel

has considered and discarded the possibility of using stony silence as her response. It might be the wisest approach, but she can't imagine being able to pull it off. The surreal horror of what she has witnessed is swirling in her head and already the words are knocking at the back of her throat, hammering to be let out. And she's also considered lying outright, saying that she and her sister were simply waiting on the platform alongside the woman in the raspberry-coloured mac, perhaps even saying that they saw her jump. But she's quickly realized that this would be stupid. For one thing, she has no idea if the station platform is equipped with CCTV. For another, she has no way of knowing what Sadie might be saying in her own interview room across the corridor. It's clear that the only real option is to tell the truth, as far as she can.

'I was with my sister, Sadie,' she says. 'She wanted to speak to the woman who—' She hesitates. To say 'the woman who died' feels odd somehow, presumptuous, although clearly there's no room for doubt. 'To the woman on the platform. I wasn't part of the conversation, but I could see that they began to argue.'

'And do you know what this argument was about?' Karen interrupts.

'I imagine it was about her husband,' Rachel says carefully. 'The woman's husband, I mean, not my sister's. Sadie has been – involved with him. She wanted to speak to his wife, to make her aware of the situation between them.'

'Were you acquainted with the woman in question yourself?' Karen asks. 'Can you tell me her name?'

Rachel shakes her head. 'Her name's Melanie, but I've never spoken to her,' she says, 'I know of her through her husband. Kaspar Kashani.' And as she speaks she sees a quick look pass between the two people opposite her, the briefest flicker of triumph or confirmation.

'Let's go back to what you saw,' the policewoman says mildly. 'They were arguing, you say, and then . . .'

'Then it became – physical,' Rachel says. 'They were lashing out at one another, trying to hurt each other, I would say. I'm sure that neither of them saw the train until it was too late, or realized that they were so close to the edge of the platform. It all happened very fast. One moment they were fighting, and the next moment the woman had fallen on to the tracks.'

Karen leans forward, her eyes shrewd and hard behind her glasses. 'Fallen,' she repeats. 'She fell? She lost her balance? Or she was pushed?'

The directness of it startles her; the way it cuts unpleasantly to the heart. She casts her mind back, tries to think. She sees the two figures in front of her, just metres away; sees her sister's arm rising up. She is not sure, not sure at all. But she notices the policewoman's expression shift minutely, betraying a flash of world-weary cynicism. Of course, she realizes, this woman expects her to protect her sister. It's the natural thing to do. Blood is thicker than water. What woman would do otherwise?

She raises her chin and does as they expect. 'She fell,' she says clearly.

The other woman watches her for a few moments, and she meets her gaze head on. 'OK,' she says levelly.

Silence stretches between them, thick and viscous. The strawberry-blond policeman's head is bent over a notebook as he scribbles away earnestly. Outside Rachel can hear the sound of some faint altercation: a shout rising and falling on the air, the rhythms of dissent and protest. She realizes that her hands are clenched in her lap, her fingernails digging painfully into her skin.

There is something rising up inside her, a powerful anger. She is furious with Sadie. For causing her to be sat in this room, for following and confronting Kas's wife, for every thoughtless word she has spoken and every thoughtless action she has performed over the past few years – from the tiny throwaway slights to the crippling restraints and burden of responsibility she has imposed on Rachel's own life.

It comes at her in a rush. At twenty-two she already feels like a mother. The mother of a wayward, defiant teenage girl who won't listen to reason and who cares about nothing but herself, and for whom love is a one-way street. She loves Sadie, but there is nothing nourishing or rewarding about this love; it simply makes her miserable. And the longer she sits in this arid, soulless room, the more she begins to realize that it doesn't really matter whether she is here or not, because even when she walks free she will still be trapped.

'Is there anything else you want to tell us?' Karen asks. She's looking at Rachel with sharp, inquisitive eyes, as if she can read her mind and doesn't much like what she sees.

Rachel bites the inside of her cheek, tasting the little well of blood. 'No,' she says. Her relationship with her

232

sister is not this woman's concern. The thought rockets wildly through her mind that if she altered her story, then things might go very differently. *She pushed her! I saw her, she meant to do it!* But it's a passing fancy, melodramatic and pointless. She won't lie, or throw out wild accusations, can no more imagine doing so than she can imagine her life being her own, free of this ever-present millstone around her neck.

'Let's go over it again, then,' Karen says. And they do go over it again – over and over, the same questions and the same brutal rehashing in ever more granular detail, until she wants to cry with frustration. Her head feels scraped out, entirely excavated. The young strawberry-blond man looks equally exhausted, slumped in his chair. She wonders if this is just another day at the office for him, how quickly he has been desensitized to drama and tragedy. But Karen doesn't seem tired at all. If anything it seems that the conversation is energizing her – her bearing ever straighter and keener, the full focus of her attention turned on Rachel.

When she finally asks a different question it catches Rachel off guard. 'So, tell me what you know about Kaspar Kashani,' she says. Her tone is almost casual, but not quite.

Rachel blinks, unsure of where the question is leading. 'I don't know him well,' she says. 'I mean, I've been in the same room as him a few times. At the club.'

'But your sister has been involved with him, you said,' Karen presses. 'You must have spent some time together?'

Rachel half laughs. 'It wasn't that sort of relationship. And besides . . .' She hesitates, not wanting to say

233

anything that might turn these people against her. But surely if Kas is known to them already, it can only be in a negative context. 'I don't like him,' she says baldly. 'He's an unpleasant, intimidating man.'

Karen regards her thoughtfully. 'What basis do you have for saying that?' she asks. And when she considers it, Rachel realizes that she has very little basis for it at all, or that she didn't, until the brief snatched conversation with Sadie on the station platform. Her dislike for him has been instinctive, unarguably so. But now it has become something else. It's justified. Validated.

Leaning forward with sudden forced intimacy, Karen speaks again, and this time it really is as if she has read her mind. 'Are you aware that Mr Kashani is currently on bail?' she asks. 'That he's been questioned in connection with murder, and that it's quite likely he'll be charged?'

Rachel doesn't reply at first, and in the brief pause that stretches between them she's acutely aware of the way the atmosphere has changed in the room. The young man is suddenly alert, sitting up in his seat, and the woman is watching her with all the avid concentration of a collector spying a rare specimen, keen for it not to get away.

'I didn't know that, no,' she says. She thinks of the haunted look on her sister's face, her hushed, broken words.

'I'll be honest with you, Rachel,' the policewoman says, and now her voice is dripping with inclusive chumminess. 'This is a separate conversation, really. We've been trying to pin Kashani down for some time. Various charges coming to nothing, you know? He's got a lot of people around him that make it pretty hard to get to him. But it's different this time. As I say, we're very close to charging him. And there's a fair bit of evidence, enough for a professional to look at and convict him.' She pauses, as if for effect, and when she continues she leans forward, her eyes intently boring into Rachel's. 'The problem is, juries aren't made up of professionals. They're just ordinary men and women, people who tend to follow their guts and think with their hearts. You see?'

Rachel frowns, lost. She tries to piece together what the woman is saying. 'They might get it wrong?' she says tentatively.

The policewoman smiles, without much warmth. 'Yes, they might. And then we'll be back in the same place we were, waiting for him to slip up and using up our time and resources trying to get him nicked. You see, Rachel, what I'm saying is that a lot of people don't care too much about *evidence*. They care about people. They'll look at Kashani looking all handsome in his nice suit, and they'll listen to a load of his mates waxing lyrical about what a great guy he is, and there's a good chance they'll fall for it. So someone like you . . .' She pauses again, and now Rachel does understand. 'Someone like you,' the woman says, 'if you did know anything and were prepared to speak out against him, could be invaluable to us.' She waits with eyebrows raised encouragingly, clearly expecting an answer.

Rachel tries to think, tries to understand what she might be committing to. It is all happening too fast, and she realizes that she is very tired. It is gone three in the morning, and there's a relentless ache spreading through her body, right up to the sharp nerves of her temples. She can't quite make sense of this, doesn't know if these people are for her or against her.

When Karen speaks again her voice is softer, and Rachel realizes that she has misinterpreted her silence. 'I can understand that you might be afraid to speak about this,' she says. For the first time, Rachel catches a flash of something human, almost warm. 'As you say, Mr Kashani is an intimidating man. But there are measures that can be put in place. Police protection. In extreme circumstances, if it was felt that you were in serious danger, your case could be approved by the witness protection programme. Do you know what that means?'

Still she doesn't speak, but this time it's shock that silences her. It's as if someone has reached inside her head, grasped hold of her brain and altered everything – a decisive, one-hundred-and-eighty-degree rotation that makes it all seem bright and clear. All this time, she's been secretly, shamefully wishing that her sister would disappear from her life. She has never even thought about the possibility that she, Rachel, could disappear from hers.

She thinks about this life and its building blocks: a decent but uninspiring job; a distant family she barely sees; friends who do little more than scratch her surface; a flat which belongs to somebody else. She's sat curled up in front of the television countless times, thinking that without Sadie's corrosive presence her life would be fine, but in reality there's very little of substance to hang on to. She has heard of witness protection – has read anonymized interviews with women who say that they are traumatized by their ordeal, still pining for the life they left behind. She tries to think about whether she would feel that way.

She nods uncertainly. 'I think so. I'd like to know more.'

'Well, that can be arranged.' Karen straightens up, clearly sensing a breakthrough. 'So, is there anything you'd like to talk to us about?'

Slowly, Rachel nods again. Her head swims lightly with tiredness, but she can feel a little pulse of excitement beating through her veins. And she knows that she hasn't properly considered this, weighed up the pros and cons and the possible implications and reverberations, but it feels right. It feels like fate.

It's almost half past four in the morning when she finally gets back to the flat, and by the time she lurches through the door she's dead on her feet, so desperate to sleep that she can't think about what has just passed. She flings herself down on her bed and it's instant – a swift vertiginous loss of consciousness that overtakes her and blacks everything else out.

Two hours later she opens her eyes again, still fully clothed, with the sickly, clinging aftermath of a headache. She's still tired, but her mind is whirring, replaying the night's events. She drags herself to her feet and goes to the kitchen, fills the kettle on autopilot and stands waiting for it to boil. Dawn is starting to creep through the dark clouds outside the window, casting a faint sheen of grey light on to the room. Her hands look pale and other-worldly. She watches them grasp a mug and hunt through the cupboard for a teabag, as if they are separate entities. When she has finally made the tea she carries it carefully across the room and drinks it standing in front of the window, looking down on to the street. She realizes she's shaking, unsure if it's the cold or some kind of delayed shock.

There's an image flashing statically in her head, again and again. The twisting of a high-heeled shoe on the platform, the skid and slide of a body falling like a stone, and then a micro-second's worth of horror, the blood and the swift obliteration of everything that held that body together. Even in her mind's relentless re-enactment of the scene, she can barely process it. A morbid part of her wants to slow it down, so that she can better understand it. She didn't know this woman. To feel sadness seems disingenuous somehow; to feel sympathy too easy and pat. She doesn't know how she is supposed to feel.

She has been sitting there long enough for the streaks of light between the clouds to widen and spread and for the streetlights to switch off, when a movement at the end of the road catches her eye. A young woman is approaching the flat. She can't see her face yet, but there's something in the way the woman walks, a kind of recklessness and looseness in her stride. Sadie is home.

Sadie

January 2000

SHE HAS NO MONEY left in her pockets and her card has been declined again so she walks all the way home from the police station and it takes hours – she walks through the dark, through the sunrise and into one of the coldest mornings she can remember. The ground is thinly covered with frost, sliding beneath her shoes with treacherous softness.

She's used to people looking at her. As early as four or five, she felt spotlit, marked out from the crowd. Women would gaze at her in the street, their features softening into delight and admiration. Such a lovely girl. She knew even then that she had been given a gift. That it made her somehow special. And then later, when she was twelve or thirteen and she changed almost overnight – her cheekbones sharpening and slanting, her body snapping into new provocative curves – she was still under observation, in a different way. The strange women on the street would look at her once, quickly, then away, tugging at their hair

239

or clothes. It was their husbands who focused on her now, but there was nothing soft or sweet in their gaze. She understood that they wanted something from her that she was not allowed to give. A couple of years later, she started giving it anyway.

She's still being watched, as she walks the streets of London, but she's no longer sure why. It doesn't seem to be just about her looks anymore. It isn't lust she sees in the eyes of the passers-by who slip through her vision like scurrying ants, but something else – something closer to fear. People veer towards her, then catch themselves and move quickly away, training their attention intently elsewhere. It's as if they know what she's done.

One foot in front of the other, for miles on end, and with every footstep she's turning it over in her head, replaying those few minutes on the platform. She remembers the way her arm shot out towards Melanie – the decisive, sharp action of it, almost as if it were outside her control. Almost, but not quite. She pushed her. She pushed her towards the tracks. She pushed her towards the tracks and she fell. She pushed her towards the tracks and she fell to her death. Every thought nudges a little further towards the truth of what has happened, but it feels less and less real. It feels theoretical, conceptual. Like she's done nothing at all.

She thinks about the police too, the way they questioned her. The swing in their attitude that she can't quite understand – that she thinks she might be able to make sense of, if she was just a bit less drunk and had had a bit more sleep. They started off solicitous, gentle. *This must have been a horrifying experience for you.*

Tissues, a steaming cup of tea. Grave, acquiescent nods when she told them that it had been an accident, just a silly little argument that got out of control – and even now, that doesn't feel so far from the truth. And then, at a certain point, the tone had changed. *So, tell us more about your relationship with this woman's husband.* Keen, inquisitive eyes raking her face. *How much do you know about his activities outside of work?* The sergeant leaning forward in the darkening lamplight, pushing the tape recorder imperceptibly closer. And then the last words she'd wanted to hear. *Do the names George Hart and Felix Santos mean anything to you?*

She had kept her face straight and denied all knowledge. She knows that this is what Kas will expect of her, and she is determined to do what he wants. She regrets the silly things she said to Rachel, when she was overwrought and stressed. Of course he isn't going to kill her. He will know that what happened to Melanie was an accident. And even if he doesn't, some small, secret part of her thinks, he isn't like other men. He respects people who go all out to get what they want. He likes people with no boundaries. That's her. These thoughts flood her head and on one level she knows she's being crazy, but she can't slow herself down, can't get back to normality now, and so she just keeps repeating these things to herself and she keeps walking, resting her hand lightly on her stomach where her baby is slowly, slowly growing.

By the time she's finally reached Covent Garden and the building where she and Rachel live is looming in front of her, she's talked and walked herself into a kind of brittle exhilaration. Somehow, this is all going to work out. There'll be a way forward, because there always is. She shoves the key into the lock and stumbles through the door, catching sight of herself in the hallway mirror. Her hair is sexily tousled around her face, her tight red T-shirt smoothly hugging her curves. She stares at herself, and half smiles. 'I'm baaaack,' she croons up the stairs, raising her voice. There's no response, so she hurries upstairs and she finds Rachel in her bedroom, sitting on the bed hugging her knees to her chest.

Her sister looks washed out, the light cutting through the window and highlighting the sallow pallor of her skin. She carefully picks up a mug of tea beside her and sips it. 'You were a long time. What did they say to you?'

'What didn't they say to me?' Sadie fires back, coming forwards into the room and throwing herself down on to the bed, pillowing her hands behind her head. 'God, it was boring as shit. Going over the same thing again and again.' She hasn't realized until this moment that she's going to play it this way; this kind of hard levity is guaranteed to rub Rachel up the wrong way, but somehow it seems the only thing to do.

Rachel watches her, narrowing her eyes. 'What did you tell them?' she asks.

Sadie shrugs and exhales. 'The truth. I think it'll be OK. Obviously they'll have to investigate it all a bit more, but I'm pretty sure they believed me. I told them that I'd started the fight with Melanie, but that that's all it was, a fight. If it had happened in the middle of the street rather than – where it did, that would have been the end of it. It wouldn't even have been on their radar.

But she slipped and fell. Boom.' She stops momentarily and frowns, the ripple of an unpleasant thought running through her. 'I mean, that's what you told them too, right?' She props herself up on the bed and looks straight at her sister. It's a question, and a challenge.

Slowly, Rachel nods. 'Pretty much. It's what I saw. What I think I saw.'

That one lingers between them for a few moments. Sadie wonders if it's as straightforward as it sounds. If she should make something of it, or move on. At last she shrugs again, nodding mildly. 'It was a shit thing to happen,' she says, 'but, well, I know this sounds bad but it might not be so terrible, all things considered. He didn't love her, you know. He loves me. And when the dust settles he'll realize that what with the baby and all . . .' She can't resist but spill out a little of what's been passing through her head, but as soon as she does so she realizes that it's pointless. Rachel's face twists with incredulity and horror, and she shakes her head.

'I don't think that's going to happen,' she says bluntly, 'and even if it did, why on earth would you want it to? After what you told me?'

Sadie sits up fully now. 'What do you mean?'

'You know what I mean,' Rachel says. 'What you told me, on the platform at the station.'

She feels a fleeting cloud of panic, but it's gone as fast as it appears. They were just words, that's all. She can't be held to them. 'I don't remember,' she says. 'Whatever I said, it didn't mean anything.'

Rachel looks as if she might press the point, but she shuts her mouth again abruptly, and her eyes flick back and forth, as if she's thinking. 'Did they say anything to you?' she asks at last. 'The police. Did they say anything to you about Kas?'

Sadie stays quiet, weighing up possible answers. The chemical ebullience that she felt when she came into the room is gone; everything feels slowed down, and very still. When at last she speaks her voice sounds different to her own ears; there's a kind of world-weariness in it that she doesn't think she's ever used before. 'Someone like Kas is always under suspicion for something or other,' she says. 'No one understands people like him. He's successful, different. It's natural for people to want to bring him down.'

'So you didn't tell them anything,' Rachel says. It isn't really a question, but it seems to demand an answer.

Sadie stands up, wrapping her thin arms around herself. She raises her chin slightly, and she catches sight of herself again, in the little mirror that hangs by Rachel's dressing table. The light that filters softly through the half-open curtains settles lovingly on the beautiful planes of her face, making her look like a film star. And she sees Rachel watching her, sees something unmistakeable in her look, even now: something like love, something like awe.

'There's nothing to tell,' she says clearly. 'There will never be anything to tell.'

She leaves the room then, closing the door very quietly behind her. The catch clicks softly as she pulls it shut. She walks into her own bedroom, pulls a blanket over herself and hugs a cushion to her chest, listening. There's no sound except for the infrequent passing of cars below. She doesn't think she will sleep, but her body takes over and before she knows it she's wrenching her eyes open in bright winter sunlight and glancing over at the clock to find that over six hours have passed.

Gingerly, she gets to her feet and moves softly down the corridor towards Rachel's bedroom, pushing the door open to peer inside. Rachel is sleeping, lying motionless with her face pressed into the pillow. She tiptoes back to her own room and pulls the large suitcase from underneath the bed, starting to pile possessions in it almost at random. Clothes and jewellery and bottles of nail varnish, stacks of paperwork that have sat there ever since she carted them out from their parents' house years ago, a few half-read books. She isn't exactly sure why she is doing this, but after the conversation last night, she knows she can't stay here. The battle lines have been drawn. No matter what she might say, her sister obviously isn't on her side. And now that she's sober and her head is clear, she's starting to wonder about exactly what Rachel said, in her own interview room. She thinks again of the way the sergeant's attitude towards her changed. She can't quite link the two together yet, but she has an instinct, a queasy tug of premonition or foreboding.

As she scoops up a bundle of clothes from the floor of the wardrobe, she notices the thin folder of photographs at the back. She had them printed a couple of months ago, she remembers, after one of her and Rachel's earliest visits to the club. The pretence was that she wanted some shots of the two of them there, but of course, the person she really wanted photographs of was Kas. She flicks through them slowly, staring at his face. He treats the camera the same way he treats most people, surveying it coolly, dead on, with little expression. As ever, he's giving nothing away.

She gathers the photos together and stuffs them into the case, then picks a few out again. She'll leave them outside Rachel's room. She's not entirely sure why she's doing it, but the motive doesn't feel pleasant. Ultimately, she thinks, perhaps it's just a reminder that her sister was there too. She might want to believe that her hands are clean, but she's been part of this, in her own way.

She steps back, surveying the near-empty room, then she crosses to the table and tears a piece of paper from the notepad, scribbles a message. *Think it's best if I stay elsewhere for a while. Didn't want to wake you to say goodbye.* She pauses, pen in hand. Is there anything else to say? She thinks for a while, but nothing comes, and in the end she just scrawls her name at the bottom of the page, the lettering large and dark. She goes out into the corridor, dragging the case behind her, and she thinks about propping the note carefully against Rachel's door, but it seems more fitting to just toss it on to the floor along with the photographs, and so she leaves it there behind her, exiting the flat without looking back.

She doesn't know where she's going at first, but she gets on the train and heads north. As it rattles along the tracks she gets out her phone and scrolls through her contacts. There are a few names there she could target, people who would probably let her crash on their couches

246

for a night or two if she just turned up and presented it as a fait accompli. Or she could call one of the men she used to see, even though it feels like a long time since she did that casual dating thing; she knows there are plenty of guys who would put her up for a while in exchange for sex on tap. But something about the idea feels grubby and sad, and she doesn't want to sleep with anyone. It feels like betraying Kas.

It's this thought that decides her. She'll go to his house. She'll find him and warn him about what the police have been saying to her. By now they'll have contacted him about Melanie. They'll have told him that she was involved. But he'll still want to know what they've been talking to her about – about George and Felix. That, surely, trumps everything else. And when he realizes that she's on his side, he'll look after her.

She gets off at Camden and trudges towards Fraser Street, pulling the case behind her. She's glad she brought her winter coat, because the air is even icier than it was yesterday and her breath is coming in clouds around her face. She can't wait to be inside, but when she reaches the street she's shaken by the way it looks in daylight. Half the houses are derelict, with broken windows and sprayed graffiti covering the walls. Even those that look more lived in are run-down and unwelcoming. Number 17, the house where she knows Kas lives, is no different from the rest. There's a small pile of rubble and rubbish stacked against the front wall, and the door is covered with cracks and scratches, as if it's been smashed and badly repaired. It isn't the sort of place she imagined him in. She thinks of his gleaming, polished appearance and the care with which he's sculpted his body. But of course that's what matters to him: himself. He doesn't care about the stuff around him; it's incidental, irrelevant.

She raises her hand and knocks on the door hard, three times in quick succession. She presses the doorbell too, even though it doesn't look as though it's worked in years. Silence, and stillness. She tips her head up and peers at the darkened windows. There's no hint of life behind them. The whole place looks abandoned. Dead.

Of course, he could just be out. Gone to visit family, or Dominic, or another associate. But something tells her that's not it. The police have come for him already. They've taken him away and he's not coming back.

She takes out her phone and scrolls to his messages. *Kas*, she types. *I know what's happened. I* . . . She hesitates. I believe in you? I'll stand by you? It feels too schoolgirlish, too melodramatic for him. *I love you*, she types in the end. She's never said this to him before, and she's wanted to for such a long time that it brings a kind of release, even if she knows he'll probably never reply. He probably won't even get this message, if he's already been arrested. But there's still a sort of satisfaction in the words. If you love someone, you're loyal to them. You give them everything.

One final knock, and then she turns and leaves, the case rattling behind her on the uneven stones. She thinks, for a few moments, about disappearing. Getting on a train and going into the middle of nowhere, relying on her wits and her charm to survive . . . But it feels like a lot of effort and, at the end of the day, she doesn't really believe she can do it. They'd find her, in the end, and what point is there in running from something that's always going to find you?

The wind is rising and there's a fine smattering of rain carried on it, settling coldly on her hair and the nape of her neck. Ahead of her the horizon stretches, curling in a grey mass of cloud. Cars are screeching down the main road, horns blaring, and there's an unruly blast of reggae music spilling out from a shop doorway. On the doorstep sits an elderly Jamaican man, smoking a spliff, raising it to her in greeting. The smell hits the back of her throat as she breathes in the cold air. She'll remember this, she thinks, this strange, harsh morning that has the quality of a lucid dream.

She turns her footsteps towards the police station. There's something fatalistic in this, walking into the hands of people who have the power to change your life for better or worse. She's tired of her hands being on the wheel. She wants to take them off, hand over the controls and close her eyes and never wake up. There's an ache in her stomach, spreading dully downwards, but she ignores it and keeps walking, driving herself forwards.

Rachel

February 2000

WHEN SHE LOOKS BACK on the weeks that have passed, Rachel finds it hard to put the memories in order. Hours at the police station, filled with soft, insistent questioning about Kas, the people he spends his time with, the patterns of his behaviour, her impression of his character, her feelings towards him. They treat her very nicely, solicitously offering drinks and snacks, asking her if she has been experiencing any difficulties.

She knows that Kas and Sadie have been charged, and that they will remain in custody until the trial. It has taken some time for her to fully realize what she has done – that by telling them what Sadie had told her she has exposed her sister's part in something about which she still knows very little. *I saw it, I saw it with my own eyes*, Sadie had whispered, and at the time Rachel had not interrogated this, not traced the thread through to its conclusion. She had not realized that this effectively made her sister an accessory after the fact, perhaps even a conspirator to murder. And she hadn't realized, either, that Sadie was already on the police's radar, already woven into the case they were trying to build.

At times she feels guilty – so much so that the crushing weight of it makes it hard for her to breathe. And yet when she thinks about the reality of these charges, she is reminded more forcibly than ever before that her sister is damaged, broken. Dangerous, even. She was always going to have to crash. She wonders, often, what Sadie is doing now. How she is feeling towards her, how much she knows about what Rachel has said – and the thought of her sister's fury at her betrayal is frightening, but she forces herself to block it out.

They ask her at the station several times if there is any possibility she would be willing to bear witness against Sadie as well as Kas, but every time she dries up, deflects the question. To her, the trial is an amorphous concept, barely even real. In the unfriendly dark of her flat, barred against the outside world, she has a hazy, queasy realization that she has little or no idea what is happening around her, to her. It is too late. The wheels that have been set in motion are far bigger than she is.

She keeps herself to herself. She finds herself staying out late less, taking the most direct route back from the office to the flat, and seeing fewer people than she used to. She spends a lot of time curled up in front of the television, staring unseeingly at the flickering static. On some level, she thinks, she's detaching. Just in case. She hasn't forgotten what they said to her about the witness protection. But as the weeks go by her life is rolling on just as it always has, and now that Sadie isn't in it, it's staggeringly uneventful.

And then one Sunday afternoon, two weeks in, she's walking to the corner shop in the rain without an umbrella, her hair plastered wetly to her scalp as water runs in tiny rivulets down the back of her neck. She hasn't planned to go out, but she's hungry and there's not much in the flat. She's waiting at the traffic lights when she sees the man. He's there diagonally across the street, leaning back against a wall, his arms folded across his chest, and he's staring directly at her.

She doesn't recognize him at first, so out of context – just feels a breath of unease at the way he's watching her, then a little tug of familiarity that she can't quite place when she sees his cropped white-blond hair and the heavy set of his shoulders. Moments later she realizes that it is Dominic Westwood.

The lights are flashing green, but her legs feel like they're giving way and it takes every ounce of her strength to force herself to cross the street and keep on walking. In the shop, she fumbles for a packet of biscuits, a carton of orange juice, keeping her head down and whispering a few pointless words of reassurance to herself. The air inside is warm and fusty, reminding her of a children's nursery. She pushes the money at the shopkeeper and goes back to the doorway, looking out on to the street.

He's still there. She sees him instantly, out of the corner of her eye, but she keeps her head directed straight ahead and starts walking fast, away from him. Behind her, she hears him say her name. She starts to run, her heartbeat thudding through her body, and she doesn't stop until she is home. Jamming her key in the lock, she whips her head round, and she sees that the road outside is empty. He hasn't followed her, but it doesn't make her feel any better. If anything, it feels even more threatening.

After that it gathers pace with relentless speed and subtlety. She sees Dominic again several times, always at a distance, but he is not the only one. The network goes deeper, reaches further than she has thought. She starts to see the same strangers' faces on the street again and again – background figures who peer at her as if through bulletproof glass, unapproachable. At first she thinks she is imagining it; seeing patterns where there are none, finding similarity in a host of anonymous faces. But deep down she's aware that this isn't true.

Once, she tries looking back steadily – facing one of these men head on and not letting her gaze drop, even though it brings her heart into her mouth. She tells herself that she will not look away first, but she can't stick to it. It's the gap in their respective knowledge that scares her: the realization from the expression in the man's eyes that he knows all about her, and that she knows nothing about him. She lets her gaze drift across the street as if she is simply bored, but she knows he isn't fooled. When she looks back, he's gone.

Strange notes appear on her doormat in the mornings; cryptic warnings and badly drawn symbols that she does not understand. She is being sent messages that she can't interpret, being set up to fail. The first time, she rips the sheet up, tearing it into tiny shreds of paper as she kneels on the carpet by the front door. She thinks that she will feel better afterwards, but this small act of defiance achieves nothing. If anything, she starts to panic that somehow they will know, and later that day she finds herself with her hands halfway down the kitchen bin, pressing the shreds of paper deep within the detritus to conceal them. She takes her hands out and stares at them, sees that they are covered with dirt and the slime of rotting food, and for a moment it's as if she has risen out of her body and is looking down at herself and detachedly reaching the judgement that she must be going mad.

And then there are the calls. Her phone often rings in the middle of the night, and when she picks it up, there is silence. Always silence, with one exception: an unfamiliar man's voice, low and vicious. *Do it, and you're dead*, it says. She has barely gathered breath to speak when the dialling tone buzzes in her ears.

She logs each incident meticulously and relays them to the police station, unsure of how much weight they are given or what picture they are gradually building. These men have never touched her or come near her – rarely even speak to her, save for the odd mumbled comment here and there as they pass by. They are simply letting her know that they are there.

She thinks that it will get easier – that she will grow to cope with this constant sense of surveillance, this continuous hair-trigger alertness that makes her turn around swiftly whenever she hears a sound she cannot place. Slowly, with increasing horror, she realizes that she was mistaken.

Three weeks in. She shuts herself in the flat as usual, double-locks and pushes a chair up against the door. She has a strange sense of foreboding, nauseous and nebulous. Unplugging the landline, she switches her mobile to vibrate. In bed she wraps herself tightly in the duvet and concentrates on her breathing. She watches the numbers click forward through the hours on the digital clock by her bedside, until they blur in front of her eyes and she loses consciousness.

When she wakes, the numbers say 08:44, and yet the room is completely dark, like the inside of a tomb. She lies there for a full ten minutes waiting for this darkness to lift, seized by a strange feeling of unreality. The flat is silent, watchful.

She rises slowly from her bed and walks out on to the landing, feels her way around the walls. It is pitch black in every room. Taking the mobile from the pocket of her dressing gown, she checks the time again, the numbers glowing greenly on the screen. Confusion rises queasily inside her, but something stops her from turning on the light.

Instead she fumbles her way down to the front door, feels for the keys by instinct in the darkness and turns them in the locks. The door swings open, and the winter sunlight pours in, hurting her eyes with its force. She steps out on to the pavement. Some realization is brewing inside her, but she does not fully understand until she takes a few steps away and looks back up at the building, and then, with a deepening shiver that passes inwards from her skin to her bones, she sees.

Someone has been there, to her flat in the night, while she was sleeping. They have painted every single one of the windows black.

The Programme officer, a woman named Deborah, is waiting for her in the little room. Karen is there too, giving her a nod of greeting. Over the weeks they have developed something between them, Rachel and this sergeant with the greying wavy hair and the determined eyes. You couldn't call it a friendship; you wouldn't want to. But there's some kind of understanding there.

'So let's sum up where we are,' Deborah says. She looks as if she is announcing a death. 'We've completed the threat assessment, and your case has been classified as a Level 1, which means we believe the threat to your safety to be serious and immediate. The Assistant Chief Constable has approved you to be admitted on to the Protection Programme. This means we will be making arrangements for your temporary, and subsequently for your permanent relocation, but before we can do so, we need you to sign the Memorandum of Understanding.' She pushes the papers towards Rachel, fans them on to the desk. 'It's important that you understand what this means.'

Dimly, Rachel hears the voice continue, but the words zoom in and out, echoing as if down a long tunnel. She looks down at the papers, the bright white pages stamped by black ink. The words blur and separate, making it hard for her to read them. She catches the odd phrase or line: . . . *agree not to give or pass on any information which could lead to the disclosure of your new location to anyone, including all friends and family members . . . forbidden to enter within the boundaries of Greater London.* Taking it in is impossible.

Deborah is still talking, her voice loud and steady. 'If you sign now, we can go ahead with all preparations for your relocation, and the formation of your new identity,' she says. 'If you do not wish to sign, the responsibility for your protection will continue to rest with your investigation team. I would strongly advise . . .'

The voice fades out again. Rachel looks down at her hands, white and still, the fingernails painted pale pink. The varnish is chipping, worn away entirely in patches to reveal the pearly, translucent covering beneath. She cannot remember when she last painted her nails. Slowly, her left hand reaches for the pen. There is a roaring in her head, a pressure that builds and builds. She thinks of Sadie, of all the years of effort and anxiety that finally came to a head on the night that Melanie died. If she went back to that night, she'd feel the same way again. Sitting in the interview room, she'd do the same again.

She presses down on the paper and writes her name. The handwriting looks shaky and erratic, the writing of a pensioner or a madwoman. Throwing the pen down, she pushes the paper away.

They come for her at dawn the next morning to take her to the safe house, in a dark blue car with tinted windows. She answers the door to a thickset man, and for a moment, despite his uniform, she finds herself searching his face, wondering if he is for her or against her. She feels her heartbeat quickening and she starts to close the door against him, but as she does so she catches sight of Deborah, peering out of the car behind him, and her body relaxes.

She leaves the flat without looking back. The previous night she had wandered from room to room, trying to find something she would miss, but it was never really her home in any case. The windows are still darkly streaked with paint, shafts of light worming through in places where she has tried to scratch it away. As the car pulls out of the street, she searches for a word for what she is feeling, and nothing comes. There is only a sense of something breaking off, a string cut somewhere inside her, leaving her strangely weightless and free.

March 7th. She wakes early, gets dressed and lies there waiting for the taxi to arrive, trying to keep her mind empty. She stares unseeingly through the window all the way across London, letting the city flow through her like water. It's only when they pull up at the rear entrance to the court that she allows herself to focus. The building is boxy and stern, pale brickwork and brushed metal, like an industrial car park. Low trees are planted at the side walls, rising from compacted soil. She does not know what she was expecting, but it was not this modern monstrosity. Slowly, she gets out of the taxi, smoothing down her skirt.

A rush of blood runs to her head. She blinks, looks

up. Long rectangular windows flanked by white stone; the imprint of a coat of arms stamped into the brickwork above. She just has time to register all this, the brief snap of a camera lens freezing it into her brain, before she is inside.

A man is coming towards her, extending his hand. 'Mark Devlin. I'm a representative from the Crown Prosecution Service. We'll get you through security and sign you in, and then I'll take you to the private waiting room.' She has been reassured about this countless times. *We'll keep you away from him and his associates, Rachel. You'll be able to wait in a room on your own before the trial. The first time you see him again will be in court.* As if this should make her feel better. She hands her letter to the woman behind the reception desk, who scans it briefly.

'Name of the principal defendant, please,' she says.

'Kaspar Kashani.' She says it automatically, closing off from the thought of him. The woman nods and glances at Mark, who is still standing behind her. 'Room 5,' she says.

Deborah is waiting in the private room, dressed in a dark navy suit with her hair pulled back from her face, showing the wrinkles around her temples. She smiles with what looks like relief. 'Got here all right?' she asks, ushering Rachel into a seat. On the table in front of her she registers a pile of magazines – bright, gossipy covers, candid celebrity snaps. Deborah follows her gaze, and smiles again. 'Hopefully we won't have to wait too long,' she says, 'but it could be an hour or two. This is the CPS's idea of entertainment, isn't that right,

259

Mark?' She raises her eyebrows at the man, and he makes some good-natured sound of agreement.

Rachel looks at the magazines. She can feel the shaking starting deep down inside her, ricocheting through her bones. Her head is swirling. 'Thanks,' she says automatically. The lurid coloured headlines are starting to jar against her brain. She looks up at the bare wall opposite. Flat pale yellow, the colour of faded buttercups.

'Try not to worry too much,' she hears Deborah say next to her. 'You're still feeling all right about giving evidence publicly? Just remember . . .' She launches into a familiar spiel, one Rachel has heard several times before. They offered her the possibility, at first, of giving evidence behind a screen, or by video link-up, but it was soon clear that this was not the desired approach. *Remember, Rachel, they already know who you are. These measures are often used by witnesses who have come forward secretly, or who don't want to directly confront the defendant. But Kashani is well aware that you will be giving evidence, so you have little to gain by not being present in the witness box.* And then the clincher, delivered in an intense monotone. *You're more likely to convince the jury if you're there in person. They're more likely to believe you, because it's harder to tell a lie to someone's face.*

'Yes,' she says, forcing the word out from the back of her throat, and finding it dry. She reaches for the jug of water and pours herself a glass, draining it in three gulps. 'I'm fine.'

When the call comes, she can see from the clock that almost an hour and a half has passed, but it seems as if the time has been dramatically compressed, folded into a few hot minutes of fear. She stands up. The door swings open ahead, and she steps out into the cool grey corridor, hearing the sharp knock of her heels against the gleaming floor. She walks slowly up towards the courtroom, counting each step. It reminds her of the corridors in an airport terminal; the same antiseptic bareness. She is becoming someone else, someone stronger and calmer, playing the part that will get her through this. The voice inside the court is saying her name. She puts the flat of her hand on to the door and pushes it open.

The room is smaller than she expected. She has imagined the melodrama of American court shows, sweeping ceilings and huge banked benches, stone columns. This room is compact and hot, packed with props like a film set. She steps into the witness box – a wooden cube, empty but for a chair that she knows she should not use unless she has to. To the right of her she sees the judge, bewigged and gowned, his face set and serious. He must be almost seventy, with bushy white eyebrows furrowing his face, lines and wrinkles mapped out across his cheeks. For an insane moment, she wants to laugh. The lights are bright as she stands and looks ahead, out at the jury seated in the opposite bank. Men and women, some of them as young as she is, dressed in suits and jackets, hands folded and expectant. Above, the public gallery, scattered with faces, her vision blurring them into one messy splurge of colour.

She is asked to take the oath, and slowly, as if in a dream, she looks down at the printed card. She reads the words out loud, hearing her voice echo around the courtroom. *The truth. The whole truth. And nothing but the truth.*

She finishes and raises her head, looking straight ahead. She knows where Kas will be. Seated to the left, directly behind the lawyers for the prosecution and defence. She does not yet turn her head and look. She can feel him, feel his presence crackling on her skin like lethal electricity.

Instead she looks at the prosecution lawyer as he stands and moves towards her. Leo Fenton – short and unassuming, with a fine pointed nose and small delicate hands with which he adjusts his white collar as he approaches. She has expected him to treat her kindly. After all, they are on the same side. But this man's eyes are sharp and his mouth is set in an unsmiling line, and she's reminded that in a way she's on trial too. There are expectations on her that she needs to meet.

'Miss Castelle,' he begins, 'I'd like you to tell me about how you first became aware of Kaspar Kashani.'

She has been told that this is how it will begin: setting the scene, easing her in. She clears her throat and begins to speak. She tells him about that first meeting with her and Sadie on the street, the invitation to the club and their subsequent visit. 'After that, she went almost every weekend,' she finishes. 'I sometimes went with her, but mostly I just came to pick her up.'

'How did you feel about going to the club?' Leo Fenton asks.

'I didn't enjoy it,' Rachel says. 'I only ever went because Sadie asked me to.'

The lawyer nods. 'Can you explain why it was that you disliked visiting the club?'

She pauses for a moment, thinking about this. In truth, there are many reasons: she has never really enjoyed clubbing, and in recent years she has not much enjoyed spending time with Sadie either. But she has sense enough to know that there is one reason that needs to dominate, and, after all, it isn't a lie. 'Because I disliked Kaspar Kashani,' she says. 'I found him unpleasant and frightening, and I didn't like the fact that my sister seemed so interested in him. I couldn't really understand why.'

She does look at Kas then; can't help her eyes sliding in his direction for a brief instant. He's staring straight at her, regal-looking and exotic in his dark suit, his face unmoving. He looks intensely contemptuous, as if all his energy is being poured into the force of his scorn.

'I'd like to understand what you observed on your visits to the club,' Leo Fenton says. 'What impression you gained of Mr Kashani and his – business,' he ends with faint distaste.

She has been over this many times and she isn't sure, even now, how much is real and how much is imagined. When she thinks back, she thinks she remembers certain things: swift transactions in dark corners, conversations between Kas and other men that seemed to have intimidation as their currency. One thing she is sure of is that people are frightened of him. So it's this on which she concentrates, describes the changes in their atmosphere and expressions whenever he appeared in the room.

The lawyer is nodding encouragingly, and no sooner has she finished than he's speaking again. 'I think I understand,' he says. 'Would it be fair to say that you always felt that this man had the capacity for serious wrongdoing? Perhaps even for murder?'

'Objection,' the defence lawyer cuts in, rising to his feet. 'The prosecution is leading the witness, Your Honour.'

The judge glances at them both, then nods. 'Please stick to the facts, Mr Fenton,' he says mildly.

Leo Fenton unfurls his hands elegantly in acceptance, but leaves a short pause, turning to look at the jury with raised eyebrows, as if asking them to consider what Rachel might have replied. 'Very well,' he says. 'Let's talk about the events of the twelfth of January of this year. You were with your sister Sadie, I believe, when Kaspar Kashani's wife fell to her death at Camden Road Station?'

Rachel swallows. 'Yes.' It feels like so long ago now, this night, and it has been so long since she has let it cross her mind except in her dreams.

'I'd like you to tell me what happened in the immediate aftermath of that event,' Fenton says, and now his voice hardens, letting her know that this is crunch time. This is when she needs to step up to the mark.

She holds her head up, keeps her voice steady. 'My sister was very distressed, and she told me some things about Kaspar Kashani,' she says. 'She told me that he had killed two people that she knew of. She called him a murderer.' The word falls harshly, and she sees the impact it has on the jury, the power of it, the way it makes them shift in their seats and glance at one another.

'Did you believe her?' the lawyer asks.

Rachel nods. 'I was absolutely sure that she was telling the truth.'

'And why is that?' he presses.

She hesitates, making sure that the words are perfectly formed in her head before she speaks. 'Because there was nothing calculated about the way she spoke,' she says. 'I think she only told me because she was so shaken by what had just happened. She was terrified, I could see that. She was terrified that Kaspar would think her responsible somehow, and she knew what he was capable of.'

'So you are sure that your sister *believed* what she was saying,' Fenton says. 'How sure are you that she was, in fact, correct? And why?'

'I'm sure,' Rachel says slowly, 'because she told me that she witnessed it herself. There didn't seem to be any room for doubt.' As she speaks, she feels a tremor of anxiety pass through her. It feels as if the conversation is starting to swerve in a different direction.

Fenton is silent for a moment, rubbing the tip of one finger contemplatively across his lip, back and forth. 'Did your sister explain the nature of her involvement in these crimes to you?' he asks. 'Did she explain why she was there, or what she did?'

'No,' Rachel says quickly. 'She didn't.'

Another pause, this time thickly charged and potent. 'Do you really believe that Mrs Kashani fell to her death that night?' Fenton asks at last.

The defence lawyer leaps to his feet again, extending his hands in supplication. 'Your Honour,' he says hotly, 'this is irrelevant. My client has not been charged in connection with Mrs Kashani's death, and it has nothing to do with the current proceedings.'

As he speaks, he glances over and across to his left, and instinctively Rachel follows his movement, and then she sees her. Sitting at the back of the defence box, dressed in a slim-fitting black jacket with her hair pulled back from her face and her lips painted dark pink. She has been so reluctant to look in Kaspar's direction, so conscious of his presence that it had not even crossed her mind that he might not be alone. But of course, he is not the only one on trial.

When their eyes meet, Rachel thinks she sees Sadie's bearing relax a little, as if she's been waiting for this moment, her body drawn tight with anticipation. It's the first time she has seen her sister in almost two months, and the oddest thing is that as soon as she sets eyes on her again it's as if she has never been away. She could have been waiting in the next room, her back turned only for minutes. She's imagined fireworks, drama. But Sadie doesn't look as if she is about to leap out of her seat and start screaming obscenities. She's watching Rachel with her eyebrows slightly lowered, frowning at her in the way that a scientist might gaze at some curious new specimen.

Rachel wrenches her gaze away, back to the lawyers. She feels the palms of her hands slippery with sweat.

'I'd argue that this line of questioning is very relevant, Your Honour,' Fenton is saying, 'considering the need to understand the nature of the relationship between the defendants, not to mention their characters.'

The judge waits, the curve of an amused smile upon his lips as he observes the lawyer for the prosecution, and she remembers that this is at least in part a game for them, or at least a professional power-play. It isn't their own lives they're holding in their hands. 'Just be careful how you frame your questions, Mr Fenton,' he says.

'Of course.' That elaborate hand gesture again. 'Let me approach this from another angle,' Fenton says. 'What is your opinion on your sister's feelings towards Mr Kashani? Was this a crush, a passing fancy? Or was it something more?'

Rachel does not answer at first. Instead she looks over at Sadie again, who is now sitting bolt upright. Her eyes are anxious and engaged, her lips slightly parted. She's sending a message, certainly, but Rachel has no idea what it might be. How would Sadie want her to answer this question? She doesn't know, and this not knowing fills her with panic. There is a sudden lump in her throat that she can't get past, and her heart is beating faster, the pulse ricocheting through her unevenly and making her dizzy. For a moment she genuinely thinks she might faint.

And then it's as if something inside her clicks and switches these feelings off. She draws a long breath, and she realizes that it doesn't matter what Sadie wants her to say. Her sister is not her master now, and she never will be again. What matters here is the truth.

'She was utterly obsessed with him,' she says. 'I don't know if I would call it love, but she was clearly completely infatuated. She would have done anything for him.'

Leo Fenton lets these words settle between them before he reaches slowly in and plucks out the one he wants. 'Anything?' he repeats.

She realizes the implication, knows that it isn't only Melanie that they are talking about here. The spectres of those two dead men are hanging over them, men about whom she knows nothing, to whom she owes nothing.

She looks at the defence box again. Kaspar has twisted around in his seat and seems to be looking hard at Sadie, sending some kind of signal that is making her clench her hands together and shake her head. In this instant, it's clear that everyone else might as well be dust. 'Yes,' she says.

Fenton nods and gathers his papers together with a snap. 'No further questions.'

'Thank you,' the judge says, and turns to his side, eyebrows raised. 'Mr Nelson, do you have any questions for the witness?'

Rachel looks at the defence lawyer properly for the first time. He's bigger and broader than Fenton, with a florid face that shines under the courtroom lights. He regards her steadily, and she looks back at him, fighting not to let her composure slip.

The silence endures for what seems like hours before he looks away dismissively, giving a theatrical shrug. 'No. No questions, Your Honour.'

She lets out a breath, confusion racing through her. Nelson is busying himself with his papers, frowning intently down at them. She glances across at the jury, and thinks she can see some of the same puzzlement she feels reflected on a couple of their faces. It can only be a psychological game, she thinks. He's trying to imply that her statement is irrelevant, contemptible. She has no doubt that he could attack her with all the savagery of a wolf tearing its prey if he chose, but he's decided to save himself for something more worthwhile. In any case that's what he wants the jury to think; she's sure of it, and she feels defiance rise wilfully in her. She would like to defend herself.

The judge looks at her blandly. 'Thank you,' he says. 'Miss Castelle, you are free to leave the courtroom.'

Rachel thinks about protesting, but almost as soon as she considers it, a wave of exhaustion hits her. She needs to get out of this place. Stiffly, she turns and steps down from the witness box, begins to move towards the exit. It's only now she is forcing herself to walk that she realizes how close she is to fainting, her head light and reeling with adrenaline.

In the brief moment before she reaches that door, she glances back, and her eyes meet Sadie's for the last time. There is no pretence now; Sadie is glaring at her with unadulterated hatred, her jaw set with fury, and as she sees her Rachel is gripped with guilt and sadness so great that she thinks she can hardly bear it. She wants to run over to her sister, throw her arms around her and bury her face in her cascade of dark blonde hair and say sorry. But she can't, and she knows she shouldn't want to.

She turns away and pushes the door open. As she walks out of the courtroom, she cannot help but notice the total silence that she leaves behind. It reminds her, she thinks, of the moment's tense anticipation in a crowded

269

theatre at the end of a performance, when it is not yet clear whether the audience will erupt into jeering cat-calls or rapturous applause.

They knock for her early the next morning, and the car takes her through central London, crawling through snarls of traffic. Familiar buildings rise up and then dip away. A phrase from the memorandum floats into her mind. She knows that under its terms she is forbidden from ever returning to London, if she wants to keep her police protection. This might, then, be the last time these streets ever imprint themselves upon her eyes. The car is moving past Trafalgar Square, and she watches as the fountains spray clear jets of water against the greying sky and drain to the ground below, foaming and scatter-ing in whirlpools. She has a moment of instinctive knowledge that this image will stay with her – that in years to come it will ambush her at odd times, a nervous twitch of the mind.

Out of London, the car gathers pace and speed, fly-ing along the motorways so fast that the motion and the unchanging lines of road lull her to sleep for a short while. When she wakes, Deborah turns round and offers her a drink, lemonade from a plastic bottle. She drains it, the sharp citrus liquid fizzing stickily on her tongue. Staring out of the window, she watches the miles fall away. Roads narrow and traffic thickens. A strange fidgety excitement is plucking at her skin, a feel-ing she remembers from childhood when, on holiday, she glimpsed the first sight of the sea.

Deborah speaks with her eyes on the road, not turning

round. 'You're clear on our itinerary for today, Rachel?' she says. 'The salon first, then the station, and then Tom will take you to the furnishings store to get stuff for the new house.'

The car is pulling up outside a small boxy building, unidentifiable as anything specific. The DC, Tom, speaks for the first time. 'Doesn't look like much, does it,' he says, 'but you'll come out a new woman.' He laughs, swinging the car into a space and screeching on the brakes. Deborah shoots him a sharp look, as if in reprimand.

'Come on, Rachel,' she says. 'Let's go in.'

Inside, the building is small and windowless, lit by artificial spotlights, the air circulating and re-circulating through the churning blades of fans. It does remind her, in a way, of a beauty salon. There is the water cooler in the corner, the mirrors lined up at intervals around the walls, the pile of magazines on a side table. The only difference is that she is the only customer. The chairs around her are empty, the radio in the corner silent.

The woman is brisk and efficient. Rachel wonders, vaguely, whether she herself is a policewoman, or simply some associate sworn to secrecy. She sits down in front of the nearest mirror and looks at her reflection.

'We'll dye first, and then give it a cut,' the woman is saying, running her hands possessively through Rachel's long blonde hair. 'And then coloured lenses and glasses, right?' She is speaking to Deborah, over Rachel's head.

She is led to a basin. She leans back as the water surges to her hairline and hands begin to work there, rinsing and cleansing, squeezing and untangling. The

271

dye is applied in stages, stiff sheets of silver foil bound all over the length of her head. She registers, somewhere in the back of her mind, that she does not know what colour it is, has not thought to ask, and now it seems too late. They offer her magazines, engage her in conversation as she waits, and she answers automatically, chatting about celebrities. When they lead her to the mirror again, she averts her gaze. She does not want to look yet, and when her eyes do slide for an instant towards her reflection, the queasy sense of unknowing that creeps over her at the sight of the woman with the long dark hair is enough to make her look quickly away.

The scissors are flashing around her face, the woman working fast and efficiently. Great swathes of hair falling on to her arms and lap, soft and sweeping, scattering like feathers. She feels a new lightness at the base of her neck, the whisper of cold air across her skin.

'Tip your head back for me and try not to blink.' The woman's fingers are pressing at the corners of her eyelids. The sensation is strange, but not painful, the slightest sense of a cool wetness which evaporates into nothing within moments. Next, the sharp pain of tweezers at her eyebrows, teasing and plucking, dragging hairs out at the root. 'There,' she says. 'Take a look.'

Rachel turns back to the mirror, and for a second, she simply stares. Looking back at her is a woman with dark hair cut into a sharp, neat bob, hanging above her shoulders. Her eyes are darker too. Tentatively, she puts a finger to her cheek. Incredibly, the new shaping of her eyebrows has changed the whole cast of her face, re-angling the structure of her bones. She takes the glasses the woman is handing her, and puts them on, but there is no change in her vision. Clear glass, she thinks. The glasses give her an air of alertness; they make her raise her chin and square her shoulders. She has the strangest sense that this woman both is and is not herself. Something is stirring inside her: the knowledge that this process is going further and cutting deeper than she imagined. This change is more than exterior – she can feel it spreading under the skin, uncomfortably mingling with everything she has always known. She is neither one person nor the other. She is weightless, no more than a concept. She does not know, yet, who she will turn out to be.

Five days later, they drive her to the house for the first time, down a long, straight street dotted with spindly trees just coming into bursts of white blossom. The houses are tall, terraced, with dark red brickwork and white-framed windows. A young couple are wandering down the street, pushing a buggy; she hears the thin, querulous squall of the baby winding through the air. The car pulls up outside number 58, and slowly she gets out, looking up at the house.

'Welcome home,' says the young DC with the chubby cheeks and the cherubic smile. His name is Drew, and he will be her primary point of contact. Deborah has dropped out of her life as quickly as she came, silently, and with no formal goodbye.

Inside, the living room is decked out with the items she chose in the furniture warehouse: the tall lamp balanced in the corner of the room, the squat burgundy sofa. For a moment, she has a strange impulse to laugh.

It is as if she is playing house, the way she and Sadie used to do as children – dragging things into their Wendy house and looking round proudly at what they had created. Back then, that was the end of the game. She remembers sitting in the little tented house and feeling at a loss. She feels the same sensation now – the same sense of having got to the end of a road.

'The bedroom's upstairs,' says Drew. 'Or up the stair, I should say.' She realizes, after a few seconds' delay, that he was making a joke; one large, wide step leads them to the bedroom door. She looks around at the bed pushed snugly into the corner crevice, the red and brown sheets she chose draped over its surface, and the terracotta curtains, neatly tied back to frame the window. Drew sees her looking and touches her briefly on the arm. 'Everything all right?' he says.

'Yes,' she says, 'it's fine, it's . . . great.' She has no idea what she is expected to say.

'Great,' repeats Drew briskly. 'I'll get back to the station, then. You know where your panic buttons are, and you've got the new phone, right? Any time you're concerned, you call.' As he reaches the front door he hesitates and stops. 'It takes a bit of getting used to,' he says. His face is kindly and understanding. 'But you'll get there.'

She nods and waves him off, closing the door quietly behind him, and stands in the sudden silence. She thinks, *my new home*. The words have an unreal ring. Uncertainly, she edges back into the kitchen, and fills the kettle with water. She stands listening to the flat, shrill whine as the water boils. Very faintly

274

she can hear the sound of someone strumming a guitar overhead.

It hits her then – the irrevocability of what has happened, and the absolute finality of the door that has closed behind her. She stares at the pretty little orange tiles that frame the kitchen worktops, and feels blind panic, desperate and childlike. Sharply, she breathes in. The kettle has boiled, but she does not move towards it. She cannot imagine sitting here and drinking a cup of tea. The thought is as strange as if she has broken in with the intention of burgling the place, and has decided instead to take a nap and tuck herself up in her victim's bed.

Abruptly, she turns and walks fast to the front door, grabbing her keys and slamming it shut behind her. Almost breaking into a run, she heads towards the centre of town, going on instinct. It is late afternoon, and the lights are starting to switch on in pubs and bars. She enters one at random. Music is spilling out from speakers and the bar is half full, scattered with laughing strangers. She looks from one face to the next, as if expecting to find one she recognizes. But there is no one.

Slowly, she walks over and orders a vodka and cranberry juice. She sips it. She can see herself reflected in the mirror behind the bar. Dark hair, dark eyes, pale-pink glossed mouth. The sight is still a novelty. The strange thought comes into her mind that she might be dead – that she has been given the freedom, in an afterlife, to roam these streets unseen.

A man is hovering at her elbow, smiling slyly at her. 'What's your name, love?' he says.

She turns to face him, smiling back. For the first time, she says out loud the new name they have given her. She hears how its syllables fall neatly, the new rhythmic cadence of her identity. For a moment, she half expects him to contradict her, expose her, but of course he's just nodding and accepting, passing on without comment. And as simply as that, it's done. Rachel Castelle ceases to exist.

PART FIVE

Alex

September 2017

THE NEXT DAY I go to the supermarket to buy some treats for Jade that I can take in next time I go. She must be getting cabin fever in the hospital. The last time I spoke to Doctor Rai, he told me that she might be discharged in a matter of days, but I haven't told her that yet. Part of me worries that she won't think it's entirely good news, and although I barely want to admit it, I'm not relishing the prospect myself. She deserves to come back to a safe haven, but how can I give her that, with no liveable home and the constant background of a threat that I don't even know how to measure?

At least Natalie has agreed to go to the police at last. We're going to call in at the station tomorrow, once I've had a chance to warn Jade that questioning may be coming her way and given her time to get used to the idea. We'll speak to them about the man in the house and the possibility that he may be someone who wants to do us harm. I can't say I'm expecting miracles from them; ever since I had that barbed conversation with the policeman outside the house who spoke to me about the burn pattern, I've heard nothing except for a terse confirmation that their investigation is ongoing. Reading between the lines, it's obvious that we're not their top priority. Still, the information that we've got for them should galvanize them – although it's frustrating not to be able to tell them more. I promised Natalie last night that I wouldn't make her go into detail about her own past, unless she has to.

Clearly, she doesn't trust the police. It's understandable, I suppose – from what she's told me, she all but sleepwalked into witness protection, placing her trust in the hands of others, and relinquishing that kind of control can be frightening. Not as frightening as your wife and daughter being caught in a house fire and hospitalized, though, I can't help thinking. Not quite as frightening as that.

I browse the confectionery aisle, thinking about Natalie and the intentness of her expression as she talked, the movements of her fingers as she traced invisible patterns in the air. The unwavering steadiness of her eyes, the perfect oval of her cheeks and the sad, resigned lines of her mouth. It was so dark by the time we finished talking that I could barely make these things out, and this darkness seemed somehow part of her – a side I hadn't seen before but which I know now is there, a long-suppressed weight with its own gravitational power. I had asked her if she regretted what she had done, and she had blinked once, considering. *No. I'd do the same again. You have to do what you feel is right.* For some reason I hadn't expected this certainty, but there were no cracks in this conviction, no room for doubt to seep through, and I found myself with nothing left to say.

I pay for the groceries, then go outside and perch on the wall, taking a picture of the bags of fizzy sweets and marshmallows that I've bought to indulge Jade's sweet tooth. I write, *Incoming delivery!! Next time I come x* – and send the message along with the photo. Within moments, she's texted back, also with an accompanying picture. It's a selfie – her thumb up, eyes widened crazily in only-half-joking glee. I smile; she's still very pale, the skin almost translucent, but I can see something of her old energy returning. As I gaze at the picture, I notice a new bunch of gaudily coloured flowers behind her on the table. She hasn't mentioned any other visitors, but maybe one of her schoolfriends dropped in. I text back: *Nice flowers. Who are they from?*

There's a brief hiatus, and then the reply appears. *Don't be mad, but they're from Jaxon . . . !!! He sent them this morning.* It's clear that she knows I won't be happy, but can't resist letting some of her excitement slip.

I frown down at the phone, my fingers moving quickly. *What? The boy you were messaging? You told me you would slow things down.*

Can't help it if he wants to send me flowerrrrrs . . . she replies smartly.

I know, but all the same. You've got to realize, Jade, he could be anyone.

I'm uncomfortably aware of the hypocrisy in what I'm saying. I can't help thinking of secretroom, and my interactions with Cali. Distasteful though the thought is, she too could be anyone: a precocious schoolgirl, a fat fifty-year-old trucker. But of course there's a world of difference between fantasy and reality, and for Jade this definitely seems to be moving into the latter.

There is a longer pause this time, and then her message pops up. *Dad you don't understand. He's not some weirdo off the Internet. I HAVE met him. Wanted to tell you yesterday but thought you might be even more mad. But maybe not . . .*

Wrong-footed, I hesitate a moment, and then I simply hit 1 on my speed dial and call her. This isn't a conversation for text.

She answers guardedly. 'Ye-es . . .'

'Hi, Jade.' I try and soften my voice, but I can't help a slight brusqueness creeping in. 'Now, what's all this about? You've met this boy? How? When?'

Jade sighs down the line, making it buzz. 'You remember a few weeks ago when the dishwasher broke? And we called someone out to fix it? Well, I came home from school and he was still there. We, um, got talking, I guess. And before he left, he kind of asked for my number.'

With difficulty, I do recall the dishwasher breaking down, and my asking Natalie to look up a local tradesman and call them out. 'Did Natalie know about this?' I ask.

'No,' Jade admits grudgingly. 'She was out of the room when he asked me. I mean, he's not going to do it in front of her, is he. Imagine if I said no.'

'How old is this boy?' I ask. 'I mean, to come out on his own on a job like that, he'd have to be . . .'

'Seventeen,' Jade supplies. 'He's on an apprenticeship.' She sounds inexplicably proud, as if being on a learning curve to fix other people's broken-down white goods is some kind of badge of honour, but I bite back the social snobbery, which after all isn't the point.

'That's three years older than you,' I point out. 'It might not sound like much, but at your age, it's a lot . . . There are things he might be into, or might want, which you, well . . .'

'Dad,' says Jade, embarrassment creeping into her tone. 'Look, he's, um, respectful, all right? I told him my age and he was happy to just message for a while, get to know each other, before meeting up. So that's what we've been doing. Honestly, it's no big deal. Sophie's had a boyfriend for four months, I've mentioned him to you loads of times, and you don't care about that.'

'Well, it isn't my job to care about that,' I respond automatically, but nonetheless something in her words has struck home. 'Look, I'll be in to see you a bit later,' I say to buy myself time. 'We can talk more then.'

'OK,' Jade says meekly. 'Love you.'

'Love you too,' I say, and then I hang up. Does the fact that Jade has met this boy make it better, or worse? I'm not sure. And is she right in what she's intimating, that under more normal circumstances I wouldn't be so up in arms over it? It's true that she's spoken to me about friends' boyfriends lately, more than once, and I've thought little of it. I remember myself at fourteen – a

283

typical teenager, all mouth and no trousers, embarking on romances that were ultimately pretty tame, no matter what I liked to tell my friends. Jade is growing up, and this is a natural part of that.

The more I consider it, the more I can't help suspecting that my judgement is off at the moment. It's hardly surprising if I'm paranoid, but the hardest thing is that I have no idea just how much *is* paranoia. I have no way of judging the real level of any threat to us. I can feel frustration rising in me, tightening my throat. This isn't sustainable – I can't carry on in this limbo, walking in the dark, waiting for something to happen because I know so little about what's going on around me. I think again about talking to the police; perhaps it will help, but I still can't muster up much faith in their ability or willingness to act fast.

I can't stop thinking about the man in the house. I don't know his name, but I do have one other fact at my fingertips: the location of the club. From what I've read online, it sounds as if it's changed both hands and image since those days, but nonetheless, it's possible that there may still be people around the area who remember Kaspar and his associates.

I look up Blackout again and find that it's a bar as well as a club, and that it's open from five p.m. I could go up there this afternoon, see what I can find. I might not have got far with Kaspar himself, but if I can track down this guy and talk to him man to man, convince him that Natalie and I just want to live our lives without trouble, then maybe it could help. Whatever's going on here, it's been sparked by ancient history, a pointless exercise in raking over old ground. This might be about revenge, but I'm willing to bet that like most crimes, it's just as much about boredom, frustration, lack of choices. I can't help thinking that there must be some way it can be resolved.

That afternoon I tell Natalie that I'm going into town and that I'll be meeting up with Gav from the office later, and she doesn't question it. Now that we're confined to a claustrophobic hotel room, there's a tacit understanding that we need more space.

'Late one, do you think?' she asks as I kiss her goodbye.

'Maybe. Gav's broken up with his latest girlfriend,' I say. 'Might want to drown his sorrows, you know, or come up with a game plan for how to get her back . . .'

'Tell him to try walking on two legs.' Natalie's always been of the opinion that Gav is a bit of a Neanderthal, but this sort of banter has been pretty scarce of late, and I realize that I miss it.

The train to London is delayed on the approach to Victoria and I end up staring out of a grimy window at grotty industrial buildings. Already on edge, when my phone buzzes in my pocket it makes me start. I pull it out and see that another message from SRUK has arrived. Remembering that last conversation with Cali, and the strange note her words sounded – *I want to know everything* – I'm tempted to delete it without reading, but something makes me open it.

Sorry about last time, the message says. *I shouldn't have asked about your wife.*

285

I hit reply, seeing that the green dot beside her name is already lit. *Don't worry about it. To be honest, I'm just not sure why you're back in touch at all.*

The reply is swift. *I've been thinking about you, that's all. Wondering about you. You're not afraid of me are you, Alex?*

As soon as I see the line of text I know that something's wrong, even if it takes me a few seconds to put my finger on it. It's not just the oddness of her question. When I realize, it makes my heart pound, though whether with panic or adrenaline I'm not sure.

How do you know my name?

I stare at the screen, waiting. Secretroom is anonymous. That's the whole point. There's nothing that could possibly link me to this locked-down profile on an under-the-radar site. At last I see the line of dots start to move, indicating she's typing a new message.

I've known who you are for a while.

How?! Why? I type back. *What's going on here?*

Look, don't worry. I was curious, that's all. We live close, you know. I'm only a few miles outside Brighton. I heard about what happened. About the fire. I was worried about you.

I exhale, wondering where to start with all this. It's increasingly starting to sound like this woman is some kind of obsessed stalker, which I could really do without. *Well, you can stop worrying,* I type back. *I can look after myself. I'm sorry, but I find this unsettling, and I don't want to be in contact anymore.*

She fires back quickly. *Has something else happened?*

I frown, and I've replied without quite considering

286

what I actually want to say. *A lot of things are happening right now.*

A long pause this time. I have no idea if what I am saying is hitting home with Cali, or whether she thinks this is all just part of some weird erotic game. I'm fidgety and restless, gnawing at the side of my thumbnail, and I'm thinking about logging off and blocking her, just drawing a line under it. But then I see that she's typing a new message.

When it appears, it knocks the breath briefly from my body.

She's told you, hasn't she?

I stare at that line of text for a few seconds. I try and think logically and fast to find the perfect reply, but before I can, the green light next to her username greys out. She's gone.

'Shit,' I say aloud, tapping uselessly at the keypad. *Come back.* But the automatic response just flashes: *Cali will receive your message when she is next online.*

Those five little words go round in my head all the way on the Tube ride to Camden Town. I still don't understand what she meant, but it feels significant, and it makes me oddly uneasy. It's tempting to dwell on it further, but I force myself to put it to the back of my mind. I have other things to concentrate on right now.

I get off the Tube and set out towards Blackout. It's been over a decade since I've been to a place like this. I don't even know if I'm wearing the right clothes – I've played it safe with a grey T-shirt and dark jeans, but for all I know this is the kind of environment where you won't be let in unless you're wearing some kind of ridiculous fluorescent trance get-up. I should have checked the dress code. For a moment I entertain the stupid but attractive thought that perhaps I should just turn around and go back to Brighton, but in the next instant, I see the club.

It's a tall dark building, the word BLACKOUT flashing relentlessly in bright neon lettering. There are a few people filtering through the doors already; mostly studenty types in jeans and leather jackets. It doesn't seem like a particularly niche crowd, but I still feel out of place. The door is half open, and as I peer past the hulking doorman I think about my wife being inside these walls, a long time ago . . . A young woman with a different name and a different life. It's only a trick of the light, but for an instant I think I can see her, moving swiftly and fluidly across the floor, her shoulders bare and her long hair falling down her back, elusive as a ghost.

I linger for a moment; then, making a decision, I stride up to the doorman.

'Go on in, mate,' the doorman says in a monotone. He's a shortish, thickset man in his forties with a shaved head and shoulders twice their natural size, squeezed into an ill-fitting suit.

'I'm looking for someone,' I say. 'I don't know if he's in there or not.'

'Go on in,' the doorman repeats with exaggerated patience, 'and then you can find out.'

I glance through the doors again. I could do as he suggests, but now that we're talking, I think it's worth pushing my luck; this man looks to be in his early forties at least, and pretty at home here. 'Look, you might be able to help me. Have you been around here for a while? Know a lot of people in the area? Did you know this place back when it was Kaspar's?'

Up until this point the doorman has been regarding me coolly and with minimal interest, but when I say Kaspar's name he folds his arms and I see something change in his posture, as if he's standing to attention. I register the power this name has, even after all this time, and a quick shudder passes down the length of my spine.

'Who's asking?' he says.

'I'm not looking for any trouble,' I say. 'I'm just trying to look after my family.' The man is wearing a thick gold wedding band, and I let my gaze drop to it for an instant before looking him full in the face again. 'This guy I'm looking for, he's quite—' I'm going to say short, but I stop myself. 'He's about your height, I think. Blond, cropped hair. Muscular. He's got an unusual sort of face, kind of . . . doughy. You know? He was a friend of Kaspar's. Do you know who I'm talking about?'

His face gives nothing away. He regards me steadily for a few seconds, but seems to reach some kind of internal decision, and I see the shutters go up. 'Can't help you.'

This feels like a closed circle, but I can't help pressing the point; something tells me that he's recognized my description. 'Please. Trust me, it's important.'

The doorman regards me thoughtfully, then turns

his attention to a few more gathering punters briefly, ushering them through into the dark mouth of the bar. He nods at his young associate by the cloakroom, beckoning him forward. 'Cover me for five minutes.' Without checking to see if I'm following, he strides off down the road. I do follow, albeit cautiously. I have no idea where he's taking me, but to my surprise we come to a halt outside an all-night supermarket. He stands in front of the fluorescent frontage, arms folded, looking at me impassively.

'What . . .' I begin, and then my gaze strays to the left of where he's standing and I see the ATM. 'OK. I see. How much?'

'Two hundred.' There's a challenge in his tone and I suspect he's expecting negotiation. I think about it, but in the end I decide it's pointless. I may as well show him how important this information is to me.

Under his watchful eye, I take out my card and withdraw the cash. I hold the wedge of notes tightly in my hand. 'Well?'

The man puts out his hand in silence. The tension between us stretches. For a moment, that ever-present instinct kicks in; if this turned nasty, could I win? I'm taller, but he's broader, and there's a dull glint in his eye, that kind of brute primal stupidity that can be dangerous. Slowly, I uncurl my fingers and pass him the notes.

'Dominic Westwood,' he says flatly. 'You'll find him in one of the pubs down Gordon Street. Who told you this?'

Wrong-footed, I don't immediately catch what he means. 'What?'

'Who told you this?' he repeats, this time with more menace.

Finally I get it. 'Not you.'

'Is the right answer, rich boy.' Without a backward glance, the doorman turns and walks off, stuffing his hands in his pockets and walking with a rolling gait that speaks of cocky satisfaction.

Gordon Street turns out to be long and winding, crammed full of pubs and bars, and I curse myself for not trying to get a bit more information for my money. I don't even know exactly what this man looks like. It's already starting to feel like a wild goose chase, but nonetheless I make a start. I quickly develop a system: work my way clockwise around the room, keeping my eyes open for any man who even vaguely fits the description – of whom there are surprisingly few – then stay close by until I either satisfy myself that he doesn't match it closely enough or hear him called by name, and then move on.

I've already combed through six or seven pubs this way before I really start thinking about what I'm doing. I'd planned to be upfront with this man – Dominic – lay my cards on the table and see how he responded. But I'm having second thoughts about the wisdom of this strategy; perhaps it would be better to engage him in conversation somehow, find out a bit more about him and where he lives or works now, so that I can simply take the information back to the police and ask them to investigate him. The more I think about it, the more sensible this seems.

The eighth pub on the street is the King and Coaches,

a down-at-heel, black-fronted building with a peeling gold sign, which is half empty. A few groups of men sit huddled around pints in the dim lamplight, several of them scowling across at the door with brief, animal suspicion as I push it open. The change in atmosphere is palpable; most of the bars I've been in so far have been packed with amiably drunk revellers, but this doesn't feel like the kind of place you come to celebrate. There's an odd, hushed quality to the stale air, and I feel the hairs rise on my arms in prickly discomfort. This is the place. I've never been one for premonitions, but I know it at once, and when I see the man sitting alone at the bar, his back turned to me, his face bounced back at me from the mirror on the far wall, I feel no surprise.

He's about my age, maybe early forties, with thickset shoulders under a khaki bomber jacket, and his hair is cropped close to his skull, so fair that it looks almost white. He's nursing a pint, but not drinking, his hands clamped around the glass as he stares into space. I see what Jade meant now about his features; he's not ugly, but there's something rough and slightly unfinished about his face, as if it's been inexpertly sculpted. I stand silently for a moment, fighting the rush of anger. Breathing deeply, I force myself to step forward calmly. I'll order a drink at the bar and stand next to him, then start a conversation – ask if he's got the football scores maybe, then take it from there.

But I don't get the chance. As I approach the bar, he glances up idly and his eyes meet mine. The change in his expression is instant – defensiveness and shock, and something else besides, something strangely like fear.

Abruptly, he pushes his stool back and stands up, abandoning his pint and walking fast towards the exit, head down.

It happens so quickly that it takes a few seconds for me to catch up. I swing round, staring after him. He's clearly recognized me, and of course I should have realized this was a possibility; he's bound to have seen me, if he's been hanging around watching Natalie and Jade. But somehow his reaction still doesn't seem quite right; everything I know tells me that this man is capable of acting brutally and without compunction, but I can't match that to the brittle edge of fear in his eyes, the speed with which he's retreating.

'Dominic!' I call, elbowing my way after him. He's already pushed his way out of the entrance, pushing the heavy door back with such force that it almost slams into my face. I catch up with him on the street, but he's looking straight ahead, his face set, as if he's trying to pretend I'm not there. 'Dominic,' I say again, and am rewarded by the slight twitch of his expression, the panic that I know his name.

'Fuck off,' he says out of the side of his mouth, almost under his breath.

'You know who I am, don't you?' I ask. 'I'm Jade's father. The girl you put in hospital.'

He shoots me a look, feigning incomprehension. 'I've done nothing.' He's powering down the road, his eyes flicking from side to side looking for an escape route.

I reach out and grab the sleeve of his jacket, but he shakes me off instantly and carries on walking. 'You know exactly what I'm talking about. I know who you are, and I know what you're doing. So you'd better fucking watch your back.' Dimly, I'm aware I've deviated from my script. There's nothing subtle or investigative about this, but the fury has taken over, blazing redly through me and leaving no space for anything else.

'Leave me out of it,' he says. He's lengthening his stride and I have to quicken my pace to keep up with him, my breath coming in hard, short gulps. 'I've done nothing,' he repeats. 'I'm out. I'm out.' He bites out the words one by one.

'Out of what?' I challenge. 'So you admit there's something to be out of. What would Kas think, if he could hear you now?'

He looks me full in the face for an instant then, his brow furrowed deeply in a frown, the colour burning hectically on his cheekbones. He shakes his head in silence, and then without warning he's broken into a full run, lashing out with one arm as he does so to knock me to the side and slam me against the wall. It's a swift jab that only winds me for a few seconds, but it's enough; by the time I've recovered and started to run after him, he's flagged down a cab that's rounding the corner of the street and dived into the back, slamming the door after him as it speeds off.

The train journey back to Brighton does nothing to calm my nerves. I can't stop going over the few seconds I spent in Dominic's presence, cursing myself for being unable to keep calm. I'm overtaken by the same sense of intense frustration that I felt after my meeting

294

with Kaspar – no matter what I do, I can't seem to get any closer to these people or understand why they've decided to threaten my family, after all these years. From what Natalie's told me, they weren't happy with the way she spoke out against Kaspar at the trial, but why have they bided their time for so long? Can it simply be that they've waited until they think she's happy and settled before they strike? My thoughts circle each other uselessly, doing nothing to stem my frustration. I'm tired of being kept at arm's length. I need someone who's on my side.

As soon as the thought pops into my head, I remember Cali. Those last few words she wrote to me, before she disappeared. *She's told you, hasn't she?* Is it possible that she could have meant Natalie, and that she knows something about my wife's past? It's clear that this woman isn't quite the stranger I thought she was – she knows my name, knows about the fire. She's repeatedly asked if I'm OK, said that she's worried about me. I need to get in touch with her again and get some straight answers.

As soon as I'm off the train at Brighton I walk to a pub near the seafront, order a drink and tuck myself into a quiet table in the corner. I use my mobile to log on to secretroom, but for the first time Cali isn't online. It seems significant, even though logically I know there's no reason why she should be there waiting time after time. I refresh the page repeatedly, jabbing compulsively at the screen, but her username stays obstinately grey and absent. It seems I've scared her off. And yet I said so little – so little that it only reinforces my belief that she already knows more about me, and my family, than she has ever let on before.

It's almost half an hour before the icon leaps to life, shining out greenly from the screen. She's there. Instantly, I type a message. **Don't go.**

A beat, and she replies. *I've only just arrived.*

I've been intending to ask her what she meant last time before she logged off, but all at once it hits me that just because I want her to be on my side, it doesn't mean it's true. I have no idea what her agenda is here. So instead I decide to take a different tack.

I spoke to someone recently, I type. **Someone you might know, or might have known once.**

The reply comes back immediately. *Who?*

I hesitate, not wanting to be too explicit. After a few moments, I type: **KK.**

She doesn't reply. I half expect her to exit the conversation at once, but she's still there, just silent, in stasis. I try and picture this woman, wherever she is, staring at her own screen. I try to imagine the expression on her face.

When it seems she isn't going to say anything, I try again. **Do you know who I mean?**

This time the pause is shorter. *Yes.*

Look, I can't get anywhere with these people, I type. **You obviously know something about me and my family. I just want to understand what's happening. I don't want any trouble.**

Yes, she replies. *I can imagine. But sometimes trouble just finds you.*

I need to keep them safe, I type. **My daughter, and my wife. You understand?**

296

Your wife doesn't need keeping safe. The reply is vicious in its swiftness. I frown, trying to understand. I see the dots rolling across the bottom of the screen again for more than half a minute, then freeze, as if she's reading back what she's written. A few seconds later the message appears.

I need to speak to you, she's written. *I don't know how much you know, or what she's told you. It may not be accurate. I know how strange this must seem to you, but it's important that you hear what I have to say. Tell me where you are, and I'll come and meet you right now.*

Who are you?? I drain my drink in a fierce gulp that makes my eyes smart, realizing that I'm angry. On and off, this woman has been in my life for well over a year.

Just tell me where you are, she replies.

I think about arguing, but I know I run the risk of scaring her off. And in any case, I can't see any other way forward now. ***I'm in the Golden Bell***, I type. ***Leonard Street, just up from the seafront. Do you know it?***

The answer comes back quick and sure. *I'll find you.*

Time passes and although I look up sharply every time anyone enters the bar, no one seems to even glance in my direction. I go to the bar and ask for a pint of water, then drain it back at my seat. I don't want to feel drunk for this, but my head still swims lightly. I realize that I haven't eaten anything all day and think about ordering some food, but just as I'm reaching for the menu I happen to glance up again, and I see her.

297

She's standing in the doorway, scanning the opposite side of the bar. It's probably only a few seconds before she turns, but each one feels stretched and liquefied, turning these brief moments into a strange elongated limbo. I recognize her instantly, from the photograph that's still in my coat pocket.

Her cheekbones are a little softer than Natalie's, her eyes slightly more slanted. She's wearing a pale pink lipstick that I can't imagine Natalie choosing and her hair is pinned up on top of her head instead of flowing loose over her shoulders. But there's something in the curve of her lips and the tilt of her nose, something in the way she moves her hand to her face and brushes a falling tendril of hair back behind her ear. The two of them are cut from the same cloth.

She turns her head and her eyes meet mine. She blinks once, twice, seeing the shock in my gaze. Then she gathers herself together and walks slowly over to the table, slipping into the seat opposite mine.

'Hello,' she says. Her voice is softer than I'd imagined, a little more cultured and smooth.

'Hello,' I echo. For an insane moment, I find the corners of my mouth twitching; I want to burst into laughter. One of our early interchanges swims into my head – when she told me that she'd always fantasized about a stranger taking her hand on the street and pulling her aside, hustling her down a dark passageway and fucking her up against a wall, his hand over her mouth, without a word exchanged. I had been that man, for a few minutes. *I've never told anyone that*, she had typed afterwards, and I had believed her.

'You're her sister,' I say, needing it to be said aloud, and she nods.

'Yes.' We stare at each other, for longer than would feel natural under other circumstances. 'Do I look like her?' she asks at last. 'I haven't seen her for so long, you know.'

'In a way,' I say truthfully. 'Not completely. But there's something there.'

She nods, looking neutral. I don't know what answer she wanted. She glances away for a moment, then returns her gaze to mine. There's something unsettlingly intense about her dark-lashed eyes and their scrutiny. 'I should apologize,' she says. 'I know that what I've done to you is wrong.'

'You mean . . .' I begin carefully. The sphere of what she might be referring to is so wide that I wouldn't like to second-guess.

'Approaching you in the first place,' she says, 'on the website. It wasn't particularly hard to do, but that doesn't mean it was right.'

'I don't understand,' I say. 'How did you even know I was on the site? How did you know my username?' With a pinch of embarrassment, I think of my profile on secretroom; the unashamed arrogance of the name I'd chosen, Alpha1. That was the kind of thing women wanted there.

'I knew where you worked,' she says, 'where you lived. These things are easy to find out. A couple of times I – engineered things so that I was where you were likely to be, at the same sort of time. It wasn't stalking. I was curious, that's all. And one time – this was a long time ago

299

now – you were in a café, and you went to the toilet, and you left— . . .'

'My laptop on the table,' I finish, unable to keep the incredulity from my tone. I'd assumed that the laptop had been taken by a teenage chancer.

'That's right,' she says, eyes downcast. 'I'm sorry. It's not hard to get past security settings, you know, not if you know what you're doing, or know someone who does. And the site was there, in your history. The laptop was still logged in to your email, so I did a search for the site and I found your username. It seemed like the best way of – connecting with you, anonymously.' She looks at me for a brief instant, then away. There's something intensely awkward in her tone. The woman I've been talking to on secretroom is shameless, brazen even, but that doesn't fit at all with the person sitting opposite me. In fact, it doesn't fit with the picture Natalie has painted of Sadie, either – but this picture is almost two decades out of date. Something's changed her, radically. Just like my wife, she's become someone else.

'But why did you do it?' I ask. 'Why "connect with me", as you put it, at all?'

She draws in a long breath, leaning back in her seat. The candlelight radiating from the little glass jar on the table between us flickers up and flows in shadows round the mouldings of her face, and I see that similarity leaping to life again. 'I had to see if you were happy with her,' she says. 'I couldn't think how else to test it. And after we started . . . Well, I didn't think you were. Or you wouldn't have – continued to engage with me.'

'I stopped it,' I say uncomfortably. 'In the end. It didn't mean anything.' These are not words you would normally say to a woman so bluntly, with no explanation or apology, but I can see she doesn't mind. I realize something as I look at her, something which floods me with guilty relief. This woman is attractive – striking, even. When I think of the things we've talked about and match them up with the face and body in front of me, I do feel an automatic twinge of desire. But the sight of her doesn't captivate me the way that first sight of Natalie did. If I met the two of them together as strangers, it's my wife that I would want to talk to; she's the one that I would want to take home.

'Yes,' she nods. 'And I'd accepted that. Started to think that I'd been wrong, and that perhaps you and her were happy. I stepped back. But then I found out about the fire. I contacted you again, because it – it worried me.'

There's something strange in the words she's chosen; they're understated, and yet I can't understand exactly what it is that might have worried her. 'Do you know who was responsible?' I ask carefully. Long overdue, I realize who it is I'm talking to here: not just Natalie's sister, but a woman who was involved with a dangerous man, involved in murder.

'I have a good idea,' she says, 'but I'm not sure why.'

We could go on like this all night, I think, circling each other delicately, testing the ground. I need to cut to the chase. 'Look,' I say, 'I never would have agreed to meet up with you under normal circumstances, but things are getting out of hand. If you're trying to sabotage

301

our lives, I need to know about it and I need to understand why.'

'Sabotage,' she repeats. 'I wouldn't put it like that.'
Incredibly, she sounds faintly offended. 'Like I said, I
just needed to know that you were happy. If I'd thought
you were, I would have left you alone. I *did* leave you
alone, when you stopped messaging me.'

'We are happy,' I say firmly. For some reason, saying
this out loud gives me an odd sensation, as if I'm swaying on the edge of a dark cliff, not quite knowing when
or if I'll fall.

'I believe that now, more than I did before,' she says.
'If she's told you about the past, and you still want to be
with her, then you must love her.'

'She can't help what happened to her,' I say sharply.
'She was forced into a situation which was hardly her
fault.' I see her opening her mouth to contradict me, but I
plough on. 'And besides,' I continue, 'I'm not sure what
our relationship has to do with you in any case.'

She shrugs miserably. 'Nothing, of course. But all the
same, it felt wrong not to check.'

Impatience flares up inside me; I don't understand
this conversation. I reach for my glass, but it's empty.
'For fuck's sake,' I find myself saying, louder than I had
intended. 'What is this? Why the hell would you think
we needed checking up on?'

'Just the habit of a lifetime, I suppose,' she fires back,
'and by the sound of what you told me earlier you're well
aware that something isn't right. Why else would you
have gone to see Kas?' Her voice drops on the last word,
and I notice the way her eyes flick quickly, reflexively,

around the room, as if she's checking that no one has heard.

'Because this situation is fucking frightening,' I say. 'Because someone set our house on fire. And if what my wife thinks is right, then you know all of this already, you're involved in the whole damn thing.'

She stares at me, her pink lips slightly parted, a frown creasing her brows. Either she is a brilliant actress, or she is genuinely confused. 'I have no idea what you're talking about,' she says. 'Why would I be involved?'

'You're lying to me,' I snap. But even as I speak I realize that I'm not sure. There's something so straightforward about her gaze, and that frightens me. 'I'm not here to play games,' I say. 'I love Natalie, and I want to protect her. That's all.'

There is a pause, and a sad little smile appears at the corners of her lips. 'It sounds so odd,' she says, 'you calling her that.'

'I can't think of her as anything else.' I don't want to get derailed, but it's something that's played on my mind too, ever since she first sat huddled on those rocks by the seafront and told me that other name. 'Rachel doesn't suit her.'

At first I don't understand what I've said, or why it provokes the reaction that it does. She draws in her breath sharply. I see her eyes move from side to side, as if she's weighing things up, fitting together the pieces of a mental jigsaw. 'I see,' she says at last.

'What?' I ask roughly. I don't like the tone of her voice, or the sudden paleness of her face, the gravity of her expression.

She leans forward, and with a shock I realize that she's reaching for my hand across the table. She takes it in her own cool fingers, the tips pressing insistently into my palm. 'You don't understand,' she says. 'She's lying to you. She's not who you think she is. The person you're talking about is me. *I'm* Rachel.'

PART SIX

Sadie

September 2017

AFTER ALEX HAS LEFT to meet Gavin, I can't settle. I prowl back and forth in the tiny hotel room, trying to get rid of this restlessness. I go to the bathroom and stare at myself in the little strip-lit mirror above the basin. That's one habit I've hung on to. I still like losing myself in the depths of my own eyes, still find it calming and serene. But this time it doesn't quite do the trick. I try a little longer, and then I give up, pulling on my coat and hurrying down to the hotel lobby. Nervous energy is fizzing through me like sherbet. I can already see a taxi lingering on the road outside. It's time.

I can't stop thinking about that little moment in the hospital earlier with Jade, when I said all that stuff about the fire and how it should have bonded us, brought us together. I'm not even sure why it came out, but I do know that in that moment I really wanted her to agree, maybe to squeeze my hand or even to throw her arms around my neck, saying that she understood what I meant and that things would be different between us from now on. That we'd be closer, tighter. That she valued me, loved me, never wanted to let me go. Stupid. After all, it's not like I feel that way about her. But if she'd said it, and if I'd really believed it, it would have made things so much easier. I wouldn't need to do what I have to do now. I could kick back, relax and enjoy my life. I've waited years to be where I want to be: free, stable and secure, with a man who loves me and who'll never leave me. I'm so nearly there, but not quite. The frustration is tangible, prickling on my skin.

For the past few days, I haven't felt like myself, whoever that is. The fire dulled my senses a little, maybe. It was easier not to think too much about the future, or the past come to that, and to just exist. It's not sustainable, though, and now that I'm here in the taxi, cold air rushing in through the window and blowing through my hair, it feels like I'm slowly returning to my own body. My thoughts are sharper, clearer. I can't block out the memories that are flooding me, kick-started perhaps by what Alex told me. I still can't get my head around him and Kas together; talking to each other, looking into each other's eyes. I feel about it the way you'd feel about walking into a room and finding someone there who you'd only ever seen in a dream. There's something nightmarish about it – the slip between reality and fantasy, between the present and the past.

I still find Kas in my head sometimes, and I haven't tried too hard to get him out, because he lives there. He isn't going away. There are time-slips even now when I wake up half dreaming and humming with desire, half of me completely lost in those early days when I first knew him. That very first time I saw him striding down the street from the club. I'd never been in love before, and it hit me so hard I could barely breathe. I've never forgotten how it felt – falling into his world, falling into him. The way the slightest look or touch could electrify me, the kick I got from those brief moments of connection that was better than any drug I'd ever taken. An obsession, an addiction. Nothing else mattered. I knew from the start that he could pull me under and I wanted to go with him.

I haven't forgotten the fear that went along with that desire either. I was confused and overwhelmed and terrified – yes, of him sometimes, as well as of the situation I was in. But somehow it wasn't enough to make me get out. I wondered for a long time if there was something wrong with me. It isn't natural not to mind about whether people live or die. Life is precious, and everyone has the right to exist. I can believe that, on a conceptual level, but I always struggled to *feel* it. George Hart, Felix Santos. They were nothing to me, not part of my life. Not everyone could say the same, of course. I remember seeing Felix's wife in the courtroom, her face pale and haggard, her eyes like black holes. It triggered something in me, the sight of her; the start of a remorse, a guilt that felt like it was so deep and fathomless that I couldn't let myself fall into it. I had to drag myself out in order to survive. And once you've managed to do that, there isn't really any going back.

It was easier with Melanie. The adrenaline and the alcohol and the conviction that she was wrong for Kas and that she was the only thing standing in our way. Trailing her through the streets and stepping out on to that platform, watching the way her forehead creased as she took me in, the little lines at the corners of her eyes. I remember her lipstick had smudged slightly, making a little dark red stain at the edge of her mouth. I was nineteen and I felt invincible, and in the end it just happened. It only took a second, that push. Everyone's done things they don't think through. You don't think it through, you just do it, and then suddenly you've killed someone. You're a murderer.

I was terrified in those first few minutes after it happened, so terrified that I lost sight of everything. It was like being shut in a long, dark tunnel, zooming down towards some point I couldn't even see, like I was suffocating and I couldn't do anything to stop it. When you feel like that, you do and say things that you're likely to regret, and I made a big mistake. I opened my mouth and those weak little words spilled out, and my sister gathered them up eagerly and deposited them at the feet of the police like they were a load of the gold medals she used to win at school sports day. It's hard to imagine, but I'm not sure I ever really understood who she was. For years she'd made out that she only cared about other people and that she martyred herself for them – for me, in particular. But when it came down to it, there were other things she cared about more. She cared more about some abstract idea of 'justice', more about principles than people. It makes no sense to me. If you love someone, surely you'd do anything for them. Lie for them, kill for them, step outside your whole belief system for them. That's the way it was for me, and the way it's always been.

I stayed true to that, with Kas. I showed him my loyalty. I stuck to my guns and I lied my arse off for him, all through the trial, even though I soon knew that it wouldn't work and there was no way we were going to get off. *Especially* then; there was nothing to lose, and everything to prove. And in the end I used up so much emotion on him – missing him, wanting him, convincing myself that one day we'd be together – that there was nothing left over. I was empty inside, scraped out. When I woke up doubled over in pain and knowing that I'd lost the baby, less than a week before the trial started, I felt nothing. When I walked into the courtroom and saw Rachel standing there at the witness box, her shiny blonde hair tied up all nicely and her pretty, soft lips uttering her traitorous words, I felt nothing. When the judge finally read the sentence and I heard that I'd been given fifteen years and that I was going to spend my twenties inside the locked walls of a prison, I felt nothing. I felt nothing. I felt nothing.

I don't dwell on those years. I'd thought that I'd be surrounded by psychos and have to sleep with one eye open, but in reality, I got pretty much left alone. If you've killed someone, or even been an accessory to murder, as I was convicted of, then you get a certain respect. It's a cliché but the boredom was the worst part, the endless days spent sitting around in the cell or trying to make conversation with twitching weirdos in the communal hours. I thought about Kas all the time.

Most of all, those few minutes in the basement. In a way I was glad that we'd only had sex that one time. It made it special. Unique. But in another way it felt as if I'd been staggering around in the desert for days with nothing to drink, and then someone had offered me a bottle of ice-cold water and snatched it away after the first sip.

I knew he would probably never get out. Two life sentences, and I'd heard on the grapevine that he was still regularly causing trouble, making it even less likely that he'd get an early release. There was a woman inside with me whose husband had a brother in Belmarsh he used to visit, and when I found out I always asked her to ask about Kas. I used to seize on these little titbits hungrily: that he'd started a fight in the dining hall and been on twenty-four-hour confinement for days, that he spent the exercise hour in a corner of the room by himself lifting weights and attacking punchbags with the kind of quiet, furious focus that quickly got him a nasty reputation. Not the kind of thing most women would want to hear about their lover, but they made me feel better. I suppose they were just proof he was alive.

But after a while the titbits got less frequent, and as the years went on I felt things shifting. It wasn't that I'd forgotten him – more that as my release date got closer and I had the exit gate in my sights, all I could think about was starting a new life. It came more and more sharply into focus, blurring everything else out. And like I said, I knew there was no chance that he would be there with me. So I put him in a different place in my head. Somewhere that wouldn't stop me starting again.

People talk about change all the time, as if it were easy. Changing their minds, changing their image, changing their opinions. Anyone can shift the dial a bit this way or that, but not many people can do what I've done. Real change is transformation. Reinvention. I had to shed my skin like a snake. And they were exhilarating, those first few months in the outside world. I dyed my hair, got a new look, changed my name. There was no particular rationale behind choosing Natalie. I just thought it sounded sort of perky and positive, like I was someone whose life had never felt a breath of trouble. I started working in a clothes store, earning enough to rent a room in a corner of south London.

I built up my life. I had a place to live, a semi-regular job and a few friends, but no one got past my force field. I invented a past, but if they ever asked about anything that touched too close to the bone, I put up a wall. A couple of my friends at the clothes store used to call me the Ice Queen – it was affectionate, but like most jokes it had a hard edge of truth. Occasionally I'd tell them about a man I'd met at the weekend, the way I'd invited him back to my place, used him for sex and then turfed him out before dawn. That was one area where I didn't need to invent anything. It was as easy as it had always been to find a man to spend a few hours with. I always insisted on having all the lights off, because it was only then, in the pitch black, that I let myself slide back into the person I had been before. They would stumble out bewildered into the street afterwards, those men, not knowing what had hit them. Afterwards they would text and call and sometimes send flowers, but I never replied.

My friends used to love those stories. They hung on every word, their eyes wide and round, marvelling at this capacity for detachment. It was something they couldn't imagine, these women whose instinct when they found a decent-looking man who didn't seem to be a psychopath was to dig their claws in and not let go. *I wish I could be like you, Natalie*, they used to sigh. *I wish I could feel like I didn't need a man*. Every time, I would smile enigmatically and say something flippant. They didn't know that I'd used up all my need early on; I'd poured it all into Kas and there wasn't a drop left over. At least, that's what I thought. And then I met Alex.

I'd gone to Brighton for the weekend on impulse, because I wanted to and because I could. I was waiting for my drink at the bar, and then he was there as if he'd popped out of a dream, intercepting the barman's hand to take the drink and swiftly giving it to me himself. *I'll buy you the next one. What's your name?* For a moment, I almost said Sadie, and that was strange because I hadn't thought of myself as that for a long time. When I analysed it afterwards, I realized that it was because when I first saw him I got it – that animal kick of lust that I hadn't felt since Kas.

I wanted him at once, not just because he was good-looking, although he was, with dark hair and eyes and the kind of body you don't get by accident. It was more the way he held himself, the self-assurance that stopped him from stuttering and blushing at me the way so many other men did. It was instant and powerful, this leap of interest. But a few seconds later I saw the wedding ring. I'd learned that lesson. A wife was an obstacle

314

I didn't want to fight to get past. If he was happy with her, he'd never really give himself to you. If he wasn't, he'd still feel tied to her somehow, the way Kas had. Either way, a wife made it too easy for a man to keep you at arm's length. Never again. So I told him that I wasn't interested, and that's when he grabbed my arm and made me look at him. *You don't understand ... My wife died years ago.*

It was inappropriate but I couldn't help smiling, because it felt like fate, it was perfect. It couldn't have been better. It would be the way it would have been with Kas, if everything else hadn't got in the way. A dead wife was no threat. Let him get nostalgic sometimes and weep over her memory if he wanted. She wasn't there, and she'd never take him away. This was it. I could see from the start how enraptured he was, and knew that he wouldn't look elsewhere. No one was going to take my place. And I gave myself up to it, in a way that I didn't think I still could. Sometimes lightning strikes twice.

It was all perfect, except for one thing. The child.

It wasn't too bad at first. Right from the start I could see the role that Alex wanted me to play: a bit of cheerleading here, a bit of help with the homework there, a bit of lounging around watching movies at weekends and 'bonding' over packets of snacks. I didn't have to do a lot of disciplining; he did that. A mother wasn't a role I saw myself in – I'd shut the door on that long ago, after I'd lost the baby and then spent my most fertile years in a sexless wasteland – but we got on OK, Jade and I. There were even moments, when she gave me a birthday card she'd made herself, or when we spent a sunny day down on the pier playing on the old arcade games, when I felt a flare of affection. Something unlike anything I'd felt before, and oddly compelling. It was always brief, though, sliding away out of my heart as soon as it had come, and difficult to hold on to.

It was more difficult after we got engaged, when she hit puberty. She was twelve, almost thirteen, and the hormones had well and truly kicked in. Stupid toddler-style tantrums out of nowhere, a lot of slammed doors and tearful accusations. It consumed Alex, more than I had expected. Even when she was in bed, he used to talk about her, going over the same ground again and again. Did I think he should talk to the school? Should he be handling it differently? Was it just a phase, or a sign of something deeper, maybe a delayed reaction to losing her mother? It coloured all our evenings, this endless speculating on Jade's mental well-being. The sofa we used to have sex on turned into a therapy couch, and that wasn't nearly as much fun.

What I found myself wanting to say, when he began to second-guess himself in this way, was that it wasn't his fault at all. It was her. I knew he wouldn't appreciate me saying it, but she was something of a burden to him. When that word first popped into my mind it reminded me of something that I couldn't quite pin down at first, and then I remembered that it was how I'd thought of Melanie, when Kas had told me that it was his duty to stay with her. The comparison stayed with me for a few minutes, and then I packed it carefully away in the back of my head.

We got married, and to be fair to her Jade was an angel that day, smiling sweetly in her pale green lace dress and scattering confetti over us like falling rain, and that rosy glow carried us through for a while. But they call it a honeymoon period for a reason, and after that everything very quickly went sort of grey and flat. Not between me and him – I was still obsessed with him, still wanting to be with him every chance I got, and I knew he felt the same. But the routine that we'd settled into, the way it all centred around Jade and her trials and tribulations . . . It was a grind. A couple of months in, I had what I thought was a brilliant idea. We should move – leave Brighton and go back to London, make a fresh start. I could get back into working, maybe move on from being a clothes sales-woman to some sort of personal shopper or something. I had a feeling I'd be good at that. Helping people change the way they looked, calculating how to move them closer to the person they wanted to be. It was an area in which I had some experience.

I'd realized when I was inside that I had a talent for being a chameleon. I'd proved that I could throw all my cards up in the air and deal myself a new hand. If you met me now, you'd meet a nice housewife in her early thirties living in a trendy seaside town, with just enough money; nothing flash, but good enough to fit in. You'd see a beautiful woman with carefully styled dark hair and a slim figure with curves in the right places, but dressed in such a way – understated, fashion editorial rather than glamour model – that you don't feel too threatened. I'm not out to steal your man. My voice is neither one thing nor the other, not posh, not common, just somewhere comfortably in between. I've always been a good mimic. I fit myself to whoever I'm with, and people like that, even if they realize I'm doing it; it validates them, makes them feel they're worth imitating. I don't put a fucking foot wrong.

I went all out to persuade Alex that the move was a good idea: home-cooked dinner, new underwear, the works. At first he was completely convinced, but the next day it was a different story. He'd had a private word with Jade, he said, and he'd realized it wouldn't be fair on her. He didn't want to disrupt her and take her away from her friends, make her start again somewhere new, not at this vulnerable age. Like she'd even be talking to most of these 'friends' in ten years' time, or like there wouldn't be a reason to call any age vulnerable, if she wanted it to seem that way. She didn't say anything to me about the idea of the move, but that night, after Alex had sat me down and told me that it wasn't going to happen, I saw her shoot a glance at me from under her eyelashes as she sat eating her dinner, and it spoke volumes. Don't think you can pull rank on me, that glance said, because I come first.

And it's true, she did. She does. He doesn't even try to hide it. *Of course, I have to think of Jade first and foremost.* I've heard that countless times. I think he thinks I like it. Maybe some women find this sort of thing noble or heart-warming. And every time he says it, I nod and smile and practically pat her on the head if she's there, and inside I can't help thinking, is this what I signed up for? Is this what I fucking signed up for?

It took me a while to really figure out what this meant,

but once I did it hit like an earthquake. I couldn't stop thinking about it. The knowledge that I'd been so focused on congratulating myself for not falling in love with a married man that I'd completely neglected to notice that a man with a child was even worse. Much, much worse. Against another woman, I'd have a chance at least; I could use every wile at my disposal to convince him that I was the one. But against Jade, I'd have no chance at all. If I went to Alex and told him that it was her or me, that he had to make a choice, he'd choose her. He wouldn't even have to think about it. It might break his heart, but he'd choose her every time.

I could decide that I'd never give him that choice, but I couldn't guarantee that she wouldn't. She tolerated me, even liked me maybe, but she was a teenager: capricious, impulsive, with the potential to be vindictive. I couldn't risk it. I know most people would have rolled over and taken that risk, accepted that they'd always be second best. But I'm not like most people. I'm not afraid of the worst things, and I know that if you want something enough, then you need to make it happen.

Alex

September 2017

I DON'T BELIEVE HER at first. I listen to her, and I watch
her – her long, slim fingers curling over the sleeves of her
pale pink jumper and worrying at the wool, the way she
moves her head swiftly to the side every so often like a
nervous tic. She's persuasive, but my overriding feeling
is that she's probably mad. I nod and make the odd noise
of encouragement as she speaks, but I'm thinking about
how I can make my excuses and leave before this situation gets any weirder.

It's not that I doubt her connection to Natalie. Quite
apart from their physical similarities, she knows too
much about her – things that it would be impossible for
any observer from afar to know. She knows about the
habit she has of staring into mirrors, losing herself in
her reflection. She knows about the unpredictable, mercurial sweep of her moods, from effervescence to apathy
within the space of a few hours. She knows the songs

she sings in the shower. I believe that this woman is her sister, but what she is saying makes no sense.

'I know this is a shock,' she says at last, 'but I have no reason to lie to you. Look. There's something else I've got that might help.' She fishes in her pocket and pulls out an old, crumpled piece of paper that she smooths out and lays on the table between us. It's a handwritten note, short and to the point. My eye goes straight to the signature: Sadie. It's Natalie's handwriting, I'm almost sure of it, but more than this, I'm drawn to the wording. *Didn't want to wake you to say goodbye.* There's an echo of familiarity to it that I can't quite catch on to, and then I remember.

Slowly, I reach into my own pocket and take out the note that Natalie left me the other day in the hotel room. *I didn't want to wake you* – I remember feeling aggrieved, that there was something disingenuous and sly about it. I place it next to the note that the woman has shown me, and I half laugh. It's almost identical. And just like that, the tide turns. Suddenly, I believe her.

Cali – *Rachel*, I think, and it's easy to fit the name to her face, in a way that it was not with Natalie – is watching me, trying to read my expression. 'It was the only thing I kept that she'd given me, and even that was by mistake – I found it at the bottom of my bag after I'd gone,' she says. 'Keeping too much from your previous life is discouraged. And anyway, I didn't want to.'

I look up at her. Her gaze is steady and open, and in this moment the conviction that I can trust her grows and strengthens. 'I just don't understand,' I say levelly. 'Why wouldn't she have told me the truth?'

Rachel shrugs, looking briefly contemptuous. 'It's not exactly something that comes naturally to her, or it never used to be. If I had to guess, I'd say that she doesn't want to come across as the bad guy. She is someone totally different from the person you thought she was, Alex. I used to try and think of her as a loose cannon, a free spirit. A bit wild and easily led astray, but essentially a good person, you know? But it just isn't true. She was wired differently from most people. It made her special, and it made her . . .' She hesitates, as if catching herself in the act of melodrama, then gives a little decisive nod. 'Dangerous,' she says, with some defiance.

'People can change.' It's all I can think of to say.

She nods, frowning a little. 'They can, of course. Once I found out that she had been released, I tried to convince myself that she'd be different now. But I didn't really believe it. Spending that long in prison, it wouldn't mellow you, would it? It would harden you even more. Obviously I couldn't be in touch with her, and I didn't want to be, but I hired a private detective to keep tabs on her when she was first out and living in London – I know,' she interrupts herself, 'it sounds mad, but I needed to know what was going on with her. I suppose despite everything I couldn't quite let go.'

'And?' I ask.

'And nothing, really. She was working, had friends, boyfriends, but nothing serious. I was told she was using a new name, Natalie Stephens, and after a while she made it official and changed it by deed poll. And then she met you, and moved to Brighton, and I thought maybe she'd settled down at last. I stopped keeping tabs on her for a while, but I was still worried. More worried, if anything.' She glances up and catches the question in my expression. 'I suppose I just couldn't see her being in a healthy relationship, to be honest. It was at odds with everything I knew about her. I was worried, mainly, for you.'

My first instinct is to dismiss this. *I don't need your concern, thanks very much*. But there's something simple and unadulterated about what she's said, and it isn't said with pity, exactly. More as if she's just letting me know that she's in my corner.

'I was particularly unsure,' she continues, 'when I found out that you had a daughter. Sadie really isn't the maternal type, and I couldn't see her in a stepmother role.' I'm about to interrupt and protest, because this is something I do know more about than she does – we've had our issues but she's good with Jade, has instinctively found the right balance between friendship and authority – but she hurries on. 'She lost a baby, you know, back when she was nineteen and she was seeing Kas. It must have happened around the same time as the trial. I don't think it's something she would have got over easily.'

She pauses, but my throat feels sewn up. I'm thinking about Kaspar – the realization belatedly hitting that it's my own wife who was involved with him, my own wife who slept with him, and the sudden understanding of that little half smile he gave as I left, as if life could still surprise him. And now the knowledge that there could have been a child, that his baby was growing inside the woman who told me from the start that she never wanted to have her own children. *I expect you're relieved, aren't you, Alex? You wouldn't have wanted to go back to the start, all the nappies and the sleepless nights?*

'She said she didn't want kids,' I say.

Rachel looks unsurprised. 'It's a strange choice then, to be in a relationship with a man who already had one. It's not like she couldn't have found someone with less baggage . . . No offence.'

'She fell in love with me,' I say, a little sharply.

'I'm sure she did.'

There is silence for a few moments, something uneasy stirring in the air between us. Rachel is frowning down at her hands, as if she's trying to fit the pieces of what we're saying together. And in that silence, a strange feeling starts creeping over me. I have an increasingly strong desire – a need – to be with Jade. It's probably just the way that Rachel has brought her into the conversation. She doesn't fit there. I already know that I'm going to have to confront Natalie about all of this, but I don't want Jade to be caught in the crossfire. It's my job to protect her, and right now she feels very far away.

That thought triggers another. 'Have you had Jade followed?' I ask Rachel. I'm aware that I sound aggressive, and I make an effort to soften my voice. 'If you have then I'm sure you had your reasons, but I need to know.'

She shakes her head, eyes wide and questioning. 'No, never. The only contact I've had, personally or remotely, has been with you.' She sucks in her cheeks in a brief moment of awkwardness, those late-night conversations shimmering in the air between us. 'And I only did that because, like I said before, I felt like I had to know if you were happy. At least, at first.' She hesitates, then seems to cut her own line of conversation off, sitting back in her chair and smoothing her hair nervously back behind her ears. 'But why do you ask?' she says.

'There's been a man,' I say slowly, 'hanging around my daughter. I think his name is Dominic Westwood.'

Rachel looks worried. 'I don't know anything about that. But I knew Dominic. He was close to Kas. Sadie would consider him a friend of hers. I can tell you that.'

The unease is growing, building painfully in my chest. I try and ground myself, remember all the moments of intimacy and tenderness Natalie and I have shared, but they don't reassure me. All I can think is that my wife is a great actress. She's someone who can hide an entire life's worth of history and then lie to me all over again even as she reveals it. I have no way of knowing if anything we've shared is real, if she's ever even loved me at all.

Abruptly, I stand up. 'I need to make a phone call,' I say. 'Just give me a minute.'

'Sure.' Rachel looks as if she wants to ask what I'm doing, but she casts her eyes down and breathes in deeply, restraining herself. As I walk away across the bar, I glance over my shoulder. From the back, she could be Natalie. The same delicate yet pronounced shoulder blades, the same elegantly curved neck.

Outside it's getting dark, the sun sinking redly behind

325

the rows of buildings. I call Jade's number, but it rings a few times and then goes straight to voicemail. It's not surprising – making calls on the ward is frowned upon, so her phone is often on silent – but my hands are shaking as I dial the number for the hospital. It takes a long time for anyone to answer. I'm staring at the setting sun as I wait, and when I glance away a little red shadow is burned on to my retina, glimmering faintly, suspended in the air.

At last someone picks up on the switchboard and I ask to be transferred to the Burns Unit, then tell the receptionist that I want to speak to Jade. She tells me to bear with her, and then puts me on hold. I listen to the scratchy looped music, rattling down the line like coins in a can.

All at once the music cuts out and the line is back. For a few seconds there's no sound except for the muffled backdrop of the ward; footsteps coming and going, murmured conversations. 'Hello?' I ask, my heart lifting. 'Jade, is that you?'

'Sorry.' The receptionist's voice comes through loud and clear again. 'I was just asking one of the nurses if she knew where Jade was, but she's only just come on shift.'

'Where she is?' I ask sharply. 'Well, she'll be in her bed, won't she? Or possibly in the toilet, or the communal area. There are only so many places.'

'The bed that was hers has been filled by another patient,' the receptionist says, clearly parroting what she's been told. Her voice is polite, but a little bored. This kind of conversation must happen to her all the time. A hospital is a vast and complex engine room, full of misunderstandings and miscommunications – and yet a sharp flare of panic shoots through me.

'Well, I suppose she's been moved for some reason,' I say, hearing my voice sound bizarrely authoritative and calm. 'Can you please find out where to? Or can you get a doctor on the line?'

'I'll see what I can do.' The hold music clicks back on. Its beat thumps in rhythm with my heart, and my breath is short, as if I've been running.

Sadie

September 2017

THE TAXI LINGERS IN traffic for a while and I take the opportunity to call Dominic again, but just like the last four times I've tried, he doesn't pick up. I decide to text him instead. I send a curt message, telling him where I'll be later and when. Whatever he thinks of my plan, I know he won't call the police – he doesn't trust them an inch, and they've got too much on him. And I haven't entirely lost hope that he'll come around. I'd still rather have his help.

I'd have expected more of him, considering all his talk about loyalty, and considering what he owes me. Back at the time of the trial, Kas and I closed ranks. We didn't bring him into the frame, and Rachel never knew that he was involved, so her little snitching performance didn't impact on him. I think the police had their suspicions; he was questioned more than once, but they couldn't find enough to charge him. There would have been no point in our bringing him down with us – it's not like it would have diluted anything. In situations like that, blame seems to multiply like magic. It seems there's always plenty of it to go round.

So when I first tracked him down and got in touch, I had the right to ask him for something and he knew it. We met in an anonymous downbeat bar just outside Brighton and I told him about Jade. I gave him the facts and he told me he understood. I didn't have to think too much about it. I didn't want to get too involved myself in her – disappearance. It was too much of a risk, and besides, something in me pushed back against it, when I thought about it. It wasn't the same as with Melanie. This was pre-planned, and there was another reluctance there, something I couldn't quite pin down. A bit of human compassion, maybe. Or just squeamishness. I don't know.

What I hadn't realized was how lightweight Dominic had become. The years had sanded off his hard edges, and while Kas and I had been inside, building up shells as hard as bulletproof glass, he'd been hanging out with a crowd that had clearly lost its focus and drive once their leader had gone. When I asked what he'd been doing, he just shrugged and muttered. Reading between the lines, he seemed to have scaled down to the odd small-scale drug deal. At one point he even mentioned working in a minimart. I raised an eyebrow and he backtracked a little, mumbling about it being good to have a front to deflect suspicion, but I wasn't convinced. He'd put on a bit of weight, too; his fingers were soft and doughy, not the ones I remembered gripping me like iron on that day down in the basement at Kaspar's, making damn sure that I didn't escape.

Still, he was better than no one. We agreed that Dominic would scope Jade out for a bit, get the lie of the land and come up with a plan. So that's what he did, only it went on for a lot longer than I'd anticipated. He hung around – not very fucking subtly, as I realized when Alex broke the news that she'd been noticing him for weeks – staring at her from across the street and psyching himself up, but that was about it. He pointed out that if he was seen talking to a fourteen-year-old girl then he'd get noticed pretty quickly, and that he wasn't sure she was likely to be seduced by him. That I definitely agreed with. And Jade never went out alone after dark, so it was difficult.

That's when I came up with the plan. I had no idea what kind of boys she was into, but I knew she spent a load of time on social media, so I created a few profiles and messaged her saying how cute she was, just throwing out bait. I made a female profile too, just in case, but she blocked that one off straight away, so I had my answer there. There was one profile she seemed more attracted by than the others. I'd taken a picture of a good-looking, olive-skinned teenager off the net – he looked a bit like I would have imagined Kas to look at that age. She'd reply to his messages with the odd emoji, a blushing face or a little heart. At first I thought it might be enough to reel her in . . . that we could chat for a few weeks and then arrange to meet. But she was savvier than that. As soon as I even dropped a hint, she backed off. But now I knew what her type was, and I knew that Dominic would know someone who fitted the bill.

Sure enough, when I asked he sent me the photo of a

friend's son, Jaxon: dark hair and eyes, a dusting of stubble at his jawline, a bit cocky looking. I got in touch and asked if he was interested in making a bit of extra cash. A one-off, and not much required from him. All he had to do was turn up at our house, dressed as you might expect a plumber to dress, chat Jade up a little and give her his number. Only of course it wasn't his number at all, just a spare pay-as-you-go phone that I'd bought in readiness. And I have to say, he played his part to perfection. I was there watching when Jade got home from school, and I saw the immediate light of interest in his eyes, and the way he straightened up slowly and gave her a look of part seduction, part innocent awe. I left the room at a suitable point and waited for the magic to happen, and after he'd gone I could see the excitement Jade was trying so hard to suppress, the way she was clutching her phone.

After that we messaged for a few weeks, taking it slowly, getting to know each other, building up to a face-to-face meeting. The plan was that we'd arrange a rendezvous, somewhere private and not too far out of town so that she could get there easily after school. 'Jaxon' would keep her waiting for a bit, send a few holding messages, until it got dark. Then, well, Dominic would show up instead. There'd be a message trail on her phone to tell the whole sorry story, and I'd have given Dominic the Jaxon phone to dispose of straight away. I'd thought of everything.

I arranged to meet up with Dominic the night before, to go over the finer points. Originally we were going to meet in a bar, but at the last minute Alex reminded me he was going out that night, entertaining a client, and that I'd have to stay in with Jade. I messaged Dominic and he suggested we could reschedule, put the whole thing off for another week or two. But I didn't want to lose momentum, just wanted it over with. So I told him to come over, later on that evening, when Jade would be in bed. He turned up about ten o'clock, and as far as I knew she was in her bedroom, lights out.

'I'm not sure about this.' Those were his first words when he came through the door and sat down heavily on the sofa. He couldn't quite look me in the eye. 'She's just a kid, Sadie.' I could never get him to call me Natalie, no matter how many times I tried.

I knew as soon as he said it that it wasn't going to work. Like I said, he'd gone soft. But I couldn't face it, the thought of all this build-up being for nothing, and so I tried to change his mind. I argued that a life was a life, that it didn't matter who it belonged to and that it didn't really make sense to have scruples about some people and not others. Unless you knew and loved them, of course, but he didn't know Jade at all. She was nothing to him. I reasoned that it would all be over so quickly, that it wasn't the hardest thing he'd done. And when none of that worked, I tried to lay down the law and remind him of what I'd done for him. I reminded him that he owed me.

He listened, and then he went off upstairs to the toilet, stayed there a few minutes before he came back. I knew he was thinking about it, but when he reappeared I could see the spinelessness written all over his face.

'I can't do it.' That's what it boiled down to, unvarnished

and simple. He spread out those podgy hands, palms upwards. 'Sorry.'

I intercepted him at the door, grabbed on to his coat sleeve. 'You're a fucking coward,' I hissed, careful to keep my voice down, but pouring as much venom into my tone as I could. 'I won't forget this, and nor will Kas. Just wait until he hears about this.' They were empty words, of course; I had never visited Kas and didn't plan to, couldn't risk having my equilibrium rocked in that way, but he didn't know that.

He shook my hand off with ease and glared at me, and for a brief nauseous moment I realized that he was still much stronger than I was and that if he wanted he could knock me out in a second. But he just shook his head and broke away, then made his exit through the back door. I stood there listening to his footsteps plodding away down the passage, and then there was silence.

Something built in me then, the kind of wild fury I hadn't felt in years. Everything I'd planned was slipping out of my fingers and I could see it, literally see it all falling to the floor and smashing around me. My vision was blurred and there was only this white-hot anger and the need to do something, do something. My hands were shaking. I lit a cigarette, and suddenly I thought about how easy it would be to let it fall on to the rug and set it alight. And how easy it would be to do the same thing in the next room, and the next, while Jade was sleeping upstairs, and then to wait just long enough before I called 999. It wasn't a well thought out plan. But in that moment it came to me with such blinding, shining clarity that it felt like the only thing to do. And so I did it.

And it was real, the heat and the light and the terror. I didn't have to fake it.

By the time Alex came home and I'd stumbled out of the building, my chest was sore and my heart was thumping like crazy and the tears came to my eyes without prompting, and when I saw him there he looked so aghast and confused and bereft, and I looked at him and thought – yes, I love you, I love you and you're worth all of this. I'm not an idiot. I knew it would be hard for him, losing her, but I'd be there for him and I'd never leave him, and he'd never be able to do without me ever again.

But of course it didn't work out quite like that. They got her out, like a cat with nine lives. I sat there in the hospital with my painted smile and my prettily crossed legs and doted on her, and I blocked it all out of my head, because I knew that if I didn't I'd lose control completely and I might just reach out my hands and tear the fabric of it all apart into shreds until there was nothing left.

The taxi rounds the corner and starts up the main road. We're almost there. I take a few deep breaths, calm myself. Crazily, I wish I could talk to Alex. I want to tell him everything and to share all the panic and frustration of the past few days with him. Impossible obviously, considering the subject matter, but that's what love is. Wanting someone to know you, and all your secrets.

I'd been wanting to tell him about the past for a long time. I'd reinvented myself, but that doesn't mean that I'd forgotten. When something is part of you, part of the blood that runs through your veins, not sharing it with the person you love more than anything else feels wrong. It drove me mad sometimes, lying there next to him and thinking that he knew so little about me – not even that, but that he actually knew completely the wrong things, that I'd just fed him a load of lies. After the fire, that feeling grew and grew. Maybe it was coming so close to death. I'd stayed in the house longer than I'd meant to, not realizing how slow and fogged my reflexes had become with the heat. The veil had been twitched back and it made me vulnerable, less able to bear things on my own.

There was only one problem. Let's just say I'm aware that, to an impartial observer, 'Sadie' might not come out of this story looking too likeable. I wouldn't have expected Alex to understand. Or more accurately, I didn't trust him to – no, not even him. I would never trust anyone enough. Also, if I was going to tell him my story, it would have involved going into some detail about my obsession with another man . . . Not the sort of thing any husband wants to hear – but if I wanted him to understand properly then I couldn't really downplay it.

I hadn't solved this dilemma, but it all came to a head sooner than I'd imagined. Alex wrong-footed me completely when he pulled out the photo of Kas and Rachel. Stupid of me to have kept it, of course. But it was a snapshot in time, that photo. I'd taken it in the early days, before it all fell apart, when I was starting to believe that Kas and I could really have something, and maybe even that Rachel and I could build some bridges. I liked to look at it sometimes, when I was on my own. Just to remind me of how it was.

Anyway, I knew in that moment that I'd have to tell Alex something – he'd forced my hand – but I couldn't tell him the truth. Like all my best ideas, it came to me quickly, a brilliant moment of clarity. I *could* tell the story, just from a different angle. I would reinvent myself all over again. And when I reached for my new self, Rachel was there waiting for me.

I hadn't thought about her too much over the past few years. Maybe it hurt too much. She was my sister, after all, and part of me could never quite believe that she'd betrayed me. I'd hung on to a few old things of hers, out of what can only have been sentiment, I suppose, but I never tried to find her. I doubt I could have in any case. And anyway, I tried to imagine it a few times, and I realized that when I thought of coming face to face with her, I had nothing to say. Or too much, maybe. In any case, not the right amount.

So it surprised me, how easily I slipped into her character. It was as if she'd been under my skin the whole time and all I had to do was scratch the surface and out she popped. It was easy to see the situation from her perspective, play up the sense of hopelessness and fear and the bitterness against Sadie. After all, it's not like I didn't get plenty of that from her in the old days. In a way it was satisfying, becoming her. Alex certainly took to her; I could see him instantly casting me in the role of wronged victim.

In the meantime, I carried on with the messages from Jaxon. I created a little teenage falling-out – he was suspicious, thinking that Jade was faking her hospitalization in order to avoid meeting up with him.

We'd smoothed it over, but now I need to step it up again. As the taxi pulls up, I take the spare phone from my bag and send another text, then make sure I put the phone on silent. And that's my cue. I swing out of the taxi and walk up to the hospital, my steps steady and sure.

She's sitting up in her hospital bed, anxiously jabbing at her phone. She looks quite fragile, her skin almost translucent, her face without make-up shockingly stripped back and revealed, the large, dark blue eyes clear and shining.

I stand in the doorway, waiting a few seconds before I step forward and speak. 'Hi again.' She starts, looking up at me, still clutching her phone. I can see at once that she's struggling to act naturally, to focus on anything except the message she's just received, and that those eyes are actually shining with tears. 'What's wrong?' I ask.

'Nothing,' she begins to say, but her voice is strained and choked. She drops her gaze, staring at the bedsheet.

I come forward into the room and sit down next to her. 'Is it this boy? Jaxon?'

She glances up at me quickly. 'I didn't know you knew about that.'

'Your dad told me.' I don't want to say too much. I'm not sure how much Alex knows about the whole thing; he only mentioned it yesterday, briefly and cryptically. So I just smile sympathetically and stroke her hand. 'Has something happened?'

Jade takes a breath, and she's clearly wondering if she trusts me enough to open up to me. The answer, under normal circumstances, would probably be no. But she's upset, and I'm the only one here, and perhaps she knows that I'll be less strict about this than her father. Because I'm not her mother. On some deep, dark level, she knows I don't really care.

'He's just texted me,' she says quietly. 'He's saying he's still not sure if I'm making it up about being in hospital, and he thinks I'm just playing with him. This is so – so frustrating. I don't want him to come here and see me like this. But he's going to lose interest, and I don't want . . .' She breaks off, rubbing a fist angrily across her eyes.

'I understand,' I say firmly.

'Really?' She shoots a slightly suspicious glance in my direction, wiping away the tears.

'Of course.' I pause, wondering whether to continue, but the mood feels right. 'Look, the reason I'm here is that last time your dad and I visited, the doctors said you were pretty much ready to get out of here. He's out tonight, so I was going to suggest that you came back with me to the hotel and we could surprise him. But maybe . . .' I let the silence stretch, as if I'm weighing it up. 'You do feel better, don't you?'

'Ye-es . . .' she says cautiously.

'Well,' I continue, with studied reluctance, 'perhaps . . . you could suggest to this guy that you meet up tonight. We could go there first, before going back to the hotel. I could take you, wait somewhere nearby so that I know you're safe.'

Jade blinks slowly, her lips slightly parted. I mentally chastise myself; I've put this on her a bit quickly, not given her time to catch up. When she's absorbed what I've said, there's a faint spark of excitement in her eyes, but her overriding expression is one of concern. 'I don't know,' she says.

I cock my head to one side, press my hands together. 'Have I misunderstood? I mean, if you don't want to, that's fine, but . . .'

'It's not that,' she says quickly. 'It's just . . .' A blush has appeared on her cheeks and she isn't quite looking me in the eye. 'I look *awful*,' she mumbles eventually. 'I haven't got any decent going-out clothes here, I've got no lipstick or blusher or anything . . . I don't want him to think I can't be bothered to make an effort.'

I want to laugh with sheer relief. 'Is that all you're worried about?' For a moment I deliberate launching into an impassioned speech about how a boy should love you for what's inside, but I change my mind. Who am I kidding? 'I can help with that,' I say decisively. 'We'll stop by the hotel on our way and I can fix you up.'

'Really?' Jade says, more eagerly now. 'Well, in that case . . .' She smiles, unable to stop herself. 'I'll text him now. Argh, I can't believe it! Do you think it'll go OK?'

'I'm absolutely sure it will,' I say, standing up. 'Let me go and find the doctor now, and get you a discharge form.'

It takes longer than I anticipate to track down the right person and the right form, and I can see the doctor isn't sure about this plan. He points out that they were envisaging Jade being in for a few more days, to be certain that she's ready. But I stand firm, telling him that there's a birthday surprise for her father and that she can't miss it. We'll bring her in for another check-up later in the week – even re-admit her if necessary – and it will all be fine. 'Now, where do I sign?' I say brightly, and although I can tell he still isn't convinced, he also knows that he has no right to prevent me.

As I'm walking back towards Jade's room I check my spare phone and see that she's sent Jaxon a text. *Hey babe, I promise I still want to meet. I can actually do this eve if you wanna?!! I'm getting out of here.*

I pause to send back a suitably encouraging reply. ***serioussss?? of course babe. i cant meet til bit later but meet u in portslade?*** I can't imagine Jade being too fussy about the location for her first date, and I have a place in mind. Stick to what you know.

She's already out of bed and tugging on her boots when I return, and she beams up at me, clearly raring to go.

'Ready?' I ask, and there's an inexplicable lump in my throat.

She nods and stands up to face me. She stumbles slightly as she does so, her legs still a little weak, and I reach out to steady her. The room is very still, a shaft of late sunlight falling through the slats of the window and shining on her face, making her look like an angel.

'Thanks for doing this, Natalie,' she says quietly. 'I really do appreciate it. I know you understand what it's like . . . What it's like to be in love.'

And it's true. I do.

340

Alex

September 2017

THE HOLD MUSIC SEEMS to last for ever. My nerves are shredded with the waiting and I'm on the point of hanging up and dialling again when the music abruptly cuts out. 'Hello?' I recognize the clipped tones of Doctor Rai. 'Mr Carmichael? I understand you're calling about your daughter?'

'Yes,' I say. 'I just want to speak to her, please.'

The doctor clears his throat, and when he speaks again his voice is a little diffident. 'Jade is no longer here at the hospital,' he says. 'She left earlier this evening, with her mother. It was contrary to our advice, but her mother was quite insistent. I assume there has been some kind of breakdown in communication and that she hasn't managed to inform you?'

For a few seconds I'm silent. My throat is suddenly dry, and I have to force myself to speak. 'Stepmother,' I say at last.

'I'm sorry?' the doctor begins to say, but his voice is

already fading from earshot as I pull the phone away and stare at it, then press the button to hang up.

When I turn around I see that Rachel has followed me outside. I don't know how long she's been standing there, but it's clear that she can tell by my expression that something is very wrong. Her eyes are searching and anxious, huge in her pale face. She puts out a hand and touches my arm, silently asking a question.

'They don't know where she is,' I say. 'The hospital. My daughter isn't there anymore. She's gone with my wife.'

Saying it aloud makes it real. I realize with a sick lurch of terror that these words don't sound as innocent as they should. 'Come on.'

I set off down the esplanade, Rachel hurrying behind me, and as I do so I call Natalie. Her phone rings, but goes to voicemail. The familiar lilting message kicks in: *Hey, this is Natalie. I'm not here right now, but I'll get back to you.* The sound of her voice is briefly reassuring – its untroubled normality. This is my wife, I remind myself. I'm letting myself get carried away with the strangeness of this situation. Whatever Natalie is doing, she'll have her reasons. Surely, it will be OK.

'Hi, sweetheart,' I say. It's an effort, but I force myself to sound calm. 'I've just been speaking to the hospital, and they tell me you've taken Jade home. Bit surprising – can you give me a ring and let me know what's going on? Speak soon.'

I hang up and keep on, turning a corner up the street that will lead us to the hotel. 'I expect they'll be back at the room where we're staying,' I say to Rachel. 'I'll just go straight there.'

'Right,' she says. Her face is still very pale, her hands clenched into fists at her sides as she walks and her hair unravelling from the bun piled on top of her head and falling around her face, making her look more like Natalie. 'I'll come with you, and wait outside. If they're there, just don't come back out. I'll wait for a while, and then go away.'

'You don't want to see her?' I ask. 'You're sure?'

She says nothing, just shakes her head and keeps on walking. For a second, something that looks like pain flashes across her face.

It doesn't take long to reach the hotel at the speed we're going, and I pause for a moment outside to catch my breath. 'OK,' I say. 'I'll go in and find them now. I'm sure they'll be here. So if I don't come back, then . . .' I pause. A goodbye feels sudden and premature, but I don't know what other parting shot there can be, and after a moment I just raise my hand in a vague gesture of fare-well, not quite looking her in the eye. She nods and leans back against the wall, turning her head away.

I hurry across the hotel lobby and into the lift, fumbling in my pocket for the room key. As I rise slowly through the levels, I try and regulate my heartbeat, take some deep breaths. I tell myself that in a few moments all this will be over. I'll be able to hold my daughter, and to look into my wife's eyes and let her know that I know the truth now, and that I'm ready to look past all the things she's done before and find the person I love still waiting there. I want us to settle down, all crowded together on the bed, and watch something tame and harmless on the television before ordering room service and maybe going for a short stroll before bed. These thoughts are flashing in my head, bright flares of hope, as I unlock the door and push it open.

I see at once that the room is empty, but I don't want to believe it, and I go inside and circle it stupidly, looking in the bathroom, calling Jade's name. The edge of the bed is crumpled, as if it's been recently sat on, and a wave of heat emanates from the shower cubicle, warm droplets of water still clinging to the glass screen. Someone has been here, very recently, but now they've gone. I turn back into the room, and that's when I see Jade's mobile, with its distinctive pink casing, lying on the floor by the bed. I bend down swiftly to pick it up, but of course it's locked and try as I might, I can't remember the pin code. My head feels soft and fuzzy, my thoughts mashing up against one another like cotton wool.

I stand there holding the phone in my hand for a minute, then cross to the window and peer down on to the street. Rachel is still standing there, leaning against the wall. She's lit a cigarette and she's smoking it in quick anxious drags, occasionally craning her head back towards the lobby, searching for me. She isn't going anywhere, I realize. She knows that her sister isn't here. She knows her better than I do.

Something starts rising up inside me, some undefinable dark horror so huge that it could entirely engulf me if I let it. I force it back down. I need to be focused. I'll call Natalie again, see if I can get through. I don't believe in God, but I screw my eyes tight shut and pray to whatever is out there as I listen to the phone ring, but no one is listening and it goes through to voicemail again. This time I don't leave a message.

When I'm back out on the street I don't need to say anything. Rachel turns round, tossing the remnants of the cigarette to the ground. 'Where else might she have gone?' She speaks levelly and with a sick jolt of foreboding I realize she's trying to keep me calm. 'Any places she particularly likes, or goes to a lot?'

'Natalie, you mean?' I try and think. 'She goes down by the sea a lot?' I'm uselessly scanning the seafront from our vantage point on the hill, my eyes searching out the rocks where we spoke the other night, but there are only a few children playing in the last of the fading light, scampering back and forth and tossing a ball between them.

Rachel shakes her head. 'No. It's too open.'

Too open for what, I almost ask, but then I realize I don't want to know the answer. I try and screw my thoughts back into place, think about my wife's habits and routines. 'I don't fucking know,' I say, my voice rising. 'I have no idea where she might be. What the hell am I going to do?'

Before Rachel has a chance to answer, Jade's mobile vibrates in my pocket. I snatch it up, staring at the screen. I still can't unlock it, but I can see the notification of a new message. **Katie:** *sorry had to have dinner. ahh this is so exciting!! you have to let me . . .* The rest of the message is cut off, but it's enough to tell me that she and Jade must have been in contact very recently.

Rachel is looking over my shoulder. 'Do you have her number?'

I shake my head. 'No, but I know where she lives.' I dropped Jade off at Katie's house a couple of months ago for a sleepover. Elmstead Road. I don't remember the number, but I have a vague memory of the house – whitewashed, with a distinctive pale yellow door.

'We should go there,' Rachel says.

'We'll have to get a taxi. It'll take too long otherwise.' I curse the inane pseudo-environmental principles that made me decide to give up my car a couple of years ago. The truth was that it had little to do with the environment and everything to do with the fact that it was an expense that I didn't really need. I need it now, when it's too late.

I'm already striding down the road towards the main stretch, scanning the street for a taxi. It's probably only a few minutes before I see one rounding the bend, its light gleaming in the dusk, but it feels like an eternity. I can't think of anything but making sure that Jade is safe. I want her right here beside me, right now, and I can barely believe that the force of my wanting this can't make it happen.

I climb into the taxi and ask the driver to take us to Elmstead Road, adding that he may need to wait and take us on to other destinations if we don't find what we're looking for. The cabbie grumbles a little at first, and I wordlessly fish in my pocket and pull out the notes I have there, hold them up for him to see. His eyes flick to the rear-view mirror, and he shrugs, then swings away from the kerb and sets off down the long sea road.

The journey to Katie's house is barely ten minutes. We sit side by side in the back seat, not speaking. Occasionally Rachel glances across at me, reaches out her hand to touch mine. I register the intimacy of this, the strangeness of it. I feel as if I'm somewhere above myself, looking down from a height, dispassionately watching this unfold.

'It'll be OK,' she says once, and I nod, then turn to stare out of the window, watching the gardens flash past, the bright smears of green lit by streetlights in the rapidly falling dark.

As soon as we pull up at the end of the street I'm out of the car, running up towards the house that I've already picked out. I ring the doorbell, long and hard. I can see some activity through the frosted glass panel, and Katie's mother flings the door open, clearly gearing up for a rant, but when she sees it's me the wind is taken out of her sails and she abruptly shuts her mouth, then smiles uncertainly.

'Oh, hi,' she says. 'Um, Alex, isn't it?'

I don't have time for niceties. 'Is Katie in?'

'Er, yes,' she says, glancing quickly behind her. 'She's just finishing off her homework before bed. Is something wrong?'

'I need to speak to her about Jade,' I say. I grope for the words that would make this feel more acceptable, and I can't find them; there's only a growing urgency, a panic rising in my chest and stifling everything else.

'We're sorry to disturb you,' Rachel chimes in, 'but it is important, I'm afraid. We need to talk to Katie about some messages that Jade may have sent her this evening.'

Her tone is reassuringly level, and I can see that Katie's mother feels more comfortable with her than with me, so I say nothing, just nod and wait.

'OK,' the woman says, if a little uncertainly, and then half turns to shout up the stairs. 'Katie! Can you come down? There's someone here to see you.'

A moment later Katie appears at the top of the stairs, all dark wavy hair, a rolled-up school skirt and suspiciously long curled eyelashes. She looks like a woman, and she's the same age as Jade. These girls aren't just growing up fast; they think they're already there, already in control, and they're so wrong. My heart tightens at the thought, and I force past the lump in my throat. 'Katie, I'm sorry to bother you. You're not in any trouble, but I really need to know if Jade has said anything to you about where she is tonight.'

'Ah . . .' Katie looks instantly guilty, stalling, and shooting a quick glance at her mother. 'I dunno.'

'I don't think that's true,' I say, fighting hard to keep my voice steady. 'Look, Jade should still be in hospital. I'm very worried about her, and I have reason to believe that something may have happened to her. If you're worrying that you're going to get her into trouble, then please don't. Punishing her is the last thing on my mind. I just need to make sure she's safe.'

Katie sidles down the stairs, folding her arms in front of her and shaking her dark curls back from her face. I can see in her eyes that she's still unsure, but also that on some level she's impressed – the drama of this situation, and her role as the one who holds the knowledge I'm after.

'Well . . .' she says slowly. 'You know there's this boy, Jaxon?' I nod, urging her on. 'Well, she said she's going to meet him tonight. Like a date?'

'A date,' I echo stupidly. I look at Rachel, but she looks as confused as I am. I can't see what this has to do with Natalie, or how it marries up with our fears and suspicions. 'The hospital told me that she had gone home with – with my wife.' Out of the corner of my eye, I see Katie's mother shoot a confused glance at Rachel, readjusting her assumptions.

Katie nods. 'Yeah, that's what she said. She said Natalie's going to take her to meet him. I thought that was pretty cool. Like, my mum would never do that.' She shoots her mother a quick venomous glance, as if this is digging up old graves, but it's all I can do not to give in to the tears that are threatening to choke me, because she doesn't understand what love is about – it's about protection, shielding.

Her point made to her mother, Katie turns back to me and smiles. 'So, I guess it's OK,' she says. 'Because Natalie's with her.'

Rachel must sense that I can't speak, because she cuts in, smiling back brightly at Katie. 'Thanks,' she says. 'You're right, that's helpful. But would it be possible to see the messages she's sent you tonight? Just in case there's anything we need to know.'

'I don't think . . .' Katie begins, but her mother cuts in.

'Just get your phone, Katie,' she says. I look at her grave expression, and I can tell that she isn't fooled. She knows there's something very wrong here.

Katie sighs and fishes in her pocket. 'This is kind of

embarrassing, you know,' she mutters. 'Like, I don't usually write messages to my mates thinking their dad's going to read them.'

I've regained some control, and I hold out my hand for the phone. 'I'm sorry,' I say, 'and I won't look at anything beyond what was sent this evening, I promise.'

Unwillingly she hands it over, and my eyes flick over the conversation, seeing it at a glance, but double-checking, making sure I haven't missed anything.

> *guess what?!!*
> *what?*
> *I'm getting out of hospital and natalie's taking me to meet up with jaxon!!!*
> *what?! u mean right now?*
> *yeah. omg I am so nervous. what if he doesn't like me anymore?*
> *don't be stupid babe. he will luuuurve u. where you meeting?*
> *I dunno exactly yet. he said portslade*
> *portslade??!! that's a fucking dump isn't it :-o*
> *yh I know :-/ but errrr maybe it's better than we think. or maybe he just knows a nice romantic place . . . oooohhh*
> *sorry had to have dinner. ahh this is so exciting!! you have to let me know how it goes*

Jade's last message was sent only forty minutes ago, about twenty minutes before we arrived at the hotel room. I can't believe she'd have voluntarily left her phone behind, and it means I have no way of contacting her, other than to go to Portslade and scour the streets. Briefly, I think about calling the police. But Jade's been missing a couple of hours, if that, and I have so little concrete information to give them. I don't want anything to slow me down – I want to get out there and do my best to find her.

'Thanks,' I say, passing the phone back to Katie. 'If she does get in touch with you somehow, will you let me know straight away?' I recite my number and she keys it in, then stares at Rachel and me wide-eyed for a moment, as if she's still trying to figure out what all this means. I grunt an awkward goodbye and thanks before turning on my heel and striding back towards the taxi.

'Portslade,' I tell the driver. 'Somewhere central.'

We're back on the road, whizzing down the long narrow streets and past Hove Park, out towards Portslade. Even though it's so close, I haven't been here for years. White Tudor-style houses, squat, neatly rounded trees; a quiet little town, where nothing much ever happens. It is almost completely dark now, and I find myself looking in the windows of the houses as we travel down the long road that leads to the high street, caught in momentary traffic. Across the road, a man pulls his curtains shut, twisting his head around as he does so to talk to a child hovering behind. A little farther along, a woman is carrying plates of food to the table, setting them down with a flourish. Ordinary people in ordinary homes. They've never seemed so seductive or desirable. I so badly want this to be another normal day, another cog grinding in the works of an untroubled routine.

The taxi pulls up again with a screech. 'All right here, mate? Are you going to need me again? Because I've got another job up in Hove.'

'I don't know.' I can't focus on the taxi driver's workload right now. 'Never mind. You can get off.' Portslade is a small town. We can get around on foot, and we're better off that way, having the freedom to search as we choose.

When he has pulled away I turn to Rachel. 'I don't know where to look.' Against reason, something in me hopes that she'll just know where Natalie is. I look frantically up and down the winding street we're standing on. It's deserted, the dim light of streetlamps faintly illuminating the pavements. 'There's nothing fucking here.'

Rachel puts her hand on my arm, steadying me. 'We just need to keep going. Ask in some of the bars, something like that.'

It's a reasonable idea and I seize on it; farther down the street I can see a pub sign bearing a painted image of a knight on horseback. I stride towards it, bursting through the door and instantly taking in the small number of punters; mostly elderly men nursing pints and staring down at the tables, lost in their own thoughts.

I approach one of them at random. 'Excuse me, have you seen a girl? About fourteen, blonde hair, maybe with a woman who could be her mother? Or maybe with a teenage boy?' My vagueness frustrates me. The man doesn't even bother to reply, just peers at me in suspicion and shakes his head in silence before returning to his contemplation of his pint glass.

I go round each of the punters in turn, asking the same question and getting the same short shrift, until Rachel gently pulls on my sleeve. 'Come on, Alex. We'll try somewhere else.'

We spend the next twenty minutes ducking in and out of pubs and late-night corner shops, asking everyone we find if they've seen Jade. After a while I realize that I should be showing them a photo of her on my phone, and the thought gives me a new injection of energy and hope, but it rapidly becomes clear that it makes no difference. No one has seen her. We've walked for what seems like miles, and no matter how much ground we cover, we don't seem to be getting any further forward.

Eventually I sink to my knees on the street, not caring who sees. 'We're not going to find her,' I say, and voicing it aloud makes it so sickeningly real that for a moment I actually think I might throw up. I know it's hopeless, but I dial Natalie's number again. This time it goes straight to voicemail.

Rachel sits down beside me, her brow creased intently in thought. 'Hold on,' she says. 'You don't have a car, right? And I don't think Sadie – Natalie – would have taken a taxi with Jade. Whatever she's trying to do here, she wouldn't want to risk being remembered by anyone. So they must have come by train, mustn't they? We should go to the station – they might have CCTV, or a guard might have seen them – someone will know something, I'm sure of it.'

The conviction with which she speaks is enough to galvanize me, and I scramble to my feet. She's right – it makes sense to go to the station.

I set off down the road, keying the location into my phone and seeing that we're less than five minutes away. My feet pound on the street, the rhythm shaking its way through my body, the sound of my own breath hard and fast in my ears. The outlines of the buildings lining the street are blurring in front of my eyes, but I force myself to keep going, running now, with Rachel at my heels. I can see the long white building of the station up ahead and as we reach it I slow down to catch my breath. But then I hear something. At first, I think I must have got it wrong. But when I turn to Rachel she's staring at me, her eyes wide, lips parted in dismay, and without a word we're running again.

Sadie

September 2017

ONCE WE'RE ON THE train I choose the emptiest carriage I can and slide into the window seat, motioning for Jade to sit down opposite me. It's a ten-minute journey at most, but the train crawls along, and we end up sitting between stations, with a bored announcer telling us that we're being held at a red signal for what feels like a ridiculously long time.

Jade doesn't say anything, but she can't stop fidgeting. I try and remember what it felt like, to be so eager to meet up with a boy that it's vibrating all the way through your body. When you're older you lose that eagerness, that lustful one-track-mind focus. But I remember how it was with Kas, when I used to travel up to the club, and for a moment it's like I'm back there, staring at my own reflection in the window against the darkening sky, imagining the look he'll give me when he sees me and the scent of his aftershave curling towards me through the air. Usually when I get these kinds of flashback I cut them off at the source, brutally, with no time for weakness. But tonight I let my memories drag me back there. It feels right somehow. It's almost like he's here, right over my shoulder, watching me.

Jade is fiddling with her pocket mirror, examining her lipstick, twisting her face this way and that to check that it's perfectly applied. It's a crimson one of mine, a shade I've never seen her wear before. It doesn't totally suit her – she's too pale. But there's something striking about the way it draws the eyes to the lips. It lets you know that the wearer wants you to be looking at them. She pouts uncertainly at herself in the mirror, then brings the back of her hand to her mouth, blotting the colour and leaving a perfect imprint of her own lips on her skin.

She sees me watching and glances up. 'Do I look all right?'

It's the sort of question I hate. If you don't know the answer, you shouldn't be asking. Still, I force a smile. 'Knockout.'

She grins, glancing down at the dark blue minidress I've lent her. It's a little looser on her than it is on me, but it skims her figure nicely enough. 'I'm sorry if I've been a bitch to you at times, Natalie. Honestly.'

I'm jolted by the way it comes out of nowhere. 'You haven't.'

'Yeah, I have,' she insists. 'It just wasn't easy, you know, getting used to Dad having someone else. It was just him and me for ages.'

'I know.' I don't want to have this conversation. Something about it is making me itchy and uncomfortable,

356

prickly heat rising up through my body. It makes her too human, too vulnerable. And I don't want her apologies anyway, because at the end of the day teenage girls are fickle and changeable and she probably wouldn't mean them tomorrow.

The train has finally lurched into motion again, and I glance out of the window, seeing we're pulling into Hove. Just one more stop, and we'll be there. I change the subject, turning the conversation in a direction I know she'll like. 'So, are you looking forward to seeing Jaxon? It's been a while you've been talking now, right?'

'A few weeks,' she says, grinning again. She's looking at me a little slyly, as if she's hugging a secret to herself – all the stored up words of those conversations that she thinks are only between her and this boy. Maybe she's remembering the interchange we had a couple of weeks ago, when he started getting a bit frisky and she told him to stop. *You're over exciting me.* Didn't take much. If she really was seeing Jaxon tonight, I'd bet he'd be getting more than a peck on the cheek. Deep down, I don't think Jade's that different from me, funnily enough. And of course that only makes her even more dangerous.

'Well,' I say, 'I'm sure he'll be pleased to see you too.'

'God I hope so.' She looks unsure again, twiddling a strand of her fair hair in her newly painted fingernails. She did those herself, in the hotel room, her head bent in concentration, and her hands were trembling just a bit too much, so that the varnish has splashed a little on to the skin at the side of her nails. It's endearing, kind of. 'I realize it might not work out,' she says now, 'but I just really want it to. It would be so great to have a boy-friend. A guy who puts me first, you know?'

'You've already got one of those,' I point out. She looks blank. 'Your dad,' I elaborate.

Her expression is half baffled, half amused. 'Well, yeah,' she says dismissively. 'But it's not, like, the same, is it.'

I'm silent, turning my attention to the lines of square flat-roofed buildings whizzing past outside the window. I've always known it, but it's gratifying to have her spell it out so baldly. It's not, like, the same, is it. That's what Alex gets for fourteen years of blind devotion. Whatever he does, it'll never be enough. He'll never be number one with her, not like he is with me.

'Look,' I say after another couple of minutes. 'We're here.'

Only five or six others get off at Portslade. Just as I'd thought, the platform is deserted within seconds. We're on the far side of the cross-bridge, sheltered from the eyes of the cameras. There's a wind picking up, and a blue plastic carrier bag rustles along by our feet, making me jump. I'm on edge. I lean back against the wall, folding my arms and looking out across the tracks. There's no one there.

'Shit.' Jade is digging in her bag beside me, suddenly frantic. 'I can't find my phone.'

I fake concern, turning to her with eyebrows raised. 'Are you sure? It hasn't just slipped down the lining or something?'

She keeps turning out the bag, pointlessly going over

the same ground. 'No . . . Oh crap, I must have left it in the hotel room. I don't get it. I'm sure I put it in here.'

'What a pain.' I congratulate myself on having thought of the phone. I took it from her bag while she was in the toilet, keeping it in my pocket and turning to throw it back into the room at the last minute as we left. I'm not stupid enough to think that Alex won't find out that Jade left the hospital with me. For this to work, I'm going to have to tell him that she gave me the slip – that I'd brought her back to surprise him, then popped out to get some treats. I've got no idea what kind of software or apps she's got set up on her phone; I can't risk the possibility that there'd be a tracking device on it, something that Alex might be able to access.

Jade throws the bag aside, on the verge of tears. 'What if he's trying to contact me? What if he's running late or he wants to meet somewhere else instead?'

'Hey, calm down,' I say, putting out my hand to stroke her shoulder briefly. 'He said he'd meet you here at the station, didn't he? So we'll just wait here. He'll turn up soon, I bet. It's . . .' I shoot a look at my watch. 'Almost nine o'clock.' It's taken longer than I thought, getting her out of the hotel room, walking to the station and then the delayed train. But maybe it's for the best; the later it gets the more this place seems to clear out.

Jade looks mollified, nodding. 'I guess so. OK.' She takes a deep breath and settles down next to me, folding her arms in an unconscious mirror of my pose.

I'm good at regulating my expressions, and I know that if someone took a photo of me right now I'd look serene, unruffled. As if I was just hanging out, doing

359

nothing special. But inside my mind is whirring at top speed, and I'm wondering exactly how and when I should do this. The trouble with premeditating is that you have too much time. Too much time to think things through and over-complicate them in your own head. This ought to be easy, for me. But for some reason it isn't.

I peel myself away slowly from the wall and walk towards the tracks. I glance at the departure board. I've got about two minutes until the next train comes in. I stand close to the edge, just by the yellow line, looking out across the tracks again. 'Come here,' I say.

She trots up obediently, peering out, trying to see whatever it is I'm seeing. 'What?'

'I thought I saw a man. A boy.' I squint into the darkness, as if I'm looking through the gap in the wall that leads to the exit. 'Maybe not.'

She's still at my side. I can smell the lime shampoo she washed her hair with before we left the hotel, the scent of it sharp and strange on the night air. When I turn my face towards her, she is so close to me that her features are barely in focus. She's all big, dark blue eyes and bright red lips, an innocent little teen-age fantasy. I take in a breath, and with the rush of cold air into my lungs I feel stronger. I open my mouth to speak again, but as I do so, I realize that my lie has turned into reality. There *is* a man opposite, walking quickly towards the footbridge that spans the two platforms, ascending the stairs. It's so dark, the one lamp on the far platform barely shedding any light, that I can't see his face, but he's definitely heading our way. I breathe out again, talking myself down. I'll just wait for the next train. He won't be sticking around. It's fine. I hear his footsteps down the steps, deliberate and slow. I twist my head to see, and then I realize that it's Dominic.

My face breaks into a smile. Relief is flooding me like oxygen, swift and pure. He's changed his mind. He's come through for me after all. I won't have to do this. I won't have to get my hands dirty, not this time.

My eyes meet his across the twenty feet or so between us. They're blank and steady, two marbles set deep in his face. And at the same moment, Jade turns round too. She's clutching my arm, whispering nervously. 'Who's that?'

'It's OK,' I say.

She looks closer, and I can tell exactly when she recognizes him. Her body goes rigid for an instant, and then she's plucking at my sleeve again, her hand shaking. 'It's him,' she hisses. 'It's the man, the man I've been seeing. The one who was in our house.' Her voice is cracking with hysteria now, her hands getting more insistent, trying to pull me away. 'Please, Natalie. We need to go.'

'No,' I say.

Dominic is walking towards us now, slowly but surely. His mouth is set grimly in a line, and he's avoiding looking at either of us now, his gaze set somewhere in the middle distance.

I look at Jade. Tears are streaming down her face, wrecking her mascara and sending it running in rivers over her cheeks. 'I'm scared,' she whispers. 'Please, please, let's go.'

I hold her steady, propping her up, and Dominic is only metres away from us, his steps slowing to a halt. His hand goes to his coat pocket. The gun is small, gleaming silver. It looks harmless, like a child's toy.

He raises it, level with his shoulder. I have the strange, hallucinatory sense that there's something not right here. But my mind can't quite comprehend what it could be. Everything has slowed down. The world is falling away, leaving me as light as air. And the funny thing is that I don't feel anything at all, nothing but an immense, spreading sense of calm.

Alex

September 2017

I'VE NEVER HEARD A gunshot in my life before but it's unmistakeable. In the few seconds it takes me to cover the ground between the station's entrance and the platform, the only thing in my head is its reverberation, shuddering through me again and again like an aftershock. I can't think – can't even begin to shape the horror of what this might mean.

The platform is almost pitch black, lit only by a small sphere of light at the far end, but I can tell instantly there's no one here. The air is empty. But I can see a ripple of movement through the blackness on the far platform, what looks like the shape of a man, walking fast and fluid, disappearing into the night. And I can hear someone screaming over and over again – a voice I'd recognize anywhere.

'Jade!' I shout, and I'm running towards the stairs that lead to the footbridge, taking them three at a time, pounding over the bridge and down the other side – and as soon as I reach the bottom she's there, rushing full pelt at me and wrapping herself around my body. It's her – the familiar smell of her hair and her skin, the long, slim lines of her arms and legs. I say her name again, but it's choked by the tears rising relentlessly – through my throat, flooding my nose and eyes, the violence of pure relief.

We sink to our knees and crouch there together at the foot of the stairs, her arms pressing tight around my neck. I can feel that she's shaking, her whole body rocked by trauma. I draw away a little, my eyes roaming her frantically and checking that she isn't hurt. She looks unmarked, just the same as always, apart from the burns at her hairline and the tops of her arms. The only thing that is different is the way she is dressed. She's wearing a short, tight dress that I've never seen before, and her cheeks are streaked with mascara, her lips painted bright red.

'Jade, what happened?' I whisper.

She shakes her head, staring at me with pure terror. And there's something else in her eyes, something I can't quite understand, something which looks like pity. She tries to speak, but she can't get the words out, her sobs rising and falling unevenly. She closes her eyes, struggles to calm herself. 'The man,' she says at last. 'The blond man, the man in the house. He was here.'

For a moment I start to my feet, looking wildly up and down the platform, although I already know he's gone. I drop back down again, take my daughter's hands in mine. 'What did he do?' I ask, my voice rough with foreboding. 'What did he do to you?'

Another shake of the head, and now the tears are falling again and she's pressing her fists into her eyes, her bare forearms prickled with goosebumps, her head bowed. 'I'm sorry,' I think I hear her say. 'I'm so sorry, I'm so sorry.'

'What?' I say urgently, gently taking her fists away, peering close into her haunted eyes. 'You have nothing to be sorry for, Jade. What do you mean?'

She draws a deep, shuddering breath, and I can see the dread in her face. She doesn't want to tell me what she has to say, and in the split-second before her lips part I have a vague, fluttering sense of premonition and I know what it must be.

'It's Natalie,' she whispers, and then she chokes, pressing a fist to her mouth.

'I know,' I say quietly.

'The man – the man had a gun. He shot her, Dad, and then he left. I think she's – I think she's . . .' She turns her head, and she's looking behind us, down the length of the platform, into the darkness.

I stand up, keeping Jade in my sights. I take a few paces forwards, holding my phone out to shed a small light ahead of me. And there it is. A body lying slumped against the back wall, completely still, a dark stain spreading across the ground. And as I take a step closer, the smell of blood that I can taste in my mouth, acrid and sour.

My head reels, and I'm dragged forwards by some nameless force. I don't want to look but I can't help it, my eyes hungrily seeking out these sights that I will never be able to un-see – the brutal demolition of that beautiful face I've gazed at hundreds of times, the inscrutable smile I used to love smashed into pulp, the white linen jacket smeared with so much blood I can barely believe it has spilled out of one body. Her eyes are untouched, and wide open. There's no nameable expression in them, but I have the strangest feeling that she sees me.

Rachel hasn't followed me. I turn my head and I see her, standing motionless on the opposite platform, staring across at where I am standing. She's illuminated by the dim streetlamp above her, the light shining around her head like a halo. Her expression is watchful, grave. I stare back at her. She folds her arms in front of her chest, and she starts walking, towards the footbridge, towards us. And I can't think of anything to do or say that could make this moment any more bearable, so I just go back to the steps and I hold my daughter, dipping my face to her cold, scented hair, my arms tightening around her for what feels like days until, finally, she stops shaking.

EPILOGUE

Alex

December 2018

I'm sitting at the kitchen table, cutting shapes carefully out of silver foil. I'm doing it the way Jade showed me, folding the foil into diamonds, then digging the points of the scissors into the centre to cut an intricate pattern that, when I fan it out, should form a symmetrical snowflake. Next will be the lights, which I'll string up around the window frames; then the finishing touches to the tree and the arrangement of cards. I've taken the afternoon off work to get this right. I know I'm being obsessive, but I want this Christmas to be perfect.

At any rate, it won't be like the last one. Both of us shell-shocked, barely functioning; still trying to process things which couldn't be processed. I had tried to gather together some semblance of celebration at the eleventh hour, but it was futile, and we'd spent the day staring at the television, watching characters from soap operas hurling insults at each other over the crackers and turkey, and even that I'd envied. At any rate it had to be better than the emptiness. We'd gritted our teeth and got through that hideous week, right up to New Year, and as the bells tolled I'd looked out of the window at the driving sleet and felt it was less than auspicious.

Slowly, though, we started to sift through the wreckage to find something salvageable. The counselling was the start of it for Jade – long hours gently teasing out the complicated knotted web of trauma and grief and guilt. I was shocked by the violence with which it all came out; the storms of tears, the shouting in the middle of the night, the digging up of old painful wounds, right back to Heather's death. But I could see my daughter resurfacing. As the months passed, she began to find pleasure in small things, and to be able to talk about the past without pain, or at any rate without that pain soaking through everything. I've clung to these small, slowly accumulating signs, and at times I could almost think that she's better. Healed.

Of course it's not as simple as that. There are still nights – albeit less frequent now – when she wakes drenched in sweat, screaming for me, her damp fingers clinging to my body. And there are times, too, when she sits mute and unresponsive, her face shuttered, her thoughts taking her beyond the normal teenage angst. She was only five when Heather died, and she barely remembers her. But she knows that to lose two mothers is almost uniquely tragic, uniquely painful. It's the same for me in a way, yet not the same. There's something darkly comic about it: to lose one wife is unlucky, to lose two looks like carelessness. *I was married twice.*

370

I had two wives. All these words do is underline the transience of such relationships. They imply desertion, divorce; they don't have that terminal stamp. *I had a mother. I had two.*

Counselling has been less helpful for me. There is so much I don't know, and will never know any more about, unless Dominic is found. So far, the police have drawn a blank, and the more time goes on, the lower I sense it slipping down the priority list. I've been back to Camden myself several times, searching around the streets where I saw him, but it's as if he's simply vanished into thin air.

I've tried to take it piece by piece, cling on to the facts I do have, but I keep coming back to that central hub; the possibility of my wife having started the fire in our home, and of having meant some harm to Jade, and why this could possibly be. Hours spent trying to make some sense out of what seemed so senseless and unforgivable. At times I've felt white-hot fury towards her, primal and intense, and I wished that she would spring back to life so that I could put my hands around her slim neck and squeeze it out of her again myself. It's a fine line, this tightrope between love and hate. I've learned not to question it, and to let myself blow from one side to the other as my mood takes me. These days, I try not to allow myself too much of this sort of contemplation. But in a way that's the hardest thing, with Jade: witnessing her grief for a woman who doesn't deserve her tears. There is no way I can rock her fragile equilibrium any further. And yet sometimes it's right there on the tip of my tongue, and I want to destroy this image she's created of a tragic martyr, a woman who died protecting her.

I can't talk to Jade about this, but I talk to Rachel. Or Caitlin, as everyone else knows her these days. I found it quite amusing when she told me that – the way she'd picked a few letters out of that new name to create Cali, her online identity. Creating falsehood out of falsehood. Strangely though, I struggle to think of her as anything but Rachel, and it's become our private name, one she only uses with me. I think she likes it, that it reminds her of who she once was, and maybe still is.

We've seen a lot of each other these past fifteen months, she and I. At first our time together felt like a necessity. We were immediately close, unthinkingly so. It was the sort of intimacy that transcended convention. We would talk for hours about Natalie – Sadie – trying to make sense of our own pain. She told me about the past, in as much detail as she could remember, or that she was willing to reveal to me. Occasionally, even now, I push her too hard, and she isn't afraid to stop me. *I don't think this is helping you, Alex*. It's strange, but I trust her judgement, in a way that I'm not sure I've ever trusted anyone's before.

As the dust settled we became more cautious. This closeness felt more loaded. I introduced her to Jade, explained gently that she was Natalie's sister and that they had been out of touch for a long time. My daughter instantly took to Rachel, and that in itself worried me. It felt as if I was introducing a new partner, setting up a new crutch, when that wasn't what this was. I didn't think I would ever want a woman near me again.

I'm still not sure. In my darker moments, even the idea of love feels like more trouble than it's worth – but sometimes, as she herself said to me once, trouble just finds you.

I unfold the foil snowflakes and the cut-out scraps scatter on to the table like silver rain. I take them over to the window and fasten them with Blu-tack, arrange them neatly in rows. Then I untangle the strings of coloured lights and start to fix them to the window frame, concentrating on the task. When I step back again, I'm pleased. The room looks right: cosy, inviting, festive, all the things I want it to be. Being here at the new house has helped. After everything that happened, staying where we were felt like an impossibility.

It doesn't mean I don't think about my wife. I still think about her all the time, wondering where the core of her was, if anyone had ever delved deep enough to find a nugget of truth, something that was unambiguously and uncomplicatedly *her*. And if they would have known it if they had. But Jade and I, we're on our own now. We've survived and we're free. Sometimes this freedom feels exhilarating – a vista of limitless possibilities, exciting and new. Sometimes it feels terrifying – free falling through a void, with no way of knowing when we'll hit the bottom. But either way, we're in it together.

I glance at the clock, knowing Jade will be home from school soon, and as I do my gaze falls on the letter that came this morning, which I still haven't put away. Quickly, I cross to the table and unfold it, scanning its contents once again. Just a couple of lines, printed blackly in large type across the page.

I saved her life. One good turn deserves another, don't you think?

It's probably just kids. Some silly pre-teen prank.

I step forwards to adjust the lights a little, and as I do so I see Jade walking up the road, her head ducked down a little against the softly falling rain. She looks thoughtful but content, absorbed in herself. I watch her for a few moments, and then I flick the switch. The window is illuminated with bright jewels of red and green and silver, and the sudden light must catch her eye, because she looks up and straight at me, and she smiles. And I crumple the sheet of paper up in my hand, shoving it into my pocket, and smile back.

Acknowledgements

The Second Wife is a book I felt passionately about from the start, but it didn't always come easily. My agent, Caroline Wood at Felicity Bryan, was a source of rock-solid support throughout and always kept me focused on the end goal, while somehow conveying the impression that she never doubted I would achieve it – thank you for persevering through my wobbles.

My editor at Transworld, Frankie Gray, was also worth her weight in gold through the whole process. Pushing an author's boundaries must, I imagine, be a sometimes difficult and frustrating part of the job; I was convinced, after my first couple of drafts, that the book was 'finished' and that it was certainly as good as I could make it. When she suggested a fairly major rethink of the structure, I won't pretend that I wasn't daunted (and just a little defensive), but working through the redraft really opened my eyes. I was left not only with a much better book, but with a new awareness that authors aren't always the best judges of when their novels are done and dusted. Luckily, Frankie is an editor with very good instincts!

Thanks as always go to the rest of the Transworld team, to Pam and Jeramie in the US, and to all the foreign markets who have taken on *The Second Wife* – I'm delighted that it will be reaching readers around the world.

I wrote the book itself in something of a vacuum, but that doesn't mean that I received no help from family and friends. Some writers work best when emotions are running high, but I need calm and clarity to get things done. To everyone who has helped me achieve that over the past couple of years – you know who you are, and thank you.

Reading Group Guide

1. *The Second Wife* is told through several different voices and perspectives. How did this structure affect your reading of the novel?

2. Family relationships, particularly the loyalties we feel towards our family members, feature throughout the novel. How does the relationship between Rachel and Sadie change over time? Can you identify any key moments that disrupt the balance of power between the two sisters? Would you have made the same choices as Rachel if you had been in her place?

3. After the fire at the start of the novel, Alex is caught between whether to trust Natalie or believe Jade. Do you think he handles the situation well?

4. Consider the use of an unreliable narrator in the novel. Did you find this effective? Were there any particular moments you found surprising or moving?

5. Was there a particular character you identified with, or felt more sympathetic towards? How did your perceptions of the characters change as the novel progressed?

6. Were you surprised by Rachel's revelation at the end of Part Five? How did this moment change your perceptions of Natalie up to this point?

7. Discuss the final chapters. Did you have any different ideas for how the novel might end while you were reading? Do you think the characters get the ending they deserve?

Also by Rebecca Fleet

THE HOUSE SWAP

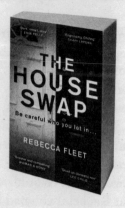

'No one lives this way unless they want to hide something.'

When Caroline and Francis receive an offer to house swap,
they jump at the chance for a week away from home.
After the difficulties of the past few years, they've
worked hard to rebuild their marriage for their son's sake;
now they want to reconnect as a couple.

On arrival, they find a house that is stark and sinister in
its emptiness – it's hard to imagine what kind of person lives
here. Then, gradually, Caroline begins to uncover some signs of
life – signs of *her* life. The flowers in the bathroom or the
music in the CD player might seem innocent to her husband
but to her they are anything but. It seems the person they
have swapped with is someone she used to know;
someone she's desperate to leave in her past.

But that person is now in her home – and they want to make
sure she'll never forget . . .

'I read *The House Swap* in one breathless sitting.
Dark, smart, sexy, gripping, totally brilliant.'
ERIN KELLY

OUT NOW